# MISS PINKERTON

# MISS PINKERTON

*Adventures of a Nurse Detective by*

## MARY ROBERTS RINEHART

———

*The Buckled Bag*

*Locked Doors*

*Miss Pinkerton*

*Haunted Lady*

———

RINEHART & COMPANY, INC.

NEW YORK    TORONTO

Published simultaneously in Canada by
Clarke, Irwin & Company, Ltd., Toronto

IN HER autobiography, *My Story*, Mary Roberts Rinehart told a little about her training as a nurse. She was seventeen years old when, in 1893, she entered The Pittsburgh Training School to become one of fewer than five hundred graduate trained nurses in America. She never forgot what she learned there: the agonizingly long hours, the depth of compassion a nurse must possess to meet human suffering, and the wisdom she must learn in order to handle those almost sacred confidences brought out by pain or fear. Above everything else, Mary Roberts Rinehart found in herself the quiet courage required to cope with any emergency. Later she would advise young writers, "Know the people you are writing about." She would say, "If you are a housewife living in the South, why try to tell a story of French Colonials in North Africa?" About Hilda Adams, America's favorite nurse detective, she knew a great deal.

The two short stories and two novels contained in this book are presented chronologically, as they were written. Years elapsed between *Locked Doors* and *Miss Pinkerton*. More years passed before Mrs. Rinehart wrote *Haunted Lady*. However, the fact that she kept drawing upon her own nursing experience gives the stories vitality and deep authenticity.

# MISS PINKERTON

# The Buckled Bag

## CHAPTER I

I HAVE broken down in health lately—nothing serious; but a nurse lasts only so long, and during the last five years I have been under a double strain. Caring for the sick has been only a part of it. The other?

Well, put it like this: The world's pretty crowded after all. We are always touching elbows, and there is never a deviation from the usual, the normal, that is not felt all the way down the line. Stand a row of dominoes on edge and knock down the end one. Do you see? And generally somebody goes down for fair. We do not know much about it among the poor; they have to manage the best way they can, and maybe they are blunted—some of them. They have not the time for mental agony. And the thing works both ways. Their lapses are generally obvious—cause and result; motive and crime.

In the lower walks of life people are more elemental. But get up higher. Crime exists there; but, instead of a passion, it is a craft. In its detection it is brain against brain, not intellect against brute force or instinct. If anything gives, it is the body.

Illness follows crime—it does not always follow the criminal; but somebody goes down for fair. There is a breach in the wall. The doctor and the clergyman come in then. One way and another they get the story. There is nothing hidden from them. They get it, but they do not want it. They cannot use it. The clergyman's vows and the medical man's legal status forbid their using their knowledge; but, where a few years ago there were only two, now each crisis, mental or physical, finds three—the trained nurse.

Do you see what I mean? The thing is thrust at her. She does not want the story either. Her business is bodies, doctors' orders, nourishments; but unless she's a fool she ends by holding the family secret in the hollow of her hand. It worries her. She needs her hands. She gets rid of it as soon as she can and forgets it. She is safe; the secret is safe. Without the clergyman's vows or the doctor's legal status, she is as silent as either.

That is the ethical side. That is what the nurse does. There is another side, which is mine. The criminal uses every means against society. Why not society against the criminal? And this is my defense. Every trained nurse plays a game, a sort of sporting proposition—her wits against wretchedness. I play a double game—the fight against misery and the fight against crime—like a man running two chessboards at once.

I hated it in the beginning. It has me by the throat now. It is the criminal I find absorbing. And I have learned some things—not new, of course: that to be honest because one is untempted is to be strong with the strength of a child; that the great virtues often link arms with the great vices; that the big criminal thinks big thoughts.

I have had my chance to learn and I know. A nurse gets under the very skin of the soul. She finds a mind surrendered, all the crooked little motives that have fired the guns of life revealed in their pitifulness. Even now, sometimes, it hurts me to look back.

It is five years since George L. Patton was shot in the leg during a raid on the Hengst Place, in Cherry Run. He is at the head of one of the big private agencies now, but he was a county detective then; and Hengst shot him from a cupboard. Well, that does not matter particularly, except that Mr. Patton was brought to the hospital that night and I was given the case.

He took it very calmly—said he guessed he would rest awhile, now he had the chance, and slept eighteen hours without moving. I made caps, I remember, and tried to plan what I would do when I left the house. My time was about up and I dreaded private duty. I had been accustomed to the excitement of a hospital, and there was something horrible to me in the idea of spending the rest of my life in darkened rooms, with the doctor's daily visit for excitement and a walk round the block for recreation.

I gave Mr. Patton his dinner that night and we had our first clash. He looked at the soup and toast, and demanded steak and onions.

"I'm sorry," I said. "You're to have light diet for a day or two. We don't want any fever from that leg."

"Leg! What has my leg to do with my stomach? I want a medium steak. I'll do without the onions if I have to."

"Doctor's orders," I said firmly. "You may have an egg custard if you want it, or some cornstarch."

We had a downright argument and he took the soup. When he had finished, he looked up at me and smiled.

"I don't like you," he said, "but darned if I don't respect you, young woman. Absolute obedience to orders is about the hardest thing in the world to get. And now send for that fool interne and we'll have a steak for breakfast."

Well, he did; and pretty soon he was getting about everything the hospital could give him. He was a politician, of course, and we depended on our state appropriation for support; but he got nothing from me without an order. He always said he did not like me, but I think he did after a while. I could beat him at chess, for one thing.

"You have a good head, Miss Adams," he said to me one day when he was almost well. "Are you going to spend the rest of your life changing pillowslips and shaking down a thermometer?"

"I've thought of institutional work; I dare say I'd be changing nurses and shaking down internes," I said with some bitterness.

"How old are you?—not, of course, for publication."

"Twenty-nine."

"Any family?"

"The nearest relatives I have are two old aunts, in the country."

He was silent for a minute or two. Then: "I've been thinking of something; I may take it up with you later. There's only one objection—you're rather too good-looking."

"I'm not really good-looking at all," I admitted frankly. "I have too high a forehead. It's the cap."

"Like 'em high!" said Mr. Patton.

I made an eggnog and brought it in to him. He was sitting propped in a chair, and when I gave him the glass, he smiled up at me. He had never attempted any sentimentalities with me, which is more than can be said of the usual convalescent male over forty.

"It isn't all the cap," he said.

That afternoon he tried to learn from me something about the other patients on the floor; but of course I would tell him nothing. He seemed rather irritated and tried to bully me, but I was firm.

"Don't be childish, Mr. Patton!" I said at last. "We don't tell about other patients. If you want to find out, get one of your men in here." To my surprise he laughed.

"Good girl!" he said. "You've stood a cracking test and come through A one. You've got silence and obedience to orders, and you have a brain. I've mentioned the forehead. Now I'm going to make my proposition. Has it ever occurred to you that every crisis, practically, among the better classes, finds a trained nurse on hand?"

"Cause or result?"

"Result, of course. Upset the ordinary routine of a family, have a robbery, an elopement or a murder, and somebody goes to bed, with a trained nurse in attendance. Fact, isn't it?" I admitted it. "It's a fault of the tension people live under," he went on. "Any extra strain and something snaps. And who is it who is in the very bosom of the family? You know and I know. The nurse gets it all—the intimate details that the police miss; the family disputes, the inner motives; the—you go to your room and think it over. And when you decide, I have a case for you."

I tried to object, but he cut me short; so I put the thermometer in his mouth and managed to tell him how I felt.

"It just doesn't seem honest," I finished. "I'm in a position of confidence and I violate it. That's the truth. A nurse is supposed to work for good; if she has any place, it's an uplift—if you can see what I mean. And to go into a house and pry out its secrets——"

He jerked the thermometer out wrathfully.

"Uplift!" he said. "Isn't it uplifting to place a criminal where he won't injure society? If you can't see it that way, we don't want you. Now go away and think about it."

I went up to my room and stood in front of the mirror, which is where I do most of my thinking. I talk things over with myself, I suppose. And I saw the lines beside my ears that said, "Twenty-nine, almost thirty!" And I thought of institutional work, with its daily round of small worries, its monotonous years, with my soul gradually shrinking and shaping itself to fit a set of rules. And over against it all I put Mr. Patton's offer.

I recall it all—the color that came to my face at the chance to use my head instead of only a trained obedience to orders; the prospect of adventure; the chance to pit my wits against other wits and perhaps win out. I put on one of the new caps and went down to Mr. Patton's room.

"I'll do it!" I said calmly.

My time was up two days later. Mr. Patton was practically well and gave me my instructions while I helped him pack his bag.

"Do the things the other nurses do," he advised. "Go to the Nurses' Home, but don't register for cases right away. Make an excuse that you're tired and need a few days' rest. When I telephone you, I shall call myself Doctor Patton—not that I pretend to do any medical work, but for extra caution."

"You said you had a case for me."

"I had, but it isn't big enough. I want you for something worth while, and it will be along soon. It's about due."

"And—just one thing, Mr. Patton: I will take my first case on trial. If I find that I am doing harm and not good by revealing the secrets of a family, I shall give it up. A doctor would be answerable to the law for doing the things I am about to do."

"You have no legal status."

"I have a moral status," I replied grimly, and he found no answer to that. Before he left, however, he said something that rather cheered me.

"You will never be required to tell anything you learn, except what is directly pertinent to the matter in hand," he said. "I would not give such latitude to any other woman I know—but you have brains and you will know what we want."

"I cannot work in the dark—I must know what you are after."

"We will lay all our cards on your table face up. I wouldn't insult you by asking you to play blindfolded. And remember this, Miss Adams—it's as high a duty to explore and heal the moral sores of a community as it is to probe and dress, for instance, the wound of a man who has been shot in the leg."

Two days later I left the hospital and took a room at the Nurses' Home he had recommended. He would arrange with the secretary, he said, that I should be called for any case on which he wished me placed.

I put in a bad week. One of the staff of the hospital located me and called me to a case. I got out of it by saying I needed a few days' rest, and he rang off irritably. Then, on the third day, I had my handbag cut off my arm in a department store, and went home depressed and ill-humored.

"You're a fine detective!" I said to myself in the mirror. "You're not so clever as Mr. Patton thinks, and if you're honest, you'll go and tell him so."

I think I should have done so—I was so abashed; but our arrangement was that I should not try to see him under any circumstances. There was to be no suspicion of me in any way. He would see me when necessary. I still had the strap of my bag, which had been left hanging to my arm; and, as a constant reminder, I fastened it to the frame of my mirror. Even now, when the department gives me its best cases, and when I have been successful enough to justify a little pride, I look at that bit of leather and become meek and normal again.

IN SPITE OF Mr. Patton's promise I went on my first case for him without any preparation. Miss Shinn, the secretary, asked me if I would take a case that evening.

"For whom?"

She was turning over the pages of her ledger in the parlor-office of the Home and she did not look up.

"A Doctor Patton telephoned," she said. "I believe he had spoken to you of the case."

My throat tightened, but, after all, this was what I had been waiting for.

"Do you know what sort of case it is?" I asked. "I'm not doing obstetrics, you know."

"It is not an obstetric case. You are to take a taxicab at eight o'clock tonight."

Miss Shinn was a heavy, rather bilious brunette, who rarely smiled; but I caught an amused twinkle as she glanced up. Quite suddenly I liked her. Clearly she knew what I was about to do and she did not disapprove; and yet she was a very ethical person. I gathered that she would be very hard on a nurse who wore frivolous uniforms, or gossiped about her patients, or went to the theater with a doctor, or cut rates. And yet she was indulgent to me—she was more than indulgent. I was certain, somehow, from the very quiver of her wide back as she marked me "Engaged" on her register, that she was wildly interested and curious. It gave me confidence.

At eight o'clock that evening I went downstairs with my suitcase and ordered a taxicab. No word had come from Mr. Patton and I had nothing but a name and address to go by. The name—we will call it G. W. March. It was not, of course. You would know the name at once if I told it. The address was a street fronting one of the parks—a good neighborhood, I knew—old families, substantial properties, traditions, all that sort of thing. Certainly not a place to look for crime.

As I waited for the cab, I searched the newspapers for something to throw light on my new enterprise. There was nothing at all except a notice that Mr. and Mrs. George W. March had returned from their summer home on the Maine coast a few days before and had opened their city home.

It looked like a robbery. I was vaguely disappointed. I had it all worked out in five minutes—Mrs. March in bed, collapsed; missing pictures or jewels; house full of trusted servants; and myself trying to solve the mystery between an alcohol rub and a dose of bromide. I hated to go on with it, but I was ashamed not to. I said to myself savagely that I was not a quitter, and got into the taxicab.

The March case was not a robbery, however. It was, strictly speaking, not a criminal case at all. It concerned the disappearance of a girl, and in some ways it was a remarkable mystery—particularly baffling because for so long it seemed to be a result without a cause. How we found the cause at last; how we located the family in Brickyard Road and solved the puzzle of the buckled bag; how we learned the identity of the little old woman with the jet bonnet, and her connection with the garden door—all this makes up the record of my first case.

The buckled bag is lying on my desk now. It is a shabby, quaint old bag, about eight inches long, round-bellied, brown with wear. It still contains what was in it when Mr. Patton found it: a cotton handkerchief, marked with a J; two keys—one a house-door key, the other a flat one;

a scrawled note in a soiled lavender envelope; a newspaper clipping of a sale of blankets.

It is one of my most painful memories that for a month I examined that newspaper cutting frequently and that I failed entirely to grasp the significance of the reverse side. We all have a mental blind spot. That was mine.

Clare March was missing. That was my case: to find her, or to help to find her, was my task at first. Later it grew more complicated. I had not thought Mr. Patton would violate our agreement about working in the dark and my confidence was justified. At the first corner he hailed the machine and got in.

"Fine work!" he said. "You're a dependable person, Miss Adams."

"I'm rather a scared person."

"Nonsense! And don't take yourself or this affair too seriously. Do your durnedest—'Angels could do no more.'"

"Is it something stolen?"

"A small matter of a daughter. It's a queer thing, Miss Adams. I'll tell you about it." He asked the driver to go slowly. "Time us to get there at eight thirty," he said. "Now, Miss Adams, here are the facts: You are going to the home of George March, the banker—you probably know the name— Mrs. March is your patient. She's not ill; she's hysterical and frightened— that's all. It's not a hard case."

"It's the hardest sort of a case."

"Well, you like work," he replied cheerfully. "The family has been away for four months. Until a month ago, Clare, the daughter, was with them. One month ago, on the third of September, Clare, who is an only child, twenty years old, left the country place in Maine for home. She traveled alone, leaving her maid in the country. The city house had not been closed; a housekeeper and two maids were there through the summer. She was expected at the house for breakfast on the morning of the fourth. She did not arrive—or, rather, she did not go home. She reached the city safely. We have traced her into the railroad station and out again—and that has been about all. She's not been seen since."

"Perhaps she has eloped."

"Possibly; but the man she is engaged to is in the city, almost frantic. Besides, there is more than I have told you. We know that she took a taxicab at the station; that before she got in, she met and accepted a small parcel from a blond young man, rather shabbily dressed; and that they seemed to be having an argument, though a quiet one. We have found the taxicab she took, and a shop where she bought a couple of books—a Browning and a recent novel. From the bookshop she went to a department store. There she dismissed the taxicab. We have traced her in the store to a department where she bought a pair of blankets. They made a large parcel, but she took it with her. From that time we have lost her absolutely."

"The third of September, and this is the fifth of October—almost five weeks!"

"Exactly," he said dryly. "That's why I've sent for you. We have tried all the usual things; we've combed the city fine—and we are just where we started. If we could make a noise about it, we should have some chance. Set the general public looking—that's the way to get information. You get a million clues worth nothing, and out of the lot one that helps. But you know these people. They won't listen to any publicity. They have only one argument—if she is dead, publicity won't help her, and if she is alive, it will hurt her."

I was conscious of a vague disappointment. In the last half hour I had keyed myself to the highest pitch. I was seeing red, really—nothing but the bloodiest sort of crime would have come up to my expectation. Certainly nothing less than a murder had been in my thoughts.

"I don't see how I can help," I said, a bit resentfully. "You've had five weeks and got nowhere," I continued, "and if you are going to ask me to put myself in her place, and try to imagine what could have happened, and to follow her mental processes, I can't do it. I can't imagine myself idle and rich and twenty. I can't imagine taking a taxicab when a streetcar would do, or having a lady's maid——"

Mr. Patton laid a hand on my arm.

"Did you ever hear Lincoln's story of the little Mississippi steamboat with a whistle so large that every time they blew it the boat stopped? . . . No? Well, no matter. I don't want you to put yourself in her place; I want a little inside help—that's all. There's a curious story behind this case, Miss Adams. We've only scratched the top. Get in there and get their confidence. They won't talk to me—too much family pride. Get the mother to talk. That's part of her trouble—family pride and bottling up her emotions. I can't get close to any of them. After five weeks Mrs. March still calls me Mr. Peyton." He smiled ruefully.

"She bought blankets! That's curious, isn't it?"

"It's almost ridiculous under the circumstances. You may not be able to imagine yourself twenty, and so on, but you can certainly get your wits to work on those blankets. If she had bought a revolver now—but blankets!"

"She was engaged, you say? Were there any other men who—who liked her?"

"Half a dozen, I believe—all accounted for."

"Any neurasthenic tendency?"

"In the half dozen? I dare say yes, when she announced her engagement; in the girl—I think not. She was temperamental rather. The picture I get of her is of an attractive and indulged young woman, engaged to a man she seems to have cared about. And yet, with all the gods smiling, she disappears."

I sat thoughtful. The cab was moving along beside the park now. We were almost there.

"She may be dead," I said at last.

"She may, indeed."

He asked the driver to stop and got out, with a quick handshake.

"Now go to it!" he said. "Go out for a breath of air between seven and eight each evening, and—keep your eyes open. I have a hunch that you'll get this thing—beginner's luck."

The March house was an old-fashioned, rather stately residence. Instead of a drawing room upstairs, there was a reception room opening into the lower hall. Behind that was a music room and, still farther back, a library.

At the very rear of the lower floor was a dining room, quite the largest room in the house, extending as it did the entire width of the building. In it was a large bay window looking onto a city garden, and in the bay, shut off by tall plants, was a small table, where the family breakfasted and even, when alone, sometimes dined.

A long flight of stairs, uncarpeted, led to the second floor. On that first evening I got merely the vaguest outlines of the house, of course. It was silent, immaculate, rather heavy. I had a glimpse of two men in the library talking—one middle-aged, rather stout; the other much younger. Over everything hung the hush of suspense—that hush which accompanies birth and death and great trouble.

A parlor maid admitted me and led me upstairs to my room.

"Mr. March would like to see you in the library when you have taken off your things," she said.

I changed quickly into my uniform—all white, of course, with rubber-soled white shoes. With the familiar garb I was myself again; I could face anything, do anything. Clothes are queer things.

Mr. March turned when he heard me at the door and rose.

"I am Miss Adams, the nurse," I said. "Do you wish to see me?"

"Will you come in, Miss Adams? This is Mr. Plummer. Have you seen Mrs. March?"

"No; I thought it best to see you first."

"I am glad of that. Perhaps I ought to tell you—we are in great trouble, Miss Adams. Our—our only daughter has gone away, disappeared. It is over a month since—" He stopped.

"That is very terrible," I said. I liked his face.

"We wish absolute secrecy—of course I need hardly say that; but you understand Mrs. March is highly nervous. I—I hope you can quiet her. What we want you to do is to be as cheerful and optimistic as possible. You know what I mean. She will talk to you about Clare—about Miss March. Reassure her if you can. Be certain that Miss March will be found soon."

"I will do what I can. Has the doctor left any orders?"

"Very few. She is to be soothed. There's a bromide, I believe. Her maid has the instructions."

There was nothing for me in that glimpse of the two men most nearly concerned—two gentlemen unaffectedly distressed and under great strain in a quiet, well-ordered house. It looked like poor material, from Mr. Patton's point of view. Mr. March followed me into the hall. "If you need anything, let me know, Miss Adams. Or will you speak to the servants?"

"I can tell better later on. If I am going to be up tonight—and I think I'd better be, this first night anyhow—I should like a lunch; something cold on a tray."

"Do you wish it upstairs?"

I hesitated. There was a picture in a silver frame on the library table— I thought it probably one of the missing girl. I wanted to see it. "It will be a change to come down."

"Very well," he said. "There will be a supper left in the dining room. There is a small table there in the bay window. It will be more comfortable —not quite so lonely."

"Thank you," I replied and started upstairs. Opposite the library door I glanced in. I had been right about the picture. Mr. Plummer had picked it up and was looking at it. I felt certain that he was the fiancé—a manly-looking fellow; not very tall, but solid and dependable-looking, with a good head and earnest eyes.

My patient was in bed—a pretty little woman in a frilly bed jacket, with a pink light beside her. She held out a nervous hand.

"How big and strong and competent you look!" she said, and quite unexpectedly fell to crying. I had a difficult evening. She was entirely unstrung—must have me sit down by the bed at once and listen to the trouble, as she called it—and as it was, indeed.

"She wouldn't go away and leave me like this!" she said more than once. "If you only knew her, Miss Adams—so full of character, so determined, so gifted! And beautiful—haven't you seen her picture in the newspapers?"

I evaded that—I never read society news.

"And happy, too?" I said. "She must have been very happy."

I saw a change in Mrs. March's rather childish face.

"We thought she was, of course; but lately—I've remembered so many things while I've been lying here. She was very strange all summer—moody sometimes, and again so gay that she frightened me."

"Perhaps she was gay when Mr. Plummer was there and moody when he was away."

"But he wasn't there at all. That's another thing, Miss Adams. She would not let me ask Walter up. She—she really kept him away all summer. I don't believe Mr. March told the detective that—he forgot so many things."

She wanted me to telephone this piece of information to the police at once, but I persuaded her to wait. I gave her an alcohol rub and a cup of hot milk; and, finding them without effect, I took a massage vibrator I found on her dressing table and ran it up and down her spine. She finally relaxed with the treatment and even asked me to use it on her face.

"I'm an old woman with all the worry," she said apologetically. "It will tone up the facial muscles, won't it? And would you mind putting some cold cream on first?"

I did not mind; and after a time she fell asleep. I was glad of a respite. In my two hours over the bed I had accumulated many ill-assorted bits of information. I wanted time to catalogue them in my mind. I have the notes I made that night on one of my records:

"C. has been missing since September third; today is October fifth—a total of thirty-two days.

"Was moody all summer—would not see Mr. Plummer, but wrote him daily.

"She had been engaged once before, to a Wilson Page, but broke engagement. Cause of trouble not known. C. suffered much at the time. Note—Have Mr. P. look up Wilson Page.

"C. usually undemonstrative, but rather affected when she said goodbye to her mother. Was she planning something, unknown to them?

"But if she was planning an elopement, why did she make careful appointments with her dressmakers and milliners? Is she more crafty than they think, or was her decision made unexpectedly?

"She forgot her jewel case, which she always carried with her. An inventory reveals only a part of her jewelry. She wore, when she left, only the sapphire ring Mr. Plummer gave her. She had less than a hundred dollars in cash.

"Wilson Page is dark. The man who met her in the station was thin and fair.

"Her picture is on her mother's dressing table—an attractive face: dark-eyed, full of character, but rather wistful. A thoughtful face. Is she living or dead? Did she go voluntarily or was she lured away? If she went voluntarily—why?"

I looked round the handsome room where my patient slept calmly, her petulant features relaxed and peaceful. I glanced across the hall to Miss Clare's room, where a light burned every evening; where an ivory dressing set, with carved monogram, was spread on the toilet table; where every luxury a young woman could demand had been gathered together for her use. And I recalled the look in the face of the man downstairs as he gazed at her picture—the tragedy in the eyes of her father. How had she gone, and why? How and why?

CHAPTER III

MY FIRST NIGHT at the March house was marked by a disagreeable and rather mystifying occurrence. I had got my patient quiet and asleep and had had a telephone talk with the doctor by eleven.

"There is very little to do," the doctor said. "I'll come in in the morning. Just keep her comfortable and cheerful. She needs someone to talk to. Let her talk all she wants."

I darkened the room where she lay and placed a screen in the hall outside the door, with a comfortable chair beside it and a shaded lamp. I had made up my mind to sit up for that one night at least. I had had nervous cases before; and I knew that sometime between then and morning she would waken, and that the sight of someone alert and watchful would be a comfort.

At midnight I took off my cap, eased my hair and loosened my uniform collar. With the neck of my dress turned in, I was fairly comfortable. It was too early to eat. I got a book from the library and read.

At two o'clock Mrs. March was still sleeping quietly and I decided to get my night supper. I slipped down the stairs as noiselessly as possible. An English hall lamp was turned on in the lower hall near the music-room door, and far back in the dining room a candle light in a wall bracket showed me where to go.

My progress in my rubber-soled shoes was practically noiseless. I made my way along the hall back to the dining room. The room was very large, as I have said before, paneled in oak, with a heavy fireplace and a tapestry in an overmantel above. At one corner, beside the deep bay window, were French doors, hung with casement cloths, evidently leading out into the garden.

I was deliberate in all my movements, I remember. I went to the fireplace and stood looking up at the overmantel; I found the switch that would throw the light over my small table and thus give me a more cheerful place to eat. The bay, walled off by palms and flowering oleanders in tubs, was dark and rather uninviting at that hour. I made no particular attempt to be silent, but I dare say it is a result of my training that I make no unnecessary noise.

One of the older nurses once said to me, "When you go out on private duty, you'll have to fuss about your night supper generally. An orange and a glass of milk is about what most cooks set out. Keep them up to the mark. Insist on cold meat or sandwiches; and if there's an alcohol coffeepot, have them leave it ready. Coffee is your best friend at three in the morning, and your next best is a shawl to lay over your knees."

I was thinking of that and rather smiling when I entered the recess and sat down at the small table. I was absolutely calm and beginning to be mightily interested in my case. The tray was ready; and there was a small alcohol coffeepot ready, with a box of matches beside it.

I lit the lamp and inspected the tray. The cook seemed to have been trained by some predecessor. There was chicken, a bit of salad, brown bread and fruit. I ate slowly while my coffee cooked—ate with an ear toward the staircase for a sound from my patient above, and with an occasional eye toward the garden below. A late moon showed a brick terrace under the windows, and three steps lower was a formal design of flower bed and path, with a small cement circle, evidently a pool in summer. Somehow the garden looked uncanny—bushes became figures, moving about, waving arms in the breeze. I was a distinct object from outside as I sat in my nook; and, having eaten and waiting only for the coffee, I stood up and extinguished the light over my head.

It was then, still standing, that I saw the hand. It was coming down the staircase rail, moving slowly and grasping tight. It was near the music room when I saw it first and therefore going away from me, but descending. There was something terribly stealthy about it. It must have been that quality in it which made me shrink back behind an oleander. Surely there was nothing unusual in people being about in a house where there was both illness and trouble, and yet . . .

At the foot of the stairs the hand, still on the rail, hesitated, disappeared. A moment later there rounded the newel post a little old woman dressed in black. She limped slightly, but for all that she came swiftly. Every detail is stamped on my mind. I can see her now, bent forward, something that was probably jet on her old-fashioned bonnet catching the faint light as she came. She had on a quaint loose black wrap—a dolman, I think they used to call them—and hanging to her arm a shabby leather handbag.

Stealthy as her movements were, they were extremely natural. Just inside the door she stopped, took off her spectacles and put them in a case, which she put in her bag, and then extracted from it another pair, which she put on. The bag was a quaint one, fastened with two straps and steel buckles. The buckles were troublesome and she was in a hurry. More than once she turned and looked back.

I waited for her to see me. It was an old servant, of course, come to tell me I was wanted upstairs. I was so sure of it that I bent down and put out my alcohol lamp. When I straightened up, she had passed the bay and was at the French door leading to the garden. She opened the door, went out, closed it noiselessly behind her, and was gone. I tried to see her in the garden, but if she went that way, she was lost in the shadows.

Even then I was rather amused than puzzled. I went over to the door and tried it. There was a lock on it. Unless she had a key, she had locked herself out.

I drank my coffee and went upstairs. My patient was still asleep. From Mr. March's room came heavy, deep breathing, telling that he was forgetting his anxieties, for a time at least. But my book—the book I had left on my chair in the hall—was gone!

It seemed rather absurd. I thought I might have taken it with me; and I searched the dining room, without result. It was not to be found. I thought of the little old housekeeper, or whatever she was—but that was ridiculous. Besides, she had carried no book. She had a black leather handbag over her arm. She might, of course, have put the book—what idiocy was I thinking! The book must be somewhere about. Everyone has laid things down and had them disappear. Sometimes they turn up and sometimes they do not—the fourth dimension, perhaps.

I met Mr. Patton the next evening as he had arranged. He fell into step beside me.

"How's it going?" he asked.

"I'm learning to be a first-rate lady's maid," I said, rather peevishly I am afraid. "I massage, manicure and give scalp treatments, and I've got a smirk from trying to look cheerful. The experiment is a failure, Mr. Patton. I'm not nursing, for there's no real illness; and I'm not helping you any. And the dreadful decorum of the house gets me. If I were twenty, I'd run away, too. Nothing ever gets dusty or out of place. No door ever slams. When I raise a window for air, I put in a gauze-filled frame to keep the dirt out!"

"Has the mother talked at all?"

"All the time—about herself. I've learned a little, of course. The girl has been moody—would not let Mr. Plummer, her fiancé, visit her this summer. Seemed to be in trouble; but confided in no one. The family relationships seem to have been all right. They adore her."

"Have you seen many of the people who come and go about the house?

Anyone who could answer the description of the man she met at the station—the light-haired chap?"

I considered.

"None, I am sure."

"She and her mother got along well?"

"I think so. They were always together."

"Is there any trace of another love affair?"

"Yes, she was engaged once before. To a Mr. Wilson Page. She broke the engagement herself."

That interested him. He said he would look up Mr. Page.

"And don't be impatient," he advised me. We had made our circuit of the block and were in sight of the house again. "These are long cases sometimes—but the longer the time the more sure I am that the girl is alive. Murder will out; it's self-limiting, like a case of measles. But take a girl who wants to stay hidden, and if she's intelligent, there's hardly any way to locate her. How many servants in the house?"

"Seven, I believe."

"Keep an eye on them. If one of them is garrulous, let her talk. They know more of the family than any member of it."

This brought to my mind the curious episode of the old woman, and I told him about it. He listened without interruption.

"When you say old, how old?"

"Seventy, I should say. She was stooped—and rather lame, but very active."

"You are sure you saw her? You could not possibly have been dozing?"

"I was making coffee; I don't customarily do that in my sleep. I think it must have been the cook. She is the only servant I have not seen. And, as to dozing, does anybody dream a handbag with straps and buckles?"

He put a hand on my arm impressively.

"It may interest you to know," he said, "that the cook is a young woman; I interviewed her myself. There is no person such as you describe in the house!"

"But why—at three in the morning——"

"Exactly," he said dryly. "Why? That's for us to find out."

He got a careful description of the old woman from me, and an account of her exit by the French door from the dining room into the garden. He was excited, for him, and rather triumphant.

"Now was it a mistake to put you there?" he demanded. "Of course not! And the next thing is to find the old lady. You can help there. Tell your story to the family. Set them to wondering and guessing. They may place her for us at once. In this business, try direct methods whenever you can. They save time."

He left me at the corner and I went on alone. Just before I reached the house, a man ran down the steps and went away rapidly. The parlor maid was just closing the door.

"Did that gentleman inquire for me, Mimi?" I asked. "I am expecting my brother." I was learning!

"No, miss. He asked for Miss March." Her eyes were wide and excited. "When I said she was not here, he ran down the steps in a hurry."

"My brother," I persisted, "is short and dark. Perhaps you——"

"He asked for Miss March," she repeated. "And, anyhow, he was thin and lightish." She turned to see whether any of the family might overhear. "He's been here before, Miss," she confided, lowering her voice—; "twice, in the last week. He—he isn't one of Miss March's friends—I know that. And tonight he left this."

She showed me her tray on the hall table. There was a note on it addressed: "Miss Clare March. Important."

"I'll take this up to Mrs. March, Mimi," I said. "And if he comes again, ask him in and call me."

"Call you, miss?"

"Call me," I said quietly. "When he asks for Miss March, merely ask him to come in. Then call me. Mrs. March has requested me to see him."

I took the letter and went upstairs, but I did not give it to Mrs. March at once. That night, while I made my coffee, I steamed open the envelope and read the contents. It was on pale lavender paper and was as follows:

"I implore you to see me as soon as posible. Come to the old place. I am up against it for sure. Don't let this go any longer! It's life or death with me!"

I made a careful copy of the note, even to the misspelled word, and sealed it again. Mr. March was out that night—a girl had been found in a hospital. He was always following some such forlorn hope, returning each time a little sadder, a little grayer.

Mrs. March was unusually exacting the next morning. She wakened at dawn with a cry and I went to her. I was sleeping on the couch at the foot of the bed. She was sitting up, terrified, in the gray dawn. She wailed that Clare needed her, was calling for her. She had heard her distinctly.

"Surely you do not believe in dreams!" I said sternly.

"Not in dreams, perhaps," she replied. She was still pallid. "But don't you think, Miss Adams, that people hear things in sleep that waking ears do not catch? You know what I mean. It's subconscious, or something."

"It's subnormal," I commented, and brought her back to earth with a cup of hot tea.

That morning I gave Mr. March the note. We were at breakfast and Mr. Plummer had dropped in, as he usually did, on his way to his downtown office. Mr. March read it without comment and passed it to the other man. He was younger, less poised. I saw him change color.

"Who brought this?" he demanded.

"Mimi got it. It was left by a thin, fair-haired young man."

They called Mimi, but she knew no more than I had told them, except for one fact: She said the man had tried to push by her into the house and that he had insisted that Miss March was at home. They sent the girl out. They seemed to have no scruple about talking before me.

"It is mystifying enough," Mr. Plummer said. "Patton ought to see it. But it doesn't help much. Whoever wrote that did not know that Clare was—not at home."

"Thin and fair-haired!" repeated Mr. March. "That's what Patton said, Walter—about the man at the railroad station, isn't it?"

"Patton is a fool!"

I gathered that the idea of the fair-haired man was extremely distasteful to him. He was almost surly.

We were sitting at the small breakfast table in the bay. I thought it a good time to speak about the little old woman. Any lingering doubt I may have had as to her right to be where I had seen her was dispelled by their manner. They were abstracted at first, then interested, then astounded.

"But, my dear young woman," Mr. March exclaimed, "why did you not rouse the house? And why did you wait for thirty hours before telling us?"

"It would be necessary for you to have seen her in order to understand. It never occurred to me that she was not a member of the household—she was so respectable. Only now, when I have seen all the servants, I begin to realize . . . She went out through that door."

"Is anything missing?" Mr. Plummer asked. "Mrs. March's jewels?"

"Still in the safe-deposit vault. We have had no heart to think of them."

Nevertheless a search of the house was made that day. Nothing was missing. Under Mrs. March's flushed directions, as she sat up in bed, I went round with great bunches of keys, verifying lists, looking up laces, locating furs. Such jewelry as she had about was safe.

As for the old lady with the jet on her bonnet, with the dolman and the buckled handbag—none of the family had ever known such a person. She answered no description, fitted into no place. Family and servants alike disclaimed her.

Life has a curious way of picking up threads and dropping them. The romantic young man with the blond hair, the little old lady with the limp, had come and gone; and for two weeks there was nothing more. Clare March remained missing. Mrs. March spoke of her in the past tense. Mr. Plummer grew thinner and took to coming into Mrs. March's room and sitting for long stretches without speech, his hands hanging listlessly between his knees.

I had my first real talk with Mr. Plummer late one afternoon while the invalid dozed in her chair. He was a good-looking man, something over thirty and already growing gray. He had sat for some time, apparently busy with his own thoughts—in reality watching me as I put away Mrs. March's various pretty trifles. She was always littered—ribbon bows, a nail file, a magazine, letters.

"Do you never make an unnecessary movement?" he asked at last.

"Frequently, I'm afraid."

"Must you put all those things away? Or will you sit down and talk for five minutes?"

I sat down near him. Mrs. March was now sound asleep.

"Do you want me to sit down and talk, or to sit down and listen?"

"To listen, and to answer some questions. Just a minute." He went quietly to the dressing table, returning with the photograph of Clare that stood there.

"You nurses know a lot about people," he said. "That's your business. You're a psychologist even if you don't realize it. I've watched you with Mrs. March. Now what do you read in that picture?"

"It is a lovely face," I replied, doing my best, but feeling utterly inadequate. Womanlike, I dare say I was anxious to say the thing he wanted to hear. "A—a pleasant face, I should say, but with character and temperament."

"What about the eyes?"

"They are well apart—that's a good sign, though cows are that way, aren't they! They are very direct and honest, too. Really, Mr. Plummer——"

"Here is a later picture, taken this summer. Now, what do you see?"

I was puzzled and uncomfortable.

"She looks older, more serious."

"Look at the eyes."

Well, there was a difference. I could not say where it lay. The effect was curious. In the early picture she was looking at the camera, and the eyes were limpid and clear. In the picture he had taken from his pocket-book she gazed into the camera also; but there was a sort of elusiveness about the eyes. It gave me a strange feeling of indirectness, evasion—I hardly know what. They might have been the eyes of a woman who had lived hard and suffered. And yet this girl of twenty had hardly lived as yet. It was almost a tragic face. I have seen the same drooping lines in eye cases, where vision is faulty and seeing an effort. What was this, then—astigmatism or evasion?

"You see it, don't you? Miss Adams, she has had some real trouble to make a change of that sort. I—I thought she was happy in our engagement; but as I look back, there are things——"

Mrs. March stirred and opened her eyes.

"I hate to waken," she said querulously. "It is only when I am asleep that I can forget, and even then I dream. Go out now, please, Walter; Miss Adams is going to use the vibrator."

That afternoon at five o'clock Mr. Patton called me on the telephone for the first time.

"I think we have something," he said. "When you go out for your walk tonight, dress for the street. There will be a taxicab at the corner and I shall be inside."

"At what time?"

"Seven thirty."

"Will an hour be enough?"

"Ask for two hours."

Mrs. March was rather peevish about my going out.

"I dare say you need air," she said, "but you could get it by opening a window. And what about my hot milk?"

"I'll ask Hortense to sit with you and she will heat the milk. I do not need air, of course. But I do need some exercise."

She let me go grudgingly. Mr. Patton would not tell me where we were going, but insisted on talking of indifferent things. As it turned out, we were headed for a police station; and at last he voiced his errand.

"We are going to show you a lot of handbags," he said. "A woman pickpocket was brought in here yesterday with four in a pocket under a skirt. I was looking over them today and it occurred to me that you might recognize one of them."

"Mine! I hope you send her up for a year!"

"Not yours. And do not jump to conclusions; it is fatal in this business."

I knew the bag at once when I saw it. Surely no other bag of that size in the city had two straps fastened with steel buckles. The handles of two of the other bags had been cut off, but the heavy leather handle of this one was entire.

"This is the one you mean, of course. Yes, it looks like the one the old lady carried; but there may be others. It is foreign, isn't it?"

"What was she doing that night when you noticed the bag?"

"She opened it and put in a pair of spectacles in a case."

He unfastened the bag and emptied onto a table a tin spectacle case, as quaint as the bag; two keys, one for a patent lock, the other an ordinary house key. Last of all he drew from a pocket inside the bag a soiled and creased lavender envelope, stamped and ready for mailing. It was addressed in pencil to Mrs. March and had been opened. Mr. Patton drew out the communication inside and watched me as I read it. It was hardly decipherable and was written on a piece of wrapping paper:

"Am all right. Clare."

I stared at it.

"Interesting, isn't it?" commented Mr. Patton. "Did she write it or didn't she? If she's all right, why isn't she home? Why do all our little communications arrive in lavender envelopes? Who's the old lady? What was she doing in the house that night? What's the answer?"

"That could be the key to the garden door," I said dully.

## CHAPTER IV

THE DOCTOR made a late call that night and dismissed Mrs. March as a patient.

"I'll drop in now and then to learn what the news is," he said as he prepared to leave. "You don't need me professionally. Just keep cheerful. It will all come out right."

I followed him into the hall. It seemed to me that if anyone knew the inside history I had failed to secure, it was he. And up to that time I had failed with him.

"I hope you will stay on, Miss Adams. I am leaving her in your hands—remember, no drugs so long as she is normal; at any symptoms of nervousness again, start them early."

"It's a trying case," I said slowly. "It takes it out of me, doctor. She asks me for theories, and—of course I didn't know the girl or her life—I cannot give her what she wants."

He hesitated. We were in the lower hall by that time.

"Just what does she want?"

"Encouragement."

"That Clare is living, of course. Well, tell her this the next time she is down. It is true enough. Tell her Clare was unhappy in her engagement and that I believe there is another man; that she has eloped with him; and that her message to the family has miscarried."

"Wilson Page?"

He eyed me. For the first time it occurred to me that he suspected my business in the house and that he was giving me information that ethically he would have refused.

"No; a blond fellow, rather thin. I have seen her meeting him in the park, and once I believe she met him in my reception room."

He seemed to regret this information the moment I had it and left immediately.

That night, after I had rubbed Mrs. March with cocoanut oil, used the vibrator, given her hot milk and finally read her to sleep, I slipped into my room and sat down by the window. The autumn garden lay beneath, with no moon to bring out its geometrical desolation. And there, elbows on the sill, the chill air blowing about me, I tried to piece together the scraps I held: the little old lady, the blond man and his frantic note, the letter in the buckled bag. And again I recalled the conversation Mr. Patton and I had had in the taxicab that evening.

"She's alive," he had said; "and she is in the city—if that note is hers, and I think it is. I'll show it to the father and the other chap in the morning. Then she is in hiding. Why?"

I lay down on a couch at the foot of Mrs. March's bed, but did not get to sleep, for some reason. The slightest movement of my patient found me wide-eyed and alert. Small sounds were exaggerated. A regular footstep that seemed to ascend the stairs for hours turned out to be a drip from a bathroom tap. The slow chiming of the hall clock set me crazy.

At two o'clock I got up and went downstairs. In the waitress's pantry, off the dining room, there were beef cubes. It seemed to me that if I drank a cup of bouillon I might sleep. As usual the light was burning in the lower hall. The dining room was dark—I no longer required a night supper—and the little table in the bay window was bare. A street light beyond the garden showed the window and the longer rectangle of the garden door. I was not nervous.

I made my way through the unlighted dining room to the pantry, a small room, painted white, with a butler's slide to the basement kitchen, and a small white glass and silver refrigerator built into the wall, where the waitress kept the dining-room butter and cream. The electric light was out of order there; I pressed the switch, but there was no answering flood of light. I had matches with me for the alcohol lamp, however, and found my bouillon cubes easily. Thus I was still in darkness when I opened the swinging door into the dining room.

Someone was trying the lock of the garden door! I do not mind saying I was terrified. The door was glass. To cross the room to the lighted hall would throw my whole figure into relief. I shrank back, breathing with difficulty, into my corner. Beyond the thin casement cloth of the door I could see a moving shadow.

The lock did not give. It seemed to me, all at once, that I knew the silhouette—that here again was the little old lady, but now without her key. My heart ceased pounding. I was able to think, to calculate. I wondered whether she would break the glass. I planned to let her get in if she could and then to cut off her retreat by advancing on her from behind. I was very calm by that time—rather exalted, I dare say, at my own bravery. I put the packet of beef cubes into my pocket in order to have both hands free.

I do not know just when I realized that it was not the little old lady—I believe it was after one of the panes had been broken and had fallen with a soft crash onto the rug inside. The figure straightened; it was much taller than I had expected. I recall that my heart almost stopped and then raced on at a mad pace; I saw what I knew was a hand put through the opening; I heard the lock turn and the cautious opening of the door. The intruder was in the room with me.

Panic possessed me then. I turned wildly and threw myself headlong against the swinging pantry door. It was madness, of course. There was no exit from the little room, no way to fasten the door. I was in a cul-de-sac and in the black dark. I believe I opened a drawer and got a cake knife; at least, eons after, I found myself clutching one. I do not remember how I got it.

The swinging door remained undisturbed. When I could hear—above the pounding in my ears—there was no sound anywhere except the hall clock's slow chiming.

Many things I have never recalled clearly about that hideous night. I do not know, for instance, how long I stood at bay in the pantry; or how my courage rose from my knees, which ceased trembling, to my spinal cord, to my pulse, which went down from about a hundred and eighty, thin and stringy, to what I judged was almost normal, still irregular, but stronger. When my courage reached my brain, which was in perhaps fifteen minutes, though I would have sworn it was daylight by that time and I had stood there most of the night, I put my ear against the door and listened. There was no sound.

The instinct of my training asserted itself. Whatever was happening, my patient must not be alone. I must get up to the sickroom. In a few moments it was an obsession. I must get back. My sense of duty was stronger than my terror.

I made the break at last, opening the door an inch or so. The room was quiet. With infinite caution I pushed the door farther open. I could see the room, solidly handsome, rather heavy, empty! I made my first few steps of progress with deliberate slowness. I knew that if I ran, panic would follow at my heels. I dared not look over my shoulder. Even the lighted hall brought small comfort, with the dark rooms opening off it, sheltering I knew not what; but I reached the foot of the stairs in safety. There I stopped.

A woman, dressed in rags, lay huddled on the bottom steps in a faint. She lay face down. Even when I had turned her over and had recognized the features of the photographs in the house, I was still incredulous. Nevertheless it was true. Bruised and torn, clad in rags, gaunt to the point of emaciation, Clare March had come home again.

It was the end of one mystery—the beginning of another.

## CHAPTER V

MY FIRST FEELING was one of horror. Her condition was frankly terrible. I even feared at first that she was dead. I found a pulse, however. I am big and strong; I got her down off the staircase and laid her flat on the floor. All the time I was praying that none of the family or the servants had been roused. I did not want anyone to see her yet.

I brought down some aromatic ammonia and gave it to her in water. Mrs. March was sleeping calmly; across the hall Mr. March also slept, audibly. I had a little time; I wanted an hour—maybe two.

She came to very gradually, throwing an arm over her head, moving a little, and finally opening her eyes. I talked soothingly to her.

"Now don't be alarmed," I said over and over. "You are at home and everything is all right. I am a nurse. Everything is all right."

"I want—Julie," she said at last, feebly.

I had never heard the name.

"Julie is coming. Can you sit up if I hold you?"

She made an effort, and by degrees I got her into the music room, where she collapsed again; and, there being no couch, I put her down on the floor with a cushion under her head. Terrible thoughts had been running through my head. The papers had been full of abduction stories, and I confess I thought nothing else could explain her condition, her rags.

"I am hungry," she said when I got her settled. "I am—I am starving! I don't know when I have had anything to eat."

She looked it, too. I had the beef cubes in my pocket and I left her there while I made some broth. I brought it back, with crackers. She was sitting in a chair by that time, and she drank the stuff greedily, blistering hot as it was.

I had my first chance to take an inventory of her appearance. It was startling. Her hands were abraded and blistered. She held one out to me pathetically, but without comment. Over one eye was a deep bluish bruise. Her face was almost colorless, and her forearm, where one sleeve had been torn away, was thin to emaciation. Every trace of beauty was eclipsed for the time. She was shocking—that is all.

Her clothing was thin and inadequate: a torn white waist, much soiled; a short, ragged black skirt; and satin bedroom slippers, frayed and cut. She had nothing on her head and no wrap, though the night was cold. She looked up at me when she held out the empty cup.

"How is Mother?"

"She has not been well."

"Was it worry?"

"Yes. Do you think you can get up the stairs?"

"Is that all I am to have to eat?"

"I'll get more soon. You mustn't take too much at once."

She rose and I put my arm around her. She had taken me for granted, childishly, but at the foot of the stairs she halted our further progress to ask me, "Who are you? You are not a servant."

"I am a trained nurse. I've been caring for your mother during her illness."

We went up the stairs and into her room.

Mrs. March wakened about the time I had got the girl to her own room.

"Don't tell Mother yet," she begged. "Give me a little time. I—I'd frighten her now."

I promised.

When I went back, half an hour later, Clare had undressed herself and put on a negligee from the closet. She was sitting in front of the fire I had lighted, brushing out her hair. For the first time she was reminiscent of the girl of the photographs. She was not like them yet—she was too gaunt.

I tried to coax her to bed, but she would not go. I was puzzled. Her nervous excitement was extreme; more than once she stopped, with brush poised, as if she were on the point of asking me some question; but she never asked it—her courage evidently failed her. It was a horrible night. I sat inside the door of my patient's room, in darkness, and watched the door opposite. I could hear the girl pacing back and forth; I was almost crazy.

I offered her a bromide, which she refused to take; but about half past three I heard her lie down on the bed, and some of the tension relaxed. I had a chance to think, to work out a course of action. Mr. Patton should be notified at once; and as soon as the girl was really composed, I would rouse Mr. March. I knew I would be criticized in the family for not rousing them all at once, but I am always willing to take the responsibility for what I do—the doctor's orders first and my own judgment next is my motto. And there have been times when the doctor's orders—but never mind about that.

I looked at my watch. It was almost four o'clock and still black dark. I went down to the library, where the telephone stood on a stand behind a teakwood screen, and called up Mr. Patton's apartment; but I could not get him.

I hung up the receiver and sat there in the darkness, meaning to try again in a moment or so. It was while I was still there that I heard Clare on the stairs.

She came slowly and painfully—a step; a pause for rest, another step. Once down in the lower hall, she made better progress. She came directly into the library, through the music room, and turned on the lights.

I was curious. It was easy to watch her through the carved margin of the screen. It was only curiosity. I had no idea there would be further mystery to solve. In the morning she would tell her story, the law would take hold, and that would be all. But I recall distinctly every movement she made.

First she went to the long table littered with magazines, with the bronze reading lamp in the center. She glanced over the magazines as they lay, picked up the framed picture of herself and looked at it for a long moment, her hands visibly trembling. Then she took a survey of the room.

There was an English fender about the fireplace, with a tufted leather top. Mr. Plummer habitually sat there, with his back to the fire. And just inside, thrown carelessly, lay a newspaper. It was the newspaper she wanted. It was not easy for her to reach it in her weakened condition. She stooped, staggered, bent again, and got it.

The wood fire had burnt itself out, but the warm bricks and ashes still threw out a comforting heat. She curled up on the floor by the fender and proceeded to go over the pages, running a shaking finger through paragraph after paragraph. I was most uncomfortable, half ashamed, and cramped from my position.

When I felt that I could stand no more, she found what she was looking for. I heard her gasp and then saw her throw herself forward, her face in her arms, crying silently but fiercely, her shoulders shaking. She paid no attention when I bent over her, except to draw herself away from my hand. When I tried to take the newspaper, however, she snatched it from my hand and sat up.

"Go away!" she said hysterically. "Stop following me and watching me. Can't I even cry alone?"

I was rather offended. I drew back, like a fool, and lost a clue that we did not find until weeks later.

"I'm sorry you feel that way," I said coldly and went out and up the stairs.

She burned the paper before she made a laborious and faltering ascent of the staircase half an hour later—at least, when I went down, there was no sign of it or of any of the newspapers that had littered the room. And, though Mr. Patton secured copies of them all later and we went over them patiently, we could find nothing that seemed to have the remotest bearing on what we were trying to learn.

She was much better by morning—had slept a little; was calmer; had a bit of color in her ears, which had been wax-white; but the bruise on her forehead was blacker.

I broke the news of her return very gently to Mr. March at dawn and left it to him to tell his wife. I went to her afterward and found her hysterically impatient to see her daughter. I induced her to wait, however, until she had had an egg and a piece of toast. I do not believe in excitement on an entirely empty stomach. We covered the bruise with a loop of Clare's heavy hair; and then her father and mother went in and I closed the door.

Somebody had telephoned for Mr. Plummer; but she sent her father out to say she would not see him just yet. It was like a blow in the face. He almost reeled.

"That's the message, boy," Mr. March said. "I don't understand it any more than you do. She's in frightful condition; we've sent for the doctor. Tomorrow I am sure——"

"But what does she say?" Mr. Plummer broke in. "Where has she been? I'll wait until she wants to see me, of course, but for God's sake tell me where she has been!"

"She has told us very little," Mr. March had to confess. "She is hardly coherent yet. She says she will talk to the police sometime today. She has been imprisoned—that is all we know."

Mrs. March's sitting room was open and Mr. Plummer went in and sat down heavily. Sometime later, as I passed the door, he called me in.

"You saw her first, didn't you?" he asked. "Will you sit down and tell me all you know about it?"

I was glad to talk—I had been bottled up for so long. I told him everything—except my reason for being down in the library behind the screen.

"Did she ask for me at all?" he asked when I had finished.

"I—I think so. Naturally she would."

He smiled at me wryly.

"You know she did not ask for me," he said and got up.

I was very sorry for him. He was so earnest, so bewildered. He waited round all morning, hoping for a message, and about noon she said she would see him. Her own maid dressed her and together we put a little rouge on her face and touched up her colorless lips. Except for the hollows in her cheeks, she looked lovely. I gave her message to him.

"Tell him I want to see him," she said to me; "but he is not to ask a lot of questions, and he is to stay only a minute or two—I am so very tired."

He was uncertain of his welcome, I think. I took him to the door. She was on a couch, propped up with pillows, and the bruise was covered. And when I saw the look in his eyes and the assuring flame in hers, I knew that, whatever else was wrong, it was nothing that lay between them. The vision of the blond man as Clare's lover died at that moment and never came to life again.

The story of the almost two months of Clare March's disappearance she told to Mr. Patton that afternoon. She would not allow her father and mother to be present, and only Mr. Patton's insistence that the nurse should be there to see that she did not overtax her strength secured my admission. The story was short and was told haltingly. It gave me the impression of truth, but of being only a part of the truth. Her descriptions of the people and of the surroundings, for instance, were undoubtedly drawn from painful memory. They were photographic—raw with truth. The same was true of her story of the escape.

"It was on the third of September that you started home," Mr. Patton said. "We know that, and that you arrived on the morning of the fourth. We lost you from the time you got into a taxicab at the station. Did you order the man to drive you home?"

"Not directly. I went to—" She named the department store to which she had been traced. "I had made my purchase when a young man came up to me and introduced himself. He said I did not know him, but that he was living in the same house with an old German teacher of mine, Fräulein Julie Schlenker. She had taught me at boarding school and I was very fond of her. He said she was—dying."

Tears came into her eyes. Mr. Patton caught my eye for the fraction of a second.

"Was this before you bought the blankets or after?"

She looked startled, but he was smiling pleasantly. If she had to reassemble her story, she did it well and quickly.

"Before. I was terribly worried about Julie," she said. "I agreed to go there at once, and I asked him what I could take her to make her comfortable. He said she couldn't eat, but perhaps blankets—or something like that. I bought blankets and had them put in the taxicab."

"What address did this blond young man give you?"

"I did not say he was a blond young man," she objected. "I do not remember what he looked like. I should not know him again."

Mr. Patton nodded gravely.

"My mistake," he said. "Was this the same taxicab?"

"No; I had dismissed the other. I got into the taxicab and the man gave an address to the driver. I paid no attention to it. I was upset about Julie. I hardly looked out. We went very fast. All the time I was seeing Julie lying dead, with her poor old face—" She shuddered. Clearly that part of the story was true enough and painful. "We drove for a long time. I was worried about the bill. When the register said four dollars I was anxious. I had checks, but very little money."

She stopped herself suddenly and gave Mr. Patton a startled glance, but he was blandness itself.

"Four dollars!" he said. "Did you know the neighborhood?"

"Not at all. I was angry and accused the driver of taking a roundabout way. He said he had gone directly and offered to ask a policeman."

"You were still in the city then?"

"Yes; but it was far out. When the driver drew up, I had just enough money to pay him. It was almost five dollars."

"Can you remember exactly?"

"Four dollars and eighty cents. I gave that man five dollars. I had only a dollar left."

"The young man was still with you?"

"No, indeed. I was quite alone. I wish you would not interrupt me."

Mr. Patton sat back good-humoredly and folded his hands. I knew why he had continually broken in on the story. I thought he had caught something, by his look.

"I got out. I had the blankets and they were bulky. The man carried them to the doorstep and drove away. I thought it was a queer neighborhood. It was a mean little house, off by itself, with only an unoccupied house near.

"I felt very strange, but Julie was always queer.

"I asked for Julie. A hideous old woman answered the door. The whole place was filthy. I felt terribly for Julie—she was always so neat. I went in and up the stairs. The stairs were narrow and steep, and shut off below with a door. All I could think of was Julie in that horrible place. There were cobwebs along the stairs. We turned toward the back of the house and stopped before a door. The old woman did not rap. She opened it and said, 'In here, miss.' I went in. The room was empty. I said, 'Why, where is Julie?' But the old woman had gone. I heard her outside locking the door."

That was a strange story we listened to that afternoon—a story of futile calls for help; of bread and water passed through a broken panel in the door; of a drugged sleep, from which she wakened to find her clothing gone and rags substituted; of drunken revels below; and of the constant, maddening surveillance through the panel by a man with a squint. She described the room with absolute accuracy and even drew it roughly for Mr. Patton: a low attic room with two small windows; a sloping roof; discolored plaster from a leak above, a washstand without bowl or pitcher;

for light a glass lamp with a smoked chimney; and for furniture a cot under the lowest part of the ceiling, and a chair.

Once a day, she said, the old woman brought her a tin basin for washing, and a towel, rough-dried. The basin had a red string to hang it up by, she said. The towels were checked—pink and white.

"Like glass towels," she said. "There was a grate for coal and a wooden shelf above it, with an old steel engraving tacked up on the wall. One corner was loose, and if I left the window open, it flapped all the time. I had a fire only once; but I did not suffer from cold—the kitchen was beneath, and the flue was always warm."

"This steel engraving—do you remember what it was?"

"The Landing of the Pilgrims," she said promptly. "Someone had colored a part of it with crayons—a child probably."

Mr. Patton looked puzzled. She might have invented the panel in the door or the man with the squint; but parts of her story bore the absolute imprint of truth: the chimney flue being warm, the flapping picture, the rough-dried towels, the basin with a red string through its rim.

"In a moment I want you to tell us how you got away," Mr. Patton said, "but first—I want a reason for all this. Was it—did they try to force you to anything?"

"Nothing at all."

"They were not white slavers then?"

She colored. "No."

"They never threatened you?"

She hesitated, considered.

"Only when I cried out—and that did no good. There was only an empty house near."

"Miss March, this is an almost incredible story. A crime must have a motive. You are saying that you were imprisoned in an isolated house for nearly two months, were unharmed and unthreatened, but under constant surveillance, and finally made your escape. And you can imagine no reason for it!"

"I haven't said that at all—I imagined plenty of reasons. Couldn't they have wanted a ransom?"

"They made no attempt to secure one."

She told of her escape rather briefly. If I can give in so many words my impression of her story, it was that here and there she was on sure ground, and that the escape was drawn absolutely from memory and was accurate in every detail.

"Every now and then they all got drunk," she said. "I—I always thought they would set the house on fire. The two younger women would sing—and it was horrible."

"You did not say there were younger women."

She was confused.

"There were two. One was married to the man. They called the old woman Ma. And there was a man with a wooden leg who visited the house. He came over the field; I saw him often. For two days they'd been drinking, and the old woman fell down and hurt herself. I could hear her groaning. And I was hungry—I was terribly hungry." She looked at me. "You know how hungry I was. I had not even water."

"She was starving," I said.

"Nobody came. I was frightened. I kept thinking that something had happened." She checked herself, started again. "All evening I lay in darkness. I could hear them yelling and singing, and now and then the old woman groaning. And I was so thirsty I hoped it would rain and the roof would leak. That's how thirsty I was. I slept a little—not very much. Mostly I walked about and worried. The house was so quiet that it drove me crazy."

"Quiet! Were they asleep?"

She looked at him quickly.

"They went away—all of them. There was only the old woman, and she was hurt. When I called, nobody answered."

"How was your door fastened?"

"On the outside."

"Couldn't you have put your arm through the broken panel and unlocked it?"

"The key was not in the lock. It never was. It was always on a nail at the top of the staircase. I could see it."

No one could have doubted her. The key was kept at the top of the stairs on a nail. It takes a perceptible second to invent such a detail. She had not invented it.

"All the next day no one came near me. One of the windowpanes was broken. I called through it for help. Sometimes there were people in the fields beyond the house. There was nobody that day except some little boys. They paid no attention; perhaps they did not hear me. I was getting weaker all the time. I thought that pretty soon I would be too weak to try to escape. The fire was out below and my room was cold. My hands were so stiff I could hardly move them. I worked a long time at the window. They had driven nails in all round it. I worked them loose."

She held out her hands. They were cut and blistered.

"I got them out at last, but I broke a pane of glass. I hardly cared whether it was heard or not. I had never been able before to see what lay below the window. There was a sort of shed there.

"I had to wait until night. The room was freezing, with the window out.

They were still away, except the old woman. She lay and groaned down below. I lay on the mattress the rest of the day and shivered. As soon as it was dark, I crawled up on the windowsill. I was frightened—it looked so far down. I lowered myself by my hands and then dropped; but I slipped. I thought I had broken my ankle. The loose boards on the shed made a frightful noise."

"How did you find your way home?"

"I walked for hours. I do not know anything about the streets. I just walked toward the glow of the city lights against the sky. When I got into the city proper, I knew where I was."

"Where were you when you first recognized your surroundings?"

"I saw the North Market."

"Do you remember from which direction you approached it?"

"The west side, I believe." Her tone was reluctant.

Mr. Patton drew a soiled lavender envelope from his pocket and took out its enclosure.

"'Am all right. Clare,'" he read. "Now, Miss March, just when and where did you write this little note?"

Her only answer was to break into hysterical crying. "Julie! Julie!" she cried. She absolutely refused to explain the note. It was an *impasse*. She could neither explain it nor ignore it. She took refuge in tears and silence.

That was the end of Clare March's story. It sounded like madness; but there was proof of a sort—her general condition; her hands; her brief but photographic descriptions. It was true—at least in part. It was not the whole truth. She had not spoken of the blond man or of the little old lady in black; and yet I was convinced she knew about them both. Mr. Patton thought as I did; for when she was quieter, he asked for a description of the old woman of her story.

"She was very stout," she said slowly, "and very dirty. She always wore the same things—a blue calico dress and an apron. She seemed to be washing all the time; the apron was always wet and soapy. And she had thin gray hair drawn into a hard knot."

"Could you tell her nationality by her voice—her accent?"

"I'm afraid not."

"Did you ever see her dressed for the street?"

"Never."

"Then you never saw her in a black bonnet trimmed with jet, and an old-fashioned dolman, and carrying a pocketbook fastened with two buckles?"

She leaned over suddenly and caught Mr. Patton by the wrist.

"I can't stand it any longer!" she cried. "What do you know? Was the paper wrong?"

When she saw by his face that he did not understand and could not help her, she sank back among her pillows. She would not answer any more questions and lapsed into a watchful silence.

## CHAPTER VI

NATURALLY I have never taken any credit for the solution of the Clare March mystery. Even now, when I am writing under an assumed name, I am uneasy. To be suspected would be my professional ruin. So far I have been able to keep my double calling a profound secret. I may have been in your house. Think it over, those of you who have something to conceal— are you certain that the soft-walking, starched young woman to whom in your weakness you talked so freely—are you sure it was not myself? Under the skin, I said in the beginning—aye, and under the flesh and its weaknesses. Do you recall that day when you and a visitor talked at the bedside and I wrote letters in a corner by a window? How do you know but that your entire conversation, word by word, was at the Central Office in two hours? Did it ever occur to you before?

I wrote many letters that week. Mrs. March was up and about, bustling and busy; Clare was my patient. I no longer met Mr. Patton in the evenings. He was combing the outskirts of the city, I believe, and interviewing taxicab drivers. I sent a daily report to him by mail:

MONDAY—I notice one curious thing: She will not let me do much for her. Hortense, her maid, does some things—not much. She gets rid of us both whenever she can. I feel worse than useless. I have offered to give her massage, but she refuses. Mr. Plummer only comes to the door—she does not wish him to come in.

TUESDAY—Still weak and inert. A box of flowers every day from Mr. Plummer. I had once thought possibly she did not care for him; but today I saw her eyes again when she looked at the roses—I believe she is crazy about him. She would like to get rid of me, but her parents insist she needs me. Her hands are healing. There is one curious thing—her wrists are abraded. Did she say her hands were tied?

WEDNESDAY—The blond man has been here. I saw him from the stairs and went down. He is not what we thought at all. He is untidy and shabby. He was waiting inside the door, turning his hat round in his hands. I told him Miss March was ill, but he refused to leave. He said, "Tell her it is Samuels, and this is the last call. She'll know what I mean." I said, "I think she has had a letter from you." He turned livid. "Then she got it!" he stormed. "And she paid no attention to it! You tell her, for me, that she'll fix things with me now—today—or I'll tell the whole story!" He felt in his watch pocket and seemed to remember that his watch was gone. That added to his rage. "You tell her that. Tell her she'll have it at the old place by three this afternoon or I'll go to her precious sweetheart and tell him some things he ought to know." I tried to follow him when he left, but by the time I'd got my hat and ulster he was out of sight. If Samuels is his real name, you can probably find him. He is blond and smooth-shaved, and has a gold tooth—right side, upper jaw; wears a tan overcoat and a soft green felt hat.

WEDNESDAY, four P.M.—I have just come back from an errand for Clare. I have been to the "old place" with a parcel for Samuels. It was money. He was so greedy that he tore it open while I waited. It seemed to be considerable—well over a hundred dollars. When he had counted it, he put it in his pocket. He looked better than in the morning and was calmer. He looked at me after he had counted it. "Don't look so damned virtuous!" he said. "This isn't blackmail. It's for value received."

The "old place" is at the corner of Tenth Street and the Embankment. We stood in the doorway of a vacant building and talked. Samuels looks decayed—as if he has seen better days. I tried to get you by telephone to follow me. You were out.

THURSDAY—A very curious thing happened today: Clare asked for some chicken cooked in cream. The cook had never done it and I volunteered. It took some time; I was in the basement more than an hour. When I came up with the chicken, she had disappeared. We were all terribly frightened. I called the office twice, but you were out as usual—you will have to arrange some way for me to get you in emergencies. She had taken her wraps and gone out by the garden door. The parlor maid had not seen her. It was two hours later when she came back, exhausted. She locked herself in her room and it was almost the dinner hour before she would admit me.

Her father had a talk with her tonight. He said, "You must not do such unwise things. You will drive your mother frantic."

"Poor Mother!" she replied. "I'll tell you before long where I was. Don't ask me."

I thought she had been crying. I believe she has pawned or sold her sapphire ring; I do not see it.

That last letter, sent special delivery, and unsigned as all of them were, brought a telephone message from the detective and an appointment for that evening.

"Ask for an evening off," he said. "I think I've got it. And I want to talk to you."

He had a taxi at the corner that night. It was when it was well under way that he began to talk.

"We've got the house," he said. "The man with the squint did it—but that's a long story. In Miss March's anxiety to tell as much as she dared of the truth, she went a little too far. Given a four-dollar-and-eighty-cent taxi-cab radius, an isolated house with two young women, an old hag and a man with a squint—put a shed on the back of the house and a bad reputation all over it—and you have perhaps two dozen possibilities. Add such graphic touches as a built-in stairway and a tin basin hung up by a red string as identification marks, and an empty house and a man with a wooden leg for neighbors, and out of the two dozen there will be one house that fits. We've found it."

"Is that where we are going?"

"To that neighborhood. I really wanted a chance to go over the whole thing with you. Now, then, what do you think? You've been close to the case—closer than I have. How much of that story of hers is true?"

"About half of it."

"Which half?"

"Well, I think she was not a prisoner. I believe she was a voluntary guest in the house she described and that she was hiding from something."

"I see. And not expecting us to find the house, she gave a circumstantial description. But what was she hiding from? So far as we can learn, her past has been an open book—she was away at school for four years, and spent a year abroad with a party of girls and a chaperone. She came out two years ago—I remember reading about the coming-out ball, something very elaborate. That first winter she went about with young Page, became engaged and broke it off. Page has been away ever since. It can't have anything to do with Page. Last spring she took on this Plummer—has been with her family all summer—has never, except during the year abroad, been away from her mother for any length of time. That doesn't look like anything to hide from. What do you think of the Julie story?"

"I don't believe it. But there is a Julie."

"Does the family know the name?"

"No. The girl is paying blackmail, Mr. Patton."

"The blond chap?"

"Yes."

"That was rotten luck, my being out of touch that day. If we had him—or if we had your friend, the little old lady!"

He stopped the taxicab shortly after and we got out. We were well out of the center of town, in a scattering suburb. I had never seen it. And before us stretched one of those empty spaces that are left here and there, without apparent cause, during the growth of the city. House builders are gregarious—they build in clusters. Perhaps it's a matter of sewers or of gas and water. To right and left of us stretched a sort of field, almost bare of grass, with straggling paths across it. Long before, a street had been cut through; its edges were still intact—a pitfall for the unwary.

I did not see all this that night. It was late October and very dark. Mr. Patton had a pocket flash, and with that and his hand I managed fairly. Our destination was before us—a little house, faintly lighted.

"I'm afraid this isn't very pleasant, Miss Adams," he apologized; "and I haven't a good reason for bringing you. But I'm up against it in a way. I want you to see this place and perhaps your instinct will tell you what I fail to make out. I've been here once today and it stumps me. They swear they've never had a girl there; that the man with the wooden leg sleeps in the garret sometimes. He's a watchman at the railroad over there. By the way, did she speak of a railroad?"

"I think not."

"It's a bad place. The police protection doesn't amount to much, but over there in the town they say it's a speakeasy. The cellar's full of beer. They say other things, too—that the old woman is a white slaver, for one thing. That bears out the story partly. And another thing does also—the hag hurt herself lately. She's going about with a cane. On the other hand—well, if they were lying today they did a good piece of work."

There was a wagon near the house as we approached. At first we thought they were moving out. Then Mr. Patton laughed.

"Getting rid of the beer and the empties," he said. "Got them scared! Now don't be nervous. You needn't speak to them. I want you to keep your eyes open—that's all."

I was nervous. There was something sinister about the very location. I have even now rather a hazy recollection of Mr. Patton's rap at the door, the imperious summons of the law, and of a hideous old woman who peered out into the darkness.

"Well, Mother," Mr. Patton said cheerfully, "here I am again. I want to look round a little."

The hag made as if to close the door, but a woman spoke from behind. "Let him in, Ma," she said. "We ain't got nothing to hide. Come in, mister."

A man came up from a cellarway with a box of bottles. I can still see his face over the bottles—his sickening pallor, his squint. He thought it was a raid, clearly. Then he saw me and his color came back.

"I guess a man's 'ouse is 'is own," he snarled. "We drink a little beer ourselves. That ain't agin' the law, I reckon."

"Not at all," Mr. Patton said good-humoredly. "I'll have a lamp, please." It appeared to be a four-roomed house. We stood in the front room, an untidy place with a bed in a corner, and heavy with stale odors. Behind, there was a kitchen containing a table littered with the remains of the evening meal. Between the two rooms was a narrow, steep staircase shut off with a door below and ending above in a small landing. From this landing two doorways opened—one into a front room, the other into a half room, or attic, over the kitchen. It was into this room that Mr. Patton, carrying a smoky lamp, led the way.

"This is the room," he said. "That is the window with the shed below. Here is where the flue comes up from the kitchen."

I looked round. It was a sordid, filthy place. The plaster had broken away here and there. Where it was intact it was discolored from a leaking roof. For furniture there was a mattress on the floor, with soiled bedding, a chair with a broken seat and a washstand. Clare had said the washstand was unfurnished, but had mentioned a tin basin. Here was a tin basin with a red string. Mr. Patton was watching me grimly.

"Well, what do you make of it?" he said.

"It looks queer," I admitted. "Only there are some things—the panel in the door, for instance. There is no door."

"I asked about that. They say it came off the hinges a month or so ago and they chopped it up for firewood."

I was still looking about. He had stooped and was examining the door hinges.

"She said she broke the glass. One window is broken, but this one over the shed is not."

He came over and ran his hand over the window frame.

"Sash is nailed in, which I believe was also mentioned!" he said. Our eyes met in the dim light—a friendly clash; he was so sure of the place and I was so doubtful.

As I stood there peering into the squalid corners of the attic, I remembered the daintiness of the girl's room at home—its bright chintz and shining silver, its soft lamps, its cushions, its white bath beyond. I remembered the exquisite service of the March household and tried to picture the hag below climbing that ladder of a staircase with a platter of greasy food. I tried to forget Clare in her lovely negligee, and to recall the haggard creature who had dropped in her rags at the foot of the staircase. And I tried to place the wretched girl of that night in this wretched place. I could not do it. There was something wrong.

Mr. Patton turned to me, gravely smiling.

"Now, then, your instinct against my training," he said. "Is this the place?"

"I do not believe she was ever here," I said. "Don't ask me why—I just don't believe it." But a moment later I felt that my instinct had received a justification. "Do you remember," I said, "a graphic description of a steel engraving that flapped in the wind?"

"By George!"

"There is not only no engraving—there are no nail holes in the plaster. There has never been such an engraving here," I said in triumph.

CHAPTER VII

I HAVE often wondered what would have happened had we taken Clare March the next day to that untidy house in Brickyard Road. Brickyard Road was the local name of the street that had been cut through and forgotten.

Would she have told the real story or not? If not, how would she have explained the discrepancy, for instance, of the missing engraving? Would she have taken refuge in silence? Had she hoped by the very detail of her description to throw us off the track? Did she wonder, those dreadful days, how the bag with the buckles had come into the hands of the police and yet had not led us further? Did she suspect me at any time?

Sometimes I thought she did. She would not let me do much for her. I gave her the medicines that were ordered, saw to her nourishment, read to her occasionally. Her own maid looked after her personally. It rather irritated me. More than once I found her watching me. I would glance up from my book and find her eyes on me with a question in them; but she never asked it.

Mr. Patton was waiting eagerly to take her out to Brickyard Road; but she was still very weak and she showed a distaste for the excursion that was understandable enough under the circumstances. Other things puzzled me, however—her unwillingness to see Mr. Plummer was one. Yet she sat for hours looking at his picture. I suspected, too, that her maid was closely in her confidence. More than once I caught a glance of understanding between them. Sometimes I wondered if Clare was quite normal—not insane, of course, but with some queer mental bias.

Outwardly everything was calm. She lay or sat in her fairylike room, with flowers all about her. Her color was coming back. In her soft negligees she looked flowerlike herself. The picture was quite complete: a lovely convalescent, a starched and capped nurse, a maid in black and white, flowers, order, decorum, with a lover hovering in the background. But the nurse was making notes on her record that were not of symptoms; the maid was not clever enough to mask her air of mystery; and the lover paced back and forth downstairs waiting for a word that never came.

On the day following my excursion with Mr. Patton, going into my own room unexpectedly, I found Hortense, the maid, in my clothes closet. She made profuse apologies and backed out. She had been looking, she said, for a frock that had been mislaid. I did not believe her.

After she had gone, I made a careful examination of the closet. A row of my white linen dresses hung there, my street clothes, my mackintosh. In a far end, where I had placed them the night she arrived, were the ragged garments in which Clare had come home. I locked my door and, taking them out, went over them carefully.

There was a worn black skirt, rather short; a ragged and filthy waist of poor material and carelessly made, put together by hand with large stitches and coarse thread. The undergarments were similarly sewed. They might have come from just such a place as the house in Brickyard Road. The skirt was different. Though ragged, it was well made, and it had been shortened.

I found something just then. On the inside of the belt was woven the name of one of the leading tailors in the city. I thought that over awhile. The skirt could hardly belong to Brickyard Road. It seemed to me that this was a valuable clue. It seemed to me that Hortense knew this also, and that there was no time to be lost.

The situation was put up to me that day in an unexpected fashion. Mr. Patton slipped on the first ice of the season and injured the leg that had been hurt before. He was almost wild with vexation.

"Just keep wide awake," he wrote me by special delivery, "and send me the usual daily bulletins. If anything very important happens, come round and see me. The people we saw are being watched. If you meet the blond chap, follow him until you get a chance to telephone. I'll send someone to relieve you. We haven't got it all yet by any means."

It rather knocked my plans, especially as I could tell by the shaky writing that he was suffering when he wrote the letter. It seemed to me that for a day or so I should have to get along alone.

But I could do something—I could perhaps trace the skirt.

I had been in the March house now for eight weeks and had had practically no time off. When I asked for two hours, Mrs. March offered me the remainder of the day.

I took it; I was glad to get it.

I took the skirt along, carrying it out quite calmly under Hortense's not too friendly eyes. I wanted to identify the skirt. If it had been made for Clare, her story of having had all her clothing taken away from her would fall to shreds. If it had not, I meant to trace it. And trace it I did that autumn afternoon, while the dead leaves in the park made crackling eddies under the trees, while the wind held me back at every corner, while fashionable women donned the first furs of the season and sallied forth to the tailors for their winter garments. I, too, went to a tailor.

I dare say I was not fashionable enough to be worth while. It was a long time before I received attention and my few hours were flying. When at last the manager turned to me, I indicated my bundle.

"I want to trace a skirt that was made here," I began. "Your name is on the belt. It is very important."

"But, madam," he said, "we cannot give any information that concerns our customers."

"This is vitally important."

"It would be impossible. We turn out a great many costumes. We keep no record of the styles."

"There is a number on the belt."

I believe he suspected me of divorce proclivities. He held out both hands, palms up.

"Madam surely understands—it is impossible!"

I turned over the lapel of my coat and he saw a badge that Mr. Patton had given me. He had said, "Don't use it unless you need to; but when the time comes, flash it!"

I flashed it. I got my information within ten minutes, but it did not help at first. He gave me the name of the woman for whom it had been made. I had never heard of her—a Mrs. Kershaw.

"You are quite positive?"

"Positive, madam. The number is distinct. Also one of the skirtmakers recalls—it was part of a trousseau a year or so ago."

A sort of lust of investigation seized me. I had started the thing and I would see it out. With a new deference the tailor handed me my rewrapped bundle and saw me to the door.

"No trouble with the Kershaws, I hope?" he said.

"None whatever," I answered at random. "She gave a skirt away and I am tracing it."

That was it, of course. I said it first and believed it afterward. She had given the skirt away.

It took an hour and a half of my shortening afternoon to locate and interview Mrs. Kershaw. She was quite affable. I did not show my badge—it was not necessary. I made up a story about some stolen goods, with this skirt among them. She was anxious to help, she said, but . . .

"I hardly remember," she said. "I gave away a lot of my wedding clothes—the styles changed so quickly. Why, I remember exactly what I did with that! I gave it to the Fräulein—Fräulein Schlenker. But stolen goods! She's the honestest old soul in the world."

"She is old then?"

"Oh, yes—quite. Such a quaint little figure. She taught me at boarding school; she seemed old even then. Poor Fräulein Julie!"

My lips were dry. Julie!

"Would you mind describing the Fräulein, Mrs. Kershaw?"

"You do not suspect her of anything?"

"No, indeed; but I should like to find her."

"Well, she is a little thing, stooped and lame. She hurt her ankle after I knew her first. She is very saving—we all thought she was rich; but I believe not. There's a brother, or someone, that she helps. She wears a rusty black bonnet with jet on it, and a queer old wrap; and—oh, yes—she always carries the same bag—a foreign one, with buckles. I really think the bag was the reason we thought she was wealthy. It seemed such a secure affair."

Julie, then, was my little old lady of the dining room and the garden door! And there was more than that—the school was the school from which Clare had graduated.

"Have you seen the Fräulein lately?"

"We have been away all summer. She may have called. I'll ask."

The little old lady had not called, however. I got her address. It seemed to me that things were closing up.

It was quite dark when I left the Kershaw house. It was very cold and I was hungry; but excitement would not let me eat. I was getting my first zest for this new game I was playing, and I was losing my shrinking horror of spying into affairs that were not my own. It seemed to me that my cause was just; for if Clare March had not been incarcerated in the Brickyard Road house, she might still, out of terror of the truth, insist that she had been. Hysterical young women had done such things before. I held no brief for the family in Brickyard Road; but if they were innocent, they were not to suffer. I was after the truth, and I felt that I should get it. I had no course of action mapped out. I wanted to confront the little old lady—I got no further.

It was seven o'clock when I reached the house. I had crossed the city again. I was hungry and shivering with cold, and I still carried the parcel under my arm. For the first time that day I was nervous. The fear of failure assailed me. I used to have the same feeling when I had charge of the operating room and a strange surgeon was about to operate. Would he want silk or catgut? What solutions did he use? Would the assistant get there in time to lay out the instruments? So now with the Fräulein—would she deny the skirt? If she did, should I accuse her of the night visit to the March house? Or of the letter in the buckled bag?

The house was a small one on a by-street, a comfortable two-story brick, with a wooden stoop and a cheerful glow through the curtains of a vestibule door. The woman who answered my ring was clearly the mistress. She wore a white apron and there was an agreeable odor of cooking food in the air.

"Fräulein Schlenker?" she said. "Yes; she made her home here. She is not here now."

"Can't you tell me where I may find her?"

She hesitated.

"I don't know exactly. We've been anxious about her lately. She went away for a vacation about two months ago. Did you want to see her about renting the house in Brickyard Road?"

For just a minute I distinctly saw two white aprons and two vestibule doors!

"Yes," I said as coolly as I could. "When—when will it be empty?"

"It is empty," she replied. "I hardly know what to do. She's been anxious to rent it; but now that she's away and no word from her . . . Would you like the key?"

The empty house in Brickyard Road!

"If I might have it."

"You'll return it soon, won't you?" She went into the hall and got a key from the drawer of a table. "She'll do anything that's reasonable—paper the lower floor and fix the roof. It's a nice little house." I took the key, still rather dazed. "It's a growing neighborhood out that way," she went on, evidently eager to do her roomer a good turn. "Some of these days that street will be paved." She had an air of doubt; she was clearly divided between eagerness and trepidation. "You'll be sure to return the key?"

"I'll have it back here tomorrow."

She watched me down the street, still vaguely uneasy. I tried to make my back honest, to step as one who walks the straight and narrow path. I had a feeling that she might suddenly change her mind and pursue me, commanding the return of the key. I hardly breathed until I had turned the corner.

I got something to eat at the first restaurant I saw. I needed food and time to think. I meant at first to telephone Mr. Patton. As I grew warmer and less fatigued I decided to go on alone. It was my first case; I wanted to make good—frankly I desired Mr. Patton's approval, and something he had once said to me came back.

"In this business," he said, "there are times when two's a crowd." I remembered that.

I ate deliberately. I never hurry with my food—I've seen too many stomachs treated like coal cellars on the first cold day of fall. And as I ate, the key lay before me on the cloth. It had a yellow tag tied to it, endorsed in a small, neat script, very German.

"Key to the house in Brickyard Road," it said. "Kitchen door."

I had, at the best, about two hours and a half when I left the restaurant. That meant a taxicab. I counted my money. I had thirteen dollars. It would surely be enough.

Brickyard Road lay a square or two away from where I alighted. I retained the cab—out there in that potter's field of dead-and-gone real-estate hopes it was a tie with the living world. Its lamps made a comfortable glow. The driver was broad-shouldered. I borrowed a box of matches from him. I have often wondered since what he thought.

The house Mr. Patton and I had examined was dimly lighted, as before. I passed it at a safe distance. The empty house, that was the only other building in Brickyard Road, was my destination. The two houses were alike—clearly built by the same builder. Only the courage of an idea took me on. In the lighted house the crone was singing—a maudlin voice. Someone was walking along the rickety boardwalk round the place—a step and a tap, a step and a tap—the one-legged man, of course.

There is something horrible about an empty house at night. A house is an intimate place; its every emanation is human. Life has begun and ended in it. Thoughts are things, I have always believed—things that leave their mark.

I had such a feeling about the little house in Brickyard Road. I was very nervous. The other house was near enough to be dangerous—too far away to be company. I felt terribly alone. There was not even starlight. I stumbled and fumbled along, feeling my way by the side of the house to the rear. There was a dispute going on next door. The crone had ceased singing. Someone broke a bottle with a crash.

I found the kitchen door at last. To reach it I had to go through a wooden shed. In the safety of the shed I struck a match and found the keyhole. The key turned easily. As I opened the door, a breath of musty air greeted me and blew out my match. The thick darkness closed down on me like a veil; I was frightened.

It was a moment or two before I could light a fresh match, and it took more than that for me to survey the kitchen. It had been in use not very long before. There was a kettle on the stove and a few odds and ends of dishes in orderly stacks on an upturned box. And there was a loaf of bread, covered with gray-green mold. There was no table, no chair—but in a corner, there was a cot bed, neatly made up. I remember distinctly the comfort of discovering that orderly bed, with a log-cabin quilt spread over it.

My match went out, but the box was almost full. I was not uneasy now. The peace of the log-cabin quilt was on my soul. I found a smoky lamp with very little oil in it, and lighted it. My nerves are pretty good. I've laid out more than one body in the mortuary at night and alone. I was not going to be daunted by an empty house. Nevertheless the glow of the lamp was comforting. I put down my bundle and went into the front room.

I had a real fright there. Something shadowy stood in the center of the room, moving very slightly. I almost dropped the lamp. I had a patient once who used to say her heart "dropped a stitch." Mine did. Then I saw that it was a woman's black dress hanging on a gas fixture and moving in the air from the open kitchen door.

I began to feel uneasy. What if the house were inhabited? Certainly it had been occupied recently. I dare say I move softly by habit, but I doubled my ordinary caution. I wanted to get away, but I wanted more than that. I wanted desperately to see whether there was a steel engraving of the Landing of the Pilgrims in the attic room over the kitchen. If I was right— if in this house Clare March had been imprisoned—if her detail of the house next door was merely what she had gained from a window—what was the meaning of it all? Where was Julie? If I knew anything, this old black silk swaying in the air belonged to her.

Not, of course, that I reasoned all this out. I felt it partly; for the next moment I heard a door open at the top of the stairs. I blew out the lamp instantly, but a sort of paralysis of fright kept me from flight. I could have made it. The stairs, as in the house next door, were closed off with a door— a dash past this door and I should have been in the kitchen; but I hesitated, and it was too late. The steps were at the lower door.

Now and then since that evening I have a nightmare, and it is always the same. I am standing in a dark room and there are stealthy steps drawing nearer and nearer. At last the thing comes toward me; I can hear it; but there is nothing to see. And then it touches me with ice-cold hands—and I waken with a scream. I frightened a nervous patient almost into convulsions once because of that dream of mine.

The darkness was terrible. Behind me the dress swayed, touched me. I almost fainted. The staircase door did not open immediately. I wondered frantically what was standing and waiting there. It showed my abnormal mental condition when it occurred to me that perhaps the old woman, Julie —perhaps she was dead, and that this on the staircase was she again, come back. I almost dropped the lamp.

I braced myself against I knew not what when I heard the door opening. Whoever it was, was listening, I felt sure. Through the open kitchen door came the sound of singing from next door and of someone hammering on a table in time. It covered my gasping breaths, I dare say. The stair door opened wider and someone stepped down into the tiny passage. We were perhaps eight feet apart.

I lived a century, waiting to hear which way the footsteps turned. They went toward the kitchen, still stealthily, with a caution that was more terrible than curses. I had a moment's respite then, and I felt my way toward the front door. If the key was there, I might yet escape. I found the door. The key was gone. Even in that moment of frenzy I knew where the key was—in the buckled bag at the police station. I was trapped!

There were various sounds now from the kitchen: a match struck, and a wavering search, probably for the lamp I held; then a dim but steady light, as though from a candle, followed by the cautious lifting of stovelids and much rustling of paper. The paper reminded me of something—my bundle lay on the cot!

I knew the exact moment when it was discovered. I heard it torn open and I shivered in the silence that followed. Then the candle went out and there was complete silence again; but this time it was the quiet of strained ears and quickened senses. I dream of that, too, sometimes—of a silence that is a horror.

I dared not move a muscle. I felt that if I relaxed I should stagger. I breathed with only the upper part of my lungs. Then, very slowly, there was movement in the next room—a step and then another. It was coming. While the light was burning I had been terrified by something desperate, but at least quick with life. Now, in the darkness, it became disembodied horror again! It came slowly but inevitably, and directly toward me. I tried to move, but I could not. The black dress moved in the air; a chill breath blew on me. Then, out of the black void all round, a cold hand touched my cheek. I must have collapsed without a sound.

## CHAPTER VIII

WHEN I CAME TO, I was lying on the floor of the empty room, with the black dress swaying above me. There was a faint light in the room. By turning my head, I saw that it came from the kitchen. Someone was moving quickly there; there was a rattle of china. A moment later a figure appeared in the doorway and peered in.

"Are you awake, Miss Adams?"

It was Clare! I struggled to a sitting position and stared at her.

"Was it—you—before?" I asked.

"Yes. Don't talk about it just now. I have a fire going and soon we can have some tea. I think you are almost frozen—and I know I am."

It was curious to see how our positions had been reversed. And there was a change in Clare—she was almost cheerful. She helped me out into the kitchen and onto the cot, and then busied herself about the room.

"I am sure there is tea somewhere," she said. "Julie was always making tea."

She was dressed for the street—suit and hat and furs. She tried to make talk as she moved about the room, but the really vital things of the evening she avoided. She fussed with the fire, filled the kettle afresh from a hydrant outside, rinsed out two cups, found tea, searched for sugar. And still her eyes had not met mine.

She found me staring at an engraving that lay on the floor, however, and she dropped her artificial manner.

"The Landing of the Pilgrims!" she said gravely. "I was going to burn it."

The sounds in the next house died away. The kettle on the stove began to boil cheerfully. The little room grew bright with firelight. Clare drew the box before the cot and poured two steaming cups of tea.

"We will drink our tea," she said, "and then I shall tell you, Miss Adams. I am very happy tonight—I have only one grief."

What that was she did not say. She had found a box of biscuits and opened it. She took very little herself. She was plainly intent on making up to me for my fright. She seemed to bear me no malice for being there. It was not until I had drained my cup that she put hers down.

"Now we'll begin," she said, and took off her jacket. Next she drew up the sleeve of the soft blouse she wore beneath and held out her arm for me to see. I gave a shocked exclamation.

"Cocaine!" she said briefly. "The other arm is also scarred. I got it first at school for toothache." I could not say anything; I only stared. "But that's all over now," she went on briskly. "Today I have—but I'll tell you about that later. I knew there was only one way out, Miss Adams—to do it myself. Father and Mother would have helped me, of course; but it would have been their will, not mine. I had to educate my own will to be strong enough. Oh, I'd thought it all out. And then—I did not want them to know. Even now, when I know it's over, I'm afraid to have them know. I've lied to keep it from them; but the detective knew it wasn't true."

She told me the whole story eagerly, frankly. It was clearly a relief. She had made her plans that summer and made them thoroughly. She had tried before and failed. This time there was the great incentive—she wished to marry.

"I wanted to bring children into the world, Miss Adams," she said. "I should not have dared—the way things were. All summer I tried and broke over. I was almost crazy. Then I got a letter from Julie—she had been my German teacher at school and I was fond of her. She had been taking care of an insane brother, who had died. She wanted to work again. Poor Julie!

"I thought she could help me. I knew it would be hard, though I didn't know—well, I wrote her the whole story and told her my plan. I had been here to see the brother with her; I knew the house. I asked her to send out after dark for just enough to keep us going for a time. I did not want the house opened. I thought there would be a hue and cry and they might trace me to Julie."

"Your father and mother said they knew of no one named Julie."

"They would have known of her as Fräulein Schlenker. They had never seen her. I came to the city, bought some blankets and a book or two, and came out here. She was here and partly settled. She was against the plan even then; but I showed her my arms and she knew I was desperate. I had a supply of cocaine—I had got it in town. I was to have it—I should have died without—but she was to reduce the quantity. I locked myself in and gave her the key."

"You had been getting the cocaine from the man with the blond hair?"

"Yes. He was in a pharmacy at first—where I got the prescription filled. He suspected me after a time. After he lost his position, he still got it for me. I met him wherever I could—on the street, in the park, anywhere; but generally we met by the Embankment. He robbed me, I think. I owed him a great deal finally. He took to bothering me about it. I used up all my allowance and more.

"I gave Julie the cocaine; and she was to reduce it—a little at a time. I suffered the tortures of the lost, Miss Adams—but perhaps you know. There were many days when I wanted to kill myself; and once Julie tied my hands behind my back. She was wonderful—wonderful! I owe it all to her. I was lost, Miss Adams—I would lie, steal, almost murder, to get the cocaine. I lived for it."

"All this was here in this house?"

"Upstairs—in the back room one window looked out over a field and could be kept unshuttered. I chose it. Besides, the fire from below heated it. We had only a little coal left in the cellar, and we could get none. Julie went out after dark and did our buying. It—it all took longer than I had thought. I planned for a month. It was more than that. We were running out of money. At the end of five weeks we were desperate—and I sent Julie to the house."

I remembered that well enough! But I did not interrupt.

"Father always gave me the fees from directors' meetings; and, as they were in gold, I dropped them under the cushion of a silver box on my dressing table. Sometimes there would be several; most of them went eventually to—to the man I spoke of. Before we went away in the summer, I had put some there; I could not remember how many—my mind was hazy—but I was sure there was perhaps fifty dollars. I had my own house keys with me and I gave Julie the key to the garden door. She was terribly frightened, but we were desperate. She got in without any trouble and got it. There was forty dollars."

I remembered something. "Forty dollars and a book," I said, smiling.

"Forty dollars and a book—was it yours? The day came when she told me I had had no cocaine for a week. I was faint and dizzy, but I wrote a line to Father and Mother. I shouldn't have written it. It could never be reconciled with anything but the truth, and I was morbid about that. They were never to know. I did not want Mr. Plummer to know—I thought he would never trust me again. But I wrote it and Julie took it out. She never came back—and I was locked in, upstairs!"

"She never came back!"

"She was killed—struck by an automobile. I thought—didn't the detective know that? He had her bag."

So my little old lady was dead after all! I was sorry. What a spirit she had!

"I was locked in," Clare was saying. "I waited—and she did not come. I had not eaten for a day or so before, and there were two days and a night without even water. I was so desperate that I tried to call the other house; but the old woman had hurt herself, and there was no one about outside. I tried to break down the door. There was a panel in it—for the brother who was crazy. I could almost reach the key on the nail outside. The last day I think I was delirious. The key made faces at me through the panel. I told you, didn't I, about getting out of the window?"

"Yes. When did you learn about Julie?"

"The night I went home. As you know, I went down to the library and searched the newspapers. I felt that she had been hurt. As soon as I was strong enough, I slipped away from the house; and—they were going to give her a pauper's burial. I pawned a ring and, at least, she did not have that."

She broke down, after keeping up bravely for so long. I gathered from broken sentences her terrible fear of having the facts known; her despair over the tissue of falsehood and truth that she had told Mr. Patton; her fear of seeing her lover again until she was sure of herself; her grief for Julie's death and her self-accusation of it; her terror that day when Hortense had told her that I had taken her skirt from my closet. But after a time she looked up, smiling through her tears.

"I am really only crying over Julie," she said. "The rest is—all gone, Miss Adams. I am cured—really cured! Today I sat for an hour with a bottle of cocaine beside me, and—I did not touch it!"

That was my first case for Mr. Patton; and, though I really discovered nothing that Clare would not have told eventually herself, he was kind enough to say some very pleasant things.

"Though," he said, wincing as he tried to move his leg, "courage carried to the $n$th power is often foolishness! What possessed you to go to that house alone?"

"I wanted to locate the Landing of the Pilgrims."

He leaned back and looked up at me, smiling.

"Curiosity!" he said. "That was the only quality I was afraid you lacked." He took an envelope from the stand at his elbow and held it out.

"Your check, as per agreement."

"I don't want money, Mr. Patton. I—don't think I am silly; but I had my reward—if I deserve one, which, of course, I don't—when I saw Mr. Plummer's eyes last night. She went straight into his arms."

"You won't take the check?"

"No, thank you."

"Then I'll bank it for you. We are going to have some interesting cases together, Miss Adams, but I wish you were back here to look after me. There's a spineless creature here who lets me bully her. Do you know— you're a queer woman! Taking as remuneration the sight of a young girl going into her lover's arms!"

"I've taken most of my pleasures and all of my sentiment vicariously for a number of years," I retorted. "And, even if it's the other person's, sentiment one has to have!"

"Yes," said Mr. Patton, looking at me curiously. "Sentiment one has to have!"

The bag is before me as I write. There are two keys—one to the house in Brickyard Road; the other to the garden door at the March home. The lavender envelope is there and its scrawled note from Clare—simply explained, as are all confusing things when one has a key. The envelope had contained the vial of cocaine that Clare took with her on her flight, and had come, of course, from the pharmacy clerk. I never examined the clipping carefully until today. It is curious to locate one's mental blind spot. I had read it many times.

The reverse is an advertisement for the cure of the drug habit.

# Locked Doors

## CHAPTER I

"You PROMISED," I reminded Mr. Patton, "to play with cards on the table."

"My dear young lady," he replied, "I have no cards! I suspect a game, that's all."

"Then—do you need me?"

The detective bent forward, his arms on his desk, and looked me over carefully.

"What sort of shape are you in? Tired?"

"No."

"Nervous?"

"Not enough to hurt."

"I want you to take another case, following a nurse who has gone to pieces," he said, selecting his words carefully. "I don't want to tell you a lot—I want you to go in with a fresh mind. It promises to be an extraordinary case."

"How long was the other nurse there?"

"Four days."

"She went to pieces in four days!"

"Well, she's pretty much unstrung. The worst is, she hasn't any real reason. A family chooses to live in an unusual manner, because they like it, or perhaps they're afraid of something. The girl was, that's sure. I had never seen her until this morning, a big, healthy-looking young woman; but she came in looking back over her shoulder as if she expected a knife in her back. She said she was a nurse from St. Luke's and that she'd been on a case for four days. She'd left that morning after about three hours' sleep in that entire period, being locked in a room most of the time, and having little but crackers and milk for food. She thought it was a case for the police."

"Who is ill in the house? Who was her patient?"

"There is no illness, I believe. The French governess had gone, and they wished the children competently cared for until they replaced her. That was the reason given her when she went. Afterward she—well, she was puzzled."

"How are you going to get me there?"

He gathered acquiescence from my question and smiled approval.

"Good girl!" he said. "Never mind how I'll get you there. You are the most dependable woman I know."

"The most curious, perhaps?" I retorted. "Four days on the case, three hours' sleep, locked in and yelling 'Police!' Is it out of town?"

"No, in the heart of the city, on Beauregard Square. Can you get some St. Luke's uniforms? They want another St. Luke's nurse."

I said I could get the uniforms, and he wrote the address on a card. "Better arrive early in the evening," he said.

"But—if they are not expecting me?"

"They will be expecting you," he replied enigmatically.

"The doctor, if he's a St. Luke's man——"

"There is no doctor."

It was six months since I had solved, or helped to solve, the mystery of the buckled bag for Mr. Patton. I had had other cases for him in the interval, cases in which the police could not get close enough. As I said when I began this record of my crusade against crime and the criminal, a trained nurse gets under the very skin of the soul.

Gradually I had come to see that Mr. Patton's point of view was right: that if the criminal uses every means against society, why not society against the criminal? At first I had used this as a flag of truce to my nurse's ethical training; now I flaunted it, a mental and moral banner. The criminal against society, and I against the criminal! And, more than that, against misery, healing pain by augmenting it sometimes, but working like a surgeon, for good.

I had had six cases in six months. Only in one had I failed to land my criminal, and that without any suspicion of my white uniform and rubber-soled shoes. Although I played a double game, no patient of mine had suffered. I was a nurse first and a police agent second. If it was a question between turpentine compresses—stupes, professionally—and seeing what letters came in or went out of the house, the compress went on first, and cracking hot, too. I am not boasting. That is my method, the only way I can work, and it speaks well for it that, as I say, only one man escaped arrest, an arson case in which the factory owner hanged himself in the bathroom needle shower—in the house he had bought with the insurance money—while I was fixing his breakfast tray. And even he might have been saved for justice had the cook not burned the toast and been obliged to make it fresh.

I was no longer staying at a nurses' home. I had taken a bachelor suite of three rooms and bath, comfortably downtown. I cooked my own breakfasts when I was off duty and I dined at a restaurant nearby. Luncheon I did not bother much about. Now and then Mr. Patton telephoned me and we lunched together in remote places where we would not be known. He would tell me of his cases and sometimes he asked my advice.

I bought my uniforms that day and took them home in a taxicab. The dresses were blue, and over them for the street the St. Luke's girls wore long cloaks, English fashion, of navy blue serge, and a blue bonnet with a white ruching and white lawn ties. I felt curious in it, but it was becoming and convenient. Certainly I looked professional.

At three o'clock that afternoon a messenger brought a small box, registered. It contained a St. Luke's badge of gold and blue enamel.

At four o'clock my telephone rang. I was packing my suitcase according to the list I keep pasted in the lid. Under the list, which was of uniforms, aprons, thermometer, instruments, a nurse's simple set of probe, forceps and bandage scissors, was the word "box." This always went in first—a wooden box with a lock, the key of which was round my neck. It contained skeleton keys, a small black revolver of which I was in deadly fear, a pair of handcuffs, a pocket flashlight, and my badge from the chief of police. I was examining the revolver nervously when the telephone rang, and I came within an ace of sending a bullet into the flat below.

Did you ever notice how much you get out of a telephone voice? We can dissemble with our faces, but under stress the vocal cords seem to draw up tight and the voice comes thin and colorless. There's a little woman in the flat beneath—the one I nearly bombarded—who sings like a bird at her piano half the day, scaling vocal heights that make me dizzy. Now and then she has a visitor, a nice young man, and she disgraces herself, flats F, fogs E even, finally takes cowardly refuge in a wretched mezzosoprano and doubtless cries herself to sleep later on.

The man who called me had the thin-drawn voice of extreme strain—a youngish voice.

"Miss Adams," he said, "this is Francis Reed speaking. I have called St. Luke's and they referred me to you. Are you free to take a case this afternoon?"

I fenced. I was trying to read the voice.

"This afternoon?"

"Well, before night anyhow; as—as early this evening as possible."

The voice was strained and tired, desperately tired. It was not peevish. It was even rather pleasant.

"What is the case, Mr. Reed?"

He hesitated. "It is not illness. It is merely—the governess has gone and there are two small children. We want someone to give her undivided attention to the children."

"I see."

"Are you a heavy sleeper, Miss Adams?"

"A very light one." I fancied he breathed freer.

"I hope you are not tired from a previous case?" I was beginning to like the voice.

"I'm quite fresh," I replied almost gayly. "Even if I were not, I like children, especially well ones. I shan't find looking after them very wearying, I'm sure."

Again the odd little pause. Then he gave me the address on Beauregard Square, and asked me to be sure not to be late.

"I must warn you," he added, "we are living in a sort of casual way. Our servants left us without warning. Mrs. Reed has been getting along as best she could. Most of our meals are being sent in."

I was thinking fast. No servants! A good many people think a trained nurse is a sort of upper servant. I've been in houses where they were amazed to discover that I was a college woman and, finding the two things irreconcilable, have openly accused me of having been driven to such a desperate course as a hospital training by an unfortunate love affair.

"Of course you understand that I will look after the children to the best of my ability, but that I will not replace the servants."

I fancied he smiled grimly.

"That, of course. Will you ring twice when you come?"

"Ring twice?"

"The doorbell," he replied impatiently.

I said I would ring the doorbell twice.

The young woman below was caroling gayly, ignorant of the six-chambered menace over her head. I knelt again by my suitcase, but packed little and thought a great deal. I was to arrive before dusk at a house where there were no servants and to ring the doorbell twice. I was to be a light sleeper, although I was to look after two healthy children. It was not much in itself, but, in connection with the previous nurse's appeal to the police, it took on new possibilities.

At six I started out to dinner. It was early spring and cold, but quite light. At the first corner I saw Mr. Patton waiting for a street car, and at his quick nod I saw I was to get in also. He did not pay my fare or speak to me. It was a part of the game that we were never seen together except at the remote restaurant I mentioned before. The car thinned out and I could watch him easily. Far downtown he alighted and so did I. The restaurant was near. I went in alone and sat down at a table in a recess, and very soon he joined me. We were in the main dining room but not of it, a sop at once to the conventions and to the necessity, where he was so well known, for caution.

"I got a little information—on—the affair we were talking of," he said as he sat down. "I'm not so sure I want you to take the case after all."

"Certainly I shall take it," I retorted with some sharpness. "I've promised to go."

"Tut! I'm not going to send you into danger unnecessarily."

"I am not afraid."

"Exactly. A lot of generals were lost in the Civil War because they were not afraid and wanted to lead their troops instead of saving themselves and their expensive West Point training by sitting back in a safe spot and directing the fight. Any fool can run into danger. It takes intelligence to keep out."

I felt my color rising indignantly. "Then you brought me here to tell me I am not to go?"

"Will you let me read you two reports?"

"You could have told me that at the corner!"

"Will you let me read you two reports?"

"If you don't mind, I'll first order something to eat. I'm to be there before dark."

"Will you let me——"

"I'm going, and you know I'm going. If you don't want me to represent you, I'll go on my own. They want a nurse, and they're in trouble."

I think he was really angry. I know I was. If there is anything that takes the very soul out of a woman, it is to be kept from doing a thing she has set her heart on, because some man thinks it dangerous. If she has any spirit, that rouses it.

Mr. Patton quietly replaced the reports in his wallet, and his wallet in the inside pocket of his coat, and fell to a judicial survey of the menu. But although he barely glanced at me, he must have seen the determination in my face, for he ordered things that were quickly prepared and told the waiter to hurry.

"I have wondered lately," he said slowly, "whether the mildness of your manner at the hospital was acting, or the chastening effect of three years under an order book."

"A man always likes a woman to be a sheep."

"Not at all. But it is rather disconcerting to have a pet lamb turn round and take a bite out of one."

"Will you read the reports now?"

"I think," he said quietly, "they had better wait until we have eaten. We will probably both feel calmer. Suppose we arrange that nothing said before the oysters counts?"

I agreed, rather sulkily, and the meal went off well enough. I was rather anxious to hurry but he ate deliberately, drank his demi-tasse, paid the waiter, and at last met my impatient eyes and smiled.

"After all," he said, "since you are determined to go anyhow, what's the use of reading the reports? Inside of an hour you'll know all you need to know." But he saw that I did not take his teasing well, and drew out his wallet.

There were two typewritten papers clamped together.

They are on my desk before me now. The first one is endorsed:

Statement by Laura J. Bosworth, nurse, of St. Luke's Home for Graduate Nurses.

Miss Bosworth says:

I do not know just why I came to the police. But I know I'm frightened. That's the fact. I think there is something terribly wrong in the house of Francis M. Reed, 71 Beauregard Square. I think a crime of some sort has been committed. There are four people in the family, Mr. and Mrs. Reed and two children. I was to look after the children.

I was there four days and the children were never allowed out of the room. At night we were locked in. I kept wondering what I would do if there was a fire. The telephone wires are cut so no one can call the house, and I believe the doorbell was disconnected, too. But that's fixed now. Mrs. Reed went round all the time with a face like chalk and her eyes staring. At all hours of the night she'd unlock the bedroom door and come in and look at the children.

Almost all the doors through the house were locked. If I wanted to get to the kitchen to boil eggs for the children's breakfast—for there were no servants, and Mrs. Reed is young and doesn't know anything about cooking—Mr. Reed had to unlock about four doors for me.

If Mrs. Reed looked bad, he was dreadful—sunken-eyed and white and wouldn't eat. I think he has killed someone and is making away with the body.

Last night I said I had to have air, and they let me go out. I called up a friend from a pay station, another nurse. This morning she sent me a special-delivery letter that I was needed on another case, and I got away. That's all; it sounds foolish, but try it and see if it doesn't get on your nerves.

Mr. Patton looked up at me as he finished reading.

"Now you see what I mean," he said. "That woman was there four days, and she is as temperamental as a cow, but in those four days her nervous system went to smash."

"Doors locked!" I reflected. "Servants gone; state of fear—it looks like a siege!"

"But why a trained nurse? Why not a policeman, if there is danger? Why anyone at all, if there is something that the police are not to know?"

"That is what I intend to find out," I replied. He shrugged his shoulders and read the other paper:

Report of Detective Bennett on Francis M. Reed, April 5.

Francis M. Reed is thirty-six years of age, married, a chemist at the Olympic Paint Works. He has two children, both boys. Has a small independent income and owns the house on Beauregard Square, which was built by his grandfather, General F. R. Reed. Is supposed to be living beyond his means. House is usually full of servants, and grocer in the neighborhood has had to wait for money several times.

On March twenty-ninth he dismissed all servants without warning. No reason given, but a week's wages instead of notice.

On March thirtieth he applied to the owners of the paint factory for two weeks' vacation. Gave as his reason nervousness and insomnia. He said he was "going to lay off and get some sleep." Has not been back at the works since. House under surveillance this afternoon. No visitors.

Mr. Reed telephoned for a nurse at four o'clock from a store on Eleventh Street. Explained that his telephone was out of order.

Mr. Patton folded up the papers and thrust them back into his pocket. Evidently he saw I was determined, for he only said, "Have you got your revolver?"

"Yes."

"Do you know anything about telephones? Could you repair that one in an emergency?"

"In an emergency," I retorted, "there is no time to repair a telephone. But I've got a voice and there are windows. If I really put my mind to it, you will hear me yell at headquarters."

He smiled grimly.

CHAPTER II

BEAUREGARD SQUARE is a small, exclusive neighborhood; a dozen or more solid citizens built their homes there in the early 70's, occupying large lots, the houses flush with the streets and with gardens behind. Six on one street, six on another, back to back with the gardens in the center, they occupy the whole block. And the gardens are not fenced off, but make a sort of small park, unsuspected from the streets. Here and there bits of flowering shrubbery sketchily outline a property, but the general impression is of lawn and trees, free of access to all the owners. Thus, with the square in front and the gardens in the rear, the Reed house faces in two directions on the early spring green.

In the gardens the old tar walks are still there, and a fountain which no longer plays, but on whose stone coping I believe the young Beauregard Squarites made their first climbing ventures.

The gardens are always alive with birds, and eventually, from my windows, I learned the reason. It seems to have been a custom sanctified by years that the crumbs from the twelve tables should be thrown into the dry basin of the fountain for the birds. It is a common sight to see stately butlers and chic little waitresses in black and white coming out after luncheon or dinner with silver trays of crumbs. Many a scrap of gossip, as well as scrap of food, has been passed along at the old stone fountain, I believe. I know that it was there that I heard of the "basement ghost" of Beauregard Square—a whisper at first, a panic later.

I arrived at eight o'clock and rang the doorbell twice. The door was opened at once by Mr. Reed, a tall, blond young man, carefully dressed. He threw away his cigarette when he saw me and shook hands. The hall was brightly lighted and most cheerful; in fact the whole house was ablaze with light. Certainly nothing could be less mysterious than the house, or than the debonair young man who motioned me into the library.

"I told Mrs. Reed I would talk to you before you go upstairs," he said. "Will you sit down?"

I sat down. The library was even brighter than the hall, and now I saw that, although he smiled as cheerfully as ever, his face was almost colorless, and his eyes, which looked frankly enough into mine for a moment, went wandering off round the room. I had the impression somehow that Mr. Patton had had of the nurse at headquarters that morning —that he looked as if he expected a knife in his back. It seemed to me that he wanted to look over his shoulder and by sheer will power did not.

"You know the rule, Miss Adams," he said. "When there's an emergency, get a trained nurse. I told you our emergency—no servants and two small children."

"This should be a good time to secure servants," I said briskly. "City houses are being deserted for country places, and a percentage of servants won't leave town."

He hesitated. "We've been doing very nicely, although of course it's hardly more than just living. Our meals are sent in from a hotel, and—

well, we thought, since we are going away so soon, that perhaps we could manage."

The impulse was too strong for him at that moment. He wheeled and looked behind him, not a hasty glance, but a deliberate inspection that took in every part of that end of the room. It was so unexpected that it left me gasping.

The next moment he was himself again.

"When I say that there is no illness," he said, "I am hardly exact. There is no illness, but there has been an epidemic of children's diseases among the Beauregard Square children and we are keeping the youngsters indoors."

"Don't you think they could be safeguarded without being shut up in the house?"

He responded eagerly. "If I only thought——" He checked himself. "No," he said decidedly; "for a time, at least, I believe it is not wise."

I did not argue with him. There was nothing to be gained by antagonizing him. And as Mrs. Reed came in just then, the subject was dropped. She was hardly more than a girl, almost as blonde as her husband, very pretty, and with the weariest eyes I have ever seen, unless perhaps the eyes of a man who has waited a long time for death.

I liked her at once. She did not attempt to smile. She rather clung to my hand when I held it out.

"I am glad St. Luke's still trusts us," she said. "I was afraid the other nurse . . . Frank, will you take Miss Adams's suitcase upstairs?"

She held out a key. He took it, but he turned at the door and said, "I wish you wouldn't wear those things, Anne. You gave me your promise yesterday, you remember."

"I can't work round the children in anything else," she protested.

"Those things" were charming. She wore a rose silk negligee trimmed with soft bands of lace and blue satin flowers, a petticoat to match that garment, and a lace cap.

He hesitated in the doorway and looked at her—a curious glance, I thought, full of tenderness, reproof—and perhaps apprehension.

"I'll take them off, dear," she replied to the glance. "I wanted Miss Adams to know that, even if we haven't a servant in the house, we are at least civilized. I—I haven't taken cold." This last was clearly an afterthought.

He went out then and left us together.

She came over to me swiftly. "What did the other nurse say?" she demanded.

"I do not know her at all. I have not seen her."

"Didn't she report at the hospital that we were—queer?"

I smiled. "That's hardly likely, is it?"

Unexpectedly she went to the door opening into the hall and closed it, coming back swiftly.

"Mr. Reed thinks it is not necessary, but—there are some things that will puzzle you. Perhaps I should have spoken to the other nurse. If—if anything strikes you as unusual, Miss Adams, just please don't see it! It is all right, everything is all right. But something has occurred—not very much, but disturbing—and we are all of us doing the very best we can."

She was quivering with nervousness.

I was not the police agent then, I'm afraid.

"Nurses are accustomed to disturbing things. Perhaps I can help."

"You can, by watching the children. That's the only thing that matters to me—the children. I don't want them left alone. If you have to leave them, call me."

"Don't you think I will be able to watch them more intelligently if I know just what the danger is?"

I think she very nearly told me. She was so tired, evidently so anxious to shift her burden to fresh shoulders.

"Mr. Reed said," I prompted her, "that there was an epidemic of children's diseases. But from what you say——"

But I was not to learn, after all, for her husband opened the hall door.

"Yes, children's diseases," she said vaguely. "So many children are down. Shall we go up, Frank?"

The extraordinary bareness of the house had been dawning on me for some time. It was well lighted and well furnished. But the floors were innocent of rugs, the handsome furniture was without arrangement and, in the library at least, stood huddled in the center of the room. The hall and stairs were also uncarpeted, but there were marks where carpets had recently lain and had been jerked up.

The progress up the staircase was not calculated to soothe my nerves. The thought of my little revolver, locked in my suitcase, was poor comfort. For with every four steps or so Mr. Reed, who led the way, turned automatically and peered into the hallway below; he was listening, too, his head bent slightly forward. And each time that he turned, his wife, behind me, turned also. Cold terror suddenly got me by the spine, and yet the hall was bright with light.

(NOTE: Surely fear is a contagion. Could one isolate the germ of it and find an antitoxin? Or is it merely a form of nervous activity run amuck, like a runaway locomotive, colliding with other nervous activities and causing catastrophe? Take this up with Mr. Patton. But would he know? He, I am almost sure, has never been really afraid.)

I had a vision of my oxlike predecessor making this head-over-shoulder journey up the staircase, and in spite of my nervousness I smiled. But at that moment Mrs. Reed put a hand on my arm, and I screamed. I remember yet the way she dropped back against the wall and turned white.

Mr. Reed whirled on me instantly. "What did you see?" he demanded.

"Nothing at all." I was horribly ashamed. "Your wife touched my arm unexpectedly. I dare say I am nervous."

"It's all right, Anne," he reassured her. And to me, almost irritably, "I thought you nurses had no nerves."

"Under ordinary circumstances I have none."

It was all ridiculous. We were still on the staircase.

"Just what do you mean by that?"

"If you will stop looking down into that hall, I'll be calm enough. You make me jumpy."

He muttered something about being sorry and went on quickly. But at the top he went through an inward struggle, evidently succumbed, and took a final furtive survey of the hallway below. I was so wrought up that had a door slammed anywhere just then, I think I should have dropped where I stood.

The absolute silence of the house added to the strangeness of the situation. Beauregard Square is not close to a trolley line, and quiet is the neighborhood tradition. The first rubber-tired vehicles in the city drew up before Beauregard Square houses. Beauregard Square children speak in low voices and never bang their spoons on their plates. Beauregard Square servants wear felt-soled shoes. And such outside noises as venture to intrude themselves must filter through double brick walls and doors built when lumber was selling by the thousand acres instead of the square foot.

Through this silence our feet echoed along the bare floor of the upper hall, as well lighted as belowstairs and as dismantled, to the door of the day nursery. The door was locked—double locked, in fact. For the key had been turned in the old-fashioned lock, and in addition an ordinary bolt had been newly fastened on the outside of the door. On the outside! Was that to keep me in? It was certainly not to keep anyone or anything out. The feeblest touch moved the bolt.

We were all three outside the door. We seemed to keep our compactness by common consent. No one of us left the group willingly; or, leaving it, we slid back again quickly. That was my impression, at least. But the bolt rather alarmed me.

"This is your room," Mrs. Reed said. "It is generally the day nursery, but we have put a bed and some other things in it. I hope you will be comfortable."

I touched the bolt with my finger and smiled into Mr. Reed's eyes. "I hope I am not to be fastened in!" I said.

He looked back squarely enough, but somehow I knew he lied.

"Certainly not," he replied, and opened the door.

If there had been mystery outside, and bareness, the nursery was charming—a corner room with many windows, hung with the simplest of nursery papers and full of glass-doored closets filled with orderly rows of toys. In one corner a small single bed had been added without spoiling the room. The window sills were full of flowering plants. There was a bowl of goldfish on a stand, and a tiny dwarf parrot in a cage. A white-tiled bathroom connected with this room and also with the night nursery beyond.

Mr. Reed did not come in. I had an uneasy feeling, however, that he was just beyond the door. The children were not asleep. Mrs. Reed left me so that I could put on my uniform. When she came back, her face was troubled.

"They are not sleeping well," she complained. "I suppose it comes from having no exercise. They are always excited."

"I'll take their temperatures," I said. "Sometimes a tepid bath and a cup of hot milk will make them sleep."

The two little boys were wide awake. They sat up to look at me and both spoke at once.

"Can you tell fairy tales out of your head?"

"Did you see Chang?"

They were small, sleek-headed, fair-skinned youngsters, adorably clean and rumpled.

"Chang is their dog, a Pekingese," explained the mother. "He has been lost for several days."

"But he isn't lost, Mother. I can hear him crying every now and then. You'll look again, Mother, won't you?"

"We heard him through the furnace pipe," shrilled the smaller of the two. "You said you would look."

"I did look, darlings. He isn't there. And you promised not to cry about him, Freddie."

Freddie, thus put on his honor, protested he was not crying for the dog.

"I want to go out and take a walk, that's why I'm crying," he wailed. "And I want Mademoiselle, and my buttons are all off. And my ear aches when I lie on it."

The room was close. I threw up the windows, and turned to find Mrs. Reed at my elbow. She was glancing out apprehensively.

"I suppose the air is necessary," she said, "and these windows are all right. But—I have a reason for asking it—please do not open the others."

She went very soon, and I listened as she went out. I had promised to lock the door behind her, and I did so. The bolt outside was not shot.

After I had quieted the children with my mildest fairy story, I made an inventory of my new quarters. I drew a diagram of the second floor, which I gave to Mr. Patton later. That night, of course, I investigated only the two nurseries. But, so strangely had the fear that hung over the house infected me, I confess that I made my little tour of bathroom and clothes-closet with my revolver in my hand!

I found nothing, of course. The disorder of the house had not extended itself here. The bathroom was spotless with white tile; the large clothes-closet, which opened off the passage between the two rooms, was full of neatly folded clothing for the children. The closet was to play its part later, a darkish little room faintly lighted during the day by a ground-glass transom opening into the center hall, but dependent mostly on electric light.

Outside the windows Mrs. Reed had asked me not to open was a porte-cochère roof almost level with the sills. Then was it an outside intruder she feared? And in that case, why the bolts on the outside of the two nursery doors? For the night nursery, I found, must have one also. I turned the key, but the door would not open.

I decided not to try to sleep that night, but to keep on watch. So powerfully had the mother's anxiety about her children and their mysterious danger impressed me that I made frequent excursions into the back room. Up to midnight there was nothing whatever to alarm me. I darkened both rooms and sat, waiting for I know not what; for some sound to show that the house stirred, perhaps. At a few minutes after twelve, faint noises penetrated to my room from the hall: Mr. Reed's nervous voice and a piece of furniture scraping over the floor. Then silence again for half an hour or so.

Then—I was quite certain that the bolt on my door had been shot. I do not think I heard it. Perhaps I felt it. Perhaps I only feared it. I unlocked the door; it was fastened outside.

There is a hideous feeling of helplessness about being locked in. I pretended to myself at first that I was only interested and curious. But I was frightened; I know that now. I sat there in the dark and wondered what I would do if the house took fire, or if some hideous tragedy enacted itself outside that locked door and I were helpless.

By two o'clock I had worked myself into a panic. The house was no longer silent. Someone was moving about downstairs, and not stealthily. The sounds came up through the heavy joists and flooring of the old house.

I determined to make at least a struggle to free myself. There was no way to get at the bolts, of course. The porte-cochère roof remained, and the transom in the clothes-closet. True, I might have raised an alarm and been freed at once, but naturally I rejected this method. The roof of the porte-cochère proved impracticable. The tin bent and cracked under my first step. The transom then.

I carried a chair into the closet and found the transom easy to lower. But it threatened to creak. I put liquid soap on the hinges—it was all I had, and it worked very well—and lowered the transom inch by inch. Even then I could not see over it. I had worked so far without a sound, but in climbing to a shelf my foot slipped and I thought I heard a sharp movement outside. It was five minutes before I stirred. I hung there, every muscle cramped, listening and waiting. Then I lifted myself by sheer force of muscle and looked out. The upper landing of the staircase, brilliantly lighted, was to my right. Across the head of the stairs had been pushed a cotbed, made up for the night, but it was unoccupied.

Mrs. Reed, in a long, dark ulster, was standing beside it, staring with fixed and glassy eyes at something in the lower hall.

## CHAPTER III

SOMETIME after four o'clock my door was unlocked from without; the bolt slipped as noiselessly as it had been shot. I got a little sleep until seven, when the boys trotted into my room in their bathrobes and slippers and perched on my bed.

"It's a nice day," observed Harry, the elder. "Is that bump your feet?"

I wriggled my toes and assured him he had surmised correctly.

"You're pretty long, aren't you? Do you think we can play in the fountain today?"

"We'll make a try for it, son. It will do us all good to get out into the sunshine."

"We always took Chang for a walk every day, Mademoiselle and Chang and Freddie and I."

Freddie had found my cap on the dressing table and had put it on his yellow head. But now, on hearing the beloved name of his pet, he burst into loud grief-stricken howls.

"Want Mam'selle," he cried. "Want Chang, too. Poor Freddie!"

The children were adorable. I bathed and dressed them and, mindful of my predecessor's story of crackers and milk, prepared for an excursion kitchenward. The nights might be full of mystery, murder might romp from room to room, but I intended to see that the youngsters breakfasted. But before I was ready to go down, breakfast arrived.

Perhaps the other nurse had told the Reeds a few plain truths before she left; perhaps—and this, I think, was the case—the cloud had lifted just a little. Whatever it may have been, two rather flushed and flurried young people tapped at the door that morning and were admitted, Mr. Reed first, with a tray, Mrs. Reed following with a coffeepot and cream.

The little nursery table was small for five, but we made room somehow. What if the eggs were underdone and the toast dry? The children munched blissfully. What if Mr. Reed's face was still drawn and haggard and his wife a limp little huddle on the floor? She sat with her head against his knee and her eyes on the little boys, and drank her pale coffee slowly. She was very tired, poor thing. She dropped asleep sitting there, and he sat for a long time, not liking to disturb her.

It made me feel homesick for the home I didn't have. I've had the same feeling before, of being a rank outsider—a sort of defrauded feeling. I've had it when I've seen the look in a man's eyes when his wife comes to after an operation. And I've had it, for that matter, when I've put a new baby in its mother's arms for the first time. I had it for sure that morning, while she slept there and he stroked her pretty hair.

I put in my plea for the children then.

"It's bright and sunny," I argued. "And if you are nervous, I'll keep them away from other children. But if you want to keep them well, you must give them exercise."

It was the argument about keeping them well that influenced him, I think. He sat silent for a long time. His wife was still asleep, her lips parted. "Very well," he said finally, "from two to three, Miss Adams. But not in the garden back of the house. Take them on the street."

I agreed to that.

"I shall want a short walk every evening myself," I added. "That is a rule of mine. I am a more useful person and a more agreeable one if I have it."

I think he would have demurred if he dared. But one does not easily deny so sane a request. He yielded grudgingly.

That first day was calm and quiet enough. Had it not been for the strange condition of the house and the necessity for keeping the children locked in, I would have smiled at my terror of the night. Luncheon was sent in; so was dinner. The children and I lunched and supped alone. As far as I could see, Mrs. Reed made no attempt at housework; but the cot at the head of the stairs disappeared in the early morning and the dog did not howl again.

I took the boys out for an hour in the early afternoon. Two incidents occurred, both of them significant. I bought myself a screwdriver—that was one. The other was our meeting with a slender young woman in black who knew the boys and stopped them. She proved to be one of the dismissed servants—the waitress, she said.

"Why, Freddie!" she cried. "And Harry, too! Aren't you going to speak to Nora?"

After a moment or two she turned to me, and I felt she wanted to say something, but hardly dared.

"How is Mrs. Reed?" she asked. "Not sick, I hope?" She glanced at my St. Luke's cloak and bonnet.

"No, she is quite well."

"And Mr. Reed?"

"Quite well also."

"Is Mademoiselle still there?"

"No, there is no one there but the family. There are no maids in the house."

She stared at me curiously. "Mademoiselle has gone? Are you cer—— Excuse me, miss. But I thought she would never go. The children were like her own."

"She is not there, Nora."

She stood for a moment, debating, I thought. Then she burst out, "Mr. Reed made a mistake, miss. You can't take a houseful of first-class servants and dismiss them the way he did—not even half an hour to get out bag and baggage—without making talk. And there's talk enough all through the neighborhood."

"What sort of talk?"

"Different people say different things. They say Mademoiselle is still there, locked in her room on the third floor. There's a light there sometimes, but nobody sees her. And other folks say Mr. Reed is crazy. And there is worse being said than that."

But she refused to tell me any more—evidently concluded she had said too much and got away as quickly as she could, looking rather worried.

I was a trifle over my hour getting back, but nothing was said. To leave the clean and tidy street for the disordered house was not pleasant. But once in the children's suite, with the goldfish in the aquarium darting like tongues of flame in the sunlight, with the tulips and hyacinths of the window-boxes glowing and the orderly toys on their white shelves, I felt comforted. After all, disorder and dust did not imply crime.

But one thing I did that afternoon—did it with firmness and no attempt at secrecy, and after asking permission of no one. I took the new screwdriver and unfastened the bolt from the outside of my door.

I was prepared, if necessary, to make a stand on that issue. But although it was noticed, I knew, no mention of it was made to me.

Mrs. Reed pleaded a headache that evening, and I believe her husband ate alone in the dismantled dining room. For every room on the lower floor, I had discovered, was in the same curious disorder.

At seven Mr. Reed relieved me, so that I could go out. The children were in bed. He did not go into the day nursery, but placed a straight chair outside the door of the back room and sat there, bent over, elbows on knees, chin cupped in his palm, staring at the staircase. He roused enough to ask me to bring an evening paper when I returned.

When I am on a department case, I always take my off-duty in the evening by arrangement and walk round the block. Sometime in my walk I am sure to see Mr. Patton himself if the case is big enough, or one of his agents if he cannot come. If I have nothing to communicate, it resolves itself into a bow and nothing more.

I was nervous on this particular jaunt. For one thing, my St. Luke's cloak and bonnet marked me at once, made me conspicuous; for another, I was afraid Mr. Patton would think the Reed house no place for a woman and order me home.

It was a quarter to eight and quite dark before he fell into step beside me.

"Well," I told him rather shakily; "I'm still alive, as you see."

"Then it is pretty bad?"

"It's exceedingly queer," I admitted, and told my story. I had meant to conceal the bolt on the outside of my door, and one or two other things, but I blurted them all out right then and there, and felt a lot better at once.

He listened intently.

"It's fear of the deadliest sort," I finished.

"Fear of the police?"

"I—I think not. It is fear of something in the house. They are always listening and watching at the top of the front stairs. They have lifted all the carpets, so that every footstep echoes through the whole house. Mrs. Reed goes down to the first floor, but never alone. Today I found that the back staircase is locked off at top and bottom. There are doors."

I gave him my rough diagram of the house. It was too dark to see it.

"It is only tentative," I explained. "So much of the house is locked up, and every movement of mine is under surveillance. Without baths there are about twelve large rooms, counting the third floor. I've not been able to get there, but I thought that tonight I'd try to look about."

"You had no sleep last night?"

"Three hours—from about four to seven this morning."

We had crossed into the public square and were walking slowly under the trees. Now he stopped and faced me.

"I don't like the look of it, Miss Adams," he said. "Ordinary panic goes and hides. But here's a fear that knows what it's afraid of and takes methodical steps for protection. I didn't want you to take the case, you know that; but now I'm not going to insult you by asking you to give it up. But I'm going to see that you are protected. There will be someone across the street every night as long as you are in the house."

"Have you any theory?" I asked him. He is not strong for theories generally. He is very practical. "That is, do you think the other nurse was right and there is some sort of crime being concealed?"

"Well, think about it," he prompted me. "If a murder has been committed, what are they afraid of? The police? Then why a trained nurse and all this caution about the children? A ghost? Would they lift the carpets so that they could hear the specter tramping about?"

"If there is no crime, but something—a lunatic perhaps?" I asked.

"Possibly. But then why this secrecy and keeping out the police? It is, of course, possible that your respected employers have both gone off mentally, and the whole thing is a nightmare delusion. On my word, it sounds like it. But it's too much for credulity to believe they've both gone crazy with the same form of delusion."

"Perhaps I'm the lunatic," I said despairingly. "When you reduce it to an absurdity like that, I wonder if I didn't imagine it all, the lights burning everywhere and the carpets up, and Mrs. Reed staring down the staircase, and me locked in a room and hanging on by my nails to peer out through a closet transom."

"Perhaps. But how about the deadly sane young woman who preceded you? She had no imagination. Now about Reed and his wife—how do they strike you? They get along all right and that sort of thing, I suppose?"

"They are nice people," I said emphatically. "He's a gentleman and they're devoted. He just looks like a big boy who's got into an awful mess and doesn't know how to get out. And she's backing him up. She's a dear."

"Humph!" said Mr. Patton. "Don't suppress any evidence because she's a dear and he's a handsome big boy!"

"I didn't say he was handsome," I snapped.

"Did you ever see a ghost or think you saw one?" he inquired suddenly.

"No, but one of my aunts has. Hers always carry their heads. She asked one a question once and the head nodded."

"Then you believe in things of that sort?"

"Not a particle—but I'm afraid of them."

He smiled, and shortly after that I went back to the house. I think he was sorry about the ghost question, for he explained that he had been trying me out, and that I looked well in my cloak and bonnet.

"I'm afraid of your chin generally," he said; "but the white lawn ties have a softening effect. In view of the ties I almost have the courage . . ."

"Yes?"

"I think not, after all," he decided. "The chin is there, ties or no ties. Good night, and—for heaven's sake don't run any unnecessary risks."

The change from his facetious tone to earnestness was so unexpected that I was still standing there on the pavement when he plunged into the darkness of the square and disappeared.

## CHAPTER IV

At ten minutes after eight I was back in the house. Mr. Reed admitted me, going through the tedious process of unlocking outer and inner vestibule doors and fastening them again behind me. He inquired politely if I had had a pleasant walk, and without waiting for my reply, fell to reading the evening paper. He seemed to have forgotten me absolutely. First he scanned the headlines; then he turned feverishly to something farther on and ran his fingers down along a column. His lips were twitching, but evidently he did not find what he expected—or feared—for he threw the paper away and did not glance at it again. I watched him from the angle of the stairs.

Even for that short interval, Mrs. Reed had taken his place at the children's door.

She wore a black dress, long sleeved and high at the throat, instead of the silk negligee of the previous evening, and she held a book. But she was not reading. She smiled rather wistfully when she saw me.

"How fresh you always look!" she said. "And so self-reliant. I wish I had your courage."

"I am perfectly well. I dare say that explains a lot. Kiddies asleep?"

"Freddie isn't. He's been crying for Chang. I hate night, Miss Adams. I'm like Freddie. All my troubles come up about this time. I'm horribly depressed." Her blue eyes filled with tears. "And I haven't been sleeping well," she confessed.

I should think not!

Without taking off my things, I went down to Mr. Reed in the lower hall.

"I'm going to insist on something," I said. "Mrs. Reed is highly nervous. She says she has not been sleeping. I think if I give her a sedative and she gets an entire night's sleep, it may save her a breakdown."

I looked straight in his eyes, and for once he did not evade me.

"I'm afraid I've been very selfish," he said. "Of course she must have sleep. I'll give you a powder, unless you have something you prefer to use."

I remembered then that he was a chemist, and said I would gladly use whatever he gave me.

"There is another thing I wanted to speak about, Mr. Reed," I said. "The children are mourning their dog. Don't you think he may have been accidentally shut up somewhere in the house, on one of the upper floors?"

"Why do you say that?" he demanded sharply.

"They say they have heard him howling."

He hesitated for barely a moment. Then: "Possibly. But they will not hear him again. The little chap has been sick, and he—died today. Of course the boys are not to know."

No one watched the staircase that night. I gave Mrs. Reed the powder and saw her comfortably into bed. When I went back fifteen minutes later, she was resting, but not asleep. Sedatives sometimes make people garrulous for a little while—sheer comfort, perhaps, and relaxed tension. I've had stockbrokers and bankers in the hospital give me tips, after a hypodermic of morphia, that would have made me wealthy had I not been limited to my training allowance of twelve dollars a month.

"I was just wondering," she said as I tucked her up, "where a woman owes the most allegiance—to her husband or to her children?"

"Why not split it up," I said cheerfully, "and try doing what seems best for both?"

"But that's only a compromise!" she complained, and was asleep almost immediately. I lowered the light and closed the door, and shortly after, I heard Mr. Reed locking it from the outside.

With the bolt off my door and Mrs. Reed asleep, my plan for the night was easily carried out. I went to bed for a couple of hours and slept calmly. I awakened once with the feeling that someone was looking at me from the passage into the night nursery, but there was no one there. However, so strong had been the feeling that I got up and went into the back room. The children were asleep, and all doors opening into the hall were locked. But the window onto the porte-cochère roof was open and the curtain blowing. There was no one on the roof, however, and I closed and locked the window.

It was not twelve o'clock and I went back to bed for an hour.

At one I prepared to make a thorough search of the house. Looking from one of my windows, I thought I saw the shadowy figure of a man across the street, and I was comforted. Help was always close, I felt. And yet, as I stood inside my door in my rubber-soled shoes, with my ulster over my uniform, my revolver, flashlight and skeleton keys in my pockets, my heart was going very fast. The stupid story of the ghost came back and made me shudder, and the next instant I was remembering Mrs. Reed the night before, staring down into the lower hall with fixed glassy eyes.

My plan was to begin at the top of the house and work down. The thing was the more hazardous, of course, because Mr. Reed was most certainly somewhere about. I had no excuse for being on the third floor. Down below I could say I wanted tea, or hot water—anything. But I did not expect to find Mr. Reed up above. The terror, whatever it was, seemed to lie below.

Access to the third floor was not easy. The main staircase did not go up. To get there I was obliged to unlock the door at the rear of the hall with my own keys. I was working in bright light, trying my keys one after another, and watching over my shoulder as I did so. When the door finally gave, it was a relief to slip into the darkness beyond, ghosts or no ghosts.

I am always a silent worker. Caution about closing doors and squeaking hinges is second nature to me. One learns to be cautious when one's only chance to sleep is not to rouse a peevish patient and have to give a body massage, as like as not, or listen to domestic troubles—"I said" and "he said"—until one is almost crazy.

So I made no noise. I closed the door behind me and stood blinking in the darkness. I listened. There was no sound above or below. Now houses at night have no terror for me. Every nurse is obliged to do more or less going about in the dark. But I was not easy. Suppose Mr. Reed should call me? True, I had locked my door and had the key in my pocket. But a dozen emergencies flew through my mind as I felt for the stair rail.

There was a curious odor through all the back staircase, a pungent, aromatic scent that, with all my familiarity with drugs, was strange to me. As I slowly climbed the stairs it grew more powerful. The air was heavy with it, as though no windows had been opened in that part of the house. There was no door at the top of this staircase, as there was on the second floor. It opened into an upper hall, and across from the head of the stairs was a door leading into a room. This door was closed. On this staircase, as on all the others, the carpet had been newly lifted. My electric flash showed the white boards and painted borders, the carpet tacks, many of them still in place. One, lying loose, penetrated my rubber sole and went into my foot.

I sat down in the dark and took off the shoe. As I did so my flash, on the step beside me, rolled over and down with a crash. I caught it on the next step, but the noise had been like a pistol shot.

Almost immediately a voice spoke above me sharply. At first I thought it was out in the upper hall. Then I realized that the closed door was between it and me.

"Ees that you, Meester Reed?"

Mademoiselle!

"Meester Reed!" plaintively. "Eet comes up again, Meester Reed! I die! Tomorrow I die!"

She listened. When no reply came, she began to groan rhythmically, to a curious accompaniment of creaking. When I had gathered up my nerves again, I realized that she must be sitting in a rocking chair. The groans were really little plaintive grunts.

By the time I had got my shoe on, she was up again, and I could hear her pacing the room, the heavy step of a woman well fleshed and not young. Now and then she stopped inside the door and listened; once she shook the knob and mumbled querulously to herself.

I recovered the flash, and with infinite caution worked my way to the top of the stairs. Mademoiselle was locked in, doubly bolted in. Two strong bolts, above and below, supplemented the door lock.

Her ears must have been very quick, or else she felt my softly padding feet on the boards outside, for suddenly she flung herself against the door and begged for a priest, begged piteously, in jumbled French and English. She wanted food; she was dying of hunger. She wanted a priest.

And all the while I stood outside the door and wondered what I should do. Should I release the woman? Should I go down to the lower floor and get the detective across the street to come in and open the door? Was this the terror that held the house in thrall—this babbling old Frenchwoman calling for food and a priest in one breath?

Surely not. This was a part of the mystery, but not all. The real terror lay below. It was not Mademoiselle, locked in her room on the upper floor, that the Reeds waited for at the top of the stairs. But why was Mademoiselle locked in her room? Why were the children locked in? What was this thing that had turned a home into a jail, a barracks, that had sent away the servants, imprisoned and probably killed the dog, sapped the joy of life from two young people? What was it that Mademoiselle cried "comes up again"?

I looked toward the staircase. Was it coming up the staircase?

I am not afraid of the thing I can see, but it seemed to me, all at once, that if anything was going to come up the staircase, I might as well get down first. A staircase is no place to meet anything, especially if one doesn't know what it is.

I listened again. Mademoiselle was quiet. I flashed my light down the narrow stairs. They were quite empty. I shut off the flash and went down. I tried to go slowly, to retreat with dignity, and by the time I had reached the landing below, I was heartily ashamed of myself. Was this shivering girl the young woman Mr. Patton called his right hand?

I dare say I should have stopped there, for that night at least. My nerves were frayed. But I forced myself on. The mystery lay below. Well, then,

I was going down. It could not be so terrible. At least it was nothing supernatural. There must be a natural explanation. And then that silly story about the headless things must pop into my mind and start me down trembling.

The lower rear staircase was black dark, like the upper, but just at the foot a light came in through a barred window. I could see it plainly, and the shadows of the iron grating on the bare floor. I stood there listening. There was not a sound.

It was not easy to tell exactly what followed. I stood there with my hand on the rail. I'd been very silent; my rubber shoes attended to that. And one moment the staircase was clear, with a patch of light at the bottom. The next, something was there, halfway down—a head, it seemed to be, with a pointed hood like a monk's cowl. There was no body. It seemed to lie at my feet. But it was living. It moved. I could tell the moment when the eyes lifted and saw my feet, the slow back-tilting of the head as they looked up my body. All the air was squeezed out of my lungs; a heavy hand seemed to press on my chest. I remember raising a shaking hand and flinging my flashlight at the head. The flash clattered on the stair tread, harmless. Then the head was gone and something living slid over my foot.

I stumbled back to my room and locked the door. It was two hours before I had strength enough to get my aromatic-ammonia bottle.

## CHAPTER V

It seemed to me that I had hardly dropped asleep before the children were in the room, clamoring.

"The goldfish are dead!" Harry said, standing soberly by the bed. "They are all dead with their stummicks turned up."

I sat up. My head ached violently.

"They can't be dead, old chap." I was feeling about for my kimono, but I remembered that, when I had found my way back to the nursery after my fright on the back stairs, I had lain down in my uniform. I crawled out, hardly able to stand. "We gave them fresh water yesterday, and——"

I had got to the aquarium. Harry was right. The little darting flames of pink and gold were still. They floated about, rolling gently as Freddie prodded them with a forefinger, dull-eyed, pale bellies upturned. In his cage above, the little parrot watched out of a crooked eye.

I ran to the medicine closet in the bathroom. Freddie had a weakness for administering medicine. I had only just rescued the parrot from the result of his curiosity—a headache tablet—the day before.

"What did you give them?" I demanded.

"Bread," said Freddie stoutly.

"Only bread?"

"Dirty bread," Harry put in. "I told him it was dirty."

"Where did you get it?"

"On the roof of the porte-cochère!"

Shades of Montessori! The rascals had been out on that sloping tin roof. It turned me rather sick to think of it.

Accused, they admitted it frankly.

"I unlocked the window," Harry said, "and Freddie got the bread. It was out in the gutter. He slipped once."

"Almost went over and made a squash on the pavement," added Freddie. "We gave the little fishes the bread for breakfast, and now they're gone to God."

The bread had contained poison, of course. Even the two little snails that crawled over the sand in the aquarium were motionless. I sniffed the water. It had a slightly foreign odor. I did not recognize it.

Panic seized me then. I wanted to get away and take the children with me. The situation was too hideous. But it was still early. I could only wait until the family roused. In the meantime, however, I made a nerve-racking excursion out onto the tin roof and down to the gutter. There was no more of the bread there. The porte-cochère was at the side of the house. As I stood balancing myself perilously on the edge, summoning my courage to climb back to the window above, I suddenly remembered the guard Mr. Patton had promised and glanced toward the square.

The guard was still there. More than that, he was running across the street toward me. It was Mr. Patton himself. He brought up between the two houses with absolute fury in his face.

"Go back!" he waved. "What are you doing out there anyhow? That roof's as slippery as the devil!"

I turned meekly and crawled back with as much dignity as I could. I did not say anything. There was nothing I could bawl from the roof. I could only close and lock the window and hope that the people in the next house still slept. Mr. Patton must have gone shortly after, for I did not see him again.

I wondered if he had relieved the night watch, or if he could possibly have been on guard himself all that chilly April night.

Mr. Reed did not breakfast with us. I made a point of being cheerful before the children, and their mother was rested and brighter than I had seen her. But more than once I found her staring at me in a puzzled way. She asked me if I had slept.

"I wakened only once," she said. "I thought I heard a crash of some sort. Did you hear it?"

"What sort of crash?" I evaded.

The children had forgotten the goldfish for a time. Now they remembered and clamored their news to her.

"Dead?" she said, and looked at me.

"Poisoned," I explained. "I shall nail the windows over the porte-cochère shut, Mrs. Reed. The boys got out there early this morning and picked up something—bread, I believe. They fed it to the fish and—they are dead."

All the light went out of her face. She looked tired and harassed as she got up.

"I wanted to nail the window," she said vaguely, "but Mr. Reed . . . Suppose they had eaten that bread, Miss Adams, instead of giving it to the fish!"

The same thought had chilled me with horror. We gazed at each other over the unconscious heads of the children and my heart ached for her. I made a sudden resolution.

"When I first came," I said to her, "I told you I wanted to help. That's what I'm here for. But how am I to help either you or the children when I do not know what danger it is that threatens? It isn't fair to you, or to them, or even to me."

She was much shaken by the poison incident. I thought she wavered.

"Are you afraid the children will be stolen?"

"Oh, no."

"Or hurt in any way?" I was thinking of the bread on the roof.

"No."

"But you are afraid of something?"

Harry looked up suddenly. "Mother's never afraid," he said stoutly.

I sent them both in to see if the fish were still dead.

"There is something in the house downstairs that you are afraid of?" I persisted.

She took a step forward and caught my arm.

"I had no idea it would be like this, Miss Adams. I'm dying of fear!"

I had a quick vision of the swathed head on the back staircase, and some of my night's terror came back to me. I believe we stared at each other with dilated pupils for a moment. Then I asked, "Is it a real thing?—surely you can tell me this. Are you afraid of a reality, or—is it something supernatural?" I was ashamed of the question. It sounded so absurd in the broad light of that April morning.

"It is a real danger," she replied. Then I think she decided that she had gone as far as she dared, and I went through the ceremony of letting her out and of locking the door behind her.

The day was warm. I threw up some of the windows and the boys and I played ball, using a rolled handkerchief. My part, being to sit on the floor with a newspaper folded into a bat and to bang at the handkerchief as it flew past me, became automatic after a time.

As I look back, I see a pair of disordered young rascals with Russian blouses and bare round knees doing a great deal of yelling and some very crooked throwing; a nurse sitting tailor fashion on the floor, alternately ducking to save her cap and making vigorous but ineffectual passes at the ball with her newspaper bat. And I see sunshine in the room and the dwarf parrot eating sugar out of his claw. And below, the fish floating in the aquarium, belly up and dull-eyed.

Mr. Reed brought up our luncheon tray. He looked tired and depressed and avoided my eyes. I watched him while I spread the bread and butter for the children. He nailed shut the windows that opened on to the porte-cochère roof, and when he thought I was not looking, he examined the registers in the wall to see if the gratings were closed. The boys put the dead fish in a box and made him promise a decent interment in the garden. They called on me for an epitaph, and I scrawled on top of the box:

> These fish are dead
> Because a boy called Fred
> Went out on a porch roof when he should
> Have been in bed.

I was much pleased with it. It seemed to me that an epitaph, which can do no good to the departed, should at least convey a moral. But to my horror Freddie broke into loud wails and would not be comforted.

It was three o'clock, therefore, before they were both settled for their afternoon naps and I was free. I had determined to do one thing, and to do it in daylight—to examine the back staircase inch by inch. I knew I would be courting discovery, but the thing had to be done, and no power on earth would have made me essay such an investigation after dark.

It was all well enough for me to say to myself that there was a natural explanation; that this had been a human head, of a certainty; that something living and not spectral had slid over my foot in the darkness. I would not have gone back there again at night for youth, love or money. But I did not investigate the staircase that day, after all.

I made a curious discovery after the boys had settled down in their small white beds. A venturesome fly had sailed in through an open window, and I was immediately in pursuit of it with my paper bat. Driven from the cornice to the chandelier, harried here, swatted there, finally he took refuge inside the furnace register.

Perhaps it is my training—I used to know how many million germs a fly packed about with it, and the generous benevolence with which it distributed them; I've forgotten—but the sight of a single fly maddens me. I said that to Mr. Patton once, and he asked what the sight of a married one would do. So I sat down by the register and waited. It was then that I made the curious discovery that the furnace belowstairs was burning, and burning hard. A fierce heat assailed me as I opened the grating. I drove the fly out of cover, but I had no time for him. The furnace going full on a warm spring day! It was strange.

Perhaps I was stupid. Perhaps the whole thing should have been clear to me. But it was not. I sat there bewildered and tried to figure it out. I went over it point by point:

The carpets up all over the house, lights going full all night and doors locked.

The cot at the top of the stairs and Mrs. Reed staring down.

The bolt that had been outside my door to lock me in.

The death of Chang.

Mademoiselle locked in her room upstairs and begging for a priest.

The poison on the porch roof.

The head without a body on the staircase and the thing that slid over my foot.

The furnace going, and the thing I recognized as I sat there beside the register—the unmistakable odor of burning cloth.

Should I have known? I wonder. It looks so clear to me now.

I did not investigate the staircase, for the simple reason that my skeleton key, which, the night before, had unfastened the lock of the door at the rear of the second-floor hall, did not open it now. I did not understand at once and stood stupidly working with the lock. The door was bolted on the other side. I wandered as aimlessly as I could down the main staircase and tried the corresponding door on the lower floor. It, too, was locked. Here was an impasse for sure. As far as I could discover, the only other entrance to the back staircase was through the window with the iron grating.

As I turned to go back, I saw my electric flash, badly broken, lying on a table in the hall. I did not claim it.

The lower floor seemed entirely deserted. The drawing room and library were in their usual disorder, undusted and bare of floor. The air everywhere was close and heavy; there was not a window open. I sauntered through the various rooms, picked up a book in the library as an excuse and tried the door of the room behind. It was locked. I thought at first that something moved behind it, but if anything lived there, it did not stir again. And yet I had a vivid impression that just on the other side of the door ears as keen as mine were listening. It was broad day, but I backed away from the door and out into the wide hall. My nerves were still raw, no doubt, from the night before.

I was to meet Mr. Patton at half after seven that night, and when Mrs. Reed relieved me at seven, I had half an hour to myself. I spent it in Beauregard Gardens, with the dry fountain in the center. The place itself was charming, the trees still black but lightly fringed with new green, early spring flowers in the borders, neat paths and, surrounding it all, the solid, dignified backs of the Beauregard houses. I sat down on the coping of the fountain and surveyed the Reed house. Those windows above were Mademoiselle's. The shades were drawn, but no light came through or round them. The prisoner—for prisoner she was by every rule of bolt and lock—must be sitting in the dark. Was she still begging for her priest? Had she had any food? Was she still listening inside her door for whatever it was that was "coming up"?

In all the other houses, windows were open; curtains waved gently in the spring air; the cheerful signs of the dinner hour were evident nearby —moving servants, a gleam of stately shirt bosom as a butler mixed a salad, a warm radiance of candlelight from dining-room tables and the reflected glow of flowers. Only the Reed house stood gloomy, unlighted, almost sinister.

Beauregard Square dined early. It was one of the traditions, I believe. It liked to get to the theater or the opera early, and it believed in allowing the servants a little time in the evenings. So, although it was only something after seven, the evening rite of the table crumbs began to be observed. Came a colored butler, bowed to me with a word of apology, and dumped the contents of a silver tray into the basin; came a pretty mulatto, flung her crumbs gracefully and smiled with a flash of teeth at the butler.

Then for five minutes I was alone.

It was Nora, the girl we had met on the street, who came next. She saw me and came round to me with a little air of triumph.

"Well, I'm back in the square again, after all, miss," she said. "And a better place than the Reeds'. I don't have the doilies to do."

"I'm very glad you are settled again, Nora."

She lowered her voice. "I'm just trying it out," she observed. "The girl that left said I wouldn't stay. She was scared off. There have been some queer doings—not that I believe in ghosts or anything like that. But my mother in the old country had the second sight, and if there's anything going on, I'll be right sure to see it."

It took encouragement to get her story, and it was secondhand at that, of course. But it appeared that a state of panic had seized the Beauregard servants. The alarm was all belowstairs and had been started by a cook who, coming in late and going to the basement to prepare herself a cup of tea, had found her kitchen door locked and a light going beyond. Suspecting another maid of violating the tea canister, she had gone soft-footed to the outside of the house and had distinctly seen a gray figure crouching in a corner of the room. She had called the butler, and they had made an examination of the entire basement without result. Nothing was missing from the house.

"And that figure has been seen again and again, miss," Nora finished. "The McKennas' butler, Joseph, saw it in this very spot, walking without a sound and the street light beyond there shining straight through it. Over in the Smythe house the laundress, coming in late and going down to the basement to soak her clothes for the morning, met the thing on the basement staircase and fainted dead away."

I had listened intently. "What do they think it is?" I asked.

She shrugged her shoulders and picked up her tray.

"I'm not trying to say and I guess nobody is. But if there's been a murder, it's pretty well known that the ghost walks about until the service is read and it's properly buried." She glanced at the Reed house. "For instance," she demanded, "where is Mademoiselle?"

"She is alive," I said rather sharply. "And even if what you say were true, what in the world would make her wander about the basements? It seems so silly, Nora, a ghost haunting damp cellars and laundries with stationary tubs and all that."

"Well," she contended, "it seems silly for them to sit on cold tomb-stones—and yet that's where they generally sit, isn't it?"

Mr. Patton listened gravely to my story that night.

"I don't like it," he said when I had finished. "Of course the head on the staircase is nonsense. Your nerves were ragged and our eyes play tricks on all of us. But as for the Frenchwoman——"

"If you accept her, you must accept the head," I snapped. "It was there —it was a head without a body and it looked up at me."

We were walking through a quiet street, and he bent over and caught my wrist.

"Pulse racing," he commented. "I'm going to take you away, that's certain. I can't afford to lose my best assistant. You're too close, Miss Adams; you've lost your perspective."

"I've lost my temper!" I retorted. "I shall not leave until I know what this thing is, unless you choose to ring the doorbell and tell them I'm a spy."

He gave in when he saw that I was firm, but not without a final protest.

"I'm directly responsible for you to your friends," he said. "There's probably a young man somewhere who will come gunning for me if anything happens to you. And I don't care to be gunned for. I get enough of that in my regular line."

"There is no young man," I said shortly.

"Have you been able to see the cellars?"

"No, everything is locked off."

"Do you think the rear staircase goes all the way down?"

"I haven't the slightest idea."

"You are in the house. Have you any suggestions as to the best method of getting into the house? Is Reed on guard all night?"

"I think he is."

"It may interest you to know," he said finally, "that I sent a reliable man to break in there last night, quietly, and that he—couldn't do it. He got a leg through a cellar window, and came near not getting it out again. Reed was just inside in the dark." He laughed a little, but I guessed that the thing galled him.

"I do not believe that he would have found anything if he had succeeded in getting in. There has been no crime, Mr. Patton, I am sure of that. But there is a menace of some sort in the house."

"Then why does Mrs. Reed stay and keep the children if there is danger?"

"I believe she is afraid to leave him. There are times when I think that he is desperate."

"Does he ever leave the house?"

"I think not, unless——"

"Yes?"

"Unless he is the basement ghost of the other houses."

He stopped in his slow walk and considered it.

"It's possible. In that case I could have him waylaid tonight in the gardens and left there, tied. It would be a holdup, you understand. The police have no excuse for coming in yet. Or, if we found him breaking into one of the other houses, we could get him there. He'd be released, of course, but it would give us time. I want to clean the thing up. I'm not easy while you are in that house."

We agreed that I was to wait inside one of my windows that night, and that on a given signal I should go down and open the front door. The whole thing, of course, was contingent on Mr. Reed's leaving the house sometime that night. It was only a chance.

"The house is barred like a fortress," Mr. Patton said as he left me. "The window with the grating is hopeless. That's the one we tried last night."

I FIND THAT my notes on that last night in the house on Beauregard Square are rather confused, some written at the time, some just before. For instance, on the edge of a newspaper clipping I find this:

"Evidently this is the item. R—— went pale on reading it. Did not allow wife to see paper."

The clipping is an account of the sudden death of an elderly gentleman named Smythe, one of the Beauregard families.

The next note is less hasty and is on a yellow symptom record. It has been much folded—I believe I tucked it in my apron belt:

"If the rear staircase is bolted everywhere from the inside, how did the person who locked it, either Mr. or Mrs. Reed, get back into the body of the house again? Or did Mademoiselle do it? In that case she is no longer a prisoner and the bolts outside her room are not fastened.

"At eleven o'clock tonight Harry wakened with earache. I went to the kitchen to heat some mullein oil and laudanum. Mrs. Reed was with the boy and Mr. Reed was not in sight. I slipped into the library and used my skeleton keys on the locked door to the rear room. It is empty even of furniture, but there is a huge box there, with a lid that fastens down with steel hooks. The lid is full of small airholes. I had no time to examine further.

"It is one o'clock. Harry is asleep and his mother is dozing across the foot of his bed. I have found the way to get to the rear staircase. There are outside steps from the basement to the garden. Evidently the staircase goes all the way down to the cellar. Then the lower door in the cellar must be only locked, not bolted from the inside. I shall try to get to the cellar."

The next is a scrawl:

"Cannot get to the outside basement steps. Mr. Reed is wandering round lower floor. I reported Harry's condition and came up again. I must get to the back staircase."

I wonder if I have been able to convey, even faintly, the situation in that highly respectable old house that night: the fear that hung over it, a fear so great that even I, an outsider and stout of nerve, felt it and grew cold; the unnatural brilliancy of light that bespoke dread of the dark; the hushed voices, the locked doors and staring, peering eyes; the babbling Frenchwoman on an upper floor, the dead fish, the dead dog. And, always in my mind, that vision of dread on the back staircase and the thing that slid over my foot.

At two o'clock I saw Mr. Patton, or whoever was on guard in the park across the street, walk quickly toward the house and disappear round the corner toward the gardens in the rear. There had been no signal, but I felt sure that Mr. Reed had left the house. His wife was still asleep across Harry's bed. As I went out, I locked the door behind me, and I also took the key to the night nursery. I thought that something disagreeable, to say the least, was inevitable, and why let her in for it?

The lower hall was lighted, as usual, and empty. I listened, but there were no restless footsteps. I did not like the lower hall. Only a thin wooden door stood between me and the rear staircase, and anyone who thinks about the matter will realize that a door is no barrier to a head that can move about without a body. I am afraid I looked over my shoulder while I unlocked the front door, and I know I breathed better when I was out in the air.

I wore my dark ulster over my uniform, and I had my revolver and keys. My flash, of course, was useless. I missed it horribly. But to get to the staircase was an obsession by that time in spite of my fear of it—to find what it guarded, to solve its mystery. I worked round the house, keeping close to the wall, until I reached the garden. The night was the city night, never absolutely dark. As I hesitated at the top of the basement steps, it seemed to me that figures were moving about among the trees.

The basement door was unlocked and open. I was not prepared for that, and it made me, if anything, more uneasy. I had a box of matches with me, and I wanted light as a starving man wants food. But I dared not light them. I could only keep a tight grip on my courage and go on. A small passage first, with whitewashed stone walls, cold and scaly under my hand; then a large room, and still darkness. Worse than darkness, something crawling and scratching round the floor.

I struck my match then, and it seemed to me that something white flashed into a corner and disappeared. My hands were shaking, but I managed to light a gas jet and to see that I was in the laundry. The staircase came down here, narrower than above, and closed off with a door.

The door was closed and there was a heavy bolt on it but no lock.

And now, with the staircase accessible and a gaslight to keep up my courage, I grew brave, almost reckless. I would tell Mr. Patton all about this cellar, which his best men had not been able to enter. I would make a sketch for him—coalbins, laundry tubs, everything. Foolish, of course, but hold the gas jet responsible—the reckless bravery of light after hideous darkness.

So I went on, forward. The glow from the laundry followed me. I struck matches, found potatoes and cases of mineral water, bruised my knees on a discarded bicycle, stumbled over a box of soap. Twice, out of the corner of my eye, and never there when I looked, I caught the white flash that had frightened me before. Then at last I brought up before a door and stopped. It was a curiously barricaded door, nailed against disturbance by a plank fastened across, and, as if to make intrusion without discovery impossible, pasted round every crack and over the keyhole with strips of strong yellow paper. It was an ominous door. I wanted to run away from it, and I also wanted desperately to stand and look at it and imagine what might lie beyond. Here again was the strange, spicy odor that I had noticed on the back staircase.

I think it is indicative of my state of mind that I backed away from the door. I did not turn and run. Nothing in the world would have made me turn my back to it.

Somehow or other I got back into the laundry and jerked myself together.

It was ten minutes after two. I had been less than ten minutes in the basement!

The staircase daunted me in my shaken condition. I made excuses for delaying my venture, looked for another box of matches, listened at the end of the passage, finally slid the bolt and opened the door. The silence was impressive. In the laundry there were small, familiar sounds—the dripping of water from a faucet, the muffled measure of a gas meter, the ticking of a clock on the shelf. To leave it all, to climb into that silence . . .

Lying on the lower step was a curious instrument. It was a sort of tongs made of steel, about two feet long, and fastened together like a pair of scissors, the joint about five inches from the flattened ends. I carried it to the light and examined it. One end was smeared with blood and short, brownish hairs. It made me shudder, but—from that time on I think I knew. Not the whole story, of course, but somewhere in the back of my head, as I climbed in that hideous quiet, the explanation was developing itself. I did not think it out. It worked itself out as, step after step, match after match, I climbed the staircase.

Up to the first floor there was nothing. The landing was bare of carpet. I was on the first floor now. On each side, doors, carefully bolted, led into the house. I opened the one into the hall and listened. I had been gone from the children fifteen minutes and they were on my mind. But everything was quiet.

The sight of the lights and the familiar hall gave me courage. After all, if I was right, what could the head on the staircase have been but an optical illusion? And I was right. The evidence—the tongs—was in my hand. I closed and bolted the door and felt my way back to the stairs. I lighted no matches this time. I had only a few, and on this landing there was a little light from the grated window, although the staircase above was in black shadow.

I had one foot on the lowest stair, when suddenly overhead came the thudding of hands on a closed door. It broke the silence like an explosion. It sent chills up and down my spine. I could not move for a moment. It was the Frenchwoman!

I believe I thought of fire. The idea had obsessed me in that house of locked doors. I remember a strangling weight of fright on my chest and my effort to breathe. Then I started up the staircase, running as fast as I could lift my weighted feet—I remember that—and getting up perhaps a third of the way. Then there came a plunging forward into space, my hands out, a shriek frozen on my lips, and—quiet.

I do not think I fainted. I know I was always conscious of my arm doubled under me, a pain and darkness. I could hear myself moaning, but almost as if it were someone else. There were other sounds, but they did not concern me much. I was not even curious about my location. I seemed to be a very small consciousness surrounded by a great deal of pain.

Several centuries later a light came and leaned over me from somewhere above. Then the light said, "Here she is!"

"Alive?" I knew that voice, but I could not think whose it was.

"I'm not—— Yes, she's moaning."

They got me out somewhere and I believe I still clung to the tongs. I had fallen on them and had a cut on my chin. I could stand, I found, although I swayed. There was plenty of light now in the back hallway, and a man I had never seen was investigating the staircase.

"Four steps off," he said. "Risers and treads gone and the supports sawed away. It's a trap of some sort."

Mr. Patton was examining my broken arm and paid no attention. The man let himself down into the pit under the staircase. When he straightened, only his head rose above the steps. Although I was white with pain to the very lips, I laughed hysterically. "The head!" I cried.

Mr. Patton swore under his breath.

They half led, half carried me into the library. Mr. Reed was there, with a detective on guard over him. He was sitting in his old position, bent forward, chin in palms. In the blaze of light he was a pitiable figure, smeared with dust, disheveled from what had evidently been a struggle. Mr. Patton put me in a chair and dispatched another man for the nearest doctor.

"This young lady," he said curtly to Mr. Reed, "fell into that damnable trap you made in the rear staircase."

"I locked off the staircase—but I am sorry she is hurt. My—my wife will be shocked. Only I wish you'd tell me what all this is about. You can't arrest me for going into a friend's house."

"If I send for some member of the Smythe family, will they acquit you?"

"Certainly they will," he said. "I—I've been raised with the Smythes. You can send for anyone you like." But his tone lacked conviction.

Mr. Patton made me as comfortable as possible, and then, sending the remaining detective out into the hall, he turned to his prisoner.

"Now, Mr. Reed," he said. "I want you to be sensible. For some days a figure has been seen in the basements of the various Beauregard houses. Your friends, the Smythes, reported it. Tonight we are on watch, and we see you breaking into the basement of the Smythe house. We already know some curious things about you, such as your dismissal of all the servants on half an hour's notice and the disappearance of the French governess."

"Mademoiselle! Why, she——" He checked himself.

"When we bring you here tonight, and you ask to be allowed to go upstairs and prepare your wife, she is locked in. The nurse is missing. We find her at last, also locked away, and badly hurt, lying in a staircase trap, where someone, probably yourself, has removed the steps. I do not want to arrest you, but now I've started, I'm going to get to the bottom of all this."

Mr. Reed was ghastly, but he straightened in his chair.

"The Smythes reported this thing, did they?" he asked. "Well, tell me one thing. What killed the old gentleman—old Smythe?"

"I don't know."

"Well, go a little further." His cunning was boyish, pitiful. "How did he die? Or don't you know that either?"

Up to this point I had been rather a detached part of the scene, but now my eyes fell on the tongs beside me.

"Mr. Reed," I said, "isn't this thing too big for you to handle by yourself?"

"What thing?"

"You know what I mean. You've protected yourself well enough, but even if the—the thing you know of did not kill old Mr. Smythe, you cannot tell what will happen next."

"I've got almost all of them," he muttered sullenly. "Another night or two and I'd have had the lot."

"But even then the mischief may go on. It means a crusade; it means rousing the city. Isn't it the square thing now to spread the alarm?"

Mr. Patton could stand the suspense no longer. "Perhaps, Miss Adams," he said, "you will be good enough to let me know what you are talking about."

Mr. Reed looked up at him with heavy eyes. "Rats," he said. "They got away, twenty of them, and some are loaded with bubonic plague."

I went to the hospital the next morning. Mr. Patton thought it best. There was no 'one in my little flat to look after me, and although the pain in my arm subsided after the fracture was set, I was still shaken.

He came the next afternoon to see me. I was propped up in bed, with my hair braided down in two pigtails and great hollows under my eyes.

"I'm comfortable enough," I said, in response to his inquiry; "but I'm feeling all of my years. This is my birthday. I am thirty today."

"I wonder," he said reflectively, "if I ever reach the mature age of one hundred, if I will carry in my head as many odds and ends of information as you have at thirty!"

"I? What do you mean?" I said rather weakly.

"You. How in the world did you know, for instance, about those tongs?"

"It was quite simple. I'd seen something like them in the laboratory here. Of course I didn't know what animals he'd used, but the grayish brown hair looked like rats. The laboratory must be the cellar room. I knew it had been fumigated—it was sealed with paper, even over the keyhole."

So, sitting there beside me, Mr. Patton told me the story as he had got it from Mr. Reed—a tale of the offer in an English scientific journal of a large reward from some plague-ridden country of the East for an anti-plague serum. Mr. Reed had been working along bacteriological lines in his basement laboratory, mostly with guinea pigs and tuberculosis. He was in debt; the offer loomed large.

"He seems to think he was on the right track," Mr. Patton said. "He had twenty of the creatures in deep zinc cans with perforated lids. He says the disease is spread by fleas that infest the rats. So he had muslin over the lids as well. One can had infected rats, six of them. Then one day the Frenchwoman tried to give the dog a bath in a laundry tub and the dog bolted. The laboratory door was open in some way and he ran between the cans, upsetting them. Every rat was out in an instant. The Frenchwoman was frantic. She shut the door and tried to drive the things back. One bit her on the foot. The dog was not bitten, but there was the question of fleas.

"Well, the rats got away, and Mademoiselle retired to her room to die of plague. She was a loyal old soul; she wouldn't let them call a doctor. It would mean exposure, and after all, what could the doctors do? Reed used his serum and she's alive.

"Reed was frantic. His wife would not leave. There was the French-woman to look after, and I think Mrs. Reed was afraid he would do something desperate. They did the best they could, under the circumstances, for the children. They burned most of the carpets for fear of fleas, and put poison everywhere. Of course he had traps, too.

"He had brass tags on the necks of the rats, and he got back a few —the uninfected ones. The other ones were probably dead. But he couldn't stop at that. He had to be sure that the trouble had not spread. And to add to their horror, the sewer along the street was being relaid, and they had an influx of rats into the house. They found them everywhere on the lower floor. They even climbed the stairs. He says that the night you came he caught a big fellow on the front staircase. There was always the danger that the fleas that carry the trouble had deserted the dead creatures for new fields. They took up all the rest of the carpets and burned them. To add to the general misery, the dog, Chang, developed unmistakable symptoms and had to be killed."

"But the broken staircase?" I asked. "And what was it that Mademoiselle said was coming up?"

"The steps were up for two reasons: The rats could not climb up, and beneath the steps Reed says he caught two of the tagged ones in a trap. As for Mademoiselle, the thing that was coming up was her temperature —pure fright. The head you saw was poor Reed himself, wrapped in gauze against trouble and baiting his traps. He caught a lot in the neighbors' cellars and some in the garden."

"But why," I demanded, "why didn't he make it all known?"

Mr. Patton laughed and shrugged his shoulders.

"A man hardly cares to announce that he has menaced the health of a city."

"But that night when I fell—was it only last night?—someone was pounding above. I thought there was a fire."

"The Frenchwoman had seen us waylay Reed from her window. She was crazy."

"And the trouble is over now?"

"Not at all," he replied cheerfully. "The trouble may be only beginning. We're keeping Reed's name out, but the Board of Health has issued a general warning. Personally I think his six pets died without passing anything along."

"But there was a big box with a lid——"

"Ferrets," he assured me. "Nice white ferrets with pink eyes and a taste for rats." He held out a thumb, carefully bandaged. "Reed had a couple under his coat when we took him in the garden. Probably one ran over your foot that night when you surprised him on the back staircase."

I went pale. "But if they are infected!" I cried, "and you are bitten——"

"The first thing a nurse should learn"—he bent forward, smiling—"is not to alarm her patient."

"But you don't understand the danger," I said despairingly. "Oh, if only men had a little bit of sense!"

"I must do something desperate, then? Have the thumb cut off, perhaps?"

I did not answer. I lay back on my pillows with my eyes shut. I had given him the plague, had seen him die and be buried, before he spoke again.

"The chin," he said, "is not so firm as I had thought. The outlines are savage, but the dimple . . . You poor little thing; are you really frightened?"

"I don't like you," I said furiously. "But I'd hate to see anyone with —with that trouble."

"Then I'll confess. I was trying to take your mind off your troubles. The bite is there, but harmless. Those were new ferrets; they had never been out."

I did not speak to him again. I was seething with indignation. He stood for a time looking down at me; then, unexpectedly, he bent over and touched his lips to my bandaged arm.

"Poor arm!" he said. "Poor, brave little arm!" Then he tiptoed out of the room. His very back was sheepish.

# Miss Pinkerton

## CHAPTER I

It seemed to me that I had just gone to bed that Monday night when I heard the telephone ringing and had to crawl out again. When I looked at my watch, however, I saw that it was a few minutes after one. A trained nurse grows accustomed to such things, of course; but I had set that particular night apart to catch up with my sleeping, and I was rather peevish when I picked up the receiver.

"Hello."

"This Miss Adams? Inspector Patton speaking."

He did not need to tell me that. I had had a sort of premonition when the bell rang that the police had turned up another case for me, and I wanted one that night about as much as I wanted hardening of the arteries. In fact, I said as much.

"Listen to me, Inspector. I need some sleep. I'm no good the way I am."

"Then you're not on a case now?" He knew that I often took what we call eighteen-hour duty, and slept at home.

"I'm still resting from that last one," I said rather sharply, and I imagine he smiled. He knew well enough what I was talking about. I had been taking care of a gangster's wife for him in order to get a line on who came to the house. But the gentleman in question kept his business and his family too well separated, and besides, she was the most jealous woman I ever saw—and a trained nurse sees a lot of them. I am pretty much given to minding my own business when I am on a case, especially when it is a police case; but the moment any female in a white cap and a uniform enters certain houses, there is to be trouble.

"This is different," he said, "and it may be for only a few hours. Better call a taxi and come over. Do you know the Mitchell house on Sylvan Avenue?"

"Everybody knows it. What's wrong?"

"I'll tell you when you get there. I'm at the drugstore on the corner. How long will you be?"

"About a half hour," I said. "I *had* hoped to get some sleep tonight, Inspector."

"So had I!" he retorted, rather testily for him, and hung up the receiver.

That was a Monday night, the fourteenth of September. If they ever have to perform an autopsy on me, they will not find Calais written across my heart, but that date.

I drew a long breath; looked at my bed; at the uniform which needed buttons, draped over a chair, and my sewing basket beside it; and then I looked through the door into my little sitting room, newly done in chintz, and at my canary, snugly covered in his cage so that he would not burst into song at dawn and rouse me. Rouse me!

I can write that and fairly weep. Rouse me! When for that night and the next four nights sleep was to be as rare with me as watercress in the Sahara. Rouse me! When just four nights later it was to look as though nothing but Gabriel's horn would ever waken me again.

Well, I am not as bitter as I sound, and that night I was merely resigned. I got down and dragged my suitcase from under my bed, threw in a few toilet articles—for it is always packed and ready—called a taxi and then got into a uniform. But I was not excited or even greatly interested. Indeed, at the last minute, finding in my suitcase a snub-nosed little automatic which the Inspector had given me, I picked it up gingerly and looked around for a place in which to hide it. It would never do for Mrs. Merwin, my landlady, to find it; so I finally decided to put it in the jardinière with my Boston fern. She never remembered to water that fern anyhow.

I suppose that is funny when I look back over it. But it is not really funny at all. Later on I planned to go back one day and get it; but it would never have done me any good, as I know now. And, as I think back over those particular five days, I realize that on the only occasion when I might possibly have used it, I was fighting madly to get air into my lungs. All I could think of was that, to get air, to breathe again. Well . . .

So I was not in the best of humor that night when I closed my suitcase and pinned on my cap. To tell the truth, I was wondering why I continued my work for the police. One way and another I had run a good many risks for them and lost a lot of sleep. I felt that I committed no breach of faith in using my profession as a cloak for other activities. I had never neglected a patient for them, and I had used hours when I needed rest to help solve some piece of wickedness or other. I knew I had been useful. Pretty nearly every crime from robbery up to murder leads to a call for a doctor, and often enough for a nurse, too. As for professional ethics, I have never known of criminals who had any, even among themselves. It has been my experience that there is no honor among thieves.

But what had I got out of it myself, except the doubtful reward of being called Miss Pinkerton when the Inspector was in a good humor? There were a good many days, and nights, too, when I sighed for the old peaceful days. Taking special duty at the hospital, and at seven or seven thirty the night nurse coming in and smiling at the patient.

"How's Miss Adams been treating you today? Holding out on food as usual?"

Wandering out into the hall with her, exchanging notes on the case and a bit of hospital gossip, and then going home. The night air cool and fresh after the hospital odors, Dick hopping about in his cage, and nothing to do until the next day.

"Sugar, Dick?"

Getting the sugar, while he watched me with eyes like small jet beads; watering the fern; Mrs. Merwin coming in at nine o'clock with a glass of hot milk and a cookie.

"It will make you sleep, dearie."

And then I had made that alliance with Inspector Patton and the Homicide Squad. By accident, but they had found me useful from the start. There is one thing about a trained nurse in a household: she can move about day and night and not be questioned. The fact is that the people in a house are inclined pretty much to forget that she is there. She has only one job, ostensibly, and that is her patient. Outside of that job she is more or less a machine to them. They see that she is fed, and, if she is firm, that she gets her hours off-duty. But they never think of her as a reasoning human being, seeing a great deal more than they imagine, and sometimes using what she sees, as I did.

With the patients, of course, it is different. They are apt to consider her as something halfway between a necessary nuisance and a confessor. Most of the time the nuisance, but take a sleepless night, with everything quiet, and about three in the morning they begin to talk. I have listened to some hair-raising confessions in my time. Sometimes these confessions had to go to Headquarters, but most of the time they did not. The police were not interested in evasions of the moral law. They were only bored with unfaithful husbands and wives, and evasions of income taxes, and what not. And to the Homicide Bureau, of course, there was only one crime. That was murder.

My exact relation to the Bureau has never been defined. One day a police captain referred to me as a "stool," by which he meant stool pigeon. I have seldom seen the Inspector so angry.

"Stool!" he said. "What the devil do you mean by that, Burke? Miss Adams is a part of this organization, and a damned important part. We've got a lot of wall-eyed pikes around here calling themselves detectives who could take lessons from her and maybe learn something."

Sometimes, as I say, he called me Miss Pinkerton, but that was a joke between us. I have never claimed to be a detective. What I had was eyes to use and the chance to use them where the police could not.

But I did not want to use them that Monday night. I wanted to shut them for eleven hours or so, and then go out the next day and do some shopping. I am ashamed to think of the bang with which I closed my bag, or of the resentment with which I lugged it down to the front door. No use letting the taxi driver ring the bell and waken everybody.

I felt better in the night air, and in the taxi I tried to put my mind on whatever work lay ahead. I had gathered from the Inspector's voice that something grave had happened, and I reviewed what I knew of the family. There were only two of them, old Miss Juliet herself and her nephew, a good-looking weak-chinned boy. He was her sister's child, and that sister had married, late in life, a man who was no good whatever. There was a story that he had squandered her money and then Miss Juliet's, but I am not sure of that. Anyhow, they had both died long ago, and the old lady was certainly impoverished and had the boy into the bargain.

I hear a good bit as I go around. In a city the size of ours, big as it is, there are always one or two dominating families, and for many years the Mitchells had been among them. So I had heard about the old lady and this boy, and I knew that she had had her own troubles with him. For years she had kept him away, at school and college, but he did no good at either, and he had been at home for some months now, sometimes working at whatever offered, but mostly loafing. His name was Wynne, Herbert Wynne, and he must have been twenty-four or thereabouts.

It was known that they got along badly, and what I anticipated that night, as the taxi turned into the neglected grounds behind their high iron fence, was that some trouble had developed between the two of them. To tell the truth, I had an idea that the boy had turned on Miss Juliet in some frenzy of anger, and possibly injured her. And I was not surprised, as the taxicab turned into the Mitchell place between old iron gates, which had never been closed within my recollection, to find that the house, usually dark, was lighted from roof to cellar.

What I had not anticipated was that, within a few feet of the entrance, the car should come to a grinding stop, and that the driver's voice should be lifted in wrath and alarm.

"Get out of there! Do you want to be killed?"

I looked out of the window, and I could see a girl in the roadway, just ahead of us.

"Please, just a minute!" she said, in a breathless sort of voice. "I must speak to whoever is in the car."

"What is it?" I called.

She came straight toward me, and by the light of a street lamp I could see her clearly, a pretty little thing, about twenty perhaps, in a light coat and a beret, and with a face so pale and shocked that it fairly made me gasp.

"What's wrong in there?" she demanded, still breathlessly. "Is somebody hurt?"

"I don't know. I imagine somebody is ill. I'm a nurse."

"Ill? Then why is there a police car at the door?"

"Is there one? I really don't know. Why don't you ask? It looks as though there are people in the hall."

She stepped back a foot or two and stood staring at the house. "They wouldn't want a nurse if anyone was—if anyone was dead," she said, apparently thinking out loud. "It might be a robbery, don't you think? If they heard someone in the house, you know."

"It's possible. Come up with me, and we'll find out."

But she drew back. "Thanks, but I'll run along. They didn't say what it was, when they sent for you?"

"Not a word."

She seemed reluctant to let me go. She stood beside the window of the taxi, holding onto it and staring at the house. Then it seemed to occur to her that what she was doing required some explanation, and she turned to me again.

"I was just passing, and when I saw all the lights and that car—I suppose it's really nothing. I just—would it be all right for me to telephone you a little later? If it would bother you, or you'd be asleep. . . ."

I looked at the house, and the police car standing in front of it, and I imagine my voice was rather grim when I answered her.

"From the look of things I'll not be getting much sleep," I said. "But you'd better give me your name, so I can leave word to be called."

It seemed to me that she hesitated. "That doesn't matter, does it? I'll call you, and you'll know who it is."

With that she left me, and I saw her going out the gate. I had seen a small coupé standing some distance off, before we turned in, and I felt certain that it belonged to her. But I forgot her almost immediately, as the taxi got under way again with a jerk that almost broke my neck.

Before me lay the old house, blazing with lights. Always I had been curious about it; now I was to know it well. To know the way it creaked and groaned at night; to see revealed in broad daylight its shabby gentility, its worn remainders of past splendors, and to hear my own voice at night echoing through its rooms while I shouted at the deaf old woman in her bed, "Can I get you anything, Miss Juliet?" Or, "Are you more comfortable now?"

For Miss Juliet was safe enough, lying there in her wide old walnut bed with her reading glasses and her worn Bible on the table beside her. Safe enough; that night at least.

I can write all this comfortably now, filling in the hours while I wait for one of those cases in which I start with one patient and end with two. Every time I take such a case, I contemplate a certain suggestion made by the Inspector at the end of the Mitchell tragedy, and I turn it over in my mind.

But in the interval I am writing the story of that tragedy, the stork—a bird which I detest anyhow—is a trifle late as usual, and so I have plenty of time. For a good many months, however, I could not even think about the Mitchell case, or the Mitchell house, or old Miss Juliet Mitchell lying there in her bed.

## CHAPTER I I

THERE WERE three or four men in the hall when the taxi stopped, and one of them, a Doctor Stewart, whom I knew by sight, came out onto the porch to meet me.

"It's Miss Adams, isn't it?"

"Yes, doctor."

"Your patient is upstairs, in the large front room. The cook is with her, and I'll be up at once. I've given her a hypodermic, and she ought to get quiet soon."

"She has had a shock, then?"

He lowered his voice. "Her nephew committed suicide tonight."

"Here?"

"In this house. On the third floor."

He was a little man, known among the nurses and hospitals for his polite bedside manner and his outside-the-door irritability, a combination not so rare in the profession as unpleasant. And I think he had hoped to impress me with his news. I merely nodded, however, and that annoyed him.

"I'll go on up," I said quietly.

The Inspector was in the hall, but he only glanced at me and looked away, after his usual custom when I take a case for him. The Medical Examiner for the department similarly ignored me. It was an officer in uniform who took my bag and led me up the stairs.

"Bad business, miss," he said. "The old lady went up to see if he had come in, and she found him."

I found myself thinking hard as I followed him. If it was suicide, then what was Inspector Patton of the Homicide Squad doing there? And why had I been called? Any nurse would have answered. Why get me?

"How did he do it?" I asked.

"Shot himself in the forehead," he replied, with a certain unction. "Knelt in front of the mirror to do it. Very sad case."

"Very sad, indeed," I said, thinking of that girl in the drive, and the look of terror in her face. She must have suspected something of the sort, I thought. And later she would call up, and I would have to tell her.

I felt somewhat shaken as I went into the room adjoining the large front bedroom to take off my coat. As I did so, I could hear voices from the other room. One was the low monotonous voice of the very deaf, the other shrill and hysterical.

"Now don't you talk, Miss Juliet. He's all right now. Past all his troubles, and safe in his Maker's arms."

Then something again that I could not hear, and the shrill voice again.

"I've told you over and over. It was an accident. He hadn't the nerve, and you know it. He'd been cleaning his gun. I saw him at it when I went in to turn down his bed, at eight o'clock."

It was evident that they did not know of my arrival, and when I was ready, I did not go at once into the bedroom. Instead, I slipped out quietly and made my way to the third floor. That, too, was lighted, and through an open doorway I saw a policeman sitting on a chair reading a newspaper, and a body lying on the floor. It looked callous to me, but of course there was nothing for him to do, until that conclave ended downstairs in the hall. The room was still filled with acrid smoke, as though flashlight pictures had only recently been taken, and the one window in the room was open, apparently to clear the air.

It was a small room, plainly furnished, a back room, looking toward the service wing at the rear. Later on I was to know that room well: the small white iron bedstead, the old-fashioned bureau, the closet beside the fireplace. But at that moment my eyes were riveted on the body lying on the floor.

It was Herbert Wynne, beyond a doubt. He lay in a curiously crumpled position on his side, with his knees bent and one arm outstretched. There was no weapon whatever in sight.

The officer looked up, and rather shamefacedly laid his paper on the bed. "Better not come in, miss," he said. "Inspector's orders. I'm sorry."

"I haven't any idea of coming in. Have you seen the cook? I shall need some hot water."

"I haven't seen her, miss."

But I lingered in the doorway, staring at that body. "I suppose there's no question about its being suicide?"

"Suicide or accident, I'd say, miss."

None of the men, outside of the Bureau itself, knew me or my connection with it. So I assumed an air of ignorance.

"It's terrible, isn't it? I didn't know they took pictures after suicide? Or even after an accident."

"There'll be an inquest," he said, as though that answered the question, and picked up his paper again. That closed the discussion, but my interest was thoroughly aroused. I knew as well as though I had seen them that the Homicide Squad had been there, working with their rubber gloves, their steel tape measures, their magnifying glasses, their fingerprinting outfits. Accident or suicide, and the Homicide Squad on the job!

It was still not much after half past one when I started down the stairs again. Just in time, for Doctor Stewart was fussily on his way up from the lower floor. I could see his bald head and, in the brilliant light, that it was beaded with perspiration. Indeed, he stopped on the landing to mop it, and that gave me time to get safely into Miss Juliet's room. She was lying in her wide old walnut bed, raised high on pillows, and a pallid neurotic-looking little woman of fifty or thereabouts was sitting beside her and holding one of her hands. She got up when she saw me, and stepped back.

"She's getting quieter, miss," she said. "You'll have to speak loud. She's deaf."

It took me only a second, however, to realize why Miss Juliet was quieter. She had lapsed into a coma, and she was almost pulseless.

"Doctor!" I called. "Doctor!"

He hurried then, and for the next few minutes we were two pretty busy people. He ordered a hypodermic of nitroglycerin, and stood for some time holding her pulse and watching it. Not until it perceptibly improved did he speak at all.

"That's curious," he said at last. "She's shown shock, of course. Been restless, and the usual flushed face and rapid pulse. There's a bad heart condition, an arteriosclerosis of the coronary arteries. But she was quieter when I went downstairs. You don't know of anything that could have excited her?"

"I've just come in, doctor."

"How about you, Mary?"

"I don't know. I was just talking to her."

"You didn't say anything to excite her?"

She shook her head. Miss Juliet had been growing calmer as she talked to her; then suddenly she had given a little cry and sat up in bed. She had even tried to get out, and asked for her slippers. Then she apparently changed her mind and lay back again.

"Did she say why she wanted her slippers?"

"I think she wanted to go upstairs again. To see *him*."

"She didn't explain that?"

"No."

Doctor Stewart considered that, his hand still on the old lady's wrist. "You didn't intimate to her that he had killed himself?"

"Killed himself! Why should I? He was yellow, through and through. He never killed himself. It was an accident."

All this time she was looking at me with unfriendly eyes. I am used to that, the resentment of all servants, and especially of old servants, to a trained nurse in the house. But it seemed to me that she was not so much jealous of me that night as afraid of me, and that she was even more shrill than usual in her insistence of an accident.

"Why shouldn't she get weak and faint?" she demanded. "She's had a plenty. And not only tonight," she added darkly.

It was some time before the old lady rallied, and still later before the doctor felt that he could safely go. He left me some amyl-nitrite ampoules and nitroglycerin for emergency, and I thought he looked worried as I followed him into the hall.

"Curious," he said, "her collapsing like that. She'd had a shock, of course, but she was all over it; and she wasn't fond of the boy. She had no reason to be. I'm still wondering if Mary didn't say something that sent her off. You see, we've maintained to her that it was an accident. If she learned that it was suicide, or might be, that would account for it."

"I heard Mary telling her it was an accident."

"In that case. . . ." He left the sentence unfinished, for one of the men who had been in the lower hall had started up the stairs. He moved slowly and weightily, and I recognized him as he approached us; a well-known attorney in town, named Glenn. He stopped on the landing.

"How is she?"

"Not so well. Better than a few minutes ago, but that's about all."

"Do you think I'd better stay?"

"If anybody stays, I'm the logical one," said the doctor. "But the nurse is here."

Mr. Glenn looked at me for the first time. As I said, I knew him by sight; one of those big-bodied men who naturally gravitate to the law and become a repository for the family secrets of the best people. He looked at me and nodded amiably.

"So I see. Well, I might as well go home; I suppose there is nothing I can do up there." He indicated the third floor.

"They won't let you in, Mr. Glenn," I said. But he was not listening.

"See here, Stewart," he said, "have you any idea why he would do such a thing? Has he been speculating?"

"What did he have to speculate with?" the doctor demanded, rather sourly.

"I suppose that's true enough. How about a girl?"

"Don't ask me. That's your sort of business, not mine!"

Mr. Glenn smiled a little, and put his hand on the doctor's shoulder. "Come, come, Dave," he said, "you're letting this get under your skin. It's bad business, but it's not yours."

They went down the stairs together, companionably enough, and soon afterward the Inspector came up to tell me to close the door from Miss Juliet's room into the hall. The door beside her bed opened close to the foot of the third-floor staircase, and they were about to bring the body down. Mary was still in the room, and I had no chance for a word with him.

Soon after that I heard the shuffling of the men in the hall, and Mary gave a gasp and went very pale. With a sort of morbid curiosity, however, she went out into the hall, after they had passed, and a few moments later she burst back into the room.

"Hugo!" she said. "They've taken him along, miss!"

"Who is Hugo?"

"My husband. What do the police want with him? He doesn't know anything. He was asleep in the bed beside me when Miss Juliet banged on that door out there."

I tried to quiet her. Miss Juliet was apparently asleep, and I was ready myself to get some rest. But she went on and on. Why did the police want Hugo? Mr. Herbert had killed himself. There he was, lying on the floor with his own gun beside him, in front of the bureau. Maybe he meant to, maybe he didn't. Hugo knew nothing. He had almost dropped when he saw the body.

I gathered, here and there through this hysterical outburst, that Hugo and Mary were the only servants in the house, and that they had been there for many years. In the old days Hugo had been the butler and Mary the cook. There had been other servants, but one by one they had drifted away. Now Hugo was everything from houseman to butler, and Mary "was worked until at night she was like to drop off her feet."

I finally got her to bed. It developed that she and Hugo occupied two rooms, a sitting room and bedroom, beyond the second-floor landing; rooms originally used by the family, so that a door on the landing connected with them. But as that door was kept locked as well as bolted, I had to take her downstairs and wait in the kitchen until she had had time to climb the rear staircase.

And it was while I was standing there that I thought I heard, somewhere outside, a soft movement in the shrubbery just beyond the kitchen door.

I put it down to nerves or maybe to a dog, but I did not like it. Standing there in the dark, it seemed to me that something was moving along the kitchen wall outside, and brushing against it.

## CHAPTER III

LIKE ALL WOMEN, I feel safer with a light. Again and again, Mr. Patton has warned me against that obsession.

"Think it over," he said dryly one day. "What is the idea anyhow? It's what is left of your little-girl fear of ghosts, and you know it. But in this business you're not dealing with ghosts; you're dealing with people, and often enough people with guns. Keep dark. Don't move. Don't speak."

But no advice in the world would have kept me from feeling about for the light in that kitchen, and turning it on. It was the light which gave me courage, so that I threw open the kitchen door. And sure enough there was something there. A huge black cat stalked in with dignity, and proceeded to curl up under the stove.

I closed and bolted the door again, but I was still uncertain. I could almost have located that sound I had heard, and it was high up on the frame wall, about shoulder height, I thought. Or maybe that is what some people call hindsight. I know now that it was not the cat, and so I think that I noticed it then.

However that may be, I put out the light and went upstairs, as the Inspector put it later on, as though I had been fired out of a gun! I imagine that was at half past two or thereabouts. I know that it seemed incredible, when I had taken off my uniform and put on my dressing gown, to find that it was only three o'clock. It seemed to me that I had been in that old house for hours.

Miss Juliet was sleeping quietly by that time, and her pulse and general condition were much better. In spite of my recent fright, I went methodically enough about my preparations for what was left of the night. But I was still puzzled. As I made my bed on the couch at the foot of Miss Juliet's big bed, as I laid out my hypodermic tray in the front room adjoining, which had been assigned to me, I was still wondering. Both Doctor Stewart and Mr. Glenn had taken it for granted that Herbert Wynne had killed himself by accident or design. Then what did they make of the Homicide Squad? Or did they know about it? I had seen the Inspector slip in a half-dozen men from the Bureau, under the very noses of the family, and nobody suspect it at all.

And had that been the cat, outside in the shrubbery?

The house was eerie that night. There was no wind, but it creaked and groaned all about me; and after I had raised the windows, the furniture began to rap. I knew well enough what it was, that the change of temperature was doing it. But it was as though some unseen hand were beating a fine tattoo, on the old walnut bureau, on the old brass fire irons, even on the footboard of the bed at my head.

I must have dozed, in spite of all that, for it was only slowly that I became aware of a still louder rapping, and roused to discover that someone was throwing gravel from the drive against a window sash.

I recognized the signal, and went downstairs at once, to find the Inspector on the front porch. There was still no sign of dawn, but I could see him faintly by the distant light of a street lamp.

"How is she? Asleep?"

"Sound. The doctor gave her a sedative."

He sat down on a step, pulled out his pipe and lighted it.

"Well, here's the layout," he said, "and I'm damned if I know what to make of it. So far as I can learn, young Wynne ate his dinner in good spirits, and spent the time until almost nine o'clock cleaning and oiling his automatic. The cook went in at eight o'clock to turn down his bed, and he was at it, and cheerful enough, she says. Shortly before nine o'clock, Hugo, the butler, heard him go out. He and Mary are man and wife; they occupy the rooms behind the landing on the second floor, and the sitting room is just behind the landing. There's a door connecting it, but it is kept locked and bolted, and the bolt is on the landing side. It's still locked and bolted, for that matter.

"But the point is that Hugo, reading his paper in the sitting room, heard him go down the front stairs shortly before nine o'clock, and says that he was whistling. We can't shake that story of his, and it's probably true. In other words, if we had nothing else to go on, it wouldn't look like suicide."

"But you have something else?"

"We have, Miss Pinkerton."

He did not tell me at once, however, and from the way he pulled at his pipe I gathered that something had annoyed him. Finally it came out. Between his department and the District Attorney's office was a long-standing feud, and now it turned out that the District Attorney was already butting in, as he put it; had put on his clothes and appeared himself.

"Afraid he won't get into the papers," he said disgustedly. "Ready to blab the whole story, and steal the job. He's working on Hugo now, so I got out. He leaves all the dirty work to us, but when it comes to a prominent family like this——"

He checked himself, grinning sheepishly and went on. The local precinct station had received a call at fifteen minutes after twelve, and the police lieutenant who first arrived on the scene had merely taken in the general picture, and had decided then and there that it had been suicide.

"Fellow's a fool," the Inspector said. "How do you get a suicide without contact marks? And it's the first hour that counts in these cases. The first five minutes would be better, but we don't get those breaks very often."

"And there were no powder marks on the body?"

"Not a mark. It took O'Brien ten minutes to notice that! And he calls himself a policeman."

He had noticed it finally, however, and he had telephoned to Headquarters.

Luckily the Inspector had still been in his office, and he got to the house at a quarter before one. It took him just two minutes, he said with some pride, to decide that it was neither a suicide nor an accident, to send for the Squad and to telephone for me.

"Not so easy, that last," he said. "Stewart had some pet or other he wanted to put on the case. Yes, Stewart was there. He got there before I did. But I tipped the word to the Medical Examiner, and he told Stewart he had somebody he could get at once. It worked."

"It did," I said grimly. "And what was it that you saw in two minutes?"

"This. That boy was drilled through the center of the forehead; and he didn't move a foot after the bullet hit him. That's certain. But where was he when they found him? He was in front of the bureau, on the floor. All right. O'Brien sized it up first that he'd been standing in front of the mirror, with a revolver pointed at the center of his forehead. But in that case where would the bullet go? It would go through his skull and into the wall at the head of the bed. But it did nothing of the sort. It hit the brick facing of the fireplace, at right angles to the bed, and bounced off. I found it on the floor."

I considered that. It was a ghastly sort of picture at best. "Maybe he didn't face the mirror," I suggested.

"Maybe not. But it's a cinch that he was standing up, if he did it himself. There's no chair in front of that bureau. And that bullet went through his head in a straight line, and hit the fireplace about four feet above the floor. He was pretty close to six feet tall, so you see what I mean."

"He might have knelt."

"Good for you. So he might. They hate the idea of falling, and I've known them to put a blanket on the floor, or a bunch of pillows. I grant you, too, that that would account for the way his knees were bent. But I still want to know why he shows no contact marks. A man doesn't drill himself through the head without leaving something more than just a hole. Of course it's possible that he'd rigged up a device of some sort for firing the gun at a distance, and there's the chance that the servants and the old lady did away with it. They had time enough before they called the police."

"It isn't an insurance case?" I asked. I had worked on one or two such cases for him.

"Well, he had some insurance. The family doctor, Stewart, says he examined him not long ago for a couple of small policies. But why would he do such a thing? Kill himself in order to leave his insurance to an old woman who hadn't long to live, and who didn't like him anyhow? It's not reasonable."

Well, it was not reasonable, and I knew it; although the trouble some people take to kill themselves so that it will look like something else is extraordinary. I believe there is a clause in most policies about suicide; if the holder kills himself within a year, the policy lapses. Something of that sort, anyhow.

"It couldn't have been an accident?" I asked.

"Well, apparently the boy belonged to a pistol club at college; he knew how to handle a gun. And most accidents of that sort occur when the cleaning is going on; not two or three hours later. He'd cleaned that gun before he went out, and left the oil and the rags on top of his bureau. But here's another thing. How do you get an accident with all the earmarks of suicide? Gun on the floor, bent knees as though he might have knelt in front of the mirror, and a bullet straight through his forehead? Straight, I'm telling you. Where was that gun and where was he, in that case?"

"If you're asking me," I said mildly, "I haven't any idea."

He shook out his pipe. "That's what I like about you," he said, smiling into the darkness. "I can talk, and you haven't any theories. You've got a factual mind, and no nonsense."

"What does the Medical Examiner think?"

"He's guessing accident. Stewart is guessing suicide."

"And you?"

"Just at the minute I'm guessing murder. I may change that, of course. But this boy was weak, and it takes more than a temporary spell of depression for any man to plan a suicide so that it looks like something else. Take that gun now; it's the one that killed him. It had been fired since he cleaned it, and there are no prints on it, except some smudged ones that look like his own. Either he'd rigged it so that he could pull a string and fire it from a distance; or somebody else held it with a handkerchief, or wore gloves."

"Nobody heard the shot?"

"Nobody. But that doesn't mean anything. The servants were pretty far away. And the old lady is deaf as a post. There was a shot fired, that's certain. Stewart, who got there before our man, says Wynne hadn't been dead for too long then; less than an hour. The Medical Examiner put the time as about a quarter past eleven. But they're both guessing. So am I. But I'm guessing that, if it's murder, it's an inside job."

He struck a match and looked at his watch. "Well, the D. A. will be wanting a little shut-eye about now. I'll go back and take over Hugo."

"What do you mean by an inside job?" I demanded. "That old woman, and two antiquated servants! Was there anyone else in the house?"

"Not a soul, apparently. And get this. Even if I can figure that this boy could kill himself without leaving any contact marks, I've got to explain one or two things to myself. Why did he go out whistling at nine o'clock, if he did, and then come back to kill himself at something after eleven? And why did he have a new suitcase in his closet, locked in and partially packed? He was going on a journey, but it wasn't one where he needed silk pajamas!"

Somehow that made me shudder, and he was quick to see it.

"Better go in and get to bed, young lady," he said kindly. "I'm going to need you on this case; I don't want you getting sick. I'll tell you the old lady's story in the morning."

But I refused to go until I had heard it. I did agree to go up and look at my patient, however, and to get my cape to throw about me. I found Miss Juliet quiet and her pulse much better, but, although she kept her eyes closed, I had an idea that she was not asleep.

When I went down again, the Inspector was sitting on the porch step in a curiously intent position, apparently listening to something I could not hear. He waved a hand at me for silence, and then, suddenly and without warning, he bolted around the side of the house. It was a full five minutes before he returned, and he appeared rather chagrined.

"Guess I need some sleep," he said. "I'd have sworn I heard somebody moving back there among the bushes."

It was then that I told him of my own experience earlier in the night, and he made another round of the place without discovering anything. But he did not sit down again; he stood and listened for some little time, his body and ears still evidently on the alert. There was no further sound, however.

I often think of that scene. The two of us there on the front porch, the Inspector's two excursions to the rear, and neither one of us suspecting that a part of the answer to our mystery was perhaps not more than fifty feet away from us while we talked. Or that he almost fell over it in the darkness, without even knowing that it was there.

IT WAS AFTER those interruptions that he relaxed somewhat, and began to do what I often think proves my only real value to him; to use me as an opportunity to think out loud.

"I want to go back to that room again, Miss Adams. No, don't move. I'm not going upstairs. Let's just think about it. Here's this boy, Herbert. Let's suppose something like this. He is sitting in a chair; sitting, because the bullet struck the fireplace at about that height. And he has started to undress, for we found that one shoe was unfastened. The door was closed, we'll say. He sees it opening, but as it was Miss Juliet's custom to discover whether or not he had come in, he does not get up. In a minute, however, he sees that it is not Miss Juliet, but someone else. Still he does not get up. Mind you, if I'm right, he was shot as he sat in that chair, and that chair was in the center of the room, between the hall door and the fireplace. Now, what do you make of that?"

"That he knew whoever it was, or that he had no time to get up."

I felt that he was smiling once more, there in the darkness. "Who says you are not a detective?" he asked. "Someone he knew, probably, if this theory holds at all. He may have been surprised; very likely he was. But he wasn't scared. He was young and active, and he'd have moved in a hurry if he had seen any reason to. He didn't; and get this. Unless we learn to the contrary tomorrow, whoever shot him didn't kill him right off. He had to get into the room and get that gun, for one thing. It was probably on the bureau, and this person picked it up. Then he walked toward the door, turned to go, wheeled and fired. Herbert never knew what hit him."

It was a horrible picture, any way one looked at it, and I felt a little sick. I've seen death in a good many forms, and some of them none too pleasant; but the thought of that boy in his chair, totally unaware that he was breathing his last breath, was almost too much for me. Breathing his last breath and looking up at someone he knew.

"Then it's your idea that, if there was a murder, whoever did it, did it on impulse?" I asked. "If he used Herbert's gun, that looks as though he had none of his own."

"We'll know tomorrow, but I am betting that he used Herbert's gun. As for doing it on impulse, well—maybe, and maybe not. Why was this unknown sneaking into the house at that hour? If we knew that, we could get somewhere. And how did he get in? There are three doors on the lower floor, and all of them were found bolted on the inside, as well as locked. That is, two of them were bolted. The third one, a side entrance, leads into the kitchen, and that is locked off at night. It also leads to the back stairs, but they go up into the servants' sitting room. Nowhere else."

"By a window?"

"Well, Hugo claims to have found a window open all right. But I doubt it. It looks to me as though Hugo, knowing that the house was always locked up like a jail at night, and wanting a murderer, had opened that window. He was a little too quick in discovering it and showing it off. But it happens that the ground is soft outside, and there are no footprints under that window. So I'll stake my reputation, such as it is, that no one got in or out of that window tonight; and that Hugo himself opened it, after the body was discovered."

"But why?" I said, bewildered.

"Listen, little sister. If this boy had insurance, the last thing Hugo wants is a verdict of suicide. If Hugo killed him, he's got to show it's an outside job. There are two reasons for you! I could think of others if you want them."

"Then Hugo did it?"

"Not too fast! Let's take the other side for a minute. To do that, we have to figure how somebody unknown could have got into this house tonight and left it, through three doors, all locked, two of them bolted on the inside. And why whoever killed Herbert Wynne killed him with his own gun as he sat in a chair between the fireplace and the door, and moved the body later so that it would look like a suicide."

"And it wasn't Hugo?"

"Think again. Why should he move that body?"

"I've told you I'm no detective," I said briefly. "You'd better tell me. It will save time. I suppose Hugo or somebody in the house could have moved it."

"Why? To make it look like a suicide, when everybody in this house stood to lose if the coroner's verdict at the inquest was suicide? Nonsense!"

"Then whoever killed him moved it?"

"Possibly. We only have two guesses, and that's the other one. Right now I think that is what happened; I believe that Hugo made one attempt to indicate a murder, but that he didn't touch the body. Miss Juliet apparently ordered them to stay out and leave everything as it stood. God knows what he'd have done otherwise, in his anxiety to prove it wasn't suicide. He did manage, however, to get that window in the library open."

"You've been over the ground around the house, of course?"

"Combed it with a fine-toothed comb," he said, and yawned. "Found the point of a woman's high heel just off the drive near the entrance, but too far from the house. Of course, we have to allow for that, too. He wasn't good medicine for women."

Strange as it seems now, for the first time during that talk of ours I remembered the girl in the drive, and told him about her. He was less impressed, however, than I had anticipated, although he stood in thoughtful silence for some time before he made any comment.

"We'll have to watch out," he said, "or we'll be hearing more people in the bushes! I'll admit that this girl looks important, but is she? It isn't unusual these days for a girl to be out alone at one o'clock in the morning, especially if she has a car. Although the car is only a guess, isn't it?"

"I'm convinced it was hers."

"All right. Far be it from me to dispute any hunch of yours. Now what about her? She knows Herbert; maybe she has been playing around with him; tonight she is driving along this street, and she sees a house not notorious for light blazing from roof to cellar. She leaves her car, walks into the drive and discovers a police car near the front door and a crowd of policemen inside the open door. She wouldn't need to be a detective to know that something had happened, would she?"

"It was more than that. She suspected what had happened. It was written all over her."

"And she wouldn't give her name?"

"No. She said she would telephone. But she hasn't."

"But that doesn't look as though she knew when she talked to you, does it? As for not telephoning, perhaps she didn't need to. We've had reporters here, or she may have stopped the doctor on his way out. Depend on it, she knows now or she'd be hanging on the wire."

"Why wouldn't she come to the house and ask?"

"I don't know, but I'll find out tomorrow—today, rather. She ought not to be hard to locate. She may simply have wanted to keep out of the picture, but we can't afford to leave her out. And while this Wynne youth was a pretty bad actor, he was also pretty well known. We'll pick her up, all right, and take her for a little ride."

Before he left, he told me Miss Juliet's story, and tragic enough it seemed to me. She had gone asleep at ten or thereabouts, and slept soundly until ten minutes to twelve. She wakened then, and looked at the clock beside her bed. She was certain of the time, and she sat up, prepared to go upstairs and ascertain if Herbert had come in. This was her nightly custom; to see if he was in the house, and then to go down and examine the front door, to be sure that he had closed it properly.

"Sometimes he came in a little under the weather," the Inspector explained here. He had certain curious reserves of speech with me. "From drinking, you know."

By which I gathered that now and then Herbert had returned to his home in no fit condition even for my experienced ears!

But while Miss Juliet sat there in her bed, looking at her clock, she was aware that someone was walking past her door, in the hall outside. She heard nothing, naturally, but like all very deaf people she was sensitive to vibrations, and her walnut bed was shaking as it always did under such conditions.

She called out. "Herbert! Is that you, Herbert?"

There was no answer, and, with the terror of burglars always in her mind, she was too frightened at first to get out of her bed. She managed that at last, and, feeling no more vibrations, she even opened her door an inch or two. There was nobody in sight, but on the landing above, Herbert's door was open and his light going.

She called again, more sharply, and finally put on her slippers and dress-ing gown and climbed to the third floor. All she had expected to find was that the boy had gone to sleep with his light burning, and apparently she went up with a sense of outrage at his indifference to waste.

What she saw, from the staircase, had sent her shrieking down to ham-mer on the door into the servants' rooms at the back. That door was locked, had been locked for years, and was bolted, too. To reach her, the servants had had to go down their own back staircase, through the lower hall and up to where she still stood, hysterically banging at that door.

She led the way back toward the upper room, but she did not go in. Hugo had done so, while she and Mary remained outside. She had told him not to touch anything, and she was certain that he had not done so. The body was lying as the police had found it, in front of the bureau, with the automatic beside it. Yes, the window was open, but it was three full stories above the ground.

She had fainted, or had a heart attack, at about that time, but she re-membered that Hugo had said there were no powder marks, and that it must have been an accident. She had asked him then to telephone for Arthur Glenn, her attorney, and Mary had apparently sent for Doctor Stew-art, for he arrived shortly after the police from the station house.

That was practically all, but the Inspector added that she had seemed anxious to believe that it was an accident and not suicide.

It was after four o'clock in the morning when he left, getting into his car and driving off at his usual furious speed. I had followed him out into the drive.

"And what am I to do?" I asked.

"Just as usual. Keep your eyes open, that's all. By the way, I've told them to stay out of that room. I want to look it over in the morning."

He put his foot on the starter, but I had thought of something.

"This boy, Herbert, he had a key, of course?"

"To the front door. Yes."

"Could he have brought someone in with him?"

"Not if Hugo is telling the truth, and why shouldn't he? He would give his neck to prove that Herbert Wynne had done just that. But what does Hugo say? He says that he was still in his sitting room beyond the landing at eleven or a little after, that he heard the boy going up the stairs to the third floor, and that he is certain he was alone."

Then he roared away, and I was left standing in the drive alone.

It was still dark, although there was a hint of dawn in the sky. Dark and cold. I shivered a little as I turned back and went into the house again.

Upstairs, old Miss Juliet still lay very quietly in that great walnut bed, her head high so she could breathe more easily, but I still had that odd feeling that she was only pretending to be asleep.

I stood and looked down at her. How old she was I have no idea even now; in her late seventies, I imagine. Possibly eighty. There were stories that Miss Juliet Mitchell had been a great beauty in her day, but there were no signs of that beauty now. She looked infinitely old and very weary. It seemed to me, as I looked at her, that surely age should have certain compensations for what it has lost, and that peace and comfort should be among them. But I wondered if she had not grown hard with the years. I was remembering what the Inspector had quoted as her words when she had finished her statement.

"He is dead," she had said, "and I will speak no evil of him. But if someone murdered him, it was for good cause. I knew him well enough to know that. And he never killed himself. He had not the courage."

CHAPTER V

It was well after four in the morning when I finally lay down and tried to get an hour's sleep on a couch at the foot of the old lady's bed. It was hard to do. She was apparently asleep, but it grew still cooler toward dawn, and if before, everything about that ancient house had seemed to creak, now it appeared to me as I lay there that ghostly figures were moving up and down the stairs. Once a curtain blew out into the room and touched me on the hand, and I had all I could do not to yell my head off.

I must have dozed again, but only for a short time. I was roused by an odd sort of vibration of the footboard of the big bed; my sofa was pushed against it, so it was shaking also.

What with the Inspector's story of some loose floor boarding or joist which connected with the hall outside, I knew what that meant, and I sat up with a jerk. Over the high footboard I could see Miss Juliet's bed, and it was empty!

I was still sitting there, gasping, when I heard the door to the hall open cautiously, and saw her come feebly back into the room. She was ghastly white, and she stopped and stood motionless when she saw me. She was in her nightgown and her feet were bare. I dare say the fright had made me irritable, for I jumped up and confronted her.

"You know you shouldn't have got out of bed, Miss Mitchell," I said sternly. "That's what I'm here for."

Whether she heard me or not, she understood my attitude.

"I've been walking off a cramp in my leg," she said in her flat, monotonous voice. "Do lie down, and go to sleep again. I'm quite all right."

She moved toward the bed, and, dark as the room still was, I felt certain that she held something in the hand I could not see, and that, with a surprisingly quick gesture, she slid it under a pillow. Right or wrong—and I know now that I was right—she refused any help in getting back into bed, or to allow me to straighten her bedclothing, or, indeed, to work about the bed at all.

"Let me alone, please," she said when I attempted it. "I don't like being fussed over."

She could not, however, prevent my putting a heater to her feet, and seeing that the soles were soiled; or taking her pulse and discovering that it was extremely fast, or watching her breathing, which was rapid and labored. Nor could she impose on me by pretending to be asleep until Mary came to relieve me for my breakfast. Neither one of us slept a wink from that time on, and I suppose there was a certain humor, hard to discover at the time, in my occasional cautious peerings over the foot of that bed, my hair flying in all directions and my very face swollen with lack of sleep; and Miss Juliet's equally wary watching, and the closing of her eyes the moment she saw the top of my head rising beyond that walnut footboard.

Whatever she had under her pillow, I did not get it, for Mary relieved me at eight for breakfast, a slim meal served by a morose Hugo in a shabby coat, with purple pouches of sheer exhaustion under his eyes. If there had been suppressed indignation for that night of interrogation in Mary's manner as she relieved me, there was a curious look of humiliation in his. He looked old, tired and rather pathetically shamed.

"I'm afraid you had a hard night, Hugo."

"I suppose it was to be expected, miss."

He did not care to talk, I saw, and so I let him alone. But as I ate my toast and drank my weak tea, I had a chance to see more fully the impoverished gentility of that house. No wonder, if the Wynne boy had actually killed himself, Hugo had tried to make it look like a murder. The threadbare carpets, the thin and carefully darned table linen, the scanty food served with such ceremony, all pointed to a desperate struggle to keep up appearances.

And to save my life I could not see Herbert Wynne in that house. He had come and gone, apparently leaving no more impression on it than if he had never been.

Mary was still in Miss Juliet's room when I went up again. The door was closed, so I had a moment or two in which to get my bearings by daylight. I could see that the house was only three stories in the front, and that the back wing, including the kitchen, the pantry and, as I discovered later, the laundry, was only two.

This back wing, a later addition, was of frame, while the main body of the house was brick. It was above the kitchen and so on that the servants had their rooms, carefully locked off and bolted from the landing on the front stairs. And it was evident that only the main staircase led to the third floor. The rear one, as Inspector Patton had said, led only to the two rooms and bath used by Mary and Hugo.

The house itself was a double house; that is, there was a long center hall leading back to the pantry and service quarters. On one side of the hall was a library with a dining room behind it. On the other was what was known as the long parlor. The doors into it were closed, but I knew that it was there. It had been rather a famous room locally in the old days, with its two crystal chandeliers and its two fireplaces, each with a marble mantel and a mirror over it.

On the second floor, not counting the locked-off rooms where Mary and Hugo lived, were three bedrooms. One of them, a small room behind Miss Juliet's, was largely dismantled, however, and Miss Juliet's was what used to be called the main chamber. It lay over the library and the lower hall along the front of the house, and opened onto the upper hall. My own room was next to it, also along the front of the house, but smaller, with a window at the rear as well as at the front and side.

The third floor, as I discovered later, was not greatly unlike the second, save that the ceilings were lower.

That morning, however, I had only time to glance at the lower floor, and on my way upstairs to stop and examine the door leading back into the servants' wing. I remembered something the Inspector had told me: that the outside door at the foot of the back stairs, the stairs which led to this wing, was the only one which lacked a bolt. In that case, the only exit which could have been made, outside of the windows, would have been by that door with its spring lock. But as that side entrance led only into a small entry, with a door to the kitchen which the servants locked each night, carrying the key upstairs with them by Miss Juliet's orders, and to the staircase by which they reached their rooms, it appeared to me that this door on the landing might have some strategic value.

But that door offered nothing. It was both locked and bolted, and the bolt was shoved home in plain sight, as the Inspector had said. Clearly no one could have left the house by that door, and bolted it behind him.

As a matter of fact, my inspection of that door very nearly got me into trouble that morning. I had just time to stoop and pretend to be tying my shoe when Mary opened Miss Juliet's door. But I thought she looked at least as frightened as I felt when she saw me, and as she scurried past me, I was convinced of something else. She was holding something under her apron.

I watched her down the stairs, and at the foot she stopped and looked back at me. Like Miss Juliet and myself the night before, we must have presented a curious little tableau for that second; but in my position suspicion is fatal, and so I turned and started back to Miss Juliet. It was then that the doorbell rang, and, listening carefully, it seemed to me that Mary, just inside the front parlor, did not answer it at once; that there was a quick movement of some sort, perhaps by the library door. But I could not be certain, and almost immediately I heard the front door opened.

It was Mr. Glenn, stopping on his way to his office to inquire about the old lady. I went down myself to tell him of her condition, and thus interrupted Mary in a flood of indignation over Hugo's experience at Headquarters. He looked annoyed himself.

"Of course it's an outrage," he said. "I'll see that it isn't repeated, Mary. And I'll talk to Hugo. You'd better get him."

Having thus got rid of her for the moment, he turned to me. But he was still irritable. "Trust the police to make a mess of it," he said. "Hugo's been with Miss Mitchell for thirty years. That ought to prove something. And what are the police after, anyhow? Either Herbert Wynne killed himself or he met with an accident. There's nothing for the police in either case. How is Miss Mitchell this morning? Did she sleep?"

"She rested. I don't think she slept much."

He stood there looking about the shabby hall, so old and worn in the morning sunlight, and apparently he felt its contrast with his own prosperous appearance, his neatly shaved face, his good, well-cut clothes, the car in the drive outside. He frowned a little.

"She has had a hard life," he said. "Not that this unfortunate event deprives her of much that she valued, but still . . . Has she talked at all?"

"Not to me."

"We'd like her to think of it as an accident. I suppose you know that?"

"The doctor said so. Yes."

He lowered his voice. "They hadn't been the best of friends, Herbert and Miss Mitchell. If she thought now that he had done away with himself, I doubt if she would survive it. All we can hope is that the coroner will see the light on this case."

Hugo arrived then, and I went back to my patient. I thought she seemed flushed, but she had no fever. When I bathed her—under protest at that, for she wanted Mary to do it—I noticed that the soles of her delicate old feet were now soft and unsoiled, and that puzzled me. Certainly she had been out of the room that early morning and soiled her feet on those carpets, which were not clean. They looked as if the dust of ages were in them.

That mystery was solved, however, when I found a damp washcloth in the bathroom. Either alone or with Mary's help the old lady had removed the traces of that nocturnal journey of hers! Then it had been a journey. There had been no cramp in the leg. She had lied, and I rather thought she was not given to lying.

I said nothing, of course. I changed her bed and her gown, and then stood back.

"Are you comfortable now?"

"Quite comfortable, my dear."

I dare say all nurses grow fond of their patients, if they are given a chance. I do not know just why, unless it is that they appeal to the maternal in us. Or perhaps it is even more than that. For a brief time, a week or a month, we become a bit of God, since it is His peace which we try to bring. But that morning I began to resent my place in that house, with its spying and watching. I wanted to help that poor old woman. And she would not allow me to help her. She never did.

Hugo and Mr. Glenn were still closeted in the library when I had finished, but Mr. Glenn left soon afterward. I could hear them in the hall below, and I thought Hugo's voice sounded more cheerful.

"Goodbye, Hugo."

"Goodbye, sir. I'll do what you say."

As he went out to his car, I saw from the window a man with a camera snapping him. It annoyed him and I could hear him angrily berating the photographer, but the man had got what he wanted. He merely smiled and turned away. As a matter of fact, the place was full of reporters and cameramen of all sorts, and it was a good thing that Miss Juliet could not hear the doorbell, for it rang all morning.

Hugo tried driving them away, but of course we were helpless, and all the noon editions of the papers showed photographs of the house. "FAMOUS OLD MITCHELL MANSION SCENE OF TRAGEDY." Also, a few morbid-minded people had stood by the gate for a part of the morning, but with the news that the body had been taken away, their interest faded, and by noon the place was practically cleared.

Only two things of any importance happened that morning. After the lawyer's departure, Hugo climbed to that room of Herbert's on the third floor, remained there about two minutes and then came down again. Listening, I did not think that he entered the room at all, but stood in the doorway, surveying it.

And after the doctor's visit that morning I prepared for an indefinite stay.

"She's a sick woman, Miss Adams," he said. "She's been a sick woman for years, and she needs care. She couldn't afford it before, but now I imagine she'll be more comfortable. That is, unless some idiotic coroner's jury decides that that poor weakling killed himself."

"There was considerable insurance, then?"

He looked at me thoughtfully. "I don't know how much, but probably enough so that the insurance companies will try to prove a suicide," he said. "It's absurd on the face of it. Why should he insure himself and then kill himself to save from poverty an old woman who hasn't long to live at the best, and for whom he showed no affection whatever?"

"It's made out to her?"

"The only policies I know about were made out to his estate. It's the same thing. He has no other relatives."

"You don't know how much it amounts to?"

"No. But I telephoned Mr. Glenn, Miss Juliet's attorney, early this morning. He's trying to check up on it now. It's a puzzle to me where he got the money to pay for it. Or why he did it at all."

"I suppose it isn't possible that he was trying to repay Miss Mitchell what his father had lost for her?" I asked.

But he fairly snorted at that. "You didn't know him, did you?" was his reply.

Naturally, the police had been around most of the morning. They had ordered the newspapermen to stick to the drive and were combing the grounds carefully. While I was bathing Miss Juliet, the Inspector had entered the house and made a final examination of Herbert's room, and I gathered that he gave Mary permission to put it in order, for later on I heard her sweeping overhead. But I had no chance to talk to him. Once or twice I saw him from a window; accompanied by a plain clothes man, he was moving slowly about the shrubbery, and at one point, near the side door, he spent some time. A little later I saw him standing off and gazing up at Herbert's window, and watched his eyes travel from it to the roof of the rear wing.

But whatever he found, if anything, I had no way of discovering. As I have said, it is one of his rules that he ignores me as much as possible on his cases, and that I use my off-duty either to see or to telephone him. As I usually take eighteen-hour duty when he uses me, I have six hours in which to do either.

I made one or two attempts to get into the library that morning, but they were entirely futile. No sooner had I got there, or even part of the way down the stairs, than some idiotic reporter would ring the doorbell again, and I would hear Hugo on his way to the door. Indeed, I would probably have abandoned the idea altogether if I had not made a rather curious discovery shortly after luncheon.

Mary had relieved me as before, and when I went upstairs again, I smelled something burning. I said nothing about it, but it did not take me long to notice that there were pieces of freshly charred paper in the fireplace, or that there was a pad of paper and a pencil on the old lady's bedside table, beside her glasses.

That renewed my suspicion, naturally. It looked as though Mary, having something to say that she dared not shout, had resorted to writing. And that what she had had to say had been so important that Miss Juliet had ordered her to burn it.

CHAPTER   VI

I HAD PLENTY to think about after that discovery and I set about to prepare for an indefinite stay: unpacking my suitcase in my own room.

What did they know, these people in the house, about what had happened to Herbert Wynne the night before? "I'm guessing murder," the Inspector had said. Murder by whom? By Miss Juliet? Absurd. By Mary? I considered that. She was one of those small tight-lipped neurotics who sometimes turn to religion and now and then to crime. By Hugo? He worshiped the old lady, and of course there was the insurance.

Yet as I had watched him, old and stooped and shabby, I somehow felt that he was not a killer. Certainly he had that combination which the Inspector regards as the basis of practically all crime, motive and opportunity. But what of that? I have had them myself!

Miss Juliet's condition was only fair that afternoon. She was restless and uneasy, and I felt that she was still watching me. She even showed a certain relief when I said that, while I would not take my regular hours off, I would like to go home and get some street clothes; I had arrived in a uniform. Said, however, is merely a euphemism for the shouts with which I attempted to communicate with her.

"That's all right," she said, when I had finally made her understand. "Don't hurry."

I did not go to Headquarters that day. I telephoned from my apartment instead, and found the Inspector in his office. I thought his voice sounded unusually grave, and he listened intently while I told him of Miss Juliet's excursion, and the discovery of the written messages between the old lady and Mary.

"You think she went up to the third floor?"

"I know she had been somewhere in the house. She hadn't worn her slippers, and when I put a heater to her feet, the soles looked as though she had been about quite a little."

"Then it's your idea that she got something, perhaps from the third-floor room, and passed it on to Mary to hide?"

"It looks like that, Inspector."

"You don't think she went outside the house?"

Well, I hadn't thought of that, although of course it was possible. He explained what he meant. The ground all around the house was hard except under the library windows. There it had been recently spaded under, and as I knew, there were no footprints there. But outside the laundry they had found that morning in a patch of dusty ground what looked like the print of a woman's foot. A small foot, without a shoe.

"Looked as though somebody had been there in her stocking feet," he said. "May not mean anything, of course. What does Mary wear?"

"A flat felt slipper. And her feet are small."

"Well, that's probably what it is. Could you get into the library?"

"No. And what would be the use? Whatever it was, it's probably gone now."

"You have no idea of what it might have been?"

"Something flat, and not heavy, I thought."

"Like a letter?"

"I thought of that. But you had searched the place. If he left a letter, he'd have left it where it could be seen."

He was silent for a perceptible time. "It's the devil of a case," he said at last. "You'd better give the library the once over if you get a chance. And by the way, Glenn—that's the family lawyer; you saw him last night —Glenn has been working on the insurance. There's a lot of it."

"How much?"

"He's not certain," he said, "but he thinks it may amount to a hundred thousand dollars."

I was fairly stunned. Here was a boy who had had no money of his own, and who had earned only a little now and then; he had tried to sell bonds, I knew, and automobiles. But the chances were that he had earned little or nothing since the depression set in, and now here he was shown taking out a hundred thousand dollars of insurance for the benefit of a woman he had disliked, and who had not cared for him.

"But how in the world . . ."

"I don't know. Ask me something easy. Apparently he would deposit sufficient cash in a bank to cover the premium, and then check it out. Most of the policies were small."

He had not a great deal more to say, and I gathered that he was disturbed and not too easy in his mind. The firearms expert of the Bureau had said that the bullet came from Herbert's own revolver, and the fingerprint men that the prints were his, although not clearly readable. There had been no other prints found, in or about the room.

Before I rang off, I asked about the girl of the night before, and while he was confident that they would find her, he had to admit that they were still at sea.

"We'll get her, all right," he said. "But I'm not sure that she's important. By the way, have you got your gun among your things there?"

"No."

"That's right. No telling who may go through your stuff, and I don't want you fired from the case. I have a hunch I'm going to need you." That was his way, to throw out remarks of that sort and not to explain them. I had to put up with it, but I must say my little apartment looked homelike and cheerful to me after that conversation. Dick was singing, and there was my sewing basket, as I had left it, and the thousand and one little things with which I have built such an atmosphere of home as is possible under the circumstances. I sat down for a few minutes, and I don't mind saying that I called myself an idiot for getting involved in other people's troubles. After all, nursing alone is pretty hard work, and when I had added to it the inside job of assisting an Inspector of Police, I had taken on more than I bargained for.

I could see myself in the mirror, and I realized that I looked tired, and older than my age. But that very mirror sent my mind back to the Mitchell case, and with that I was on my feet again, and gathering up what I needed. The game was in my blood, after all.

Before I left, I looked at Dick. He looked little and woebegone, but he chirped as I moved to the closet.

"Want a piece of sugar, Dick?"

He stared back at me, with his head cocked and his eyes glittering like small jet beads.

Well, that was on Tuesday. Herbert Wynne had been found dead late on Monday night, and the inquest was to be the next day, Wednesday. That evening Doctor Stewart, Mr. Glenn and the Inspector held a three-cornered conference in the library, but I had no chance to speak to the Inspector, and nothing new to tell him. At nine o'clock it was over, and the doctor came upstairs and saw Miss Juliet. He left a bromide for me to give her, and by half after ten o'clock she was settled for the night.

That was the first opportunity I had had to search the library, and I took it.

Hugo had looked dead to the world all evening, and by ten o'clock he and Mary had locked up the house and gone to bed. At least, listening at the door on the landing as I went downstairs at eleven o'clock, I could hear nothing.

I had taken my pocket flash along, so that I turned on no lights, and I went at once to the library. It was a dark and dismal room at any time, and I remember that, as I searched, there were innumerable creaks and raps all around me. I would find myself looking over my shoulder, only to face a wall of blackness that seemed to be full of potential horrors.

And, not unexpectedly, the search produced nothing. It was not my first experience of the sort for the police, and I flatter myself that I did it pretty well, considering that I had not the faintest idea what I was looking for. I ran my hand down behind the cushions of chairs, felt under the edge of the rug, and even behind the rows on rows of dusty books. But I found nothing at all, save behind the books near the door a scrap of dirty newspaper, which I left—luckily, as it happened—where I had found it.

Just why, after completing this search, I should have decided to investigate the long parlor across the hall I do not know to this minute. I did not believe that Mary had gone in there, for the high old double doors were always kept closed. But I was less nervous by that time, and I own to a certain curiosity as to the room itself. Perhaps it rather pleased me to enter uninvited into a parlor which had been, in its day, so rigidly guarded and so exclusive!

I opened the doors carefully and let my light travel over the room. No trace of its former grandeur remained, however. If the library had been dingy, this once-famous long parlor of the Mitchell house was depressing. It was done in the worst of the later Victorian manner, with figured wallpaper and a perfect welter of old plush chairs and sofas, and there were a number of windows with heavy curtains and an additional one at the rear, looking out over the service wing and the entrance to it.

It was not until my light had traveled to that window that I started. It had never occurred to me that the room might be tenanted. But tenanted it was, and by Hugo. He was sitting, only partially dressed, in a large easy chair just inside the window, and he was sound asleep.

Mysterious as this was, I had no intention of arousing him, so I slipped back into the hall again and closed the doors. I must have turned my light off at that time, for I recall standing in the hall in the dark and listening, afraid I had awakened him. No sound came from the parlor, however, and I proceeded to grope my way up the stairs. I dare say I moved very quietly in my rubber-soled shoes, for my memory is of silence, utter and complete. Silence and black darkness. I know that I was halfway up the stairs when the hall clock began to strike midnight, and that the wheeze it gave before it commenced sent a cold shiver over me. But it was not until I reached the landing that the real shock came.

There was something there on the landing with me, something blacker than the darkness, which moved and swayed in the corner by the door. And not only moved and swayed. It seemed to be coming toward me.

I could hear a voice screaming, but I did not even realize that it was mine. And I must have backed down the stairs, although I have no recollection of that retreat; for when Hugo came running, he stumbled over me, halfway up the stairs. I still remember his ghastly pallor when, having turned on the light, he bent over me and found that I was uninjured. Then he shook me, not too gently.

"What was it? What happened?"

"There was something on the landing. Somebody. It came at me."

"There's nobody there, miss."

"There was somebody there. I'm not an idiot. Do you think I want to scare myself to death?"

I saw then that he had a revolver in his hand, an old-fashioned single-action gun.

But the careful search which followed revealed nothing whatever. The door on the landing was locked and bolted. Miss Juliet was gently snoring in her bed, and from beyond, in the servants' sitting room, Mary was hysterically demanding to know what was wrong.

We went over the entire house together that night, Hugo and I. It was certain that, if anyone had been on the landing, he could not have passed me to get down the stairs, and so we directed our main attention to the third floor.

There were two front rooms there, unoccupied and sparsely furnished; a small storeroom; and the rear one where Herbert had been killed. But we found nothing in any of them, nor any indication that anybody had entered them. Hugo persisted long after I was willing to abandon the search and to try to get some sleep. He still had his revolver in his hand, but he offered no explanation for it, or for his appearance from the parlor when I screamed.

It was full daylight before I dropped off into an uneasy sleep. My mind was abnormally active and filled with questions. Why had Hugo kept that vigil of his at the parlor window? What did he know that he would not tell, about the whole mystery? And who had been on that landing? For someone had been there. I was willing to stake my reputation on it.

It was not until the next morning at breakfast that Hugo saw fit to enlighten me as to how he had come from the parlor in answer to my scream, and with a revolver at that.

"You may have wondered at my having a gun last night, miss," he said, as he put down my cup.

"I had plenty of things to wonder about," I said dryly.

"I suppose you couldn't describe what it was you saw?"

"It looked like a ghost. I don't suppose that helps any!"

"Tall or short, miss?"

"I was a little excited," I admitted. "It was rather like a tall man, stooping. It was there, and then it wasn't, if that means anything."

There was no question that he was disturbed, and that he was trying to connect what I had seen with what turned out to have been an experience of his own the night before. Briefly, and corroborated by Mary, his story was that both of them had retired shortly after the doctor left. As I have said, the doctor had remained after the others, to pay Miss Juliet his final visit.

At half past ten or thereabouts Hugo had put out the light and gone to raise a window; but that particular window looked down over the rear end of the long parlor, and as he stood there, he thought he saw somebody in the corner below, close up against the wall.

He put on some clothes, took his revolver and went down the rear staircase. At the side door at its foot he stopped and listened, but he heard nothing, so he groped his way to the parlor and looked out the window there. The room was dark, and he could see nothing suspicious outside. But he was very tired, having had no sleep the night before, and when everything remained quiet, he sat down and finally dropped off.

That was the story, and what I had seen bore it out. But I wondered if it was all of the story, although it was possibly all that Mary knew. It seemed to me that he was vaguely on the defensive, and now and then he glanced at his wife as though for confirmation. Or perhaps to see the effect on her! Who knows, even now? I had an idea that he was not in the habit of confiding in Mary.

The Inspector called me up as I finished breakfast, and after our usual custom when this is necessary, I pretended that he was a doctor.

"Listen," he said, "I want you to do something for me."

"Yes, doctor."

"Take a bit of air this morning, and look close to the house for marks of a ladder; a pruning ladder. I'll explain later."

"I'm terribly sorry," I said, for Hugo's benefit. He was in the dining room. "But I imagine I'll be here for several days. I'd like to take the case for you, however. Don't forget me later on, will you?"

"Do it soon, and come in this afternoon," was his reply. Then he hung up.

The servants and I had agreed to keep the story of the night before from Miss Juliet. She was not so well that morning, and although I did not think she was grieving for the boy, it was as plain as the rather aquiline nose on her face that she was worrying about something. I put it down as anxiety over the inquest, which was to be held that morning. After all, poor old soul, the verdict would mean a great deal to her, and she could not bring the boy back to life. I saw her looking at the clock now and then. She spoke only once, and that was when I had rubbed her back with alcohol.

"You have good hands, my dear."

And once again I detested my job, sneaking into that house under false pretenses and fooling the poor old creature into being even mildly grateful to me. I had to harden myself deliberately, to remember that very probably she had found and hidden an important piece of evidence, before I felt equal to going on with the work. An important piece of evidence, perhaps, for which the detectives for the insurance companies would have given their eyeteeth!

That was on Wednesday. The inquest was to be held at eleven, and both Hugo and Mary left the house at ten thirty that morning. Miss Juliet was drowsing, and so I had an opportunity to make the search the Inspector had ordered without any interested supervision. I had only the faintest idea of what constituted a pruning ladder, but any ladder leaves twin impressions, and so I made my way slowly around the house, beginning at the front door, continuing around the library, the kitchen wing and back to the long parlor.

But I found no ladder marks, and it was at the side door, just behind that rear window, that I passed a clump of shrubbery and suddenly confronted the girl who had stopped me in the drive the night Herbert Wynne was killed. She was standing in the corner, backed up against the wall, and if ever I have seen a girl look scared to death, she did.

## CHAPTER VII

SHE RELAXED, however, the moment she saw me.

"Good heavens! I thought they'd come back!"

"Who had come back?"

"The servants. I waited until I saw them go out, and then I slipped in."

Well, I had had time to have a good look at her, and I saw that if she had not looked so utterly stricken, she would have been really beautiful. Now, however, she looked as though she had not slept for a week; her eyes were swollen, and now and then she gave me an odd little defiant look.

"What are you doing here, anyhow?" I asked her.

"I came to see you," she replied rather breathlessly. "After all, you're a nurse. You'll understand, and I have to talk to someone or I'll go crazy. You see, he never killed himself. I don't care what the verdict is. He never did."

"How do you know?"

"Because I knew him very well. I was—engaged to him. And he knew he was in danger."

"What sort of danger? Who from?" I said.

"I don't know. He said he was being followed. That's why he was cleaning his gun. He said somebody was trying to get him."

"But he must have said something to explain all that."

"He wouldn't tell me. There was something going on, but he wouldn't tell me what it was."

"You haven't told the police?"

She shook her head. "I don't want to be dragged into it," she said. "But he knew it might happen. And he knew something else. He told me once that if anybody got him, they'd try to get me, too."

"But that's ridiculous," I expostulated. "Why should anyone want to kill you? And why do you think that all this wasn't an accident? They do happen, you know."

She shook her head again. "He was murdered," she said, looking at me, her eyes swollen with long crying. "He was murdered, and I know who did it."

I was not so certain that she knew, however, when she had finished her story. But before I let her begin, I made an excuse of going back to Miss Juliet, and did a thing which I loathed, but which was essential. I telephoned to Headquarters and left word that the girl was at the Mitchell place, and to have somebody ready to follow her when she left.

Miss Juliet was quiet when I ran up to her. I suppose she knew that the inquest was being held that morning, but she had not mentioned it to me.

"I'm all right," she said in her flat voice. "You needn't stay in the room. Go out and get some air."

When I went back to the girl, I found her crouched on the doorstep, a small heap of young wretchedness that went to my heart and made me feel guiltier than ever. But she told her story clearly and well.

She had been in love with the dead boy, and he with her. She knew his faults. He was lazy, and not too scrupulous, I gathered, but that had not made any difference, apparently; except that it had caused her people to dislike him, and finally to forbid him the house. After that, they had had to meet outside, wherever they could. Sometimes they took walks, or drove in her car. She had a small coupé. Sometimes they merely sat and held hands in the movies. I gathered, too, that there was another young man who cared for her, and who was likely to make trouble if he saw her with Herbert, so they had had to choose remote places.

"What sort of trouble?" I asked sharply.

She started and colored, but her chin went up. "Not what you think. That's ridiculous." She looked rather uneasy, however, and she expatiated on this other youth's good qualities at some length. Then she went back to Herbert again.

It appeared that they had been quite happy, until a month or so ago. At that time Herbert had changed. Sometime in the spring he had got a little money, she didn't know where, and had put it into the market on a margin. Stocks were very low, and he had thought he would make some money. But all summer they had remained low, and even dropped. That had worried him.

"But not enough to make him kill himself," she hastened to explain. "He was anxious, but he was sure they would do better this fall. And he didn't worry about money anyhow. He was like that. It was something else. He began to act as though he was afraid of something."

"He didn't say what it was?"

"No. But he said that he was being followed, and that he was in danger of some sort."

"Did he know who it was?"

She hesitated. "He thought it was my father, at first. It was someone who had a car, and of course he knew my family was watching me, or trying to. I knew it wasn't Father; I thought at first that Herbert was just excited. He liked to imagine things, you know. But one night I saw the car myself. It trailed us along a country road. At first I thought it was someone else, but I know now that it wasn't."

"You thought it was the other man, I suppose?"

She nodded. "But it wasn't. It wasn't his car." She looked at me searchingly. "I'm telling you the truth. I know his car well, and it wasn't his."

"It wasn't your father's?"

"Father and Mother dined out that night, and played bridge. They came in after I did, together."

"Then who was it? Who is it you suspect?"

She looked around before she answered. "Hugo," she said. "Miss Juliet's butler."

"Hugo hasn't got a car. There's no car here."

"He could rent one, couldn't he? Or she could rent one for him."

"But why? Aren't *you* imagining things now?"

"I'm not imagining that Herbert is dead, am I? Look at it! The papers say he had taken out a lot of insurance. Where did he get the money to do that? And why would he do it? He knew they had no use for him. And— maybe you don't know this—that old woman in there was pretty desperate. She was going to be put out of the house."

"But even that . . ."

"You don't know her," she went on, her voice rising. "She hated Herbert. She had hated his father for marrying his mother and then losing her money. And she's proud. She's always been a great lady in this town, and she'd rather kill than have a Mitchell go to the poorhouse. You've seen her. Is she grieving? Is she even decently sorry? You know she's not."

"If she was as desperate as that, how would Miss Juliet have obtained any money to insure Mr. Wynne?"

"I don't know. Maybe Hugo had some. Herbert used to say that he was as tight as the paper on the wall. He'd probably saved a lot."

However all that may be, Herbert had been less depressed for the past ten days. He told her that he was getting everything ready, and that soon they would go away together. He had a plan of some sort, but he didn't say what it was. All he told her was that she was to be ready to go at any time.

"To be married, I suppose?"

"Certainly. What do you think I am?"

I thought she was less frank about this, however. There was a change in her manner. She seemed to be choosing her words. But there seemed to be no doubt as to the essential facts. They were to go away as soon as he could sell his stocks without a loss. He had put five thousand dollars in them.

"Five thousand dollars," I said. "Where did he get it? From Miss Juliet?"

"She's never seen five thousand dollars at one time in her life," she replied scornfully. "No. I don't know where he got it last spring. He just said he had had a windfall. He wasn't very communicative, at any time. I—well, I asked him if he was bootlegging, and he just laughed. He said it was all right, and that the only dealing he'd ever had with a bootlegger was to buy a quart of gin."

Then, about a week before, they had both had a bad fright. They had been motoring along a country road again, and they were both certain that they had not been followed. They had stopped by the side of the road, and he had turned on the light on the instrument board to look at a railroad schedule. They were planning the elopement. Both of them, I gathered, were bent forward so that they saw nothing, but a car raced by them and fired several shots. Neither one was hit, but the glass in the windshield of her coupé had been shattered.

They gave up driving about after that. Herbert was in a bad way. His hands shook and he said he couldn't sleep. For two or three days they did not meet at all, although he called her now and then over the telephone.

"And still you had no explanation of all this?" I asked incredulously.

She hesitated. "I thought it was someone else. But I know now that I was wrong."

"You thought it was the other young man?"

"Well, I did and I didn't. I'd been engaged to him when I met Herbert, and he was pretty bitter about it. After that shooting, of course, I knew it wasn't. He's not that sort at all. And anyhow," she added naïvely, "he wouldn't have risked killing me."

Then came that last night. She told it clearly enough, although she constantly dabbed at her eyes with a moist ball of a handkerchief.

They had met about nine o'clock at a small neighborhood moving-picture theater. Herbert was uneasy, she said, and he told her that he had brought his revolver along. But he would tell her no more than that, and they sat quietly enough through the picture. When they went out, she found that her bag was missing, and she went back and found it, on the floor under her seat. When she emerged again, he had bought a copy of the evening edition of the *Eagle*, and was looking at the financial page.

"It looks as though everything has gone to hell," he said to her, and folded the paper and put it in his pocket. But he did not seem particularly depressed. He put his arm through hers and took her to the corner, and once he turned around and looked back. He seemed satisfied that he was not followed, however, and he put her into her car there, and, leaning in, kissed her good night.

"Just a day or two now," he said, "and we'll be on our way. On our way and sitting pretty!"

He was whistling as he went down the street. And that was the last she ever saw of him.

Up to that final farewell of Herbert's I felt sure that she had been telling the truth, although possibly not all of it. It was when it came to the later incident in the drive, when she had accosted me, that I was less certain.

She had not gone home at all, she said. She often drove about at night by herself, and this night she had had a good bit to think about. Her people did not like Herbert, and she was as good as committed to going away with him in a day or so. She drove out into the country, and somewhere on a remote road she found she had a flat tire. It took a good while to change it, and she was on her way home when she passed the Mitchell house and saw the lights there.

Well, it might have been true. Girls do queer things these days, although a car has to travel a good many miles, even with a flat tire to change, to use up two hours or more. True or not, however, there was no doubt that she believed with every ounce of her that Hugo had killed Herbert Wynne, and that with the tacit agreement of the old woman in the bed upstairs.

But she stubbornly refused to give her name, or to go to the police, although I warned her that they would find her, sooner or later. She only shrugged her shoulders at that.

"Why?" she said. "The verdict will be accidental death, and that closes it, doesn't it?"

"Not necessarily."

"Well, I've told you what I came to tell you. You can pass it on to the police if you like. But tell them to leave me out of it. I'm telling you; they did it." She indicated the house. "And they'd kill me, just as if stepping on a bug, if I got in their way."

All this time, of course, I had been watching for some indication that my message to Headquarters had reached Inspector Patton. Now, as she rose to go, I saw that it had. Across the street and down a half block or so was a dark inconspicuous car, with the engine running. But I felt cheap and unhappy when she turned to me and held out her hand.

"It's done me good just to talk to you," she said. "You see, I have nobody else."

I watched her go out the drive and climb into her gay little coupé, and then and there I swore to sever my connection with the police after this case was over. It was dirty work. I did their dirty work for them. What was I but a stool pigeon, after all?

The police car moved forward as she got under way.

## CHAPTER VIII

SHE HAD BEEN GONE less than an hour, and Hugo and Mary had not yet returned, when I heard a newsboy calling an extra. I went out to the street and bought one, and I saw that the verdict had been brought in: accidental death, and seemingly fair enough of course, with that gun laid out for cleaning and no powder marks found on the body.

Doctor Stewart came in soon afterward, brisk and cheerful, and he was the one who told Miss Juliet. She took it quietly, although I was watching for some sign. She merely sighed, and asked if Hugo and Mary had returned. It was Mr. Glenn, coming in at lunchtime, who explained the full significance of the verdict to her: that there would be considerable insurance. If he had expected her to show surprise, he was disappointed, although I thought she moved uneasily.

"Nothing can bring him back," he said, "so I can see no reason for not considering the change this makes in your circumstances." He had to repeat that, raising his voice, and she said nothing for an appreciable time. Then she raised herself on her elbow.

"So I keep my house after all!" she said. "On blood money!"

"I wouldn't look at it that way, Miss Juliet."

"What else is it?"

"It's a good many things; it is security and comfort in your old age. It means that you keep your home, the house which has stood for a great deal which is fine in this town for a good many years. That's something, isn't it? And these are hard times. Most of us are having our own troubles."

He drew a long breath, and she saw it rather than heard it.

"If I can help you, Arthur——"

"No, no," he said hastily. "I'm all right. I spend a lot, but then I make a lot!"

"Not from me," she said dryly.

He only smiled at that, and got up. As he looked down at her, his smile faded.

"One thing this ought to do, Miss Juliet," he said gravely. "It ought to reassure you about Herbert. It was an accident. Just remember that, and stop worrying."

I found myself wishing that the girl could have heard that conversation, and could have seen Miss Juliet's face. It was inconceivable that she could be acting for my benefit, or Mr. Glenn's. Yet even as I thought that, I was remembering that curious stealthy opening of the hall door the morning before. The door opening, and Miss Juliet slipping something under her pillow, hiding it from me.

I took my regular off-duty that afternoon, leaving Mary in the sickroom, and met the Inspector at his office at half past two.

"Well," he said, when I entered. "I suppose you saw the verdict? And thanks for the message. We've got the girl. That is, we know who she is, and we can lay our hands on her if we need her."

"Who is she?"

"Paula Brent."

"Paula Brent!"

He smiled at my astonishment. If the Mitchells had once been the leading family in the city, the Brents were now just that. With the usual difference, of course, that whereas no Mitchell ever allowed a picture in the paper or a reporter within a mile, the Brents were constantly featured. I thought fast. No wonder her family had objected to Herbert Wynne. The only wonder was that I had not recognized the girl. She had been a debutante the year before; I must have seen dozens of her photographs.

"It doesn't seem possible."

"That's what makes this business interesting. Nothing's impossible in it."

I was to remember that later.

He listened to her story attentively, as I told it. Here and there he asked a question, and he made a note about the shattering of the windshield on her car.

"Easy to check that," he said.

But on the whole he was less impressed than I had thought he would be.

"We'll get her in and talk to her. But all she has, so far as I can see, is a dislike of the old lady that she has translated into suspicion. It's not as easy as all that. It does account for that suitcase, though. It's been bothering me."

He was more interested, apparently, in my account of what had happened the night before, and particularly in my discovery of Hugo in the parlor.

"It's possible he saw someone, as he claims," he said thoughtfully. "On the other hand, it's always possible that he knows more than he's acknowledging. Remember, we're dealing with somebody who is no fool; that is, if this *is* a murder. And if it is supposed to be a murder by someone outside, what better proof that the house has been broken into once than to pretend that it's been done again? Still, if you saw the thing yourself, and are sure it wasn't simply nerves——"

"If I had any nerves of that sort," I said rather sharply, "I would certainly not take this work for you!"

"It was there, eh?"

"Something was. It was there, and then it wasn't."

"And it moved toward you?"

"It seemed to. I can tell you here and now, if I'd had a gun in my hand, I'd have shot it."

"And quite right, too," he said soothingly. "That's one reason I told you to leave your gun at home."

He leaned back in his chair, drew out his pipe and filled it thoughtfully.

"I gather that you found no ladder marks."

"None whatever."

"Well, think this over and see what you make of it. Between three and four on Tuesday morning, that would be three hours after the crime—if it was a crime—a man named Baird, who lives half a block from the Mitchell place, telephoned in to the precinct station nearby. He said that he was tending a sick dog in his garage, and that he had just seen a man enter the next property, which is the Manchester place, carrying a ladder. He had notified the people in the house, and they were investigating.

"A couple of men went around there, and they found the ladder all right. It was not where it had been left the night before, but it belonged to the Manchester place, right enough. In other words, somebody had carried that ladder away, used it for some purpose, and then brought it back."

"How long a ladder?"

"Long enough to reach to the roof of that ell on the Mitchell house."

"And then, I suppose, whoever it was flapped his wings and flew into the window above."

He laughed a little. "That's it," he said. "If that window was only above the roof we'd have something to go on. But it isn't. It's a good four feet to one side. But the time is interesting, isn't it? We got the body out at two, and I came back to talk to you at three, or something after three."

"Then that noise you heard——?"

"Possibly; although I'd hate to admit that while I sat on that front porch, somebody had put a ladder to that roof so that somebody else could get off it! If that ever got out, I'd be through, *finis!*"

"The sound I heard from the kitchen was earlier than that, of course," I said. "Did you get any description of this man?"

"Not much. Tall, and apparently strong, Baird says; he carried the ladder easily. He'd come across lots, avoiding the street. But here's an odd thing, although Baird is probably mistaken. He says that this fellow with the ladder wore a dinner jacket! Baird couldn't see his face. The man had a soft hat, well pulled down, but he'll swear to the shirt front and so on. But why a ladder? I've looked at it, and if anybody could get into that third-floor window with it, he's a human fly; that's all."

"There were no ladder marks, anyhow."

"They could have been erased, of course."

I must have started, but he had walked to the window and was standing there with his back to me and did not notice.

"You see where we are," he said, still at the window. "This girl of yours has it all doped out. Those three elderly people did it, so Miss Juliet wouldn't have to go to the poorhouse! And old Hugo rented a car and followed him, so the boy began to carry a gun for self-defense! What sort of story did that lad invent to tell her, and why did he invent it?"

"It may just possibly be true."

"Possibly. But why should Hugo, having, we'll say, followed him for some time, and at least once fired at him outside, have chosen to shoot him in his own room, where, under the circumstances, he was bound to be suspected? Tell me that, Miss Pinkerton in the red hat. By the way, it's a nice hat."

"Thanks. I need a few kind words."

He laughed at that, and, coming back to his desk again, sat leaning back in his chair.

"Well, as I may have said before, it's the very devil of a case. We have only two alternatives: either the boy was putting up a front that night in order not to distress this girl, and then went home and killed himself. Which doesn't seem likely, if she's telling the truth. Or this fear of his had a sound basis, and he was killed. If he did it himself, how did he do it? If he didn't do it, then who did, and why, and how? That's the way it has to be, and here I am, with the whole Homicide Squad ready to go and no place to go. What's the use of tailing Hugo? To the grocery store and back again? And time is passing, and in crime it's the first hundred minutes that are the hardest—for the criminal. After that every hour helps him."

I asked him about the fingerprints on the gun, and I learned that the verdict at the inquest had largely been based on them.

"They're Herbert's, all right," he told me. "Smeared, but faintly readable. Of course the coroner knows, and I know, that that gun may have been held in a handkerchief, or fired through a pocket; or that the killer, if there was one, could have worn gloves. But a suicide usually freezes to the weapon until it's all over, and leaves a pretty clean print. Still, I don't mind telling you that if I could think of some method by which that lad could have shot himself in the forehead without leaving any contact marks, I'd go home and call it a day."

I did not remind him of the position of the body, or of that bullet mark on the fireplace. He knew all that better than I did, and he had no intention of calling it a day. That was shown by his next move, which was to open a drawer of his desk and fling out three photographs.

"Study these," he said. "Maybe you will see something I don't. I've looked at them until I can't see them any more."

I did not like them much, but a nurse has to see a good bit of death, one way and another, and so I took them to the window and inspected them carefully. One was a close-up of the body; another showed the body and the bureau; and a third, taken from the doorway, showed almost the entire room, including the fireplace. But the second one showed a small spot of white on the floor, between the body and the bureau, and I found myself staring at it. It was a roughly triangular bit of white, perhaps two inches across.

"See anything?" the Inspector inquired.

"No . . . but what's this bit of white on the floor? Is it a defect in the film?"

"A defect! Don't use that word where Johnny Nicholson can hear you. You'll break his heart!" He sauntered over and glanced at the picture in my hand.

"Where?"

"There, a little underneath the bureau."

"It looks like a bit of paper," he said. "Why?"

"I don't know, I just wondered. I suppose—isn't that the *News* on the bureau?"

"It is. Our famous tabloid."

"But it was the *Eagle* he bought, according to Paula Brent. He bought the *Eagle* and looked at the financial page."

"That doesn't mean that he took it home with him. Still, I wouldn't mind seeing that paper. It's just possible——" He took the magnifying glass and inspected the picture again, with what I thought was a certain excitement. Evidently under the glass he saw something he had not seen before, for he turned to me abruptly.

"What became of that newspaper? Have you any idea?" he demanded.

"Not the slightest. The last time I saw it, the officer you had left with the body was reading it."

And then he blew up. "The infernal fool!" he shouted. "The double-distilled idiot! I'll break him for that. And somebody ought to break me! I don't belong in this job; I ought to be in a stable somewhere, being fed with a pitchfork. I suppose the room was cleared that night, after we took the body away?"

"Not until the next day; then you told them they could clean it. And they did."

"They would," he said grimly. "They knew, or guessed. Or maybe that was what Miss Juliet went after. She'd heard of it somehow. Damn Kelly. If that paper had been where I left it——"

Well, I knew the routine pretty well by that time, and that nothing should have been moved or touched. At the same time, the Squad had finished its work when Kelly took that paper; even the photographers had gone. And it is dreary work sitting up with a body, as well I know. But I said nothing, while the Inspector sat biting on an empty pipe and muttering to himself.

"What becomes of the papers from the Mitchell house?" he asked at last. "Are they saved?"

"Hugo burns them."

"He would!" he said viciously. "He'd burn that one, sure. And to think I never guessed it! I look all around for some sort of contrivance so he could kill himself and leave no powder marks; and there it lay, the simplest contrivance in the world. Look at that scrap on the floor. Does it suggest anything to you?"

"Not a thing."

"Well, you're not alone in that." His tone was still vicious. "It didn't suggest anything that night to a half-dozen bright young men whose job it was to find just such things."

"Are you trying to tell me that Herbert Wynne killed himself?"

"I think it's damned possible. And I think that that scrap on the floor should have told it to a lot of braying jackasses who were going around acting like detectives, including myself, if they'd had one good brain among the lot. There was a case like this in New England last spring. Probably Herbert saw it in the papers, and maybe the old lady saw it, too."

He picked up a newspaper, laid it flat on the top of the desk, but with a few inches hanging over the side, and then knelt in front of it.

"Now watch. I'm going to kill myself, but I carry a lot of insurance, so I want it to look like murder or an accident. Here's how it's done."

## CHAPTER IX

HE GOT OUT his fountain pen, and showed it to me.

"Now see," he said. "This pen is my gun. I'm going to shoot myself with it, but I don't want any powder marks. So I lift two or three of the top pages of the paper out of the way; not too far. I want them to fall back later and cover the others. And I leave some of the bottom ones, too. Then I hold up these half dozen in the center. Do you get the idea?"

"I think so."

"Good. I'm going to shoot myself, but through these center pages. Then the powder marks will be on the paper, not on me. And as I let go and drop, the top pages will fall over and cover the others. Picked up and glanced at, that newspaper is all right. The front and back pages show nothing. I looked at that newspaper, and you say Kelly picked it up and read some of it. But the inside pages had a bullet hole through them just the same; and powder on them. And there was powder on that scrap, too, unless I'm crazy. It wasn't torn off; it was shot off. He was a smart boy, Miss

Adams, and if I can prove how smart he was, I'd save the insurance companies a lot of money."

"I don't believe it," I said stubbornly.

"Believe it or not, that's the way it looks. The chances are that that scrap wasn't on the floor at all when our fellows went over the place. It was loose, though, and the first flash dislodged it."

"And the cleaning rags and the oil, set out on the bureau?"

"Camouflage, Miss Pinkerton! Darned good camouflage, if I do say it."

I could only shake my head. "You talk to this girl," I told him. "I don't believe that that boy went to the movies that night, bought a paper to look at the financial page, kissed his sweetheart goodbye, told her to be ready to run away with him in a day or two, said that they would soon be sitting pretty, as he expressed it, and then went whistling down the street to kill himself. It's nonsense."

He looked slightly crestfallen. "You didn't tell me all that, before. I'll get her here, and get the truth out of her."

"She'll tell you just what she told me. Maybe he did kill himself, but he didn't expect to do it when he left her. He left her around eleven, and Miss Juliet found the body about twelve. That gave him less than an hour to get home and to have something happen which would lead him to kill himself. And where did he get that copy of the *News*? Don't tell me he stopped and bought it so he could use it as you say, when he had the *Eagle* in his pocket. You talk to Paula Brent, and then find whoever put that copy of the *Daily News* on that bureau. If it's possible to have a suicide arranged to look like a murder, why not a murder that looks like a suicide?"

"But it didn't look like a suicide. Remember that."

"Well, like accidental death. That's the verdict, isn't it? And here's another thing, Inspector. I don't believe he invented that story about being followed. And who shot at him, that night in the country? You'll find that that's true."

"Plenty of that going on these days," he retorted. "I still insist that if he meant to kill himself, and wanted it to be considered a murder, he would make up a story just like that, and tell it where he knew it would be repeated."

"Why should he want it to be considered a murder? If he set that stage, as it was set, with the things for cleaning his gun all over the place, then he meant it to be considered an accident. If he meant anything at all."

And with that for him to think about, I went back to my patient.

I did not go directly back. I was annoyed with the Inspector and rather upset myself. For the first time in my experience I found not only my sympathy but my judgment opposed to that of Headquarters. I did not believe that Herbert Wynne had killed himself. I believed Paula Brent's story, vague as it was, and I dreaded the ordeal of interrogation which I knew was before her.

I was undecided when I reached the street. I called a taxicab, and stood with my hand on the door, still hesitating. Then I gave the address of the Brent house in Rosedale, crawled in, and gave myself up to an emotional orgy of irresolution and remorse. I was on my way to warn Paula. I knew police methods. Who better? They would not use physical force with her, of course, but they would discover at once that she was not telling all she knew. After that, they would not stop. They would keep after her, poor little thing; firing questions at her until she was exhausted, playing tricks on her, waiting until she was utterly weary and then pouncing.

I was pretty much exhausted myself when I got to Rosedale. Once a suburb, it is now a part of the city, and I knew the Brent house by sight. It was one of those large brick Colonial houses which should be set back among trees, and instead took up almost all of the lot. At the rear was a garage, and behind that an alley. The block was almost solidly built up, and the alley on both sides lined with similar garages, brick and frame.

Paula was at home, and her mother out. This last was no surprise to me. Mrs. Brent was on the Woman's Board of St. Luke's, and when she was not there, running her finger around for dust and prying into the refrigerators in the diet kitchens, she was somewhere else doing the same thing. I knew the type; the sort who leaves her daughter to a governess until she is old enough to come out, and then wonders why she gets into trouble.

The butler showed me into a large living room, and I found Paula there. She had apparently been curled up in the corner of a davenport until I came in, and I had a feeling that she had not been alone there; that someone had left the room by a rear door as I entered. I thought she looked somewhat better, and she even managed a smile, although I saw that she was startled.

"Then you knew me, all along," she said.

I had not thought of that, and it took some quick thinking. "I've seen a good many pictures of you, Miss Brent."

"Funny! I never thought of that."

But when I told her that the police would probably want to ask her some questions, she sat down suddenly, as though she had gone weak in the knees.

"What makes you think that?"

"They saw you with me this morning, and I think they followed you home," I said shamelessly. "I thought maybe I'd better tell you. They have a way of getting the facts, you know."

She lighted a cigarette, and I thought her hands were unsteady. But she looked at me again with that queer look of defiance that I had noticed before.

"I'll tell them just what I told you."

"If there is anything else——"

"There is nothing else. Herbert was killed by someone in that house, probably Hugo, and that old woman knows it. If the police are out to whitewash the Mitchell family, I'll call in a bunch of reporters and tell them so! You can tell them that, if you like."

But it was bravado. So was the cigarette, and her whole general attitude. She was very pale, and the next thing I knew, she was crumpled up in a heap on the davenport, crying as though her heart would break. I found myself trying to quiet her, and from that moment on, through all that was on the way for all of us, I found myself unconsciously on that child's side, and against the police.

And that in spite of the fact that I was fully aware, as the butler showed me out, that she had already started back for that rear door, where somebody unknown had been waiting and probably listening.

Miss Juliet ate a fair supper that evening, and I must say that everybody around the place seemed more cheerful than I had yet seen them. The meal, too, was the most substantial I had seen served, and Hugo moved almost lightly around the table. After all, why not? No one there had had any affection for Herbert Wynne, and his passing and the verdict meant a clear hundred thousand dollars for them. I began to think, not that the death had been as the Inspector now believed, but that it had had its compensations. After all, comfort and security for the old age of three elderly people were not such bad things in exchange for a boy who had obviously been of little value to the world, save to one girl, who would soon forget him.

I was, however, rather surprised to learn that certain plans had been made in my absence. Hugo told me of them when he brought in my dessert.

"I beg pardon, miss, but I thought you would like to know. Doctor Stewart and Mr. Glenn are going to be in the house tonight."

"Both of them? What for?"

"The gentlemen consider it advisable, miss. Mr. Glenn will be here until two o'clock, and Doctor Stewart will spend the remainder of the night. I understand that he has a case which will keep him until about that time."

"They haven't said why?"

"No, miss."

I lost patience at that. "Now listen to me, Hugo. If you know anything, it's your business to tell the police. What is it? Who was here last night, on that landing? And who are they afraid will get in again tonight?"

But he had no explanation beyond what I already knew. The two men had met there late that afternoon, and Hugo had told them about the night before. It was Mr. Glenn who had suggested the watch on the house.

"After all, miss," Hugo went on, "if somebody got in on Monday night and again last night, there's no telling when they will try again."

"But for what purpose, Hugo? Why should somebody try to get in?"

"I haven't any idea, miss."

And somehow I believed him.

Nevertheless there was an element of humor in that night's vigil as kept by the two men who had arranged it, and also a bit of drama. One or two small things, too, rather roused my curiosity.

Thus, although the general atmosphere had certainly improved, I thought there was some sort of trouble between Mary and Hugo that evening. She stood sullenly over her stove while Hugo prepared Miss Juliet's tray, and once, when he spoke to her, she ignored him. Also, while she relieved me for my dinner, she must have said something to the old lady which upset her, for her pulse was faster when I went back to her.

Some of the humor lay in Mr. Glenn's rather ponderous and meticulous examination of the house when he arrived at nine o'clock. He spent some time in the kitchen with Mary, and then proceeded to go over the entire place, including the cellars; and the only good laugh I had during that entire week was when he somehow managed to knock over a can of red paint at the top of the cellar stairs, slip on the top step, and bump all the way to the bottom.

He was not hurt, but he was outraged to the very depths of his soul. I could hear him swearing clear up in the sickroom, and I was just in time to see him emerging, apparently covered with blood, and in a vicious humor. He had to send home for other clothes, and the house smelled of paint all night!

Mary was sullenly viewing the wreckage when I went back again.

"How on earth did he do it, Mary?"

"I don't know, miss. He'd do well to keep to his own part of the house. That's all."

After that we settled down. Apparently Mr. Glenn had brought some work with him, for at ten o'clock his confidential secretary arrived, and as it turned out, it was she—her name, I learned later, was Florence Lenz—who provided the only bit of drama we had that Wednesday night.

I had seen her when she came in, and I did not like her much. She had evidently made a special toilet for the occasion, and she stopped in the hall to powder her nose. I knew her sort the minute I saw her. They never forget that their employer is a man, and when he is, like Mr. Glenn, pretty much a man of the world and not married, that he may represent anything from a tidy flat to a marriage license.

But she was evidently an efficient secretary, and they worked together in the library with the door open until midnight. Now and then he would emerge, make a round of the lower floor, and then go back again. I could hear his voice, monotonously dictating something to her, and only broken by these tours of duty.

Then, at twelve o'clock, he let her go, sending her out to his car and calling to the chauffeur to take her home. And it was not more than three minutes later, when I had at last settled down for some sleep, that I heard the doorbell ringing furiously and Mr. Glenn running to the door.

I was a trifle scared myself when he opened it. There was the chauffeur with the secretary in his arms, looking as helpless as men always do at such times.

"What's the matter? Is she hurt?"

And with that she released herself, stumbled through the doorway and dropped gracefully on the floor at Mr. Glenn's feet! I ran down at once, in my dressing gown and bare feet, and I had only to touch her eyeballs to know that she was no more in a faint than I was. It did not take me long to go back to the kitchen and get a bottle of household ammonia. I had seen plenty of this fake fainting, and I have never known anything quicker than a good whiff of that stuff to bring them around.

It did not take her long. She choked and coughed, and when she opened her eyes, she gave me a look of plain hatred! But she came around all right, and it turned out that she had something to tell after all. I had not believed it at first, nor, I think, had Mr. Glenn.

"Sit up, Miss Lenz, and don't be an idiot," he said. "What's the matter? What happened to you?"

"A man," she said, still coughing from the ammonia. "A man. He knocked me down and ran over me."

"*Knocked* you down? He attacked you?"

"He knocked me down and ran over me."

"You've said that before! Where was all this?"

"Around the corner."

"What corner?"

"Around the corner of the house."

And there was certainly some truth in what she claimed, as we realized when we looked at her. Her knee was cut—she wore her stockings rolled, of course!—and she had a considerable bump on her head. Mr. Glenn asked no more questions. He went out the front door in a hurry, leaving Florence glaring at me.

"That's a dirty trick you pulled!" she said.

"It revived you."

"It damn near killed me."

Well, there was enough truth in that to send me rather remorsefully upstairs for some dressings and adhesive plaster. I was still working over her knee, and she was making a lot of fuss about it, when Mr. Glenn came back and she told her story.

She had started for the car, and then decided to go around the house and take what she elegantly called a look-see. All her life she had heard of the Mitchell place, and now she was inside the gates.

"I told Mac to wait," she said—Mac was evidently Mr. Glenn's chauffeur —"and that I was going to walk around the house. But as I rounded the corner at the back, this fellow bumped into me, and how! Well, he knocked me flat, but did he stop? He did not. He simply jumped over me and beat it. You can ask Mac. He heard him running."

Well, it might or might not be important. I didn't know. We got rid of her at last, loudly calling on "Mac" to bear her out, and limping so that Mr. Glenn had to help her to the car. But that was the only dramatic incident of the night. When the doctor arrived at two o'clock, his reaction to the Lenz girl's story was characteristic.

"Somebody's chauffeur, going home late across lots," he said dryly. "Probably worse scared than the girl, at that."

And I gathered, after the lawyer had left, that the doctor considered the whole idea a silly one.

"I'm ready to do my bit," he said to me. "I'm used to losing sleep, if it comes to that. But what the hell do Glenn and Hugo think anyone wants out of this house? A lot of secondhand furniture?"

After which he proceeded to settle himself on the old sofa in the hall, and to sleep there comfortably for the rest of the night. I could hear him snoring as I lay on my extemporized bed at the foot of the big walnut one, so I finally dropped off myself. I needed sleep that night, and I got it.

## CHAPTER X

THAT WAS ON Wednesday night.

I wakened early the next morning, and lay on my sofa, thinking over the newspaper incident and the Inspector's theory about it. It seemed to me, not only that if a suicide could be planned to look like a murder, a murder could also be planned to look like a suicide; but that in this latter event the newspaper became extremely important. For suppose a charge of murder was made, against Hugo, for example? What would be simpler than for Hugo to produce that paper and thus demonstrate that Herbert had killed himself, but had carefully arranged it to look like murder or accidental death?

In that case the paper would not have been destroyed. It would be carefully hidden, perhaps somewhere in the library, where I had missed it, or better still, in that back flat where Hugo and Mary lived their silent lives together.

At seven o'clock I heard Doctor Stewart moving in the hall below. There was an old-fashioned marble washstand built in under the stairs, and I could hear him washing there. Soon after that he went outside, and I could see him from a window making a round of the house. Apparently he discovered nothing suspicious there, for when he had had a cup of coffee, he came up to see Miss Juliet, and he was scornful about the whole business.

"I don't believe there was anyone there at all," he said. "What I think is that that girl, whatever her name is, fell over something and then cooked up a story for Glenn. Makes her interesting! And Glenn's not married."

He left soon after that, and I went down to get my own breakfast. But I found myself watching Hugo that morning with a sort of indignation. What manner of man was this, if I were right, putting down my coffee with a steady hand, bringing in my bacon, and placing the morning paper before me almost with a flourish: "WYNNE VERDICT ACCIDENTAL DEATH." I looked up and caught his eye, and I thought he looked away.

"So they've settled it, Hugo!"

"It's all settled, miss. Apparently."

But for all his flourish, he seemed quiet and depressed. There was no talk going on in the kitchen when I got the old lady's tray, and Mary was still sullen and morose.

Just what was it that Mary knew, and Miss Juliet? For that they shared some guilty knowledge I felt convinced by that time. Why must Mary write her messages to the old lady and then destroy them? Why had she resented Mr. Glenn the night before?

I have lain awake at night since, wondering if poor old Miss Juliet ever felt that I suspected her of some tacit connivance in that crime, and thinking of the price she had to pay to convince me that she was innocent. Poor old Miss Juliet Mitchell, succumbing to her one moment of temptation, and so sending herself in all innocence to what the Inspector called the black-out! I was glad that she never knew that. And I am glad to remember that if, from that time on, there was little kindness in my care of her, at least I did my duty by her. And I hope a little more.

They buried Herbert that morning, Thursday, from a mortuary chapel in the town. I gathered later that there was a small attendance of old friends of the family, and an enormous crowd of morbid-minded people there.

And that at least one person attended in simple grief and with utter reck-lessness of consequences—Paula Brent. Hugo did not go at all, but at ten o'clock Mary appeared in the doorway of Miss Juliet's room, clad in the black raiment which certain people keep for such occasions, and shouted to the old lady.

"I'm going, Miss Juliet."

"Thank you, Mary."

That was all.

At noon the Inspector called me up, to say that he was going to talk to Paula Brent that afternoon, and would like me to be there.

"You'd better come down and check on her story," he said. "Watch out for any discrepancies. She's pretty much haywire just now, but she'll have settled down by the time you get here."

I looked about, but Hugo was in the kitchen, and Mary had not come back. I lowered my voice. "You might have given her a little time, after this morning!"

"She's had three days," he said, rather ominously, and hung up the receiver.

I was considerably upset when I went upstairs again. What did he mean by that three days?

Mary came back soon afterward, and when I went upstairs after lunch, I found that she had been carrying down the dead boy's clothes, and piling them on the stairs to the third floor. They lay outside Miss Juliet's room, on the lower steps, piled in neat bundles; his shirts, his collars and ties, his suits of clothing. There was something dreadful to me in that haste of hers to get rid of the last vestiges of that unlucky youth, and I called Mary into the hall and said so.

"What is the hurry?" I asked. "That could wait, couldn't it?"

"It was her idea," she said sourly. "She wants to look them over. They're to go to the Salvation Army. And what's wrong about it? He'll never need them again."

When I went in, I found Miss Juliet's pulse fast again, and not too good. I gave her some digitalis, and I advised her to let the clothing wait for a day or two.

"You're in no condition to do things like that, Miss Juliet," I told her sternly. "A day won't matter, and I won't be answerable to the doctor if you don't obey orders."

She nodded. "Mary wanted to get them out of the house," she said. "Certainly there is no hurry."

Well, I could make what I wanted of those two statements, Mary's and hers, although I was pretty much puzzled. Had they been going over his clothing together, those two old women, searching for something? I thought of that as she nibbled without appetite at the food on the tray I had carried up. Were they afraid he had left something, a letter perhaps, which would weaken or destroy the verdict which meant so much to them? A letter was the usual thing left by suicides.

Still, if he had killed himself, why take all that trouble to make it look like something else, and then leave such a letter? Unless it was a letter he might have received, from Paula perhaps. Almost certainly she would have written to him.

The only thing I could work out from that was that Paula might have written him something about the danger he was in, and that those two women suspected that she had. But, of course, that implied that they knew both of this danger and about Paula. I was not sure that they knew either. Actually I was sure of only one thing, and that was that they had made a systematic search of the dead boy's clothing.

That theory was verified when I saw that the coat which Mary had hastily laid on the stairs as I appeared had a pocket turned inside out. Of course that really proved nothing. Everyone goes over clothing before giving it away. Or the police might have done it. It was only the haste and stealth of the performance that looked queer to me.

I would rather have had a tooth pulled than go into the Inspector's neat and tidy office that afternoon. Unlike the Police Commissioner's room, which was a sort of murder museum with revolvers, dirks and even a bit of charred human bone glued to a card, the Inspector's office was bare to the last degree. A chair or two, a big desk, and two telephones were all that it contained. But I stood for some time with my hand on the knob of the door, before I could make up my mind to go in and face Paula Brent. Nor was my discomfort lessened when she looked up at me with a dreary little smile.

"So they've got you, too!" she said.

"It looks like it."

"Well, I hope he believes you. He doesn't believe me. He thinks Herbert killed himself."

"If he was sure of that, you wouldn't be here," I told her.

And that turned out to be the case. The interrogation had barely commenced, but I saw at once that the Inspector had at least temporarily abandoned the suicide theory.

She bore up under it very well, although watching her as she sat in her straight chair—facing the light, as did everyone called for questioning into that office—I saw what struck me as rather pathetic; that she had put on a black dress and a little black hat for the funeral.

It had its effect on the Inspector also, for he handled her with rather unusual gentleness. And I must say that the story she told him was the story she had told me, word for word. Now and then he looked at me, and I nodded. It was not until he began to question her that she seemed less assured.

"Now, about your being on the Mitchell place that night. You hadn't, by any chance, been in the house with him?"

"What do you mean by that?"

"I'm asking you, Miss Brent. Don't get the idea that I think you killed him. I know better. But if you had quarreled, and after you left, he had decided to—you see what I mean."

"Never. We had never quarreled."

"Tell me about the two hours between the time you separated, and the time you saw the house lighted and a police car in the drive."

"I just drove around," she said vaguely. "I was nervous."

"Drove for two hours? Where did you go?"

"I really don't know."

"You must know," he said sharply. "You know the roads around here. You had to get back home. Come, come, Miss Brent! Don't you want us to learn the truth about all this?"

"What I did has nothing to do with that. I didn't kill him."

"Well, where were you when you had the trouble, on what road?"

"Trouble? What sort of trouble?"

"Didn't something happen to your car?"

She remembered then, and glanced at me suspiciously. "I had a flat tire. It was outside of Norrisville. It took me a good while to change it."

And then, while she was still confused over that temporary lapse, he flung a bomb at her.

"Just why did you get that ladder?"

She stared at him, her lips slightly parted. For a moment she could not speak.

"I don't know what you mean by a ladder."

"I think you do," he said quietly. "And I warn you against concealing anything which has a bearing on this case. You got a ladder and dragged it across two lawns and through the shrubbery of the Mitchell place; and a good trail you left. If you want to see it, I have a rough drawing here."

But she made no move to look at it. She sat huddled in her chair, her face white and drawn. "I don't understand," she said weakly. "I don't know what you're talking about."

Nor did I, for that matter. The afternoon before, he had told me that a man had carried that ladder, and now here he was accusing this girl. He has his own methods, however, and in the next question he had apparently abandoned the ladder, and shifted to something else.

"You told Miss Adams that Herbert's family, or rather Miss Mitchell and her household, did not like him."

"They hated him."

"How do you know that?"

"He always said so. Lately it had been worse. For a month or so."

"What do you mean by worse?"

"He got frightened. They were following him."

"That's rather absurd, isn't it? Old Miss Juliet could follow nobody."

"Somebody was following him. He began to carry his revolver."

"He never said who it was?"

"He didn't know. I think now that it was Hugo."

"Why Hugo?"

I need not repeat that part of her story. It was much like what she had told me. But she added something which was new. This was to the effect that, while Herbert had refused to explain his fears and suspicions to her, he had told her he had written a letter, so that if anything happened to him, she would understand. And that on Wednesday morning, when I had surprised her in the yard, she had been trying to get into the house to find it.

"That's the truth, is it?"

"I've told you."

"You weren't there to see if that ladder had left any marks, and to erase them if you found them?"

"What ladder?"

But the questions had evidently alarmed her, for now she began to cry. She didn't know anything about a ladder. She wished he would let her alone. She wanted to go home. After all, she hadn't killed Herbert, although the Inspector acted as though she had. When she was quieter, I noticed that he had tactfully abandoned the ladder.

"This letter you speak of, did he tell anyone else about it?"

"He wouldn't. I'm sure he never did."

He nodded, and shortly after that he got up.

"You understand, of course, that you are not under arrest. That would be ridiculous. But I shall ask you a few more questions, and I'll see that your family is notified of your safety. You'll be home tonight, all right. In the meantime the matron will see that you are comfortable, and we'll have some food sent in."

"Why not ask them now?" she said. "If I'm not guilty, you have no business to hold me."

"Maybe not." He smiled down at her. "But I can't ask my questions yet; and after all, you and I want the same thing, don't we? We want to know who killed Herbert Wynne, if he was killed. And why."

SHE WENT, chin high and her bearing faintly defiant, when the matron came. The Inspector followed her out with his eyes, and waited until the door had closed.

"How about it, Miss Adams?"

"It's the same story."

"She almost forgot the tire!"

"That doesn't prove anything, does it? She has had a lot to distract her. How on earth did you learn that she had dragged that ladder, Inspector?"

"I didn't," he said calmly. "We found the tracks, all right. They led toward the Mitchell house. But we found none leading back. In other words, it looked as though someone without strength to carry it had taken it to the house; that might be a woman, or a girl. But it had been carried back; somebody had had strength enough to do that, and as you know, this man was seen."

"And that footprint was hers?"

"That's my guess. She wore high heels, and so she slipped off her pumps. She's intelligent, and if she was scared that night, she was still using her brains."

"Then you think she got somebody off that roof? On Monday night?"

"I do indeed, Miss Pinkerton!"

"Who?"

But he ignored that for the time. He got out his old briar pipe and carefully filled it.

"It's like this," he said finally. "When there's a question between murder and suicide, we have only one choice. We have to go on the murder theory until that's disproved. That doesn't mean that it is a murder. It only means that it may be a murder. But in this case there are a number of things that begin to confirm my first impressions. The coroner didn't have all of them. I can't see that boy in front of the bureau when that shot was fired, and I know he didn't move a foot after it *was* fired. But I can't see that ladder either, unless it was used to let somebody escape from that roof who had no business to be there. Any more than this fellow in the grounds had any business there last night."

"You know about that, do you?" I asked, surprised.

"I know a little about a lot of things," he said. "And not enough about any one of them. For instance, why the deuce let those two amateur sleuths take over the job of the police?"

"It was their idea, not mine. I'd told you I had seen something on the landing the night before," I said indignantly. "But you were too busy shooting yourself through a newspaper to pay much attention."

He grinned at that, but he was sober enough as he went on. "Well, we both slipped up there," he agreed. "The point is that Hugo was scared last night, and that he didn't want the police. So he gets the two men he trusts; and we lose something that might be important."

He filled his pipe and leaned back in his chair. "After talking with this girl," he said, "I notice that there is one element which she has been mighty careful to keep out of her story. That's her family. She's frightened, and so she emphasizes the fact that the Mitchell household disliked him.

"But somebody else may have had more than dislike for him. He was a weakling, with the unbridled passions of his type, and here was a nice girl in love with him. Who had a reason for putting him out of the way? Maybe more of a reason than we know?"

"I suppose you mean Mr. Brent. But I don't think——"

"No? Well, fathers have a way of looking after their daughters. And remember, this boy was a bad actor. He may already have—well, let's not get carried away. She looks like a girl with character, but just the same she has a father; and it's pretty certain that that father was afraid of him, and of what might happen. Mind you, I'm not accusing the father. He just enters the picture as a possibility, provided this turns out to be a murder.

"Now go back to that night. Herbert Wynne may have killed himself, but he was a fellow with a weak chin and that sort are pretty careful of their skins! Also, if she is right about his whistling when he left her and all that, we have to suppose that something happened between eleven and twelve o'clock that night which changed his cheerfulness into despair. That's a pretty short time. What had he done, or what had he learned, to effect that change? Had Paula thrown him over? She doesn't act as though she had."

"She hadn't," I said positively. "Whether she was in love with him or simply infatuated, I don't know. But she's still wearing his ring, if you noticed."

He nodded. "I did notice. Nice ring, too. I'd like to know where he got the money for it. . . . But let's get on to Mr. Brent again. And by the way, that story of the broken windshield is true enough. We've checked it."

"So Mr. Brent drove past his daughter's car, and fired at it! How did he know he wouldn't kill her?"

That annoyed him, although he laughed. "I've said that there is a good bit of indiscriminate shooting going on just now. Let's leave that for a minute. Suppose that the girl's father has followed them, seen them in the movies, and when the girl drove off, has followed him home. He goes in with him, there's a quarrel, the boy's revolver is on the table, and—because it has turned out that he deserves it—the father shoots him. Probably he didn't mean to, but there's the boy's gun on the bureau. Perhaps it was that shot that aroused Miss Juliet, although she doesn't know it. She opens her door, sees a light above, and starts up the stairs. The father is there, trapped!

"What does he do? He only has a few minutes. He drags the body in front of the bureau, bends the knees, and—using his handkerchief, of course—he puts the revolver on the floor beside him. Then he escapes, by the only way possible."

"By the window?"

"By the window. I believe a strong man could swing over to that roof of the ell, and do it safely. And now take the rest of the story. The girl watches those two go off, either together or the one following the other; and she knows there may be trouble. What does she do? She follows them and hangs around outside the house. That story about a flat tire near Norrisville is pure invention. She hangs around the Mitchell place, and she's not deaf, or asleep. She hears a shot fired.

"What can she do? She sees the lights going on, and knows that the household is alarmed and up. But so far as she knows, Mr. Brent is still in the building. She sees the police go in, and later on a Headquarters car. She still hangs around. She stops you, but you can't tell her anything. And she has to know, somehow.

"Now we get to the ladder. We'll say that Mr. Brent is on that roof. He can't get down, and he's gone if he's found there. It isn't hard to imagine that he saw her below and signaled to her, or that she waited until we had gone and then got that ladder. Of course, this is only conjecture, but something like that happened Monday night, if there was any murder at all."

"And so on Wednesday morning," I said, "when she knew that the servants were at the inquest, she went back there to——"

"Precisely. To look for the ladder marks and to erase them. You surprised her, and so she told you that story."

I sat for some time, thinking this over. It fitted together too well to be ignored, but I was not certain of one or two things.

"He didn't go in with Herbert," I said at last. "Herbert had started to undress."

"Then he followed him later."

"How did he get in? The doorbell rings in the servants' bedroom as well as in the kitchen. It would have wakened them."

"He might have called, or thrown gravel. You and I know that that can be done."

But I was not satisfied. "Herbert wouldn't have admitted Mr. Brent," I said. "Not if Paula's story is true. He'd have known that it meant trouble."

But he only shrugged his shoulders. "One thing will happen if I'm right," he said. "We'll let the family know where Paula is, and if there is anything to this idea, he'll burst in as soon as he hears it. He'll probably do that anyhow," he added ruefully.

He let me go soon after that, merely saying that he would probably come up that night, to look over the roof and the window sill of Herbert's room.

"If this was a murder, then somebody was on that roof all the time we were examining the body and the room," he said. "As a matter of fact, I looked out over the roof myself. But there's a sizable chimney there, and whoever it was, Brent or someone unknown, may have been behind it. But this girl knows who it was. You can bank on that.

"And don't forget this," he added, as I started to go. "That theory doesn't apply only to Brent. It applies to anyone who was interested in the girl."

It was four o'clock when I left the office, and four thirty when I got to the Mitchell place. I bought an evening paper on the way, and I saw that the press already knew that Paula Brent had been interrogated. "SOCIETY GIRL QUERIED IN MITCHELL CASE," was the heading. Following as it did on a coroner's verdict of accidental death, the *Eagle* had certainly made the most of it.

I was not surprised when I saw the doctor's car in the drive, but I was startled at Hugo's face when he let me in.

"She's had a bad turn, miss," he said. "The doctor's asking for you."

I went in, without changing my uniform, to find Miss Juliet lying back on her pillows, and both the doctor and Mary bending over her. The doctor was holding a towel to her nose, and the pungent odor of amyl-nitrite filled the room. When I took her wrist, her pulse was very rapid, and I noticed that her sallow face was flushed.

It was a full ten minutes before the doctor straightened and gave me the towel. "I think she'll do now," he said. "Did anything happen to cause this, Mary?"

"I don't know, doctor. She had been quiet enough. I had got her the paper and her reading glasses. Then I heard her give a quick breath, and let the paper drop. I called Hugo, and he called you."

Doctor Stewart stayed until almost seven. By that time Miss Juliet was better, but far from being herself. Most of the time she lay with her eyes closed, not speaking, although she was perfectly conscious; and she refused to take any nourishment whatever. It was only when the doctor was about to leave that she opened her eyes and said a few words.

"I want to see Arthur Glenn."

"Not tonight, Miss Juliet. Tomorrow will do, won't it?"

She nodded and closed her eyes again.

I followed the doctor into the hall, and he stood for a few minutes, apparently thinking hard.

"I'm not quite satisfied with the look of things, Miss Adams," he said. "It seems to me—did you notice the *Eagle* on the bed? I have an idea that what sent her off was an article stating that a young woman named Brent had been held for questioning by the police on this case."

"I saw that," I agreed cautiously.

"Well, that's understandable. The girl's grandfather had been a lover of Miss Juliet's years ago. Of course he is dead now, but it must have been a shock. Quite aside from that, however, is the fact that the police are interrogating anybody, after the coroner's verdict."

"I suppose they are not satisfied, doctor."

He eyed me impatiently. "That's a mild way of putting it, anyhow! What the hell do you think I'm talking about? Of course they're not satisfied. What I want you to do is to keep any suspicion of that away from the old lady. Let the police get themselves in the newspapers if they like. Miss Mitchell is an old woman with a bad heart. It may quit on her at any time. I don't want any more shocks for her; that's all."

He turned to go down the stairs, then turned back again. "Has she said anything about making a will?"

"Not to me, doctor."

"She may. She's worth money now. There's an old one somewhere, with legacies for Mary and Hugo in it. Pretty substantial ones, I imagine. But if the will question comes up, let me know, will you? I might get some money for St. Luke's."

Well, I suppose that was natural enough. He had got a good bit of money for St. Luke's, one way and another. But I felt rather resentful as he went down the stairs. I made up my mind to keep my own counsel if the will question came up, and I was unusually tender with Miss Juliet that evening.

I was thoughtful, too. So there were already substantial legacies for the servants!

## CHAPTER XII

I HAD PLENTY to think of as I prepared Miss Juliet for the night, straightening her bed and once more rubbing her thin old back. I settled her early, for I knew that the Inspector was coming. And it was while I was folding up that copy of the *Eagle* and putting it away for later reading that something came into my mind. I have had this happen before; I can puzzle over a thing until I am in a state of utter confusion, give it up, and then suddenly have the answer leap into my mind without any apparent reason.

Yet there was a connection, in a way, I dare say. I straighten Miss Juliet's pillows, and remember that she had hidden something there. I put away the *Eagle,* and I remember that search in the library for what I was certain Mary had concealed there. And then I am reaching behind the books, finding a dirty scrap of newspaper and leaving it there.

My first impulse was to go down at once and look for it. Hugo, however, was still on the lower floor, and I decided to wait until the house was quiet; or perhaps until the Inspector arrived. One thing I have learned from the police, and that is never to take a risk by being in a hurry.

It was eight o'clock, and the Inspector had not yet arrived, when Miss Juliet roused from what I had hoped was a sleep, to ask me if I had telephoned to Mr. Glenn.

"Not yet," I said. "Won't the morning do?"

But she was insistent. He was to come in the morning, and to come prepared to take down something she had to say; so in the end I went down to the telephone and called him.

"What does she want?" he asked. "Have you any idea?"

"She's going to make a statement of some sort. This affair of the Brent girl seems to have upset her."

"A statement, eh? What on earth does she know that requires a statement? Have you any idea?"

"No. But she has had something on her mind ever since this thing happened. Something she thinks has a bearing on the case."

"I'll come around now," he said. "I'm on my way to the theater, and I'll stop in."

That satisfied Miss Juliet when I told her. She was excited, I thought, and somehow I got the impression that she was frightened also; that she had determined to do something which she was afraid to do. I was standing at the window, watching for the lights of Mr. Glenn's car, when she spoke to me.

"I used to know Paula Brent's grandfather," she said, in her flat voice. "Why should they question Paula? She couldn't know anything about Herbert."

"I wouldn't let that bother you," I said, as gently as I could while shouting at her. "They've questioned a lot of people."

"Why? If they think it was an accident?"

"Well, you know how these things are. The insurance company wants to be certain. That's all."

"Certain of what?"

I hesitated, but I had gone too far. She was watching me, and to save my life I could not think of any evasion.

"Of course it's nonsense, Miss Mitchell. They simply want to be certain that he—that it didn't happen by design."

"That he didn't kill himself?"

"Yes."

She closed her eyes, and although it was difficult to be sure in the dim light, I thought I saw tears oozing from beneath her wrinkled lids. But the next moment she apparently felt what I had not even heard, the vibration of Mr. Glenn's heavy car in the drive, and she visibly braced herself.

"There is Arthur," she said. "Will you tell him to come up? And then will you go out, my dear, so that I can talk to him?"

I did not go far; only into my room, which adjoined hers. But I could hear nothing after her first words. To tell the truth, I did not care to. Long ago I had made my position clear to the Inspector, that I was no eavesdropper, listening with my ear to a keyhole. I left them there, Mr. Glenn large and resplendent in dinner clothes, with two black pearl studs and a carefully tied black tie, and that frail old creature on the bed. Perhaps she did not realize that I had not yet closed the door when she spoke to him.

"Arthur," she said. "I have connived at a great wickedness, and now I am going to save my soul."

It was then that he followed me to the door and closed it behind me.

He must have been very late for the theater that night. The conference lasted about a half hour; if one can call a conference what sounded like expostulation from him, and a monotonous sort of insistence from that walnut bed. Whatever she wanted to do, he was opposed to it. Once or twice, indeed, he raised his voice so that I actually heard what he said.

"I don't believe it," he said. "I don't care what he told you. I don't believe it."

And again: "You've had a bit of good fortune when you needed it. And if you'll look back, you'll see that it was coming to you."

But I doubt if his arguments had any effect whatever on her. At something before nine he went downstairs and out to the kitchen, and I heard Hugo calling up the back stairs to Mary, telling her to come down. Evidently she refused, and soon after, I heard Mr. Glenn banging out of the front door and driving away in his car.

When I went back to Miss Juliet, she was looking tired, but happier than I had seen her since I came.

"I feel much better, my dear," she said quietly. "Now I think I shall sleep."

And sleep she did, for at least part of a night which was to be filled with horror for me.

The Inspector did not arrive until half past nine, but I had no opportunity to get into the library during that interval. Hugo was prowling about the lower floor, now in the long parlor, now in the library. He looked disturbed and anxious, as well he might if my idea of Miss Juliet's talk with

Mr. Glenn that night was correct. And as I sat in that dim room and checked it over, I myself could find no flaw in it.

I had a complete picture in my mind by that time; of Miss Juliet's salvaging that copy of the *News* from wherever Kelly had left it, and of finding the scrap on the floor and placing it inside. Almost certainly the scrap had still been inside when Mary got it and hid it, but when the paper was next moved, it had dropped out behind the books, and it had not been missed.

Then, if that were true, there had been no murder. Herbert Wynne had killed himself, and Miss Juliet's crime had consisted of withholding that knowledge. "I don't care what he told you," Mr. Glenn had said. What could that be but a reference to a possible method for making a suicide look like something else? And, although, as it turned out, I was entirely wrong in a good many things relating to this case, in that, at least, I was correct. Miss Juliet did know about that newspaper device.

At nine thirty the Inspector arrived, bringing a deputy inspector with him. I heard the three men, Hugo in the lead, going to the third floor, and after some considerable time I gathered that the deputy was on the roof of the rear wing, and that they were having trouble getting him off it.

I slipped into the hall and listened.

"All right, Evans," the Inspector was calling. "We'll get a ladder."

I had only time to slip back when the Inspector and Hugo came down the stairs. The Inspector was talking.

"There must be one in the neighborhood. A pruning ladder would do."

And Hugo's voice, quiet and respectful: "I believe the Manchesters have one, sir. That's quite a little distance, however."

"I guess we can manage it."

So Hugo knew of that ladder! I sat on the stairs and tried to think that out, until by the sounds outside I gathered that the two men had started for the Manchester place. Then, still confused, I slipped into the library. Confused, because once again the Inspector and I had shifted opinions on the case. That night, searching behind the books for that scrap of paper, I was as convinced as though I had been present that Herbert Wynne had shot himself; and at the same time the Inspector had veered once more to murder, and was out hunting a ladder to prove it.

So absorbed was I that I did not hear the men returning. I was having some difficulty in locating the scrap again; indeed, at first I was certain that it had been removed, and it was necessary to take out certain books and pile them on the floor before I found it. But at one glance I was satisfied. It was not only the proper size and shape, but it was scorched and stained with powder.

I had just tucked it into the waistband of my apron when I heard a sound in the hall, and turned to see Hugo in the doorway. His face gave me a very real shock, for if ever I have seen uncontrolled rage in a human countenance it was in his. He could not even speak for a perceptible time, and then it was an effort.

"What are you looking for, miss?"

"For a book to read," I said shortly.

He had regained control of himself by that time, and his voice was more civil. "If you have found one, I'll wait and put out the light."

"This will do," I said, and took one at random. It was only later on that I found it to be a highly technical discussion of ancient Greek art, and with it under my arm I marched out. I do not believe that his eyes left me for a second, from the time he discovered me until I turned the bend at the top of the stairs. Then, listening, I heard him go outside again, and I gathered that the unlucky deputy inspector was being rescued. Apparently he and Hugo returned the ladder, for the Inspector came back into the house and took advantage of that chance to talk to me.

"We're right so far," he said cheerfully. "Somebody got out of that window Monday night. Hung by his hands and swung over to the roof."

"You mean that you found prints?" I asked incredulously.

"They're there, but they're not clearly readable. As he swung before he let go, he smeared them all over the place. Still, we've learned that much."

But when I gave him the scrap of paper, he looked rather crestfallen.

"Powder stains, all right," he commented. "Well, your guess is as good as mine on this case. And so's my bootblack's! Why would a killer shoot through a newspaper? What's the idea? Unless you hit it the other day, when you said that a murder might be planned to look like a suicide. And who stood to gain in this case by a suicide?"

He stood turning the scrap of paper over in his hand. There was no reasonable doubt that it was the one shown in the picture, or that it was a corner of the *Daily News*; and his own idea was that it had not been on the floor when the Squad had gone over the room, that scorched and torn as it was, it had not dropped until possibly the concussion of the flashlight for the pictures had loosened it.

"Would it be possible," I asked, "for someone to plan a murder so that it would look like an accident, or even suicide? But so that, in case he was suspected, he could produce this paper as a sort of alibi?"

"It would work, of course. But not if the paper is destroyed, young woman."

And then I told him of the strained relations of the past day or two between Mary and Hugo. He listened gravely.

"And then what?"

"It's clear, isn't it? Miss Juliet gave Mary that paper, and she destroyed it. Now Hugo finds you still on the case, and his alibi is gone."

He whistled, but the next minute he smiled. "And so it was Hugo who got out of the window? And Hugo for whom Paula Brent brought the ladder? It won't wash, Miss Pinkerton! It won't wash."

He went on to say that he had decided to release Paula Brent after I had gone that day; and that a check-up on Mr. Brent as to Monday night showed that he had been out of the city.

"So that's that. And now where are we?"

Then, without warning, a new element was introduced into the case.

## CHAPTER XIII

THE DOORBELL RANG, and a little fussy man who gave his name as Henderson was at the door. He wanted to see the Inspector.

"I telephoned and learned that you were here," he said. "I'd like to see you alone." He eyed me.

"You can talk before this lady."

"Well, it's like this. I didn't pick up the paper until about an hour ago, and I saw that you had been questioning Paula Brent. I live near the Brents, Inspector, and I may know something. I don't know how important it is."

"Everything's important in this case," the Inspector said.

Mr. Henderson's story was brief and to the point. He lived behind the Brents, on the next street; that is, their back yards adjoined, or almost. There was an alley between, and so their garages were across from each other, with only about twenty-five feet, the width of the alley, between them. Next door to the Brent house was the residence of a man named Elliott, also with a garage.

On Monday night Mr. Henderson had taken his family to the theater, arriving home at eleven o'clock. He had put his sedan away and gone to the house when his wife discovered that she had left her purse in the car. Somewhat annoyed, he had gone back to the garage, entering it by the narrow door toward the house.

At that moment Paula Brent drove her coupé into the Brent garage, and stopped the engine. Mr. Henderson was groping in the dark for his wife's bag, and she could have had no idea that he was there. But apparently someone had either been waiting for her in the garage or just outside of it, for the next moment he heard voices. One was hers; the other was that of Charlie Elliott, the son of the family in the next house. There was no doubt as to who it was, for she named him.

"Good heavens, Charlie Elliott! You scared me. What's the idea?"

"You know the idea, all right. Look here, Paula, haven't you made a fool of yourself long enough?"

"That's my business."

"And how about your people? What would they think if they knew what I do?"

"What *do* you know?"

Mr. Henderson was interested by that time, and rather thrilled, I gathered. But after that, their voices dropped. They were quarreling, he said, and he was sorry to hear it. Everybody in the neighborhood liked them both, and up to six months before they had been together most of the time.

"Looked like a real love affair," Mr. Henderson said. "I kind of liked to see it, myself. Good-looking young people, you know, and all that."

The quarrel was apparently a bitter one, for at last the Elliott boy had said that he was going to settle the matter once for all; see somebody and have it out with him.

"Not now!" Paula said.

"Right now!" was his reply, and he started down the alley. Mr. Henderson listened, and he was certain that Elliott did not go into his place at all, but went on down to the cross-street.

"But wait a minute," he said. "I've got ahead of my story. Before he left, he took something from her. I heard a sort of scuffle, and she said sharply, 'Give me that. Give me that, do you hear?'"

Mr. Henderson stopped to wipe his face with his handkerchief. "I came as a matter of duty, you understand," he said, in a different tone. "I like them both, and I don't believe that Charlie Elliott would kill anything. But I talked it over with my wife that night, and when she saw the paper this evening, she insisted that I see you."

"What time was it when young Elliott started?"

"About eleven fifteen, I imagine. And she didn't leave for ten minutes or so afterward."

"Oh! She left again?"

"Yes. She stayed there in the garage for some time. I gathered that she was crying and was pretty well upset, and I waited because—well, I was interested, and I didn't much like her being there alone and in trouble. As a matter of fact, I was seriously considering going over to see what I could do, when she started her car and went out again."

"What time was that?"

"It may have been eleven thirty, or thereabouts. Long enough, anyhow, for my wife gave me the devil when I got back. She's rather nervous," he added sheepishly.

I could believe that. He offered a complete picture of the subdued and dominated husband as he stood in the Mitchell hall that night, giving evidence that he would infinitely have preferred keeping to himself.

He had little more to add. He had not heard Paula's car come back, but his wife said that she had got in shortly after three thirty. They had a clock which chimed the hours. He hated the thing, but his wife liked it. She didn't sleep very well, and it was company for her.

Mr. Henderson left shortly before Hugo and the deputy inspector returned, and I had little or no time to discuss the new turn events had taken before I was compelled to retreat to the sickroom. I noticed that the Inspector looked unusually grave, however.

He sent the deputy inspector away about a quarter to eleven, and then, with Hugo leading the way, he proceeded to make a minute inspection of the house from the basement to the upper floor. I saw him stop on the landing and inspect the locked and bolted door to the servants' quarters, and he even stooped and glanced at the clothing still lying on the stairs. He saw the inverted pocket, I imagine, for he straightened and glanced at Hugo. But Hugo was imperturbable.

It was midnight when he went away. Miss Juliet had wakened by that time, so I went down at half past twelve and heated a glass of milk for her. But I must admit I was not comfortable down there. A wind was blowing outside, and the kitchen wing seemed to be even more out of repair than the rest of the house. It creaked and groaned, and once I would have sworn that the tea-kettle moved right across the top of the stove! If it had been possible to gallop upstairs with a glass of hot milk in my hand, I would have done it! As it was, I went up with my head turned over my shoulder, until I got almost to the top of the stairs. Then I fixed my eyes on the landing, and if Miss Juliet had appeared there at that minute in her white nightgown, I dare say I would have died of heart failure.

But I got to the room safely enough, and after the old lady drank the milk, she grew drowsy. Just before she dozed off, however, she asked me if Hugo had gone to bed, and seemed disappointed to learn that he had.

"I want to see him," she said. "I must see him before Arthur comes back, in the morning. He has a right to know."

She did not explain that, so at one o'clock I put on my kimono and fixed my couch for the night.

Something roused me after I had been asleep an hour or so. It sounded like a door banging somewhere, and I looked at the luminous dial of my watch. It was two o'clock, and there was a real gale going outside, although the room was quiet enough. But as I lay there, a sudden gust came in over the transom, and I could dimly see, by the distant street lights, that the curtain at the window was blowing out, and flapping in the wind.

Out, and not in! That took a moment to register in my mind, and then it meant only one thing. Someone somewhere in the house had opened either an outside door or a window.

I sat up and stared over the foot of the bed at the door into the hall, and I admit that if the handle had so much as turned, I was prepared to let out a shriek that would have reached to the police station. But it did not, and I was drawing a real breath when something happened which set my heart to hammering again. Something fell in the hall, or rather on the stairs to the third floor. There was no crash, but a dull thud, and then a complete and utter silence. I knew at once what it was.

Somebody had been going up those stairs to the third floor, and had stumbled over the clothes piled on them.

## CHAPTER XIV

FOR JUST a moment I had an irresistible impulse to crawl into bed beside Miss Juliet and cover my head with the bedclothes. The next, however, I was in the center of the floor, and listening intently. There was no further sound, and I moved to the door and put my ear against it.

There was no room for doubt. Someone was stealthily climbing the stairs to the third floor. The old stairs creaked one after the other, and one of the boards on the landing gave with a loud crack.

The next second I was out in the dark hall and feeling my way to the locked door to the back flat. I wanted Hugo; I wanted Hugo and Mary. I wanted somebody near, and the fact that, in spite of everything, I still suspected Hugo of the murder seemed at that minute to have no importance whatever.

In a condition approaching panic I groped my way through that awful darkness, and flung myself against the door. "Hugo!" I called. "Hugo!"

The next second I was falling, and that is all I remember.

When I came to, I was lying flat on my back in a room I had never seen before, and Mary, in her nightgown, was sprinkling water on my face and listening to a crashing noise overhead which sounded like the breaking down of a door. Hugo was not in sight.

"Where am I?" I asked feebly.

"In our sitting room, miss," Mary said shortly. "You fainted."

I managed to sit up and look about me. From somewhere out in the grounds a man was calling, and from overhead came that continued battering, as though a heavy body was throwing itself against a door. Mary had left me and was standing in the doorway, listening; in the doorway, for that long-locked door onto the landing was standing wide open. But a strangely changed Mary. If ever I have seen a woman look tortured, she did that night. When I spoke again to her, she did not reply.

"It's a strong door," she said, as though she was talking to herself. "It looks old and easy to break, but it's strong."

"Who's in that room?" I demanded. "Is it Hugo?"

That seemed to register. She turned and gave me a strange look. "Hugo!" she said. "Hugo is up there helping the police."

And as if to prove it, there was a call above for an axe, and Hugo passed the open doorway on a run, going downstairs apparently to get one.

I got up then, rather dizzily, and surveyed the site of my recent disaster. The door from the little sitting room onto the landing was open, as I have said, and I could see readily enough what had happened. I had thrown myself against it, and it had been partly open. In my fall I must have struck my head, perhaps on the rocker of a chair nearby, for I found a sharp bruise on my forehead later on.

The room itself was small and dreary enough, although it was very tidy. In a corner a small staircase led down into darkness, and I knew that it ended at the side door behind the parlor window. All this I took in at a glance: the room, the staircase, the open door and Mary in it. I moved unsteadily toward the doorway, to find her planted squarely in it.

"Better sit down and wait a minute, miss. You've had a bad knock."

"Let me out, Mary. I'm going upstairs."

She eyed me. "Nobody's going up those stairs," she said doggedly. "Let them fight it out themselves. You stay here."

"Don't be idiotic, Mary. I can at least go to Miss Juliet."

She moved aside, unwillingly. "I wouldn't wonder there'll be some shooting," she said. "He'll be desperate."

"He? Who?"

She shrugged her shoulders, under her cheap cotton nightgown. "You'll find out soon enough now," was all she would say, and again fell into that somber attitude of waiting and listening. For what? Even now I am uncertain as to how much Mary knew that night, or how much she merely suspected.

I looked in at Miss Juliet. She was wide awake, and staring at the door as I entered.

"What is it?" she asked anxiously. "Who is running up and down the stairs?"

Well, there was no use mincing matters. I shouted to her that the police were in the house, and that they had apparently trapped a burglar on the third floor; that he had locked himself in one of the rooms, and they were breaking down the door. But if I had expected her to show excitement, she did not.

"I hope they won't break the door," she said. "My father was so proud of the doors in this house. They are all solid walnut. Ask them to do as little damage as they can."

And that was that! I gazed at her in astonishment, but she only waved me toward the hall.

"Tell them, please."

I went out obediently, and over those piles of clothing to the upper hall. It was all a part of the strangeness of that night that I should find the Inspector there outside the closed door into Herbert's room, with Evans, the deputy inspector from Headquarters, and a lieutenant in uniform, and that none of them paid any attention to me. I can still see them, the Inspector with his gun in his hand, and the lieutenant now working with the axe. But as I arrived, the Inspector stopped them.

"Pretty solid door," he said. Then, raising his voice, he called, "Stand aside in there. I'm going to shoot this lock."

He waited a few seconds and then fired. The explosion fairly rocked the old house, but the door swung open, and the three men burst into the room. I was just behind them, and I saw standing against the wall by the head of the bed a tall, very good-looking young man, ghastly white, but with a faint smile on his face.

He moved away from the wall and faced us all squarely, still with that faint whimsical smile. "Pretty good door!" he said. "Don't make them like that any more."

"Good, but not good enough," said the Inspector, fumbling in his pockets. "Look him over, Evans."

"I'm not armed."

"I'm not looking for a gun. I want a bunch of keys."

He shrugged at that, and submitted quietly while the deputy searched him, laying out on the bureau in methodical order what he found: a monogrammed handkerchief, a gold cigarette case, a wallet, some loose money, and last of all a key ring with a number of keys. The Inspector took these last, and the young man smiled again.

"Sorry, Inspector," he said. "I can identify them all; office key, keys to my car, keys to my home. That's all. You can try them out if you like."

"I wouldn't be feeling funny, if I were in your place," said the Inspector grimly. "Take these down and try them, Jim." He passed the keys to the lieutenant, who disappeared. "How did you get into this house?"

"Maybe I found the doors open."

But the Inspector merely grunted, and went to the window.

"O'Reilly," he called, "did this bird throw anything out of the window?"

"Didn't hear anything, Inspector."

"Well, take a look around. I want a bunch of keys."

He turned back to the boy. "I'm arresting you, Elliott. I guess you know why."

"Housebreaking?"

"That will do until we find those keys."

"And then what?"

"Then I'll arrest you for the murder of Herbert Wynne, in this room, last Monday night."

He fumbled in his pockets and brought out a pair of handcuffs, and for a second or so I thought the boy was going to faint. Then he straightened himself and smiled again, faintly.

"So I killed him," he said quietly. "I killed him, but I couldn't stay away from the scene of my crime! Like a dog returning to his vomit, eh?"

"I've told you it isn't funny."

"I'm not trying to be funny. I'm trying not to cry, or fight. You don't need the bracelets. I'm coming all right."

"You bet you're coming."

We stood there, waiting. The lieutenant brought back young Elliott's keys, reporting that none of them fitted the doors in question. In the grounds, O'Reilly and Evans, the deputy inspector, were searching below the window, presumably with a flashlight. In the doorway Hugo stood like a man carved out of stone, and down in Miss Juliet's room I could hear Mary shouting to her that they had caught the burglar.

Suddenly the boy lost his debonair manner. He looked at the Inspector with rather desperate young eyes. "I'd like to stop and tell my mother," he said. "She'd take it better from me. She hasn't been well, and this will be a shock for her."

"It's a little late to be thinking about a shock for her, isn't it?" the Inspector said coldly.

The boy—he was not much more—made an odd little gesture, throwing out both hands in a helpless fashion that went to my heart. Then he got hold of himself again, shrugged his shoulders and put his hands in his pockets.

"Sorry!" he said. "My fault! Forgive these tears! And may I have a cigarette? No poison in them, save the natural poison of the natural leaf."

When no one spoke, he went to the bureau and took one from his case. In that brilliant light, with all eyes on him, he looked like a bright-haired young actor, rehearsing a bit of business. When he had lighted his cigarette, he flicked his eyes over us, and they came to rest on me. He stood looking at me thoughtfully.

"You, there," he said. "I don't know your name. Will you telephone a message for me?"

"To your mother?"

"I'll attend to that. To Paula Brent. You know her. In fact, I think you owe her something, don't you? If it hadn't been for you—but never mind that. Tell her there has been a slip-up, but she is not to worry. Will you?"

I glanced at the Inspector. But at that instant we heard the tramp of feet below, and soon after, Evans and O'Reilly came into the room. Evans held out his hand, without speaking. On his palm lay two keys on a silver ring, and he confronted the Elliott boy with them.

"These what you threw away?"

"That would be telling. Think it out for yourself," he said, with that white-lipped flippancy which fooled nobody.

"These are Herbert Wynne's keys, to the side door and to the door on the second-floor landing. His initials are on the key ring. How did you get them?"

"That," said young Elliott quietly, "I regard strictly as my own business."

CHAPTER XV

IT WAS ABOUT half past two when they took him away. He walked down the stairs jauntily enough, and he went down without the bracelets after all. I think the Inspector felt a sort of grudging admiration for the way he had carried it off, and after all there were four of them to guard him. I stood in the hall and watched that heavy-footed procession go out the front door, and something in me rebelled. That boy a killer!

Yet I knew that the case against him was practically complete, so far as the police were concerned. He had a motive, as Mr. Henderson and a good many other people knew; he had been in love with Paula Brent, probably still was. He had left her in anger on Monday night, to go and settle the matter with someone unknown. She had been frightened and had followed him somewhat later; and that the somebody he meant to settle with was Herbert Wynne was certain, for it was to the Mitchell house that she had gone.

It was one of those neatly fitting cases that the Inspector loved, as I knew. Every piece fell into place, now that he had the keys. Here was the Elliott boy in Herbert's room that night, and old Miss Juliet unconsciously cutting off his retreat; and here was the open window, and his strong young arms to swing him to the roof below, and safety. But not immediate safety.

There must have been a bad time when the Inspector threw his flashlight out onto that roof; the boy cowering behind the chimney, and the flash playing on both sides of him.

Just how Paula had discovered him there I did not know. It seemed certain, however, that she had, that she had then gone in search of a ladder, dragged it to the house and so enabled him to escape. And I had not the slightest doubt that it was Charles Elliott who, as the man in the dinner jacket, had returned the ladder to the Manchester property.

Tragic as the situation was, I had to smile at the sheer audacity with which that entire escape was carried through, and at the thought of Inspector Patton smoking quietly on the front porch, while those two youngsters calmly used that ladder and then politely returned it to where it belonged. As a matter of fact, later on we were to learn that when the Inspector left me Monday night to investigate a sound at the rear of the house, he almost fell over that ladder as it lay on the ground.

That was one time when his theory of working in the dark failed him!

But I only learned that later, and after much grief and further trouble had made all that relatively unimportant. What I knew that night, as they took the boy away, was that he was in line for the chair; and I felt I could not bear it.

I knew well enough what would happen. I had seen it too often. The District Attorney's office would make its case, using only what it required to do so, and eliminating everything which conflicted with it. That scrap of powder-stained newspaper would never be brought into evidence; nor another thing which occurred to me as I once more prepared for what was left of the night. Herbert had started to undress when he was shot. That didn't look as though Charlie Elliott had entered the house with him; and if he had not, then how had he got in?

It was easy enough to explain his presence this night, provided he had killed Herbert. He could have taken the keys from his pocket. They were Herbert's own keys. But on Monday night he would not have had those keys. And again, even granting that he had killed Herbert Wynne, why had he taken the keys from him? What mystery lay behind them, and his reckless entrance tonight into the house which, above all others, he should have avoided? And was this his first visit? What about that figure I had seen on the landing, the night I had found Hugo asleep in the parlor? What about the man who had bumped into Florence Lenz? Had Charlie Elliott been that figure, that man?

I sat down on my sofa and held my head. I had a lump the size of a goose egg on it, and my brain felt like a cheese soufflé, but I had to do my thinking then, if ever; I knew that something terrible was going to happen if I did not.

Miss Juliet was awake but quiet, and in the lower hall I could hear

Hugo at the telephone, reporting the night's events to Doctor Stewart and to Mr. Glenn. Mary was nowhere in sight; I had seen her face as Charlie Elliott was taken downstairs, and it had puzzled me even in that moment of stress. She had looked at the boy, and then she had turned hard relentless eyes on Hugo, following the others. But he had not looked at her.

It was the door on the landing, I found, which most puzzled me. That is, outside of Charlie Elliott being in the house that night at all. I gave that up. It seemed plain idiocy to me, for if he had left anything incriminating there, he must have known that the Homicide Squad would have found it, unless it was that he was afraid he had left some prints on the window sill.

That was possible, and after Hugo had hung up the receiver below and gone to bed, I invented an excuse and went up to look. But if Charlie Elliott had left any readable prints on that sill—and I had the Inspector's word that he had not—there was no sign of them now. Only in one corner a bit of the print powder which the police had used on them.

I stood there, looking around that bare little room. Like the rest of the house, Herbert Wynne might never have lived there, for any trace of occupancy he had left. But I noticed something that the police had apparently overlooked. The bed had been moved somewhat. It stood four or five inches away from the wall, and not entirely straight.

It must have been three o'clock by that time, and three o'clock in the morning is a low hour for nurses as well as patients. But I had to look under that bed, and around it. I hated the room; I hated the whole job. Nevertheless I examined it carefully, and, finding nothing, I got down on the floor and crawled under it. I had had one case where an important paper was hidden under a bed slat, and I was not going to make another mistake.

But as I have said, that room was filled with ghosts for me, and my head was jumping anyhow. I got underneath somehow, and on my back at that; and I had no sooner done so than something touched my ankle. I lay there, helpless and absolutely paralyzed, and the next minute it gave another soft shove against my knee.

Then I yelped, and I imagine I hold the world's record for the lying broad leap. I simply gathered my muscles together and shot out, and why I didn't carry the bed with me I do not know. I was out in the hall before I dared to look back. Then I saw that it was Mary's cat again; and if I had bitten it that night, it would have died of tetanus.

I suppose, in order to make it interesting at this point, I should have gone back into the room and found a clue there. But it has not been my experience that criminals go about dropping cuff-links for the police to discover. And I did not go back into that room. Not that night, at least.

A nurse has to learn to act, and so I probably looked calm enough when

I went back to Miss Juliet. She was still awake. Although she had accepted the story of a burglar calmly, I was not sure that she had believed it, and I have wondered since if some inkling of the truth had come to her that night. Did she know she was in danger? How could she know?

I cannot think so, and yet something she requested might be so construed. I had been rubbing her with alcohol, after that experience on the third floor, when unexpectedly she said, "I shall want to see my clergyman tomorrow, Miss Adams."

"Very well, Miss Juliet."

"I want to make a statement to my lawyer first, and then to speak to my clergyman. Mary knows who he is. You can tell her."

"A statement? Can't that wait until you are stronger?"

"I may never be any stronger," she said, in her flat voice. And added, as if to reassure me, "After all, I am an old woman, my dear. I am living on borrowed time at the best."

I did the usual thing, of course; told her she was getting better all the time, and so on. But my mind was occupied with only the one thing. She was going to make a statement of some sort! A formal statement, signed.

I took that to my sofa with me later, along with my bump and my headache. What sort of statement? Would it involve Charlie Elliott still further? After all, what had she seen that night when she climbed the stairs? What had she told Mr. Glenn so that he would say, or shout, "I don't believe it. I don't care what he told you. I don't believe it."

I had thought that that had referred to Herbert, but did it? Suppose that when Miss Juliet went up the stairs Monday night, she had found Charlie Elliott in the room above? Suppose, then, that all the time she lay in her bed, and I on the couch at its foot, she had known that he was on the roof? And suppose that her later excursion to the third floor while I slept was to see if he was still there, or had escaped?

Then all those days she had lain in her bed, knowing something which she had concealed. And now she was about to tell it, and to send that boy to the chair. To save her own soul, and send him to the chair! Her lawyer and then her clergyman, and that bright-haired boy her burnt offering.

It made me shudder.

I was convinced that I was right, but it was daylight before I thought of a plan, and that not a very hopeful one. Yet, in a way, it had possibilities. After all, it was her indignation that Paula Brent had been questioned by the police which had apparently crystallized her resolution. Evidently that ancient love affair of hers with Paula's grandfather had never been entirely forgotten. And my plan was simply to get Paula there before the attorney came, and to have her plead with the old lady for silence.

I think now that it would have worked, and I put it among the tragic failures of my career that I did not make myself clear when I finally got Paula on the telephone. She understood well enough. She agreed to come. But what with her terror and excitement over the news of Charlie Elliott's arrest, she somehow mistook the hour. I had told her nine o'clock, and she came at ten.

She was just an hour too late.

CHAPTER   XVI

I HOPE NEVER to live through another morning like that one of Friday, the eighteenth of last September.

The first thing that went wrong was the arrival of Inspector Patton, slightly smug with success and, what is rare with him, inclined to be garrulous. That was at half past eight, and Paula was due at nine. He had apparently settled the case and thrown all caution to the winds, for he called me down into the library and closed the door.

"You look half dead," he observed, inspecting me. "You'll need a rest after this case. But I guess it's over."

"Naturally!" I said with some bitterness. "I know it. Who better? Why should you care whether he did it or not? You've got your case, and that's what you want, isn't it?"

"You're like all women. Because a man happens to be good-looking, you can't believe he's a rascal."

"I can't believe he's a fool, either. Why did he come back again, last night? And maybe a night or so ago, too? Tell me that."

"What does it matter, now? We're not interested in last night, or the night before. We're interested in Monday night, and that's all."

"You would be!" I said. "Personally, I don't think you've touched this story. You've got your case, but you have enough left over to make another. Why did Charlie Elliott fire that shot through a newspaper?"

He smiled. "Who said he did? That scrap of paper was from a *News* of the week before."

I stared at him. "A week old?"

"Our fellows looked it up. No mistake about it, Miss Pinkerton! And as for his coming back, you know why he did that, and so do I."

"I suppose you mean the prints on the window sill?"

"I thought you'd get that. Yes."

He settled down in his chair and drew out his pipe, and I had a cold sensation of despair. He was going to go over the whole story. I knew what that meant. So long as he remained around the place, I could not smuggle

Paula into Miss Juliet's room. And it was no use to try to escape. When I said my patient needed me, he merely called to Hugo to tell Mary to stay with her, and calmly went on talking.

Under any other circumstances I would have been interested, to say the least; and even as it was, I followed him clearly enough, if I did spend most of the time watching the drive for Paula Brent. He explained first what, to me at least, had remained a mystery so far, just how and why he had had the house surrounded, and had caught Charlie Elliott as he had. After that semi-absurd watch of the night before, divided between Mr. Glenn and the doctor, he had put a man on the grounds "on general principles," as he said. But also, after hearing Mr. Henderson's story the evening before, he had had young Elliott "tailed." He had put a good operative on the case, and then had gone back to his office.

"You see, I held something out on you that I'd known for a day or two," he said, eying me. "No use making you nervous, you know. That bolt on the door upstairs, the one on the landing, wasn't much use. Not any, in fact. It had been sawed off, so that it appeared to be on the job, but wasn't. It fooled me for a while. It fitted pretty closely, and there was no key to unlock the door and test it. It stood to reason, then, that anybody with keys to that door and to the side door below could get in and out whenever they wanted. That's what Herbert Wynne did, anyhow. In spite of the old lady, he could come and go at night pretty much as he liked, provided, of course, the servants had gone to bed."

"Did Hugo know about the bolt?"

"He says he didn't."

"And you believe that?"

"I believe this. I believe Hugo was as worried about this fellow getting into the house as anybody, and as puzzled."

But that door, and its sawed-off bolt, had played their part in what he called the solution of the crime.

"Elliott had to get in somehow," he said. "He got in Monday night and committed the murder. He got part of the way in on Tuesday night, and you spoiled it. He escaped through the door on the landing, of course; again on Wednesday night, when he knocked down Glenn's secretary and gave her a sore knee for him to be sorry for." He grinned. "And again last night.

"Now it isn't hard to know how he got in. He'd taken those keys from the body, so that was simple enough. But how did he get in the first night? That's the question."

"He won't tell you?"

"No."

"You surprise me!" I said, with the sarcasm he detests.

"Still fighting for the blond-haired boy!" he observed. "Well, that comes of letting a woman in on a thing like this. She gets carried away by her emotions."

"*Letting* me in? I was dragged in, and you know it."

He let that go, and went back to the story of the night before. After Mr. Henderson's statement, he had put the operative on the case, and then gone to his office at Headquarters. He often sleeps there, and he had had a hunch that something might happen.

It did. At half past one the operative watching the Elliott house had seen young Elliott slip out quietly, using a rear door and not taking his car, and having followed him to the Mitchell property, found the policeman hidden in the shrubbery on the other side of the house and notified him. Then he had hurried to the nearest telephone and called Headquarters.

When the Inspector and Evans arrived, young Elliott had already entered the house by the side entrance, and they found the door there standing open. They had brought a police lieutenant along also, and he remained outside at first, to watch with O'Reilly for a possible escape.

The Inspector and Evans had gone in by the same route, moving very quietly, and they had just reached the top of the stairs when they had what amounted to a real shock, there in the servants' sitting room and in black darkness. Something had given a terrible shriek and then pitched into the room almost at their feet, and not moved.

"That was you," said the Inspector, "and the only reason I didn't turn and bolt down those stairs was because Evans was behind me!"

Well, they turned a flash on me, and at first they thought I had been killed.

"It was a bad thirty seconds or so," the Inspector said, smiling grimly. "It looked as though he'd got you. I don't mind telling you that I thought I'd lost my most valuable assistant!"

But the beans were spilled by that time, he said. There had been enough noise to rouse everybody in the house, and to warn Elliott.

"He was warned all right. A dynamite explosion couldn't have done it any better! But he couldn't get out this time. He might have tried the roof again, but he had no little lady friend to help him down, and he probably saw our fellows below anyhow. What he did was to lock the door and then wait. He hadn't anything to gain by it, but that's what he did. Just to make it harder!"

"Or to gain time to look for whatever he was after," I said. "I suppose that hadn't occurred to you?"

"The prints on the sill? He'd had plenty of time for that."

"But he didn't touch them, did he?"

He looked at me thoughtfully. "Well, no. Now that you speak of it, he didn't. But he didn't have to. As he swung off, he'd smeared them pretty well, and he'd realized that. What are you driving at?"

"I'm intimating that he was there to get something," I said rather sharply. "And that it was not fingerprints, unless they were under the bed."

"Under the bed? Nonsense!"

"Then why was the bed moved away from the wall? Or perhaps you didn't notice that?"

He got up, and grinned rather sheepishly. "One up for you," he said. "No, I didn't notice it. I'm a rotten policeman, but you're the only one who knows it! I'll go up and take a look around!"

But he did not go at once. "What are you thinking about this case?" he asked. "You've got an opinion. I can see that. And it's not mine."

"It is not. There was a time when you were certain this case was a suicide, and I believed it was a murder. Perhaps you remember that? Now you would stake your reputation that it was a murder, and . . ."

"And that I have the murderer. I certainly would. Well?"

"I'm still trying to explain to myself why that scrap of newspaper had powder marks on it. And whether, after all, Paula Brent doesn't believe that Herbert left a letter explaining that he had killed himself, and sent that boy to get it. How deep was he in the market?"

"All he had. That wasn't enough to drive him to suicide."

"Well then, something which might explain this danger he was always talking about."

"How do you know there was such a danger? Or that the girl didn't invent that story later on, to protect this Elliott boy?"

"He was carrying a gun. Monday night wasn't the first night Herbert had carried that gun."

"How do you know he was, before that night? That's her story, too."

"All right," I said. "Then tell me where he got the money to take out all that insurance? And enough more to speculate with on a margin? That's what you've got left over, isn't it? You've got your case, but you have all that left over. What are you going to do about it?"

He did not answer that, for the telephone rang, and as it was the District Attorney, he had to leave at once and go downtown.

When I saw him again, it was too late. The second tragedy had happened.

WHEN HE HAD GONE, I took a final despairing look outside, but Paula was still not in sight, and so I went up to Miss Juliet. To my surprise Mary was not there, and it was Hugo who stood by the bed. It was the first time I had seen him in the room, and if ever I have seen a man both alarmed and angry, he was that morning. He was standing by the bed, and Miss Juliet was talking, in her low monotonous voice. The door was open, and when he heard me on the landing, he made a gesture of caution and her voice ceased.

He brushed past me without a word, and soon after that Mr. Glenn arrived, and I heard Hugo talking to him in the lower hall. He was still upset, apparently, and Mr. Glenn seemed to be conciliating him. However that was, Hugo came up in a few minutes to say that the lawyer wanted to see me in the library, and so I went down again.

Rather to my surprise, I found the secretary in the hall. She was standing in front of the mirror powdering her nose, and she grinned at me in the glass.

"You don't feel weak, or anything?" she sang out at me.

"Weak? Why?"

"I'd like to try that ammonia stunt on you, for a change!"

"The next time you throw a fit like that, be sure there's no trained nurse around," I told her, and went into the library.

Mr. Glenn was there, neat and immaculate and rather too well dressed, as usual. But he was nervous, too. He was pacing up and down the room when I entered it.

"This is a bad business, Miss Adams," he said.

"Very bad indeed."

"Does Miss Juliet know about it?"

"Not yet. No."

"That's right. Keep it from her as long as you can. Tell Mary not to carry her a paper. I can trust Hugo, but not Mary." He took another turn about the room, while I stood waiting. "As a matter of fact, I think the old lady knows already that this boy is guilty, Miss Adams. She intimated as much to me last night."

"Then why keep the arrest from her?" I asked. "After all, if she knows . . ."

He hesitated. "I suppose I might as well tell you. She intends to make a statement this morning. Or perhaps you know that."

"I do."

"Well, this statement should be as unprejudiced as possible. She saw something last Monday night, and that is what she wants to tell."

"She saw Charlie Elliott, I suppose, Mr. Glenn?"

"That's for her to say," he said shortly. "The point is that, right or wrong, she thinks she has not long to live, and she wants to tell her story before she goes. As a matter of fact, it was to be kept in my safe, and only used in case of some miscarriage of justice. But this arrest changes things. She needn't know that, however."

"She needn't make the statement at all!" I said. And then, what with Paula not getting there in time and strain and lack of sleep and all the rest, I simply made a fool of myself and burst into tears.

I could hear him talking, but I could not stop crying. He said the police had the case anyhow, and that everybody knew that Charlie Elliott had been crazy about Paula for years; and jealous of her, too. But when he went upstairs, I was still crying, and that gibbering idiot of a Florence was standing in the doorway staring at me with hard amused eyes.

"And did she get her feelings hurt!" she said. "And didn't he pet her, or anything?"

"Oh, for God's sake keep quiet," I said, and went out on the porch for air and to escape from her. I found Paula just coming up the steps.

She was white and distracted, and I had to draw her around the corner of the house, for Florence was watching from the hall. I was ready to shout at her, to tell her what the delay had cost; but one look at her was enough, and anyhow it was too late. She looked as nearly frantic as I have ever seen a human being look, and she simply caught at me and held on.

"Is the Inspector here?" she demanded. "I've got something to tell him. Are they all crazy, down there?"

"They found him, here in the house."

"Is the Inspector here? Don't talk. Tell me!"

"The District Attorney sent for him. Now listen, Paula. Try to be quiet and listen to me. There's no hurry. You've got months; weeks, anyhow. What you have to tell the Inspector can wait."

"But it can't wait. Why should Charlie Elliott be under arrest, when I ought to be?"

I almost shook her. "Don't talk like that. You didn't kill Herbert Wynne, and you know it."

"I got Charlie into this mess," she said doggedly. "I've got to get him out. Listen, Miss Adams, I gave him those keys he had last night. They were mine."

"*You* gave them to him?"

"Don't look at me like that. I don't care what you think about me. I gave him those keys, to get something of mine that I'd left in that room."

It is not easy to shock me, but I was shocked at that moment. By and large, I know as much as anyone about the free and easy ways of this generation of youngsters, and I have always believed that the free and easiness is a matter of manners, not morals. It seems strange now, but my first reaction had nothing to do with murder, but with the fact that this girl, wide-eyed and young, had had keys which had enabled her to visit Herbert Wynne in that upper room of his; and that she had done so.

But I rallied myself, and I hope my face showed nothing. Not that I think she would have noticed, anyhow.

"What was it that you had left in that room?"

"My bag."

"And when?"

She hesitated, and looked at me with quick suspicion. "I'd rather talk to the Inspector."

"And make things worse!" I said. "I'm friendly, at least. I warn you now that the Inspector is not. Nor any of the police. When did you give Charlie Elliot those keys?"

"I don't see——"

"Listen," I said brutally. "Do you want to send him to the chair? Don't you see what I mean? If you go to the police and tell them that Charlie Elliott had your keys on last Monday night, that's the end of him."

She paled, and drew a quick breath.

"I'll tell you this, for your own sake," I went on. "They know a lot that you don't realize; they know about the ladder, and they think they know who got it, for one thing. Maybe they can't prove that, but they'll try. And they know that Charlie Elliott was jealous of Herbert, and that you two quarreled about him on Monday night. What's the use of making things worse by telling about those keys until you have to? And damaging your reputation into the bargain?"

She lifted her chin at that. "I've done nothing I'm ashamed of," she said. "And I've told you part of the truth anyhow. Charlie Elliott came here last night on an errand for me."

"To get your bag? Don't be foolish."

"To get something."

I turned as if to go. "All right," I said. "I've done my best for you. Maybe you'd better run to Police Headquarters and let them work on you for a little while. I have a lot of things to do."

But she ran after me and caught my arm. "Listen," she said. "I've got to talk to somebody, and I know you're friendly. It wasn't a bag. It was a letter. I've told you there was a letter."

"You'll have to go further than that," I said shortly. "If you know something that will help Charlie Elliott out of this trouble, I'm simply telling you that I'd be glad to hear about it, and to help if I can. If that isn't enough, then I'll go back to my patient. What about this letter, and where is it? You'd better come clean."

"I'll tell you," she said in an exhausted voice. "Can't we sit down somewhere? I haven't slept or eaten for days."

She looked it, too, poor child. I found an old bench in a corner of the grounds, somewhat screened from the house, and there she tried to tell me what she knew. It was not a great deal, as it turned out, and it sounded rather fantastic, to tell the truth, when I finally did get it.

Some of it, of course, I already knew. Within the last few months, Herbert had got mixed up in something shady. She thought that it involved Hugo, but whatever it was—and obviously she did not know except that it was "not bootlegging"—it had finally dawned on him that Hugo, or whoever it was, was not playing fair with him; and that he was possibly in danger of his life.

It was after they were fired at that he began to talk of their going away together. She knew then that he was frightened, and she tried to get from him what the trouble was, and who was after him. But he would not tell her. But here came the matter of the letter again.

"I'll put that in a letter and leave it for you," he told her. "So if somebody gets me, you can pin the rap on the proper party!"

He had said it with a laugh, but the idea had taken hold of her, and she insisted that he do it.

"You can see why," she told me. "It wasn't that I wanted it for that reason; but if he wrote such a letter, and Hugo, or whoever it was, knew there was such a letter, it would keep him from—bothering Herbert."

Well, it was not a bad idea at that, and it appeared that Herbert had thought so, too, after a long delay. There had been no more trouble, apparently, after that one attempt to shoot him; and on that last night, Monday, he had been very cheerful.

"I've got it all set down, honey," he told her. "But I think it's all right anyhow. We'll be getting out of here pretty soon. As soon as the market settles down."

He had promised to give her the letter the next day, and she was to place it in a bank vault. In the meantime he had hidden it in a safe place; she thought in his own room.

I have said that it sounded fantastic; like the juvenile vaporings of an immature mind, trying to impress a romantic girl by working on her fears and her sense of drama. But there is something fantastic about all unusual crimes, and after all, there was that shot to account for. Also I remembered something the Inspector had said to me when I took my first case for him. "Working on crime is a lot like working in a steel mill; never sit down on anything until you spit on it first. It may be hot."

But the point of all this was that, after Monday night, first Paula herself, and later Charlie Elliott, had set to work to find that letter, and had failed. I tried to think that out.

"Then," I said, "it was this letter that Charlie Elliott was trying to find last night?"

"Yes. I'd tried to once myself, but you came up the stairs. You may remember. You screamed."

Did I remember! I could have shaken her then and there, small and woebegone as she looked.

"And nothing else? Just a letter?"

I thought she was less assured when she replied to that. "What else could there be?"

"And it hasn't been found?"

She shook her head. "I don't think it is there," she said. "I think they got it and destroyed it."

And by "they" once more I knew she meant the people in the house.

## CHAPTER XVIII

STANDING THERE with the wind blowing my uniform about me, I had a moment of doubt. Never before had I worked against the Inspector, and I felt disloyal and uncomfortable. Yet the Inspector wanted the facts, and if this girl offered one way to get at them, then it seemed to me that it was my duty to use her.

But I was convinced that Paula had not told me all the truth. Indeed, had it not been that the letter had not been found, I might have gone so far as to suspect her of planting such a letter after the crime! Certain as she was that someone inside that house had killed Herbert Wynne, she might conceivably have gone even to such a length to bring out what she felt were the facts.

But the letter had not been found, and inside that house I was certain that old Miss Juliet Mitchell was at that moment making her peace with her God, and was about to sign Charlie Elliott's death warrant.

I was roused by Paula touching my arm. "Listen," she said. "Why can't you get me into that house and upstairs? Now."

"I might, if you had come clean as I asked you."

She colored faintly. "I've told you all I can," she said. "I'll give you my word for this, Miss Adams. I'll show whatever I find to you. Absolutely. And you can tell the police."

"Then, you know where this letter is? Or was?"

"I think I do. I'm not certain."

"Why not let *me* look?"

But she made an impatient gesture. "Why should I?" she demanded. "I've trusted you, and I think you're friendly. But this is a life and death matter, and after all *they* employ you." She changed her tone. "I'm sorry, but you'll not regret it. I promise you that."

I agreed, at last. Agreed with an uncomfortable feeling that Paula was probably being shadowed all the time, and that the Inspector might come down on me with one of his rare rages when he found it out. She followed me to the front of the house, and rather to my surprise it was empty. Florence Lenz had disappeared and there was no sign of Hugo. The house was very quiet, except for Mary, scrubbing viciously somewhere in the rear.

I turned and nodded to Paula, and she slipped in, looking about her nervously. Everything was quiet as we reached the landing; Miss Juliet's door was still closed, and from behind it came the faint monotonous sound of her voice. But just as I reached the door leading into my own room, which adjoined Miss Juliet's, I heard Hugo's heavy step in the hall overhead. He was coming down from the third floor.

Both of us stopped, petrified. Then I caught Paula and shoved her— there is no other word—into my room and followed her. As I closed the door, Hugo was on the stairs above! I stood for a moment, facing the door and holding the knob, and I confess that my heart was beating a good hundred and fifty, and then some. Hugo did not stop, however. I thought he hesitated outside of Miss Juliet's door, but he went on again, and I waited until I could hear him in the lower hall before I turned.

Florence was in front of the dressing table, staring at Paula with her hard curious eyes. She had been powdering her nose, and using my powder to do it. The puff was still in her hand.

"Miss Brent, isn't it?"

"Never mind," I said shortly. "This young lady wants to talk to me. If you have anywhere else to go, I'd like my room for a few minutes."

But she was quite impervious to sarcasm. Indeed, I doubt if she heard me at all. There was a twisted little smile on her face by that time, and she ran her eyes over Paula, beginning at her feet and ending at her face.

"I'm Florence Lenz," she said. "Maybe you've heard of me?"

She meant something by that. I knew it, and Paula knew it. She drew herself up and gave the other girl look for look.

"Possibly. Is there any particular reason why I should?"

"There's plenty of reason, and you damned well know it," Florence retorted, reddening under her coating of powder. But she seemed to make an effort then, and pulled herself together.

"Mr. Glenn sent for me to come up," she explained to me. "Then the old woman in there thought of something else, so I wandered in here. I'm a notary, and she is to sign something." Her eyes flickered to Paula again, standing stiff and straight, and then to me. "Making a will, isn't she? She's got plenty of money now."

That, too, I felt, was for Paula. The scene, if it could be called that, had no meaning for me; but it had meaning. I knew it, or felt it. And I felt that for some unknown reason Paula was slowly reaching a breaking point. She was entirely colorless by that time, and rigid.

I went to the hall door and opened it, but although Hugo had disappeared, Mary was in the hall now. Ostensibly she was moving that clothing which still lay, trampled from the night before, on the stairs. Actually she was close to the door of Miss Juliet's room, and although her arms were loaded, I was certain that she had been listening with her ear to the door.

She started and moved away when she saw me, and I waited until she had gone down the stairs. Halfway down, she looked up again, and I began to think that I was developing a complex about Mary; that I was always looking down at her from those stairs, and she looking up with wary eyes, watching me.

Maybe I only imagine all that. Maybe, as I look back over the case, I remember certain incidents and give them a value they did not have at the time. But Mary looked back right enough, and then stumbled over a dragging garment and almost fell. And back of me in that room Paula Brent certainly stood, icily still, while Florence made up her mouth and watched her in the mirror.

I gave Paula a quick look, and motioned to the hall. "We'll have to talk another time, Miss Brent," I told her. "If you don't mind waiting somewhere, I can see you later."

I closed the door behind her when she went, and I knew well enough that she was on her way to the third floor almost before I could turn around. I glanced at the dressing table, and sure enough there was powder all over it; over my instruments and my hypodermic tray as well, and I gave that young woman a piece of my mind as I straightened it. But I might as well have reproved one of the old silhouettes framed on the wall. She never even heard me.

"Is there any particular reason why I should know her!" she repeated. "I'll say there is. And I'll say she's got a hell of a lot of nerve, hanging around this house!"

Only the opening of the connecting door saved me from a charge of assault and battery with intent to kill. It was Mr. Glenn, and he seemed relieved to find me there.

"Come in, Miss Adams," he said, "and you, too, Miss Lenz. I want you to witness a signature."

He looked disturbed and very sober, and I saw that he had a paper in his hand. To my surprise I found Hugo there, also. Miss Juliet, her eyes closed, was lying back on the pillows; and I saw that Florence, well dusted with powder, was gazing at her with an expression of avid interest. From the bed her eyes traveled about the room, taking in every detail of its worn dignity, its shabby gentility.

Mr. Glenn had approached the bed. "You won't think better of this, Miss Juliet?" he said.

She sensed what he said rather than heard it, and shook her head. "I must do what is right, Arthur. I'm sorry; but I have told you the truth. Now let me sign it."

He turned to us. Hugo had not moved.

"I have read this statement to Miss Mitchell. She acknowledges it to be correct, but while she wishes to sign it before witnesses, she prefers to keep the contents secret, for the time at least. Is that correct?" He looked at her.

"It is correct, Arthur."

So the four of us stood by while she signed with his pen, in a wavering old hand that still had some faint distinction: "Juliet Mitchell." Then she herself took it, folded it over so that only the signature showed, and Hugo and I both wrote our names in the opposite corner. Hugo's hand, I noticed, was shaking. That finished, Florence affixed her notarial seal and Mr. Glenn put the paper carefully into his brief case, and went back to the bed.

"I suppose you realize the importance of what you have done, Miss Juliet?" he said impressively. "What it means to several people."

She nodded. "I know you have tried, Arthur. But I have not long to live, and I must right a great injustice."

I thought she glanced at Hugo as she said that. But he said nothing. He turned and went out of the room, and Mr. Glenn followed him almost immediately, taking Florence with him.

I had plenty to think about for the next fifteen minutes or so; so much that I almost forgot Paula. For one thing, Miss Juliet's pulse was thin and reedy, and she seemed exhausted to the point of coma. It was not until I had telephoned for Doctor Stewart and had gone into my room for some spirits of ammonia that I really thought of Paula at all, and then it was because I found her there, looking utterly dispirited.

"I can't get out," she said. "Hugo is sweeping the hall."

"Did you find anything?"

She shook her head hopelessly. "They've got it," she said. "And if that old woman in there knows it, then death is too good for her."

She did not mention Florence at all.

I went back to Miss Juliet. I had not told the girl about that scene which had just ended, and I did not intend to. It seemed to me that if that statement of the old lady's incriminated Charlie Elliott, Paula would learn it soon enough; and I had a shrewd idea, too, that in spite of everything she was more fond of Charlie Elliott than she realized. That Herbert's death had horrified rather than grieved her, and that her romance or infatuation, or whatever it might have been, had been almost over when he died.

I did not see Paula again until that evening. When Doctor Stewart came and I went in again for my hypodermic, she was gone.

All this which I have just written took place on Friday morning, the eighteenth of September. Herbert Wynne had been dead for almost four days, and Charlie Elliott had been under arrest since the night before. From the absence of reporters at the doorbell and in the grounds I gathered that public interest now centered around Police Headquarters; but shortly after Mr. Glenn left, somewhere around eleven o'clock, I saw two young men in paint-spattered overalls carrying a long ladder in through the gates, and I went to the back window of my room and watched them as they went around the house.

They were quite businesslike, but apparently they had forgotten their paint! They put the ladder up against the wall not far from my window, and both climbed to the roof of the ell.

Well, my patience was pretty much exhausted by that time, so I got a broom from the housemaid's closet in the hall and, reaching out the window, I gave that ladder a good shove. It fell with a crash, and the last I saw of those two reporters they were peering dejectedly over the tin gutter of the roof, and muttering to themselves. Later on I learned that they had stayed on that roof for five hours, not daring to call for help! And it was a tin roof, and a hot September day.

I never thought of them again. It appears that one or two cameramen from other papers appeared, and that they appealed for help from them. But one rude young competitor only put his thumb to his nose at them, and another took their pictures. It was the police who rescued them at last, after threatening to leave them there all night.

Sometimes I think of them, marooned on that roof while, inside the house, a tragedy was taking place; probably seeing the Medical Examiner's car in the drive and people coming and going, going slowly crazy while another story broke, and nothing to do about it except, like Charlie Elliott, either to fight or cry.

But they served a very important purpose, nevertheless, in the answer to our mystery. When the dénouement came, it was as though we had been putting together one of those jigsaw puzzles, and they had found the key to the picture.

Mr. Glenn had not left the house until after eleven o'clock, and so it was probably nearly twelve when the doctor arrived. I knew that it was after one when the Inspector, hurriedly sent for, was reached while he was eating his lunch, and he got there shortly afterward.

Just when Paula Brent left the house I do not know.

What happened, as accurately as I can remember, was as follows:

The doctor had ordered a hypodermic of nitroglycerin for Miss Juliet, and he remained with her, his fingers on her thin wrist, while I went down to the kitchen for some sterile water with which to give it. Mary was alone in the kitchen, and gave it to me herself.

I cleaned my hypodermic, and then, going back to my tray, I got the tube of tablets. There was no mistake about it. I remember looking at the label of the tube, which was not a fresh one, shaking out the tablet, dropping it into the glass barrel of the syringe, and watching it dissolve there. I remember all that, just as I remember pinching up the flesh of Miss Juliet's withered old arm, and her wincing at the jab of the needle. I remember, too, that Doctor Stewart still held his fingers on her pulse, and that I moved about the room, straightening it after my habit; and that I then went into the bathroom, where I washed my hypodermic needle and cleaned it with alcohol.

I was there when the doctor called to me. Miss Juliet looked rather strange. She had grown tense and was twitching somewhat. The doctor was leaning over her.

"What is it? Pain?"

She did not say anything, and he looked puzzled.

"What did you give her?" he asked me.

"Just the usual dose of nitroglycerin, doctor."

That apparently satisfied him, and he drew up a chair and sat beside the bed. After ten minutes or so the twitching stopped, but she still seemed rather rigid, so he ordered another hypodermic. The interval between them was perhaps a half hour. I could feel that curious rigidity when I gave the second injection, but I had seen angina before, and some people stiffen under the pain.

I repeated my previous procedure, went to the bathroom, cleaned the syringe, put away my tray. I was in my room when I heard the doctor again, and this time he was fairly shouting for me.

I ran back, to see Miss Juliet in a convulsion on the bed.

Over and over again I have lived those next few minutes. I have even dreamed about them. In these dreams I am once again beside the big walnut bed, with Doctor Stewart across from me and staring down at the old lady, and she is having that convulsion, jerking and twitching; and on her unconscious face that dreadful *risus sardonicus*, the sardonic grin which almost at once began to fade into the mask of death.

How long that lasted I do not know. Time means nothing in such a situation. As the grin began to fade, I remember that I glanced up at the doctor, and at that instant she gave a final convulsive shiver and then relaxed.

The doctor stared at her, then straightened and looked across the bed at me.

"She is dead! For God's sake, what did you give her?"

## CHAPTER XIX

I STOOD THERE, stupidly looking down at her. My own heart seemed to have stopped, and my mind, too. I was certainly not thinking.

"Wake up, woman! She's dead, I tell you. What was in that hypodermic?"

"What you ordered. You can look at the tube. You gave it to me yourself, Monday night."

"Bring that syringe here."

"I've washed it, doctor."

"Then bring me the tube. Bring in your tray."

His hands were shaking as he examined it, but he went over it carefully. There was not much on it; the usual morphia, but the tube containing it still sealed; the amyl-nitrite ampoules; some cotton and alcohol; and the nitroglycerin. One of these tablets he shook out in his hand and then put to his lips. Whatever he had expected to discover, he was evidently disappointed.

I was terribly frightened; more frightened than I had ever been in my life. I had not even time for pity. Every ounce of me was concentrated fiercely on self-protection.

"I gave her exactly what you ordered."

"How do I know you did? She's dead, and nitroglycerin didn't cause that spasm."

"I've never made such a mistake in my life!"

"Mistake or—something else."

"Good God, doctor! What do you think I gave her? Or why would I want to kill her?"

He made no reply to that. He came close to me, and I saw that his forehead was beaded with fine drops of perspiration. He got out his handkerchief and wiped it.

"Listen, Miss Adams," he said. "I believe that this unfortunate woman here has been poisoned. I don't know why, or by whom. I'm making no accusations. I'm not even certain of the fact. But I believe she was poisoned, with an alkaloidal poison of some sort."

"What sort?"

"Strychnia," he said grimly. "Strychnia. That's my guess, and it is yours."

"I don't know what you mean," I said wildly. "There's no strychnia on that tray."

"Not now." He put his handkerchief away, turned to the bed, and then faced me again.

"I prefer to say nothing more until I have called the police. You will remain in this room, please, until they arrive."

I tried to laugh, then. "And make me a prisoner! You can't mean that, doctor."

"I do mean it. And"—he added more slowly—"I begin to wonder if Hugo was right after all."

"What has Hugo to do with it?"

"He hasn't trusted you, for one thing. You can tell your story to the police when they get here, but I'll say just this. I don't know what you are doing here. You were not my choice, if it comes to that. But Hugo has suspected all along that you were here for some purpose of your own. He has found you where you have had no business to be, and he wanted you sent off the case; he asked me to do that yesterday."

"I wish you had," I said bitterly. "I'd have been glad enough to go."

"That's as it may be. And I'll take that hypodermic, if you please. You were pretty quick about washing it!"

He slipped the case into his pocket, along with the other tube from the tray, and started out. But he hesitated at the door. His intention was clear enough; he wanted to lock me in. But he did not quite dare. I stood in the middle of the room and defied him.

"If you do that, doctor," I said clearly, "I shall shout for help from a window!"

He went out then, and in spite of that quiet old figure on the bed he slammed the door behind him. Then I could hear him running down the stairs, and shortly afterward, shouting at the telephone. He was trying to get through to the Inspector, who was evidently still closeted with the District Attorney. But he did get the Medical Examiner. I could hear that.

My anger had left me by that time. I went over to the bed, and looked down at the quiet figure lying there. Death had smoothed that terrible grin from Miss Juliet's face, so that now she looked younger, and very placid. I had no fear of the doctor's accusations, but I had a real regret for the method of her passing. Perhaps she had not had much time left, as she had said the night before; but little or much, she had been entitled to it. And she had not seen her clergyman after all!

I was still dazed, of course. I made no move when the door opened, and Mary came in. She was not crying. Her face was a sort of bluish white, and she paid no attention to me whatever. She stood on the other side of the bed, looking down at the body, and then she did a queer thing. She made the sign of the cross over it, in the air. Only after that did she speak to me at all.

"Hugo's feeling poorly, miss. I said I'd tell you."

"You'd better get the doctor, Mary. He wants me to stay here."

She looked at me. "What's the use, now?" she said. "It's all over, isn't it? All over and done?"

"I'm afraid it's all over for Miss Mitchell, if that is what you mean."

She went out again, and I followed her to the landing. In the hall below, the doctor was pacing back and forth, his head sunk on his breast. He heard me, and told me sharply not to disturb anything; to leave the body alone, and the room. Then Mary told him about Hugo, and he went back with her toward the kitchen.

I suppose it was a half hour before the Medical Examiner got there, and with nothing to do I had plenty of time to think. I looked at Miss Juliet, lying so peacefully on her bed, and I had a bitter moment when I felt that, since she was to go, it was a pity that she had not gone before she signed Charlie Elliott's death warrant. For that it was, I knew. And now there would not even be the respite of a few days. Mr. Glenn would have to produce it, and at once.

It was only then that I began to see a possible connection between Miss Juliet's murder, if it was murder, and that confession. Suppose it had been intended that she never make that statement? Suppose someone, with access to that tray of mine, had skillfully plotted to kill her, so that it would never be signed?

I stood at the window, twisting a curtain cord in my hand, and tried to think that out. Who had had access to my tray recently? Recently, because I had already given her more than one hypodermic from that tube, with perfectly normal reactions. Hugo and Mary, of course, and even the doctor that morning, while I was downstairs getting water. And of course there had been Florence Lenz.

I thought about Florence. Had she been acting all the time, and was she really the blatant and rather disagreeable person she seemed to be? Or was there something else behind that frivolous manner of hers? Had she known Herbert Wynne? Would she have had any motive for putting Miss Juliet Mitchell out of the way? What lay behind her slipping into that room when she came upstairs? She had stood directly over the tray. It was covered with the powder she had been using. Wasn't it possible that that very powder was a sort of blind? Suppose she had been working over the tray, putting something into that nitroglycerin tube, when she heard me just outside?

We had come up the stairs very quietly. She could have had only a second or two of warning. Then what was more likely than a wild dash at my powder, spilling it in her excitement, in every direction?

But, once again, all of this was simply one of those devices to which we all resort when we want to protect ourselves from some thought which is not bearable. I knew all along that I would have to come to Paula Brent.

She had hated Miss Juliet, and was convinced that she had had something to do with Herbert's death. Suppose that visit of hers that morning had been deliberately devised so that she could get into the house? The story of the letter an invention, and Paula determined that Miss Juliet, knowing something vital to Charlie Elliott's safety, should be put out of the way before she decided to talk?

She knew Doctor Stewart. She knew Mr. Glenn. Suppose the doctor had told her that Miss Juliet was being stimulated with nitroglycerin? Or the attorney had revealed that the old lady knew something, and was bound to tell it sooner or later? And the girl desperate, distracted.

I went back again over that little scene when the two girls met in my bedroom. There had been some deep and secret antipathy there. I had an idea that, while they had not met before, each knew about the other; and my mind once more went back to Herbert Wynne.

The Medical Examiner arrived while I was still standing there. I saw his gay little car come in, and he himself emerge, dapper as usual. I have sometimes thought that his bright car and his dandied dress were a sort of defense which he set up against what was often a gruesome business.

He was followed out of the car by a tall thin individual whom I recognized as the laboratory man from Headquarters. Doctor Stewart brought them both up, and the Medical Examiner seemed rather put out that the Inspector was not there.

"What makes you think it was poison?" he demanded.

"How would anybody know it? She was weak, but she wasn't dying. Then she gets these two hypodermics. She reacted very badly to the first, so I ordered a second."

"How far apart?"

"A half hour. The second caused the convulsion. There was *risus sardonicus,* very marked; and if you've ever seen angina cause that, you've seen more than I have."

The chemist had said nothing, but now he asked for the hypodermic and the tubes. He got them, handling them carefully and dropping them in an envelope, and then glanced at me. He knew me, but, like the Examiner, he made no sign that he did.

"Cleaned, I suppose?" He always spoke with a drawl, and now it seemed more marked than ever.

"Thoroughly. With alcohol."

"What do you think of this case?" he asked me.

Doctor Stewart glanced up angrily. "That's a question for the police, isn't it?"

"Oh, I don't know," he drawled. "After all, this young woman gave the stuff. She ought to know something, if there's anything to know."

"I think she was probably poisoned," I said quietly. "I don't know how it was done, but I venture to guess that, whatever was put into the nitroglycerin tube, whoever did it placed it there within the last twelve to fourteen hours. I had used nitroglycerin tablets before that, and they worked as they should."

He took out the tube, holding it in his handkerchief to do so, and, like the doctor, shook a tablet into his hand and put it to his tongue.

"No strychnia here, anyhow," he said. "Well, let's get busy, doctor."

"What will you want?" I asked.

"Nothing much. Some towels. We have everything else."

I shall not go into details of what followed. There was some talk of strychnia affecting the central nervous system, and so they took some spinal fluid as well as a specimen of blood from the jugular. I know that the laboratory man wanted the stomach, too, but he did not get it. The Medical Examiner wanted his lunch.

"Going to be hard enough to discover anything," said the laboratory man. "And even when these things are given by hypodermic, some of them resecrete in the stomach. Give us a chance."

"If you can't find it with what you've got, the chances are that it isn't there," said the Medical Examiner briefly, and drew off his rubber gloves.

The laboratory man lounged about the room while the other was preparing to go. He whistled softly as he moved, and Doctor Stewart eyed him without much favor. He was quite unconscious of it, however.

"Queer case, isn't it?" he drawled. "Here they have one murderer all safely locked away, and another one turns up!"

"If it *is* murder," said the Examiner, picking up his bag. "You get the idea of murder going, and you can see it everywhere. I'm still not sure that poor devil upstairs didn't kill himself, last Monday night. He may have worked out something. You never can tell."

Then they went away, quite cheerfully. I could hear them arranging to lunch together as they went down the stairs. The tall man turned back to say that there would be a tentative report that night, but that it might take longer. I thought later that it was merely an excuse, for he leaned forward and said something in a low tone.

"Watch out for yourself, little lady," he said to me. "When these poison bugs get started, they don't know where to stop."

It was while Doctor Stewart was still below with them, and while I was cleaning the rubber sheet in the bathroom, that I heard a sound in Miss Juliet's room. I went to the door, to see Hugo on his knees beside the bed, his shoulders shaking. He got up when he heard me, and started out of the room, but he seemed unsteady as he walked. He had suddenly become an old man, a tired and feeble old man.

## CHAPTER XX

IT WAS AFTER they had gone that the Inspector arrived. He said later that his car did not have to be steered any more; that it just naturally took the route to the Mitchell place and turned in there. And he took hold at once, hardly listening to the doctor's excited story.

"Examiner's been here already?" he asked. "Well, that's quick work. All right, Hugo. Go and sit down somewhere. And Miss Adams, I'll put you in charge of that room up there. Don't let anybody in. Now, doctor, if you'll come into the library, we'll talk this over."

"I protest against leaving Miss Adams in charge upstairs," said the doctor truculently.

Hugo had gone by that time, and the Inspector smiled at me and then patted me on the shoulder. "I know this young woman, doctor," he said. "It's perfectly safe to leave her here. Safe for us, anyhow. I'm not so sure about the lady!"

A chance statement which I was to remember with considerable bitterness a few hours later.

But the Inspector was not smiling when, a half hour later, he came upstairs alone and into Miss Juliet's room. He closed the door behind him.

"I've sent Stewart off," he said. "He's an ass. A pompous little bald-headed ass! But he's pretty much worked up. I have an idea that he had hoped for a new will before she died, and this ends it. Don't let him worry you."

He glanced at me with a sort of half apology, and going to the bed, stood looking down at the sheeted figure on it.

"Life's a queer business, Miss Adams," he said, "but death is sometimes queerer. Now you take this old woman. Who would want to put her out of the way, if she *was* put out of the way? She hadn't long at the best."

"No. But she should have had that, at least."

"Precisely. She's got a little money. She's going to be comfortable and without worry. Then somebody decides to get rid of her, and—she's gone. Like that!"

"But she *is* gone," I pointed out. "We can't help her now; and you'll admit that Charlie Elliott had nothing to do with this. I take it he's still safely locked away?"

"He is, and he'll stay locked away."

"He hasn't talked, I suppose?"

"He talks all right, but he doesn't say anything. You heard him last night." He felt for his pipe, but after a look at the bed he took it out and held it, unfilled and unlighted, between his teeth.

"You know," he went on, "by and large I've seen a good bit of murder in my time, but this case gets me. We've got one suspect locked up, and this happens."

Well, I dare say my nerves had commenced to go, for I found myself laughing, half hysterically.

"Maybe he did it, at that," I said, while he watched me carefully. "Maybe he wandered into my room last night on his way upstairs, and dropped a tablet or two into that tube on my tray. Why stop at one murder? He may have got a taste for it, like eating olives."

"You need a rest and a bromide," he said. "That is, if that's hysteria. If you're merely trying to be funny, for God's sake don't. I've had enough of it with that blond-haired killer at Headquarters. He'd better do his laughing now. He won't laugh long."

"You are as sure as that, are you, Inspector?"

"Sure enough."

"As sure as you were of suicide, and that scrap of paper?"

"What's that got to do with it? It was a week old. I've told you that."

"But it did have powder stains, didn't it?"

"Certainly it did. That doesn't necessarily mean anything. That was a pruning ladder that Paula Brent brought here that night, but she didn't prune any trees, did she?"

Well, I might have told him that there were two young men on the roof at that minute who had brought a ladder, too, but not to paint a roof. I refrained, however, for I saw that he was gravely troubled by the turn events had taken. He left the bed and moved about the room, and when he spoke again, it was in his usual businesslike manner.

"No use wasting time bickering over this case," he said. "You and I may not always see eye to eye, but we're likely to see a lot between us. I suppose you agree with the doctor? It's poison, eh?"

"I think so, Inspector."

"And you've no idea how it got there?"

"I can think of a half-dozen ways. I'm not sure of any of them."

"Let's see where that tray was kept."

I led him into the other room, and he stood for some little time, surveying it. He opened the door into the hall, and glanced out.

"I suppose anybody could get in here. You didn't keep this door locked?"

"No."

I knew his methods. He preferred to get his own picture first, so I volunteered nothing. But he gave a quick look at my dresser, and then at my face.

"Who used the face powder? There's none on you."

Then I knew that the time had come to tell him of Miss Juliet's statement. I had dreaded it all along, but it had to come. We went back into Miss Juliet's room, and with that rigid thin old body on the bed, I told him my story.

I told of the article in the paper about Paula Brent, and its effect on Miss Juliet. I told of her bringing Mr. Glenn there the night before, and of the long argument and his protest, which had followed; and of Hugo's presence beside Miss Juliet's bed early that morning, before Mr. Glenn came, and his attitude of resentment.

"But she was determined to make that statement," I said. "She had something on her conscience, and she felt guilty. She wanted to make it, and then to see her clergyman."

He looked up quickly. "Why? Had she any idea that there was trouble coming for her?"

"I think not."

"And Glenn has this statement now?"

"He took it away with him. Hugo and I witnessed it, and the Lenz girl, his secretary, is a notary. She attested it. But Miss Juliet didn't want it made public, Inspector. Mr. Glenn said—and she corroborated it—that it was only to be used in case a grave miscarriage of justice threatened. I suppose she was thinking of Paula Brent."

"You didn't read it, of course?"

"No. She folded it down, so none of us could see it."

"A grave miscarriage of justice, eh? Now what did that mean? I'll get hold of Glenn and have a look at it."

He left me then and went down to the telephone. I could hear him there, trying to locate either Florence or Mr. Glenn; but they were both out of the office at lunch, and Mr. Glenn had a case in court that afternoon. The Inspector came back in a very bad humor, having left word to trace them and get them to the Mitchell house as soon as possible. Then he went back to the kitchen and had a few words with Mary, and when he came back, his face was set.

I knew something had happened when I saw him. He stood for a moment, eying me coldly. "How many people have had access to that room of yours, and that tray, this morning?" he demanded. "The doctor, and the Lenz girl, and Hugo and Mary, I suppose. Is that all?"

"Don't use that tone with me, Inspector."

"Why didn't you tell me that Paula Brent was here this morning? And that she was upstairs, at that!"

"I suppose Mary told you that."

"So she was upstairs? No, Mary didn't know that, but she saw her going out. Now listen to me, Miss Adams. Whether we see eye to eye on this case doesn't matter a damn. What does matter is that you decide whether you're working for me or for Paula Brent."

"She never poisoned Miss Juliet Mitchell, Inspector."

"Was she in that room?"

"Yes. But Florence Lenz was there at the same time."

It was only after I had said it that I remembered that Paula had been in that room later on as well, and alone. But he gave me no time to go on. He flushed angrily, and banged his hand on the arm of his chair.

"I'd break a man for doing a thing like that," he said. Then he relented, I suppose when he saw my face. "What story did she put up, to make you do a fool thing like that, and then keep it from me?"

"A story I believed. I still believe it, for that matter. And as for your breaking a man, you can break me and welcome. I'm about broken now anyhow. If I wasn't a darned fool, I'd be at home this minute, feeding sugar to my canary!"

That restored his temper, and he listened patiently while I told him Paula's story of the morning, and after some hesitation, that the keys they had found on Charlie Elliott were hers. But I did not tell him that Charlie

Elliott had had those keys on Monday night. Why should I? Under oath I might have to, but not then.

"So she was going to Herbert's room!" he said. "Well, I give up. One thing is certain, however. If Elliott had those keys later, he had them on Monday night, too. I imagine they are what our friend Henderson heard him taking from her. Well, we'll soon know."

He leaned back and started to light his pipe, but after a look at the bed he put it in his pocket.

"We'll soon know," he repeated. "But this morning is a horse of another color. So far as I can figure out, about six people have had access to that room of yours and that tray, in the last dozen hours or so: Hugo, Mary, Glenn, Paula Brent, Florence and Doctor Stewart.

"Hugo and Mary we know about. They had a motive and they had opportunity. But they were pretty loyal to the old lady. Glenn seems fairly well accounted for. He didn't want that statement made, but take the average man of his type, and he'll stand up for a boy like Charlie Elliott as against the law any time. If you think all lawyers are sold on the law, think again! Now take the doctor. What motive would *he* have? But the doctor, according to what you say, had a pretty good chance."

"He asked me last night about her will."

"Well, that's natural enough. She has left a good bit of money, and he knew she hadn't long."

"He said there was an old will, and that Hugo and Mary are left legacies in it."

"How much? Did he know?" he said quickly.

"He didn't say."

"I'll have a look at that will." He made a note in the small book he carries, and sat looking at it. "Both Hugo and Mary?"

"So he said."

"Well, let's get on. How about this Florence Lenz? I gather you don't like her."

"I don't."

"Why?"

"I know her type, and I don't like it," I said shortly. "She's playing up to Mr. Glenn, for one thing. Rolls her stockings and lets him know it. And she staged a faint here that night when she was scared in the grounds. It wouldn't have fooled anybody. It didn't fool me, anyhow."

He began that sort of noiseless whistling which often accompanies his thinking, and slid farther down in his chair.

"Of course," he said finally, "in a way, poison is a woman's method. She isn't strong enough to use a knife, and it's messy anyhow. She hates blood. In a majority of cases she's afraid of firearms. But poison is different. She can understand poison. I don't suppose you can connect this Florence with the case?"

"I'm not certain. I think she hates Paula Brent, but I don't know why."

I told him then about the encounter that morning, and he listened carefully.

"It was Florence who was the aggressor?"

"Yes. But Paula Brent knew her, or knew who she was. She was almost rude, herself."

He looked at his watch. "Well, the Lenz woman ought to be here soon. It would be interesting to find out whether she knew Herbert, or this Elliott boy. In that case . . ." He shifted to something else. "How about Mary? She's been taking strychnia for her heart, if this was strychnia. But in capsules, not hypodermic tablets. She's a queer woman, fanatically religious, according to the doctor, and neurotic. But sane enough."

"She cleaned my room this morning."

"Well, you dressed in it probably. That doesn't mean you killed this poor old woman, does it? No. Take it all in all, Miss Pinkerton, and what does this second murder look like? For I think it was murder. What happens when any crime is committed? The first step is to escape and leave nothing incriminating behind. The next step, once the escape is made, is to protect that escape.

"That is, the murderer's fear is not for the thing he knows about and can clear up, but for the thing that turns up later on. He lies awake at night and worries about that. The somebody or something which he hasn't counted on, and which may destroy him.

"Now take this case. Here's the way it looks just now. I'm not saying it's right. Herbert Wynne was killed last Monday night, and we think we have the killer. We have every reason to think so. But here is Miss Juliet hiding something, and finally deciding to spill it. Something damaging to the killer, of course. That has to be suppressed, or at least the old lady put where she can't confirm it on the stand, we'll say. So she is poisoned."

He looked at me. "I would give a good bit to know," he said, "just how many people knew in advance that she was going to make that statement. Did this Florence?"

"She seemed to think it was a will. That is, until Mr. Glenn explained."

"Well, Hugo knew; and probably Mary. But maybe not. I have an idea that he isn't very communicative with her."

"She may have known. I found her listening outside the door this morning."

"The doctor didn't know, did he?"

"I think not. But I've just thought of something. I don't believe two hypodermics of strychnia, say, a fifteenth of a grain in each, would have killed or hurt most people. It was only in her condition that it was fatal."

He sat up and stared at me. "It wasn't a poisonous dose in itself?"

"I couldn't buy a hypodermic tablet of strychnia that would be poisonous in itself, unless I wanted to use it on a horse! And I want to ask you something, now. Paula Brent says that there was a letter left in Herbert's room, and if the people here haven't got it, it is still there. Have you ever given that room upstairs a real search? One based on the conviction that something is really hidden there?"

"I've been over it. You know that."

"Then go over it again," I said half hysterically. "Go up the chimney, or tear off the floor boards. Look around that bed. I tell you there was something else. It may be gone, but it was there. And I think it will solve these crimes."

It was at that moment that the doorbell rang, and Hugo announced Florence Lenz.

## CHAPTER XXI

I WAS NOT PRESENT at the Inspector's interview with Florence. I could hear her in the lower hall, loudly explaining that she had notified Mr. Glenn and that he would be here as soon as court adjourned; and from the delay there I fancied that she had stopped as usual before the mirror to make up her face.

That must have irritated him, for I heard his voice, sharp and edged. "Come, come, Miss Lenz," he said. "This isn't a beauty parlor."

"I'll say it isn't!"

She flounced into the library, or so I imagined, and he closed the door.

I had nothing to do for the next half hour or so but to worry. I had been told not to touch anything in the room, and so far the press had apparently not been notified of the death. But it does not take long for such news to get about, and as I looked out of the window, I saw the usual car driving in through the old gates, and the usual young man with a soft hat and businesslike manner getting out of it.

Hugo answered the bell, and I called to him softly as he went through the hall, telling him to give simply the facts of the death, and the hour. It must have been two o'clock by that time, or even later. I had had no luncheon, and Mary had apparently retired to her room and locked herself in. But soon after that, Hugo rapped at my door with some crackers and milk. He did not look at the bed as he crossed the floor.

"My wife is ill, miss," he said. "I'm sorry. She'll get up to cook dinner."

"What about that reporter, Hugo?"

"I did as you said, miss."

He looked inscrutable to me, seen in the strong afternoon light that day. Old and suddenly feeble, but inscrutable. On an impulse I followed him as he turned to go, and put my hand on his arm.

"She's gone, Hugo," I said. "Perhaps she didn't need to go so soon, but —well, she's gone. Why not tell all you know? You will feel better for it, and she would have wanted it."

"She has told it, miss," he said heavily. "She told it this morning."

The Inspector called me down soon after that. Florence was still in the room, dabbing at her eyes with her handkerchief, and the Inspector's face was stern but not unkind.

"I think we have got to the bottom of some of this, Miss Adams," he said. "This young woman was at one time engaged to Herbert Wynne, or so she claims."

"I was," she broke in, but he raised a hand for silence.

"This engagement, however, was broken last March, and she had not seen him since. But she knew that he was being seen constantly with Paula Brent. That explains her attitude to Miss Brent when they met today.

"This morning she came to the house with Mr. Glenn, to attest what she had expected to be a will. She waited downstairs until sent for; then something additional was apparently to be added to Miss Juliet's statement, and she was left in the hall. From there she went into your room for face powder, and she was there when you brought Paula Brent in. Miss Brent left the room soon after that.

"Following that, she went with you into the large bedroom to witness the statement, and did so. But on leaving that room to go back to the office with Mr. Glenn, she opened the door into the upper hall, and she says that she saw Miss Brent again. She was going into your room."

"That is true, Inspector," I said. "I found her there. She had been to the third floor, and as someone was in the hall, she couldn't get out. She didn't want to be seen."

"Why didn't you tell me this before?"

"Because it is absurd to suspect Paula Brent of poisoning anybody."

And at that, that vixen in the corner let out a yelp of laughter, and I could cheerfully have killed her.

"How do you know she had been to the third floor?"

"I should know," I said with some bitterness. "She's been trying to get there all week, and you know it."

"Faithful, wasn't she?" Florence jeered. "Well, I'm on my way if that's all, Inspector. Bye-bye! Be good!"

The Inspector let her go without a word, and I was just bracing myself for a defense when Mr. Glenn's car drove up. That saved me for the time, although, by the very manner in which the Inspector told me that I could go, I realized that his faith in me was pretty thoroughly shaken.

Mr. Glenn breezed in a moment later, and I knew well enough what that meant.

As I went up the stairs, I was determined to get off the case and out of the house. I was heartsick and homesick. I wanted to get back to my little apartment, and see Dick's eyes when I went to the closet for sugar. I wanted to sleep for twenty-four hours.

It may sound funny now to say that, when the Inspector came up, I was packing my bag to go, and that I had put on my hat, although I still wore a uniform. It was not funny then. That impulse to get out was nothing but a premonition; I know that now. I had not a doubt in the world that day but that Charlie Elliott would go to the chair, and I was not so certain that Paula would not go with him.

I heard Mr. Glenn going, and the Inspector coming up the stairs. He walked heavily, like a tired man, and when he came into my room, I even thought that, like Hugo, he looked older. He sat down without saying anything, and got out his pipe and lighted it.

"I dare say it's bad news?" I asked.

"I suppose that depends on the point of view. It doesn't cover everything, but it covers enough. I suppose you'd like to read it. You certainly deserve to get the low-down on this case, if anyone does."

Which I took to be his apology. After all, he could afford to be lenient; he had his case in his pocket, and he knew it. He produced the statement and passed it to me, and well enough I knew it; Mr. Glenn's careful writing, Miss Juliet's signature, my own signature in the corner, then Hugo's, and below them Florence's seal.

"You'll find," he said, "that the early portion of the story is substantially as Miss Juliet told it before. It is only at the end that it differs."

But I read it from start to finish nevertheless, with a slowly sinking heart. Clearly she had dictated it in her own words, although here and there was the evidence of a legal mind.

"I, Juliet Mitchell, being of sound mind and in the full possession of my faculties, wish to make the following statement, which I hereby state is the truth and nothing but the truth. I say this realizing that before long I shall have to face my Maker.

"My previous testimony to the police was also true to a certain extent. It is true that, on the night of Monday, September the fourteenth, I was awakened at about ten minutes before twelve by someone passing outside my door, and looked at my clock. It is true that I then prepared to go up the stairs to see if my nephew had come home, and that while preparing to get out of bed I felt by the vibration of the floor that someone was passing in the hall. It is true that on going to my door and seeing the light burning in his room above, I called to him and received no answer. And it is also true that I then put on my dressing gown and slippers and went up to his room to put out the light."

Here, however, this rather formal style ended, and Miss Juliet began to tell her story in a more ordinary manner, and to this effect:

She had got halfway up the stairs that night, from which point her head was slightly above the floor level above, and she could see directly into the room. To her horror, she saw her nephew lying on the floor in the center of the room, not moving.

What followed, according to that statement, must have had for her the stark drama of a silent motion picture shown in a dark theater. She could hear nothing, of course, and the brilliantly lighted room must have been like a stage, seen through the open door. However that may be, she was clear enough as to what followed. From a space which she could not see, but which was apparently the location of the closet or the bed, she saw a man approach this body and stoop over it; a young man, fair-haired and well dressed. To her horror, she then saw him drag what she now realized was Herbert's dead body toward the dresser; and stooping again, saw him deliberately bend the legs and lay a revolver beside it.

Up to that moment the full import of what she was seeing had not dawned on her. But with this man still stooping, she had found her breath and began to shriek. The figure turned and looked toward her, and then made a leap toward the window. Whether he escaped that way or not she was not certain. As she had only gone down the stairs to arouse the servants, however, he couldn't have passed her. She was convinced that he had gone by way of the roof.

But, although she had recognized the guilty man, she did not tell either Hugo or Mary when they appeared, and Hugo had at first believed that it was suicide. Also, Hugo had said that if it was suicide, it would invalidate certain insurance policies held by Herbert, and suggested moving the body away from the bureau. But this she would not allow. She was back on the stairs again at that time, with Mary holding aromatic ammonia to her nose. She had not been able to climb all the way to the room.

It was Hugo who discovered that there were no powder marks around the wound, and called to her that it was either a murder or accidental death. There was some unimportant detail here, and then Miss Juliet entered into a defense of her course of action which was typical and yet almost incredible. She went on to state that she had given Herbert a home, and what she could of support, and he had rewarded her with cold ingratitude. She would not pretend, even now, that she felt any grief at his death, or that the world had suffered any loss. And she was entirely engrossed that night, she admitted, with the situation in which she found herself.

There had never been a scandal of this sort in the Mitchell family. They had made their mistakes, but if Herbert had been murdered, she was convinced that it had been for good and sufficient reason. She dreaded the publicity, the stirring up of some filth—the word is mine—which would disgrace what had been a proud old name, and she was prepared to take any steps possible to avoid this.

Also there was another reason. She had recognized the boy. He belonged to a good family, and had at one time been engaged to Paula Brent, the granddaughter of an old friend of hers. She had made up her mind, sitting weakly there on the stairs that night, to keep her knowledge to herself!

She broke off here, to say that she did not know when or where Hugo had opened a window downstairs. She learned later that one had been found open; and she believed that he had done so in his anxiety to prove the case not one of suicide. He had been a loyal employee, and he knew that there was some insurance. Nor did she know when he had sent for the police. She herself had asked him to telephone to Mr. Glenn, and he had arrived shortly after the police got there. But she had had no chance to talk to him that night. Mary had sent for Doctor Stewart, and he had ordered her to bed.

Then she went back to her story. It was much later on Monday night, toward morning, indeed, that, as she lay in her bed, it had occurred to her that this man was probably still on the roof and unable to escape. She had felt fairly safe until then; Mary had reported that the police thought it was either suicide or accidental death, and probably an accident. But if he was still on the roof, it meant discovery, so she got out of bed and went upstairs. She leaned out of the window and called to him, but he must have escaped, for he did not answer to his name.

That name was Charlie Elliott.

## CHAPTER XXII

THERE WAS MORE of it, but nothing of importance. All the week, it was evident, Miss Juliet had struggled with an increasing sense of sin. She believed in the Bible, and there was the law of an eye for an eye, a tooth for a tooth. She had allowed her pride and a sentiment for an old friend to defeat the law, God's law and man's. It was when she learned that Herbert had taken out a large amount of insurance, and that his death had released her from serious financial worry, that she began to see where her duty lay.

She could not profit by his murder and protect his murderer; if, indeed, it were a murder. And when she saw by the paper that Paula Brent had been dragged into the case, she determined to do what she should have done at once.

It was that astounding document, which meant the chair for that blithe boy who had faced us all down that night in that upper room, which Hugo and I had signed. Here was Miss Juliet's wavering signature, here was Hugo's shaking one, and my own scrawl.

I stood, holding it in my hand and gazing at nothing. So Paula had known all along that Miss Juliet had seen Charlie in the room, and that the old lady could destroy him with a word. Here was Florence, telling the police Paula had gone back to my room that morning; had been there alone. Inspector Patton was watching me, a curious look on his face.

"Now you know what I've been talking about," he said. "I don't claim that I knew the old lady had seen Elliott in that room. But I do claim that I've known all along that Paula Brent knew more than she was telling. Then what do you do? You go out of your way, and forget your duty into the bargain, to tell her that Miss Mitchell is about to confess something! And I'll tell you something maybe you don't know. Paula's in love with this Elliott boy. Maybe she doesn't know it either, but that's the fact. It sticks out like a sore thumb. She's in love, and she's desperate."

"How could she know I was giving that nitroglycerin?"

"Well, that's not hard, is it? Maybe you told her; you seem to have told her a good bit, one way and another. Maybe Doctor Stewart told her; he's the family doctor for the Brents. Maybe she got into your room on Tuesday night and saw your tray. As a matter of fact, maybe that's why she got into the house. I don't uphold that theory. I only mention it."

"I've given half a dozen hypodermics since then."

"Still, she might have seen what you were using. And there were only two tubes on that tray. One of them was morphia, and it had not been opened. The other was nitroglycerin. Just remember that."

"And I suppose Paula Brent knew what was the matter with Miss Juliet's heart! And what it could stand, or couldn't!"

But I was remembering something else. "Listen, Inspector," I said earnestly. "You couldn't buy strychnia in hypodermic tablets so that two would be a poisonous dose. If those two injections killed Miss Juliet, that was because of her heart condition. Whoever substituted those tablets must have known that. Do you think a girl like Paula Brent could possibly have known such a thing?"

"You're certain of that, are you?"

"Ask the doctor."

He was silent for a few minutes, evidently turning that over in his mind. Then he got up and wandered to the bureau, standing in front of it and surveying it with care: my silver brush and comb; the tray, looking strangely empty and useless; my box of powder. With his back to me, he spoke again.

"I suppose you wouldn't notice if that tube had been tampered with?"

"It was a fresh tube. I had opened it, but I had not used it."

He wheeled. "A fresh tube? Then, supposing two tablets had been put into it, two others would have had to come out."

"Yes. Although I hadn't thought of it."

He looked around then. The bathroom, as in most old houses, was reached only by way of the hall. He glanced at the carpet, got down to examine some of the powder Florence had spilled on the floor, found it only powder, and then, rising, glanced at the rear window, which was open.

"What about that window? Was it open all morning?"

"It was."

"Let me see one of those tablets."

"The laboratory man took them."

He muttered something, and then, without another word, he went out of the room and down the stairs.

I looked at my watch, and I had to hold it to my ear to be certain that it had not stopped. It was only a little after four, and it seemed to me that I had lived a lifetime since morning. The house was as still as only a house with death in it can be. There was no sign of Hugo, or of Mary; but from that rear window of mine I could see Mary's black cat, moving stealthily across the grass toward the building. When I went closer to the window, I saw what had attracted it. The Inspector was furiously moving that ladder from where I had thrown it, and loudly demanding to know how it had got there!

Well, it had been a bad day for me, and was slowly growing worse. And evidently the two youths on the roof felt rather the same, for they never peeped while he was below.

He flung the ladder away, and then began to go over the ground with minute care, getting down on his hands and knees to do so. His tall figure in its gray sack suit was concentration personified, and I drew my first real breath when I saw him pick up some small object, lay it in the palm of his hand, and then drop it lightly in one of those small glass vials which the Bureau provides for such purposes.

But when I turned away from that window, I knew one thing, and knew it beyond a doubt. Miss Juliet had been murdered; deliberately and skill-fully murdered.

The Inspector did not find the other tablet, apparently. Or he was satis-fied with the one. I heard him coming back into the house, and up the stairs. But he made no explanation to me. He passed my door as though I were not in the room, and moving with that peculiar catlike rapidity which is his when he needs it, he went on up the third-floor stairs and into Her-bert's room.

Some ten minutes later he was down again, and at my door. "Can you get me a hammer?" he said. "One with a tack puller on the other end, or something of the sort?"

"There is a drawer of tools in the pantry. But I imagine Hugo is there."

"Then don't try it." He scanned the room quickly. "Have you a nail file, or a strong pair of scissors?"

Well, I had both, and I gave them to him. "They are my best surgical scissors," I told him. "Don't break them."

"My God!" he said. "What a contradictory person you are, Miss Pinker-ton! You go calmly through murder and sudden death, and now you don't want your scissors broken. Take that hat off and stop being ridiculous! And if Hugo shows up, ask for something from downstairs. Tea, molasses, I don't care what. Just hold him."

He was excited; I could see that. He is seldom facetious except at such times. Excited and happy, like a dog which has followed a cold trail for a long time, and suddenly finds it a hot one.

"I gather that you found something, down below that window."

"I did," he said dryly. "I found that a hardhearted young woman had left a couple of reporters on a hot tin roof, and that it is only by the grace of Providence that in venting her personal spleen she didn't destroy some valuable evidence."

He grinned at me, and then he was on his way upstairs again, taking the steps two or three at a time.

He was upstairs for some fifteen minutes. Then I heard him coming down, and at the same time Hugo's slow steps on the staircase, coming up. They met just outside my door, and neither one of them seemed to realize that I was there. I can still see Hugo, stopping and looking up, and the Inspector moving down on him, stern and implacable.

But it was Hugo who spoke first. "I was going to ask about the funeral arrangements. I suppose we can go ahead with them?"

"Why not?"

"You know that better than I do, sir. But if she died a natural death, why bring the Medical Examiner? You don't think she did; nor I either." Then, without any warning, he broke down and began to weep, the terrible unwilling tears of age. To weep and to talk. "I killed her, Inspector. I'd have done anything for her, and—I killed her!"

"Pull yourself together, Hugo," the Inspector said sharply. "You are not confessing a crime to me, are you?"

But Hugo only shook his head, and would have passed on. The Inspector caught him by the shoulder.

"Why don't you come clean about this?" he said. "What's the use now, Hugo? She's gone."

"I have nothing to say, sir."

"You've said something already, too much or too little."

"I've got my wife to think of, Inspector. If anything happens to me, what will become of her?"

"What could happen to you?" the Inspector demanded roughly. "I know about the insurance, and your fear that Herbert's death would be considered a suicide. I know that you wanted to move the body away from the bureau up there, for that reason. And I understand that better than you think. But I know a lot of other things also. For instance, why Miss Juliet got out of bed that night and went up to the room again."

"She told that, sir?"

"She did."

"It was my fault that she didn't do it before, sir."

The Inspector nodded. He still had his hand on Hugo's shoulder.

"Isn't it time you told what you know, Hugo? Or what you suspect? What's the use of holding back now? If you're afraid, I'll take steps to protect you."

"Protect me! You couldn't protect *her*, sir."

"But if I tell you that I know the whole story? What then?"

Hugo did not answer. He caught hold of the stair rail, looked blankly ahead of him, and then crumpled up on the floor in a dead faint.

It was some little time before he recovered sufficiently to be moved from my room, where the Inspector had carried him, and still later before he was strong enough to be taken to Headquarters for interrogation. Up to the time he left, he had stubbornly refused to talk, and much of that time the Inspector had spent in pacing up and down in the lower hall. I had gone down to the kitchen and on up the back stairs to tell Mary, but although she was clearly startled, it was some time before I could induce her to open the door and let me in.

She was not in bed. She had apparently been sitting by the window, and she was fully dressed. She was pale, even for her, and I had to assure her that I was alone before she would unlock the door. She was suspicious even then, for she kept looking over my shoulder into the sitting room.

"Where is he?" she asked.

"In my room, Mary."

Then, for the first time that day, so far as I knew, she broke down and cried.

I took her to Hugo, and she bent down and touched his forehead with her work-hardened hand.

"I told you," she said. "I told you. But you're a stubborn man."

He opened his eyes and looked at her, and I saw then that, whatever had separated them, there was a strong bond between them; the bond of years and habit, and maybe something more. He took her hand.

"My poor Mary," he said weakly. "My poor girl."

It was about that time that the Inspector ordered the release of the two boys on the roof. Instead of leaving at once, however, I saw them in deep conference with the Inspector in the lower hall. One of them had something in his hand, and the Inspector took it and looked at it.

I could not see what it was.

CHAPTER XXIII

THE REPORTERS had barely gone, to the sound of considerable badinage from one or two cameramen in the drive, when the doorbell rang.

That was nothing new that afternoon. The neighbors, the Manchesters and the Bairds, had already heard our news, by that sort of grapevine telegraph which travels from kitchen to kitchen, and had called to offer condolences and help. Indeed, it had been all I could do to keep Mrs. Manchester from settling in the house that afternoon.

"There should be a woman around," she said, looking at me with wide protruding eyes.

"I am here. And Mary."

"Mary!" she said with a sniff.

So I expected a reporter, or a neighbor, when I opened the door. But it was Mr. Henderson who stood on the front porch. Apparently he had already learned of Miss Juliet's death, for he had his hat in his hand, and he tiptoed in after the manner of most people in a house of death, and spoke with his voice decorously lowered.

"Is Inspector Patton here?" he half whispered. "I've been to Headquarters, and they said he was here."

The Inspector emerged from the darkness of the rear hall.

"I'm here, Henderson. Want to see me?"

"I don't like to intrude at a time like this, but my wife felt that I should see you. Perhaps if we could go outside and talk . . ."

"Speak right up. It's all right."

"Well, it's like this." He stood turning his hat in his hands and hesitating. "I don't like to repeat gossip myself. Live and let live is my motto. But Mrs. Henderson has a way of receiving people's confidence. You'd be surprised how much she hears. And lately she has learned something about Paula Brent. It seems that our cook is friendly with the Brents' butler, and she has a sort of cock-and-bull story that my wife thinks you ought to know."

Well, it was just one of those things that might be important, or might be simply backstairs talk. As the Inspector said after Henderson left, "I've got an idea that that henpecked little man, as well as his wife, has been holding an opera glass on those two houses across the alley ever since the murder."

But stripped of his apologies and so on, it ran as follows:

According to this butler, about a month before, Paula Brent had gone to a house party. But something turned up over that weekend, and when her family called her by long distance, they found that she was not there. On Sunday night she came home, in her car, and according to the butler there was a terrific scene. Her father shouted and raved like a madman, and one of the things he said was overheard. He said, "If I find out who the man is, I'll kill him."

Paula was crying, and so was her mother; and apparently they locked her up that night in her own room. She was locked up for two days. The servants were told that she was ill, but no one entered her room but her mother, and she carried in Paula's trays. She ate little or nothing, however. The trays went down practically as they went up.

"I didn't much care about reporting this," said the little man, "but as a decent citizen I suppose I should." He seemed to draw a long breath. "Mr. Brent is a good friend and a good neighbor. We're on the School Board together. Of course it is Mrs. Henderson's idea that if Mr. Brent had anything to do with all this, he had justification. But she has just heard of Miss Juliet's death, and what with Charlie Elliott locked up and all——"

The Inspector looked up sharply. "So that's the talk, is it?"

Mr. Henderson spread his hands. "You can't keep people from talking, Inspector. Mrs. Henderson heard that Miss Juliet was dead, and she called the Brent house. But it was Paula who came to the telephone, and my wife says she never said a word. Just hung up the receiver. My wife was pretty much upset about it."

"What are they saying about Miss Juliet's death?"

"I didn't listen to it all. But Doctor Stewart called on Mrs. Brent this afternoon, and I believe the butler heard something."

"Something? What?"

"Well, the doctor seemed to feel that the death wasn't natural."

"Oh, damn the doctor!" said the Inspector, with feeling. "And why in God's name would Mr. Brent do away with Miss Juliet Mitchell?"

The little man cleared his throat. "It's my wife's idea that possibly—well, suppose the old lady found Paula Brent in that room that night, as well as Charlie Elliott?"

"*And* Paula's father. Quite a crowd, wasn't it?"

He spread his hands. "I don't think that, Inspector. I'm only telling you the talk in our neighborhood."

"Well, go home and tell them to shut up," said the Inspector savagely. "I don't need any help on this case; when I do, I'll ask for it."

The little man creaked out soon after that, and the Inspector remained thoughtful when he had shut the door behind him. He did not speak again until we were both in the library with the door closed, and he was methodically filling his pipe.

"Funny thing," he said, "how the public clamors for a victim, isn't it? Brent was out of town last Monday night; and I don't mean maybe."

He took a turn up and down the hall. "What do you make of all this?" he asked suddenly.

"I think," I said dryly, "that when Miss Juliet died, the defense lost an important witness. And that somebody knew it."

"A witness for the defense! Now that's interesting. Why?"

"The old lady didn't claim to have seen the shot fired, did she? All she saw was the boy in the room."

"She saw him moving the body."

"How do you know that? I'd give a good bit to know if she had taken time that night to put on her distance glasses! She couldn't see across a room without them."

He was watching me, with that unblinking gaze of his.

"And how about this gossip we've just listened to? Suppose young Elliott hadn't known about that excursion a month ago, and just heard it, last Monday night?"

"Well," I said stubbornly, "I don't know anything about this young generation, and thank God I'm not its moral censor. But I'll never believe Charlie Elliott is guilty of that murder."

He had been moving uneasily about the room. Now he took his pipe from his mouth and grinned at me.

"You're an obstinate young woman, Miss Pinkerton," he said. "But you've got a certain amount of common sense, along with your weakness for blond youths! And I'll admit that several things today have me out on a limb, and with no Paula Brent to come along with a ladder. That old woman was poisoned; I don't need a laboratory report to tell me that."

"You found the tablets?"

"I found one of them. That's good enough. If it hadn't been for your vindictive act with that ladder, I'd probably have both of them."

"That ought to let Charlie Elliott out," I said, with a certain relief. But he merely sucked at his pipe and followed his own line of thought.

"Now we have two murders. The first one is a case for the Grand Jury; no doubt about that. The D. A. has young Elliott in a barrel with the lid nailed on. He's out for an indictment, and he'll get it as sure as God made little fishes. But I want no miscarriage of justice, and there isn't a doubt that if our little friend Henderson goes on the stand with his story of last Monday night in that alley, it's a case of just too bad for Charlie Elliott. What he took from Paula Brent that night was probably her bag, with the keys to this house in it.

"But I've been lying awake at night over this whole affair, and it puzzles me. A furiously jealous man commits a crime of passion. He's out to kill, and he does it. He's not a calculating human being; he doesn't fire a shot while holding a revolver in his handkerchief, and then set the stage to look like a suicide. For one thing, there isn't time. A shot isn't like a knife wound. It makes a devil of a lot of noise. Then, here's this statement of Miss Juliet's that he moved the body. Maybe you're right, and she imagined that. But it will send this boy to the chair just the same."

"There is another thing, Inspector. How did he know that shot wouldn't be heard? He probably knew that Miss Juliet was deaf, but what about the servants? I don't believe he had ever been in this house before. Whoever fired that shot either took a long chance that it wouldn't be heard, or—knew that it wouldn't."

"Meaning Hugo, I suppose?"

"Hugo knew about it. Or knows about it. I haven't watched him all week for nothing."

He nodded, and smoked in silence for some little time.

"Just what do you know about this Florence Lenz?" he asked.

"Nothing, except that she's a hussy."

He threw back his head and laughed. But he sobered almost at once. "Nevertheless, hussy or no hussy," he said, "it might be important to find out, for example, if she knew by any chance that Paula Brent had married Herbert Wynne."

"What?" I screeched. "Married him!"

"She did, indeed," he said gravely. "She has kept her secret pretty well, but that accounts for that weekend excursion of hers. It's a pity we can't see the Henderson woman's face when she learns it, isn't it? Yes, she married him, and one of the things she has been ttying to get from this house is her wedding certificate, poor child. I have a suspicion that she knew that marriage had been a mistake, even before he was killed. But that's what she did, and—if it relieves your mind—that is why she carried those keys."

"But why break in for that certificate? I don't understand. Surely she didn't need a certificate to prove the marriage?"

"I've been thinking it over, and the only explanation I have is that they were married at night, possibly in some remote place he had selected, and that she was excited or frightened, and didn't even know where it was done."

"Where did you find it? The certificate? I suppose you have found it?"

"I did, and by the way, I owe you a new pair of surgical scissors. It was behind the baseboard at the head of the bed. Herbert had ripped off the molding and dropped it there. I had the devil of a time fishing it out."

"And there was no letter?" I asked.

"There was a letter, but it doesn't tell us much. I'll come to that in due time. Let's keep on with this girl, Paula. Now, if she had done the normal thing, she'd have told that at the start. But few of us do the normal thing when we're frightened, and she was pretty thoroughly scared. For one thing, while she didn't believe young Elliott had killed Herbert Wynne, she wasn't sure. She isn't sure even now. She only has his word for it. And she was in dead wrong with her people. For whatever reason, Wynne wanted that marriage kept secret; the minute he died, she wanted that certificate to show her people. But it's a curious bit of psychology that people in trouble always believe that the police are against them. We'd have turned up that preacher for her, but does she tell us? She does not.

"Let's follow her a bit. She's in trouble, all right. On Tuesday night she gets into this house and scares you into a fit. Scares herself, too! On Wednesday she tells Charlie Elliott the whole story, and he makes a try, but Florence runs him off the place. And on Thursday he finally makes the grade, and we get him. He may be guilty of the murder; guilty as hell. Or he may be as innocent as an unborn babe. But we've got him."

"But the letter!" I said impatiently. "Doesn't that tell anything?"

"It does and it doesn't. I'm not going into that too far just now. But I'll tell you this. The whole thing started as an insurance swindle, and nothing else. He—Herbert—was to take out a considerable sum of straight life insurance. It is cheap at his age; and the idea was to arrange a drowning; or rather a pseudo-drowning. It was his own scheme at first. He wanted a lump sum for carrying it out; enough to get away, and a payment later to make a start somewhere else. He went to Hugo with it, and at first Hugo refused. Then he agreed, I suppose, for two reasons. It would provide for the old lady in her need, and it would ensure his legacy, and Mary's.

"But here's the devil of it. Hugo gave him the money for the premiums, either from his own savings or borrowed elsewhere. He didn't know, and in the end it was Hugo this boy was afraid of. You see, he had held up the plan, and Hugo didn't like it. Miss Juliet was about to lose her home.

"He had got his advance money, and he had gone into the market with it. But the market had gone down, and he didn't want to 'die' until he could get his money out again, and a little more. For by that time he had met Paula Brent, and fallen in love with her. You can see how it was; the boy keeps postponing the date of his pretended death by drowning. The summer goes by, the obvious time for such a trick, and still he hasn't done it. What's more, he is apparently stalling. He's fallen in love, and it looks as though he might quit the game. Hugo takes to watching him, and he knows that he's out with this girl at night a good bit.

"What's more, he may marry her! That is fatal to the scheme; his wife becomes his heir, and not the old lady. That's why Herbert hid the certificate and swore Paula to secrecy, although I doubt if the girl knew anything about the plot. And no wonder he was rather cheery on that last night! He could pull that drowning as before, but Paula would get the money. They could ship off to Europe or South America, and live happily ever after. Only he waited a day or two too long."

"And Hugo murdered him, after all?"

"I haven't said that, have I?" he said. He got up and shook the ashes out of his pipe. "If Glenn gets here within an hour or so, tell him to call me up, will you? I'm taking Hugo with me. And here's a last thought for you. Suppose the Lenz girl knew about this plot, and expected to marry him and share the profits? It's an interesting idea, isn't it?"

But I noticed that he had told me nothing about what those two reporters had found on the roof.

CHAPTER   XXIV

WHEN I went upstairs again, the morticians, as they call themselves now, had been at work for some time in Miss Juliet's room, and soon after, they called me in to look at her. All traces of her sickness and trouble had disappeared, and she lay, like an old marble statue, in her wide walnut bed. They had put a little color on her face and arranged the lights, and when they called me in, I was almost startled. She had become the great lady again, majestic and almost beautiful. It was not hard to believe that she had once been a beauty, and that Paula Brent's grandfather had been passionately in love with her.

Mr. Glenn did not arrive until five o'clock, and I gave him the Inspector's message. He called up at once, and I heard him saying that something was in Miss Juliet's box at the bank, and that he would locate it in the morning.

Hugo had not returned, and I was glad that there was someone in the house besides Mary, strangely set and brooding in her kitchen. For the afternoon papers had carried the notice of Miss Juliet's death, and almost immediately people had commenced to arrive. They came in numbers and dignity, these elderly folk, some merely leaving their cards, others coming in. Some arrived in cars, but here and there was an ancient victoria, used only for ceremonial occasions, and driven by an equally ancient coachman in shabby livery. When they came in, it was with the careful movements and the lowered voices proper to such occasions. Old gentlemen leaning on sticks, elderly women rustling after the fashion of years ago, they came and went, a little sad, a little alarmed; for the death of the aged was to most of them a warning that they themselves had not long to live, that soon the same decorous gathering would be for them.

Almost none of them asked to see the old lady.

I was rather surprised, however, to find Mr. Henderson among those who did so. Led by the doctor, he came up and stood by the bed, in silence at first.

"Knew her when I was a boy," he said jerkily. "They say she grew hard, but she wasn't hard then. Beautiful, she was."

He tiptoed out on creaking shoes, but as he went, he gave a sharp look at the stairs to the third floor.

"It's a pity she didn't go before *that* happened," he said.

I was surprised to see tears in his eyes as he creaked down the stairs again. I have often thought of him since, that little man; finding his bit of romance vicariously in the Miss Juliets and the Paula Brents, and living his drab suppressed existence with the woman he always referred to as "my wife."

And we were not through with him. I was to see him once more before anonymity closed down on him, and that under strange and tragic circumstances.

Rather to my surprise Hugo was back and served the dinner that night. Mr. Glenn paid little attention to him, being apparently absorbed in his own thoughts. But once, when Hugo was out of the room, he spoke about him.

"Looks pretty well broken," he said. "Aged, don't you think?"

"Very much," I agreed.

"What do the police want with him anyhow?" he said irritably. "I don't suppose they think for a minute that he had anything to do with what happened here today. If anything did happen!"

"You don't think it did?"

"I think Stewart is pretty excitable. After all, the old lady has had angina for a long time. She was due to go soon, in any event. And she was pretty feeble when I left about noon."

Then Hugo returned, and nothing more was said.

Soon after that the telephone rang in the hall, and I answered it. It was Inspector Patton.

"Miss Adams?"

"Yes, doctor."

"Nothing doing with the old man. He won't talk. But I've got an idea that he'll try to get word to somebody; he knows something, or suspects something. Or he may come back here. I rather think he will. And be on hand at eight thirty. I'm bringing Elliott up."

"Very well, doctor," I said. "I shall probably be free tomorrow."

"And again you may not, Miss Pinkerton!" he said, almost blithely for him, and hung up the receiver.

We finished the meal in comparative silence. To tell the truth, it was an indifferent meal indifferently served, for the inevitable flowers had commenced to arrive, and there were long intervals while Hugo received boxes, signed for them and took them back to the pantry.

Doctor Stewart came in before we had finished, looking grave and self-important; and he waited until Hugo had left the room before he said what he had evidently come to say.

"Well, I've had the report."

"What about it?"

"It looks like poison, all right. Maybe you'll listen to me the next time, Glenn."

"What makes you think there will be a next time?"

I suspected some friction between them, but the doctor was off on the *risus sardonicus* and the other symptoms, while Hugo once more answered the doorbell. Mr. Glenn's face showed distaste, and at last he got up and flung down his napkin.

"For heaven's sake, Stewart!" he said. "I've had enough this week. I'm no medical man. Keep your knowledge for the police. They eat up that sort of thing."

Then he stalked out. He met Hugo in the hall and spoke to him briefly. Then, still irritated, he banged out of the front door. The doctor looked after him and smiled.

"Nerves!" he said. "Well, I don't know that I blame him. I'm a bit jumpy myself. And he's got a hard job ahead of him."

"What sort of job?" I asked.

"I happen to know that Paula Brent saw him, late this afternoon, and asked him to defend young Elliott. He has his own attorneys, but she wants him to help. He's not a criminal lawyer, but she's no fool. Glenn and his father before him have been close to the Mitchells for fifty years. It might be a shrewd move."

He left soon, and Hugo followed him out onto the porch. There they talked for a short time, and then the doctor drove away. That must have been at seven thirty.

I wondered then if that quiet talk on the veranda was the attempt to get word to somebody that the Inspector had anticipated. But the doctor's final words, which I had overheard, sounded open and reassuring enough. He had spoken from some little distance, raising his voice to do so.

"Think about it, anyhow," he said. "We don't want any more trouble, Hugo."

"You may be right, doctor."

I wandered out onto the porch myself after he had gone, and stood there for a while. The September night air was cool and bracing, and I remember taking long breaths to fill my lungs with it, and to help to clarify my mind. Think as I might, I could not put together the pieces of that puzzle. I tried to fit in Florence Lenz, but I could not. I believed that she was as capable of putting poison into that tube as any Borgia, but I could see no reason why she should. She was capable, too, of shooting Herbert Wynne; but again, why?

She was cool enough, for all her pretended fainting when Charlie Elliott had bumped into her that night. She knew Herbert. She might even have learned from him that trick of shooting through a newspaper. But again, why?

I was still standing there, in the light from the front hall, when Hugo appeared from around the corner of the house and stopped near me.

"I am going out, miss," he said. "I'd be glad if you would keep an eye on my wife. She is very nervous tonight."

"I'll do that, of course."

"And—if she should decide to give you something, miss, I'll ask you to put it away carefully."

"Give me something, Hugo? What?"

"She will tell you herself. But I don't advise mentioning it to her. She might resent that. Let her bring it. If she doesn't . . ."

He made a small gesture, put on his hat and went down the drive. I was never to see him again. It seems strange to think of that; to see again in my mind the hall light falling on his white hair and his old face, to remember him going down that drive, on his way, like Herbert, like Miss Juliet, to his death.

Was he murdered? I don't suppose we will ever know. But from the direction he took, he was on his way to Headquarters, and it is easy now to see why it was determined that he should never get there.

Sometimes I think that I had a sort of premonition that night, for I found myself shivering, and I had turned to go in when I heard Paula Brent's voice. She was standing in the shrubbery at the end of the porch, and she spoke in a low voice.

"Don't go in. I want to talk to you. Close that door."

"Hugo has gone out."

"I saw him. But that wife of his is still there, isn't she?"

I closed the door and moved over to her. Even in the dark I could tell that she was excited.

"Listen," she said. "There's a story going around that Miss Mitchell was poisoned. Is that true? Do you think it's true?"

"They suspect it," I said cautiously.

"Well, that lets Charlie out, doesn't it?"

"Not necessarily, Paula. But things would look better, of course."

"Tell me how it happened, and then I'll tell you something. Did that Lenz girl have anything to do with it? She was in your room, remember. And there was stuff on your tray, right under her nose."

"I haven't an idea. Yes, she could have. The question is, did she?"

And then she brought out her own news. "I've just remembered something," she said. "Although why I come to you with it I don't know! I suppose it's because I have nobody else. I can't go to my people. They think Charlie did it, and they won't talk to me. You saw the Lenz girl this morning, and the way she looked at me?"

"I did, indeed," I said briefly.

"I'd never met her before, but I knew who she was. You see, she used to be a friend of Herbert's. They were pretty close friends until he met me. Then that was over, and I guess she didn't like it much."

Well, I could imagine that Florence had not liked it much; and I began to wonder if Paula had come that night to admit her marriage, and to say that Florence had learned about it. It turned out, however, to be something entirely different, and possibly more important.

On Monday night, as she had said before, she had met Herbert at the movies, and they went in and sat together. The theater was dark, and she had paid no attention to who sat near her. When she left, she discovered outside that she had dropped her bag, and went back for it.

It lay under her seat, and she got it and went out again. Herbert was looking at a paper, and while he did so, she examined her bag to see if her money was there. It was, but the two keys to the Mitchell house, which she always carried, had disappeared. She looked at me defiantly as she mentioned the keys, but I pretended not to notice it.

"They were gone," she said. "I had had them that evening, but they were gone."

But the point was that, while they were still standing there, the Lenz girl had come out of the theater. Herbert had not seen her. He had been rather annoyed about the keys, and he had reached into his pocket and got his own, on a key ring marked with his initials. He took one key from the ring for himself and gave her the other two. It was those keys of Herbert's which Charlie Elliott, trapped upstairs on Thursday night, had thrown out of the window.

"You are certain it was Florence?"

"Certain. I knew the other day upstairs that I had seen her somewhere, and not long ago. It just came to me tonight."

"And you're sure those keys were in your bag?"

"I had to be sure. I couldn't leave them at home!"

"Nobody at your house could have found them and taken them? Before you left?"

She considered that, and I thought that she was uneasy. But the next moment she dismissed the idea. Nobody there knew she had them. No, they had been stolen in the theater, and whoever took them had suspected they were there, and had slipped her bag from her knee.

"You didn't notice the people around you?"

"It was dark, of course. I didn't recognize anyone. No. But she was there. Near, too. Maybe beside me. How do I know?"

"Why don't you go to Headquarters with that?" I asked. "After all, if somebody else had keys to this house that night, and Charlie Elliott didn't, whoever it was could get in, couldn't he? Or she?"

She shook her head. "But he did," she said miserably. "He did, and they'd get that out of me. We had a quarrel that night, and he took them from me. He took my bag, with the keys in it. He knew they were there. That's why I followed him, and why I had to get the ladder. I knew he could get into the house. But if somebody else had keys, too—don't you see? They got there earlier, and that's what he says they did. He says Herbert was dead when he got into the room; that he was just dead, at that."

"Then why did he move the body?"

"He never moved the body. Where did you hear that? He heard somebody below, and he swung out the window onto the roof."

"Miss Juliet made a statement before she died, Paula. She said she had seen him move the body."

"Then she lied!" she cried angrily. "She never saw that. When Charlie found him, he was in front of the bureau, with the revolver on the floor beside him, and some oil and rags on a newspaper on the dresser, as if he'd been cleaning his gun. Charlie thought it was an accident, but he didn't want to be caught there. He knew how it would look. He hid behind the chimney on the roof until the police left."

And at that minute a police car turned into the drive.

## CHAPTER XXV

AMONG THE other unrealities of that sickening night—Hugo's face with the light shining out on it, Paula and her shadowy figure and her eager voice on the end of the porch—is my recollection of that police car; of Evans getting out first, followed by Charlie Elliott, and then by the Inspector.

I can still hear Paula's gasp, and see that boy, handcuffed to Evans, standing gazing at the house; and his expression change from a sort of dogged patience to sheer joy when she rushed to him.

"Charlie! Charlie darling!"

"Sorry, honey. Only have one arm. Other's in use."

And then I can see her with her head on his shoulder, and the two police officers looking fierce and uncomfortable at the same time. They gave them their minute together, however, and let her cry her heart out, as she proceeded to do almost immediately. And Charlie Elliott tried to cheer her after his fashion.

"My turn now," he said. "Suppose you stand up and let *me* cry. Listen, dampness! How would you like to get into the car and bring me some doughnuts and a cup of decent coffee?"

But his voice was husky, and he tightened his hold on her when his humor had no effect on her.

"Now stop it," he said. "These fellows aren't as sure as they were, or why would they drag me from my warm cot and bring me to this cold, cold spot? Do you get that, sweetheart? These minions of the law are trembling in their boots right now, because they know they're off on the wrong foot. You *are* trembling, Inspector, aren't you?"

"Shaking as with a chill," said the Inspector gallantly.

Somehow this nonsense steadied her. She looked up at Charlie Elliott and smiled.

Nobody had paid the least attention to me, and now I spoke.

"You're not the only person with a chill," I said.

The Inspector saw me then, and came to me on the porch. "What about Hugo?"

"He's gone out."

He nodded. "I thought he would. I'm having him tailed. The chances are that he made for Headquarters. If he didn't, we'll soon know where he did go."

But when I told him of the talk about Mary before Hugo left, he whistled softly.

"And what might that be?" he said. "A gun? A bottle of strychnia?"

"It just might be what Miss Juliet gave her. The newspaper is my guess."

"So things are getting pretty hot, and it's time to produce the alibi!"

"That's my idea. I may be wrong."

"You're not often wrong, Miss Pinkerton!" he said, and went back to his prisoner.

Then followed one of those quietly dramatic experiments which now and then a police officer with imagination will stage. Charlie Elliott was there to reproduce as faithfully as possible every move he had made in the house and on the grounds on the Monday night before. Evidently he had "come clean" to the extent of admitting that he had been there, and had agreed to duplicate his actions.

From the moment that small drama began, both the Inspector and Evans were absorbed in it. I doubt if they even know that Paula and I were following. Now and then the Inspector asked a question, but much of it took place in silence, save for the boy's own explanations as they went along.

He led first to the street, and turned from there into the next property. "I got out of the taxi at the corner," he said, "and turned in here."

He went back perhaps a hundred yards and stopped there. The house was not much more than a shadow from there, and he stopped and surveyed it.

"I'd been here before," he said. "I'd followed Paula one night. The side door is over there."

After that he moved through the shrubbery, still leading Evans by that handcuff, and partway across the lawn he stopped again.

"This is where I was when I saw somebody coming out of the side door. I've told you that. You can see how dark it is, and why I couldn't tell whether it was a man or a woman."

"And they went toward the rear of the house?"

"Yes."

The Inspector was still standing, gazing toward the side door. "Listen, Elliott," he said. "You must have thought something about that figure. After all, why should anybody slip out of that door at that hour of the night? You must have thought a lot about it, if your story's the right one."

I thought young Elliott hesitated. "I tell you," he replied, "I have thought about it. I haven't thought of much else. Remember, I didn't see who it was. But at the time I sort of took it for granted that it was either Hugo or Doctor Stewart. I knew the old lady had a bad heart; everybody knew it."

"But you couldn't see the doctor going toward the kitchen. Is that it?"

"Well, hardly that. His car wasn't in sight, and he might have cut across lots from another case nearby. There are no fences. No, it isn't that. Why would he shoot Wynne? What would be the idea? That's where I bring up every time."

"All right. Let that ride. What then?"

"Just what I've told you."

We moved toward the house, and at the side entrance he stopped.

"This part was easy. I'd got Paula's keys, as I've explained, and I had no trouble with this door; but I was pretty well lost when I got to the top of the back stairs. I could hear Hugo snoring, however, in the back room, so I tried the other key on the door there. I had lighted a match to do that, and I found myself on the landing of the second floor."

We went on up, and he repeated what he had done. Apparently Mary was still in the kitchen, and unsuspicious. In the hall on the second floor Charlie Elliott stopped and smiled faintly.

"I stopped here," he said. "I'd been blind crazy up to that minute, but the job began to look too much like housebreaking about that time. I don't mind saying that up to this point, I might have killed him if I'd had a gun. After that I began to feel pretty much like a damned fool."

But the light had been burning overhead, and so he had kept on.

Halfway up to the third floor, or a little more, he stopped again.

"If somebody will go ahead, and turn on that light, it will help," he said. "I was here when I saw him first."

The Inspector went on up, and we stood there waiting. In the semi-darkness I saw Charlie reach down his free hand and grope for Paula's; and so they waited, those two children, until the light went on.

"I was here," he said. "I stopped and looked across into the room; and at first I thought he was looking for something under the bureau. But his position was queer, and when he didn't move, I saw that something was wrong. I nearly turned and ran then! But of course I couldn't. Whether he was sick or hurt or just blind drunk, I had to go on. And I did."

Up in the room itself he repeated what he had done. He had stooped over the body, but had not moved it. He saw the wound, and knew at once that Herbert was dead.

"How long dead?" said the Inspector. "Was he still warm? Was he limber?"

"I don't know. Or was that a trap? I didn't touch him, I tell you. I thought at first of lifting him onto the bed. Then I remembered not to touch anything. First order of all good policemen."

"But you went over and looked at the bed?"

"I don't think so. I was still stooping when I heard somebody on the stairs, and I had to get out. I knew of the roof, and I can show you how I did it, if you like."

"And have to get off with a ladder again? Not on your life! And how do I know you haven't got a ladder there now, my lad?"

Well, that was meant as a joke, and so we received it. Any relief in that grisly business was welcome. But the Inspector was sober and business-like enough immediately.

"How long had you stood in that shrubbery?"

"Only long enough to get my bearings."

"And you heard no shot?"

"I may have. I wouldn't have paid any attention. Too many backfires these days."

"You didn't connect what you found with the figure you'd seen?"

He hesitated. "I'd rather not answer that."

"Go on, Charlie. Tell them," said Paula unexpectedly.

"How did I know that it wasn't Paula?" he said slowly. "I know now that it couldn't have been, but you see what I mean. I didn't know then that they were married, but I did know she couldn't see him at her home, and that she came here."

"You'd just left her, hadn't you?"

"He had to look for a taxi," Paula said bravely. "I could have got here before he did, and he knew that. I didn't, but that's what he thought."

"You had her keys, didn't you?"

"She could have whistled, or something. I'd better explain what I mean. I didn't think she'd killed him. You understand that. I didn't think any-one had killed him. But if she had told him something . . ."

"That I cared for you, and not for him," Paula put in bravely.

"Well, you see what that would mean. I just didn't want her mixed up with it. That's all. And of course I wasn't sure that it was Paula." He glanced at her. "Sorry, Paula, but you know it, too. Wynne always had a girl or two on the string. He was that sort."

The Inspector flicked a glance at me. "All right," he said. "Now we'll go over the ladder business. I'll need you for that, Miss Brent."

But they never did go over the ladder business. When they had reached the front door, passing solemnly by that room where Miss Juliet lay in state, surrounded by her flowers, it was to find an officer in the lower hall, with a message for the Inspector.

He turned to me with a grave face. "Break this to Mary as gently as you can," he said. "The old man was knocked down by a hit-and-run driver not very far from the house, and died on his way to the hospital."

## CHAPTER XXVI

THAT NIGHT remains to me one of the most horrible in my experience.

It was necessary to break the news to Mary, and she went into utter and complete collapse. Hugo's body was still in the hospital mortuary, and it was useless to ask her what her wishes were with regard to it. By ten o'clock I had got the doctor, and he gave her something to keep her quiet; but when he had gone, I found myself virtually alone.

A dim light burned in Miss Juliet's room, and the entire house was redolent with the sickly odor of funeral flowers. I had opened the door on the landing, so that I could go back now and then to see Mary, and I sat in the room which had been mine, and which adjoined the large front room where Miss Juliet lay in state.

I was very tired. It was Friday night, and the amount of real sleep I had had since the Monday before was negligible. But as usual in such cases, I was too weary to sleep. I threw myself, still in my uniform, on my bed; but once down, my mind began to fill with clues, conjectures, what not.

Once more I tried to reconstruct what had happened in that upper room on Monday night, but with the same lack of success. I could see Herbert, entering by the front door, and cheerfully enough. He would still have the *Eagle* in his pocket, at least probably. And I could see him in his room later on, preparing to undress, taking out his revolver first, and laying it and then the newspaper on the bureau. I could even see someone entering that room, but it would not have been Charlie Elliott, or Herbert would not have remained in that chair. He would have leaped to his feet, surely; have sensed trouble, even reached for his revolver.

But he had not gotten up. He had looked up, perhaps, from untying his shoe. He had almost certainly not been alarmed at all, although he may have been surprised. But he had stayed in his chair, perhaps for some time. There had been conversation of some sort, with the killer getting out his handkerchief under some pretense or other, or keeping on his gloves, and edging toward that revolver on the dresser. But Herbert had not expected to be killed. He had looked up, and had got a bullet in his forehead, perhaps even before he sensed that there was any danger.

I could go as far as that, but no further. I believed Paula's story, and Charlie Elliott's. I believe that Herbert had been dead when Charlie Elliott entered that room. But nothing in all of this explained how the *Eagle* had become the *News,* or why that scrap of paper had had powder marks on it, or had been a week old. Nor did any of it bear any relationship to a plot about life insurance.

I went over Miss Juliet's statement in my mind. Perhaps young Elliott had moved to the bed; he was excited. Perhaps she had seen him coming forward as she said, and then stooping over the body. But she had said that he had moved it, dragged it across the floor! Had she seen that, or had she imagined it later?

I was roused at eleven by the doorbell, and I went wearily down the stairs. It seemed to me that I had made a million excursions up and down those stairs; that I had worn hollows in them with my feet. I had expected a reporter, but it was the Inspector himself, looking even more grave than the circumstances seemed to warrant.

He stepped into the hall, and closed the door behind him. "Look here," he said, "have you your automatic?"

"You told me not to bring it."

"Well, I've brought you one," he said, and laid it on the table beside me. "Just remember to take off the safety before you snap it at anybody."

"I don't want it," I said. "I don't want it. I want to go home and go to sleep forever."

"You'll take a good chance of going to sleep forever if you don't keep a gun handy in this house," he retorted grimly. "I'm not trying to scare you, but I put you on this job and I'm responsible for you. I'm not sending you after Hugo."

"After Hugo?"

"I think Hugo was murdered, deliberately run down and killed as he crossed the street by the Manchester place. Our man saw it done, but he had only a glimpse of the car."

"He was murdered!"

"He's dead, anyhow."

He looked at me, and I must have been pale, for he put a hand on my shoulder. "You're a brave young woman, Miss Pinkerton," he said, "and you're not going to quit on us now. Nor are we going to quit on you. Just remember that. And now I'm going up and talk to Mary."

He was closeted with her for some time, and after that I heard him moving about the rear of the house. He stopped at the washstand in the hall to wash his hands, and he was drying them when he came back to me, in the library.

He put me into a comfortable chair before he said anything.

"Just lean back and listen," he said. "I think I've got this thing doped out, and I've made some plans to close it up. But I can tell you a certain amount. Here was what at first looked like a suicide, but with no contact marks. There were two possibilities. This boy had a fortune in insurance, and he knew that the old lady was desperate for money. It might, of course, have been accidental death, but Herbert wasn't cleaning his gun when it happened. He'd done it earlier that evening, between eight and nine. And if the bullet mark on the fireplace and other signs meant anything, he had been in a chair when it happened, taking off his shoes.

"Still, there are ways of committing suicide so that it looks like something else, and that newspaper would probably have thrown us off the scent entirely, if I had happened to open it. As a matter of fact, I picked it up and looked at it, but as you know, the front and back pages were whole; no bullet marks on them. It wasn't until you found that scrap here in the library and gave it to me that I began to veer toward the suicide idea. But even there I was puzzled. The scrap was from a paper a week old, and by all the evidence it should have been from the *Eagle*. It wasn't. I put our fellows on it, and it was from the *News*.

"That might mean a lot, or it might not. I can tell you now that I got that newspaper from Mary just now. She'd had it hidden from Hugo all week, but she told me a little while ago where to find it."

He took it from his pocket and gave it to me. It was much as he had described such a paper, that day in the office. Closed, it was whole; opened, it showed part of a bullet hole, and certain powder marks and scorchings. One corner was missing, and the Inspector took out the scrap from his wallet and fitted it into place.

"Now we have to think of this," he went on. "Miss Juliet confessed a certain amount, but not all she knew. She had seen that newspaper, and Mary admits that she knew from Herbert how such a trick could be pulled. She got that newspaper that night and gave it to Mary to hide. Hugo was not to know about it, or anybody.

"What I figure is that she lay in her bed that night, and she suddenly remembered that newspaper on the bureau, and had her moment of temptation. Mary may have told her that night that there was considerable insurance. Mary had a way of learning things she was not supposed to know. You can see Miss Juliet's argument. After all, she was poor and insurance companies are rich. And she couldn't bring that boy back to life."

"I don't believe it. I don't believe she would lend herself to a thing like that. To profit by her own nephew's death . . . !"

"Nevertheless, that is what she did. And that's our scrap of paper."

"And he killed himself after all!"

"Who said he killed himself? All I'm saying is what whatever opinion she formed later, that night she believed that he had killed himself. It wasn't until we began working on the case that she began to doubt it. She had seen young Elliott escaping, but she knew him. It wouldn't occur to her that a boy she knew would kill. You know the idea; she'd known his people. He'd been engaged to Paula. An accident, or a suicide, but not murder. Not then, anyhow."

"She came to murder, just the same," I said with some bitterness.

"Surely she did. So did you. So did I. But let's get on with this. I have to go." He looked at his watch.

"Now take the other side. Here's a clear case of murder against Charlie Elliott; so clear that the District Attorney is going to have to be restrained if anything happens to it. Young Elliott was jealous. More than that, he was frantic. He had followed the girl, and he knew she was coming to this house at night. Pretty hard to swallow, all that, for Herbert Wynne was no good and he knew it.

"Now, it's at least conceivable that, leaving out the matter of the insurance, young Elliott might kill Wynne. Here's the girl's story about Wynne being followed, and having to carry a revolver. It all fits. But there are one or two things left over; this newspaper, for one thing. It's hardly conceivable that Elliott fired at Wynne through that paper. But if he did, for any reason, why was the paper a week old?"

"You mean, it had been prepared in advance?"

"Good for you. That's just what I do mean. You said something that day in the office, when you said that a murder could be made to look like a suicide. The only answer to this newspaper is that this murder was to look like an accident, and that if trouble came there was the alibi—the paper. Only one thing slipped up. Mary got that paper and hid it. She hid it, if you want to know, in a mason jar and set it into a crock of apple butter in the cellar!"

I gazed at him with eyes that must have been sunk deep in my head. "Then it was Hugo, after all?"

"It was not Hugo. I only know this; that if some plans I've laid work out as I expect them to, I ought to be able to tell you in the morning. Or sooner!"

And with that he went away. Even now, looking back, I find it hard to forgive him for that. He might have told me something, have given me some hint. He could trust me; I had worked hard for him. But he did not even tell me how he had planned to protect me.

I think he had his own moment of doubt as he went away, for he stood in the hall and looked at me, and then at the stairs behind me.

"Good night," he said. "Don't do too much running about; and take the gun upstairs with you." Then he went away, and as I locked and bolted the door behind him, I again had that curious little shiver of fear.

The house was certainly eerie that night. It creaked and rapped incessantly, and over it all hung the heavy funereal odor of those flowers in the front room. The hall was filled with it, and it had even penetrated back to Mary's room.

I had taken the gun upstairs with me, but I don't mind saying that after a time I began to feel that no revolver would be of any use against the phantoms with which my mind insisted on filling those old rooms; with Miss Juliet and Herbert, and now with Hugo. Only Mary left, out of that family of ghosts, and she sleeping the sleep of drugs and exhaustion in that back room.

At half past twelve I went back to look at her, but she was quiet. Even seeing her, at least alive and substantial, calmed me somewhat; and I was quiet and somewhat comforted when I left her. Somewhat comforted! That is even funny now. For it was that visit to Mary which precipitated my own catastrophe.

Her cat was lying on her bed, and I picked the animal up to carry it into the front hall. Perhaps it is a superstition, but I do not like cats around where there are dead, and it was my intention to put it out.

On the landing, however, it escaped and ran up the third-floor stairs. I disliked intensely the idea of following it, but at last I decided to, turning on the hall light first, and then going on up, calling it as I went.

"Here, Tom!" I called. "Come here! Tom! Tom!"

The sound of my own voice in that quiet house sounded cavernous, and I was not happy to catch a glimpse of the animal, and going into Herbert's room at that. But I had started, and I meant to see the thing through. So I followed him in.

There was a faint light in the room from the hall below, and by it I worked my way toward the dresser and the bracket light beside it. I could see it, faintly gleaming; and then suddenly I could not see it at all. Very quietly the door had closed behind me!

I was paralyzed with terror. I stood perfectly still, my arm upraised toward the bracket, and now I was certain that there was someone in the room. Yet nothing moved. There were only the usual creaks and groans of the old house, swaying in the September breeze. Then, I was certain that the creaks were approaching me. I had my back to the room, but I could hear them, coming closer; and just as I opened my mouth to scream, I felt hands close on my throat. I was being slowly strangled from behind.

CHAPTER XXVII

WHOEVER IT WAS, those hands were prodigiously strong. I was utterly helpless. Sometimes, even now, I waken at night, dripping with a hot sweat, again feeling that terrible struggle for breath, and once more trying to loosen those deadly fingers.

I was incredulous at first, I know. This thing could not be happening to me. It was not possible that someone was trying to kill me. Then I knew that it was possible, and that I was about to die. I can remember that, and I can remember when I began to lose consciousness. My knees went first; I could not stand. I was sagging, falling. Then I must have gone entirely, although I have no memory of that.

I came to myself very slowly. It was difficult to breathe. My throat was swollen and I could not turn my head. And the air, when I did get it, seemed to do me no good. My lungs labored; I could hear myself gasping.

I tried to move, although my head was bursting. But I could not move. I seemed to be in a half-sitting position, in a narrow space, and as I became more conscious, I put out my hand. I touched a wall, and in another direction, only a couple of feet away, I touched another wall. It was some time, in my dazed condition, before I realized that one of these walls was a door, and a still longer time before the facts began to dawn on me; that I was locked in the closet of Herbert's room, and that the air supply was very bad.

So completely was I engrossed with my own position and with that struggle for air, which was partially due to the œdema of my throat, that it must have been several minutes before I so much as attempted to orient myself. It was even longer before I became aware of the complete and utter silence in the house. Then I tried to call out, but I could only make a hoarse and guttural noise which could not have been heard beyond the door of the room, so I gave that up. It took air which, apparently, I could not spare.

The closet was stiflingly hot, and my legs began to cramp. I tried to stand up, but I was too weak to rise. My mind was clearer, however.

I tried hammering on the door, but the really dreadful silence continued. And then, far away, I heard a sound. It might have been anything, but it began to sound like someone climbing the stairs. And that, I realized very soon, was what it was. Whoever it was came very slowly, and seemed now and then to stop; but that inevitable progress continued. The stairs creaked, the railing groaned, as if someone was holding on to it. Suddenly it occurred to me that it was the murderer coming back, and I had an attack of panic so terrible that, even as I write this, I find myself in a hot sweat of fear.

The footsteps reached the third floor at last, still with that curious wavering advance, and the unknown seemed to stand in the doorway for some time, like a runner who has finished a race. Then they came into the room and stopped there. I could hear a sort of gasping for breath, and then there followed another stealthy movement; a movement toward the closet door and, after what seemed like a moment of listening, the turning of the key in that door.

Even now I wonder about that. Was there a sort of late repentance for it? A final decision to give me a chance for life before I smothered? I cannot believe it. But I do know that with the turning of the key I tried to scream, and that my vocal cords would not respond.

Something else did, however. Just what strength I received at that instant I do not know. I have a vague sort of recollection of suddenly being able to stand, and of being stronger than I had ever been before. I recall that, and that as the key turned I pushed against the door with a frenzy born of desperation. It flew open, and it evidently struck whoever stood outside, and struck hard; for I heard a grunt in the darkness and then a heavy fall and silence. I actually fell over that inert figure as I rushed out, and the next instant I was flying down the stairs, and almost straight into the barrel of a revolver held by Inspector Patton.

"In Herbert's room," I croaked. "Quick! In Herbert's room."

Then, almost on the spot where poor Hugo had collapsed that very day, I fainted again.

When I came to, I was lying on my bed in my own small room adjoining Miss Juliet's. The Inspector was standing beside the bed, and there was a sound of shuffling feet outside. The Inspector frowned and hastily closed the door into the hall, but I knew only too well what that shuffling meant: the careful carrying of a stretcher, where men do not keep step, but walk with a broken rhythm to avoid the swinging which might jar whoever lies on it. When the Inspector came back to the bed, I was looking at him, he has said since, and making strange noises in my throat.

"Don't try to talk. How do you feel? All right?"

I nodded. "Ice," I croaked. "Ice on my throat. Swollen."

I realized then that there was a policeman just outside the door, for the Inspector sent him for some cracked ice in a towel, and then looked at me gravely.

"I'll have to be running along," he said. "But I can't go without saying that I owe you a number of things, including one of the profoundest apologies of my life; and a policeman's life is full of them! I told you once that down at Headquarters we had a lot of wall-eyed pikes who called themselves detectives. Well, I'm the king piker of the lot. All I can do is to thank God it's no worse, little Miss Pinkerton."

"Who was it?" I croaked. My lips were still swollen, and my tongue felt thick in my mouth. When he said later that I was hissing like a teakettle with excitement, he was pretty nearly right.

And, of course, the policeman chose that moment to come running with a piece of ice as big as his head, and on top of that I heard the telephone ringing wildly downstairs. Somebody below answered it and called up.

"You're wanted, Inspector. Fellow seems to be in a hurry."

"Who is it?"

"Name's Henderson, he says."

The Inspector flung out of the room, and I could hear him running down the stairs. I got off the bed, and went as far as the landing, feeling weak, my knees shaking. When I had got a firm grip on the stair rail and looked over, it was to see the Inspector at the telephone, a tall lank figure in a gray suit; the front doors wide open and men standing on the porch, and beyond them again, something shining and black; the police ambulance.

The Inspector was barking into the telephone.

"What's the matter, Henderson?"

He listened for a minute.

"How long ago?" he shouted. . . . "An hour or more? Good God, man! Get over there and break a window. I'll be right along."

He gave a few orders, and then, seeing me on the stairs, he called to me.

"How are you now? Strong enough to take a ride? You won't have to talk!"

I nodded, and was about to turn back for a coat when he called again.

"If you're coming, come now. We've got no time to spare."

With that he shot out of the front door and down the steps. I followed him as best I could, and I was barely in the car, and had not managed to close the door, before he had let in the clutch and we were on our way. Never before have I traveled at such a rate, and I hope never to do so again. A motorcycle policeman had materialized from nowhere, and he preceded us, keeping his siren going, and clearing the way. We dashed through traffic lights and past pedestrians, having only a glimpse of their astonished faces, and in all that time he spoke only once.

"It's Paula Brent," he said, not looking at me. "She's in the garage; locked in, according to Henderson. And he can't make her hear him."

To my surprise I found that I could speak, although huskily.

"Locked in! She hasn't tried to kill herself?"

"I rather think," he said slowly, "that someone has tried to do that for her. And we can thank little Henderson if it wasn't successful. I don't even know that yet."

"How?"

"Carbon-monoxide gas, apparently. But it is a large garage. There's just a chance . . ."

His voice trailed off, and at that moment we turned into the alley behind the Brent house.

There was no trouble in finding what we were looking for. Halfway along the block was a private garage, brightly lighted, and inside of it a small group of people bending over something on the floor which I could not see. Even before we had got out of the car, a figure detached itself from the group, and I saw that it was Mr. Henderson.

"We've sent for the ambulance, Inspector. It ought to be here any minute."

"Then she's living?"

"Yes."

"Thank God! Who is in there?"

"Her father and mother, and my wife. Our roundsman, too, but he has just come. It was my wife who sent for the ambulance."

And I seemed to feel his pride in that, even as I climbed out of the car and went into the garage.

Paula Brent was lying on the cement floor, very still and barely breathing.

CHAPTER    XXVIII

SHE LAY at the rear of her own small coupé, and as the group about her moved back, I examined her, but I had had little experience of carbon-monoxide cases, and I was rather at a loss. I suggested artificial respiration until the ambulance arrived; and it was the motorcycle man who gave it. I myself was still too weak.

I found the Inspector bending over me as I stooped.

"Any marks on her? Has she been hurt?"

"I'm not sure. There is a lump on the back of her head, but she may have fallen."

He left the group and I saw him prowling about the garage, but apparently he found nothing, and I think he expected to find nothing. There was glass on the floor under the window, where Mr. Henderson had broken his way in, but that was all. I saw him talking to Mr. Henderson, and soon after that he took a pocket flashlight and went out into the alley. When he came back, with little Henderson trotting at his heels, he was carrying a small key in his handkerchief, and he wrapped it carefully and put it in his pocket.

If I had had any doubt that an attempt had been made that night to murder Paula Brent, it died then. She had been locked in that garage, and left to die.

The ambulance arrived very soon after that, and we followed it to the hospital. A queer-looking object I must have been, at that. I had worked at St. Luke's, and the night porter knew me well.

"Looks as though you'd been in some sort of a mix-up, Miss Adams," he said.

"Mix-up is the word, John," I said, "and if there is anyone still in the kitchen, I'd like to have some strong black coffee."

He promised to send it to me, and I followed the Inspector to the Emergency Ward. There were five or six people around the table there, and they had sent for the pulmotor. What with a couple of internes, the night supervisor and what not, I could get only a glimpse of Paula, lying there still and rather childish. Then the group closed in, and somebody brought me my coffee.

They worked over her most of what was left of the night, and it was gray dawn before she was out of danger. The Inspector had disappeared as soon as she began to improve, but he returned again shortly after daylight, to pace the hospital corridor until he was allowed to see her. When that time came, he cleared the room, except for me, and then drawing up a chair beside the bed proceeded to question her; rather gently, as one might interrogate a child.

But she knew very little. After that experiment at the Mitchell house she had meant to go home, as the Inspector had ordered. She was happy and excited, however, for she felt certain that the police meant to release Charlie Elliott. She had told the Inspector, too, about Florence and the keys, and all in all she was very hopeful.

So she did not go home. She drove about until half past eleven or so. Then she went home and put her car in the garage. She had cut off her engine when she heard someone walking in the alley. That did not disturb her, and she was on her way to close the garage doors when she saw a man entering. There was a light in the alley, and her first alarm came when she saw that he had something dark tied over the lower part of his face.

That frightened her, and she turned to escape by the small door leading to the house. It must have been then that he struck her down, for she remembered no more until she awakened in the hospital.

That was all she knew, and it was Mr. Henderson, still waiting below, who supplied some of the gaps in her story.

Apparently it was as Inspector Patton had said the day before, that the arrest of Charlie Elliott, and his own part in it, was the nearest to drama that his life had ever touched. However that may be, apparently from the time on Monday night when he had heard Paula and Charlie quarreling in the alley, he had taken an avid interest in their affairs.

On that Friday night, then, he had heard Paula taking out her car about eight, and when she was not back by ten or thereabouts, he grew a little anxious.

"I've got no children," he explained, "so I've always been fond of Paula. And of Charlie Elliott, too," he hastened to add.

By eleven, when she still had not returned, he spoke to his wife. She, however, was not as fond of Paula as he was, and she told him to go to bed and quit worrying about a girl young enough to be his daughter. He said nothing more to her and he did go to bed; but he lay awake and listened, and around eleven thirty or maybe a quarter to twelve, she drove in and cut off her engine, and soon after, he heard the garage doors close.

He turned over then to go to sleep, but after five minutes or so he heard the engine going again. He got up and looked out. The garage across the alley was dark, but there was no question about the motor. It was going, and going hard. He would have gone over then, but his wife was indignant by that time, and so he had crawled back into bed.

"You'd think that child didn't know anything about a car," she told him. "If she wants to try out her engine, let her do it."

"But there's no light in the place."

"How do you know that? She's probably using a hand flash. Now go to sleep."

He did not go to sleep, however, and it was perhaps a quarter to one when his wife at last seemed settled for the night. All that time he had heard the motor running, but at that time or thereabouts he heard the engine stop, and he went to the window again. He was worried, for some reason or other. He went to the window, he said, so that when Paula left the garage by the small door, he could see her and then settle down. There was a light on at the Brent place, and he could always see anyone who left the garage at night and went toward the house.

But she did not leave the garage. He waited for perhaps fifteen minutes, and then he resolutely put on his clothes and went carefully down the stairs and out of the house. He felt, I gathered, rather foolish, and he did not want his wife to waken and find him gone.

"You know how women are," he said to the Inspector, as if that explained it.

He found the Brent garage doors locked, both the double ones on the alley and the small one toward the house, and the garage itself dark and quiet. He began to feel foolish, but that odd sense of something wrong still persisted and at last he went back to his house and got his flashlight.

His wife wakened as he fumbled for it, and he made an excuse of hearing a noise downstairs, and said something about burglars. It was the wrong thing, evidently, for she tried to keep him from going down at all; and at last he simply went, asserting himself in a fashion that still evidently startled him. He mopped his face as he told it.

But he took the flash and went across the alley and around to a side window, and he was sure that he could see Paula lying on the cement floor, behind the car. It was then that he went back and telephoned, first to Headquarters and then to the Mitchell house.

As to the stopping of the engine at a quarter before one, he believed what later proved to be the fact—that it had stopped because the gas tank was empty.

Most of all that I only learned later, of course. I was still with Paula when the Inspector came back and again began to question her. She was much better by that time, although she was still very white.

"Can you tell me what you did yesterday, Paula?" he asked. "Go through the day, as briefly as you can."

Well, her day had been fairly full, all things considered.

It began with my telephone message, and her mistake in the hour. She had reached the house at ten, had been too late to see Miss Juliet, and had asked me to take her into the house.

"I know all that. I found that certificate, Paula. It's safe."

She colored faintly, but went on. She had met Florence Lenz in my room, and learned who she was. Florence had been rude to her. She had had trouble in getting out of the house, but had managed it, and gone home to lunch. Early in the afternoon a woman named Henderson, a terrible person apparently, who browbeat her nice little husband, had telephoned that Miss Juliet was dead. She was the sort who could not wait to pass on bad news, and Paula resented her tone. She had simply hung up the receiver.

But she was frightened just the same. If Miss Juliet's statement was damaging to Charlie Elliott, there would be no way of disproving it now. It was not until later in the afternoon, when Doctor Stewart came in to see her mother, that she learned the possibility of poison.

"But if it was poison, doctor," she had said, "wouldn't that exonerate Charlie? They couldn't blame him for that."

The two of them were alone in the library by that time, and she made up her mind to tell the doctor at least a part of the story. She had done that, and while she did so, something had occurred to her for the first time. If she was married to Herbert, she was entitled to that insurance money. And if she had that money, she could afford to employ a lawyer.

When the doctor left, she had telephoned to Arthur Glenn, but he was still in court. She went to his office, however, and waited for him until he came in at something after four. She had thought of him, because he had been Miss Juliet's lawyer, and his father had represented the Mitchell family before him. If he worked with Charlie's attorneys, it would show that he really believed him innocent.

But sitting there waiting, with Florence busily typing in another room, she had had time to look at her. And it was then that she had remembered where she had seen Florence before; coming out of that moving-picture theater on Monday night, and giving her a cold stare as she passed.

CHAPTER XXIX

STRANGE AS it seems now, in all the strain of that night and the frenzied endeavors to save Paula Brent, I had given little or no thought to my own experience. And now, in that hospital room, all I craved was sleep. Curiosity was dead in me. I found my head drooping while she talked, and when, later on, the Inspector bundled me in his car and drove me home, he tells me that I slept all the way.

But we did not leave immediately when Paula had finished. Instead the Inspector got up and, opening the door to the hall, beckoned to someone. The next moment Charlie Elliott was in the room and bending over Paula's bed.

"Darling!" he said thickly. "You poor darling."

"Somebody gave me the rap, Charlie!"

"I know about that."

But if I had expected any emotional scene between them that morning, I did not get it. True, they had a tight grip on each other, as though they meant never to let go. But these modern youngsters camouflage what they feel, so what she said was, "You need a shave, you know. What did you do? Break out with dynamite?"

He glanced at the Inspector, benignly watching them.

"Those bozos down at the jail said that after almost a week they'd be glad to pay me to get out."

"I don't blame them! I suppose you tried to be funny."

"*Be* funny!" he protested. "I *was* funny. Ask the Inspector; *he* knows. Tell her that joke of mine about the Marines and the cow, Inspector."

But it was camouflage, and the next minute he grinned at us, and waved toward the door.

"We're about six months behind in our necking," he observed, "and I'm old-fashioned about necking. I don't like an audience."

When I glanced back through the open door a minute later, he was on his knees beside Paula's bed, with an arm thrown over her. And she was crying.

I was almost beyond noticing, however. Somehow the Inspector got me down to his car, and as I have said, I slept all the way home. I remember getting out of the car and climbing the stairs to my sitting room. I have a faint recollection of Dick hopping about wildly, and then I was on my couch and I did not waken until the stealthy clatter of dishes roused me. I looked up, and Mrs. Merwin was carrying in a tray for two.

"Here's some breakfast, dearie," she said cheerfully. "And some for the gentleman. . . . You look a wreck. It must have been a bad case," she added, appraising me carefully. Then she left.

I began to laugh. I laughed until I found the Inspector holding a cup of coffee under my nose and sternly telling me to drink it and quit it.

"Quit it!" I said hysterically. "I have quit. I'm through. Washed up."

He paid absolutely no attention to that, and while I sipped my coffee, he went over and talked to the canary.

"Well, Dick," he said, "your mistress is in a bad humor, and there will be no sugar for either of us for a while. I don't know that I blame her, either. And we have to remember that. But outside of the temper, she's rather a dear person, and I'm fond of her. In fact, I'm very fond of her."

"Stop talking nonsense," I said sharply. "And tell me about last night."

"It's a long story. I need food first."

"If that gun you gave me wasn't in the jardinière . . ."

"In the jardinière!" he said. "My God!"

And then, between mouthfuls of a hearty breakfast, he began his story.

"As a matter of record," he said, "I owe a part of the solution of these two crimes—or maybe three—to you. You did a good piece of work without knowing it, when you marooned those two poor devils on the roof yesterday. And I repaid you by getting you damned near choked to death! You can consider last night's apology repeated, and then some. But I have an excuse, such as it is. We were there all right, outside the house. But we were watching the doors. We knew that this person we were after had keys to that side door and, by all the laws of probability, would use them.

"What we did not know was that a window would be unlocked and subsequently used.

"When we found that open window, it was too late.

"But let's get at this in orderly fashion. I'll say this. Up to between four o'clock and five yesterday afternoon you knew almost as much as I did. You knew about the insurance, and that Herbert Wynne hadn't carried out the plan as he was supposed to. You'd seen Miss Juliet's confession, and you knew that it definitely implicated Charlie Elliott. And you knew, too, that she had been murdered in her turn.

"Charlie Elliott couldn't have done that. And as you said yesterday after you read that statement of hers—or did I say it?—that statement left out certain facts which were important. What about that newspaper? Why had she left that out of her statement? That set me to thinking.

"Now, what sort of woman was Miss Juliet Mitchell? She was honest, wasn't she? And all week she has been lying in her bed and worrying about the thing she had done. At last she decides to make a statement, telling about what she found in that room that night; that is all she had to tell, but she was determined to tell it. Yet after Mary produced that paper last night, I knew what I had already suspected: that Miss Juliet hadn't told all she knew. She never mentioned that paper. Why?

"But let's forget Monday for a minute, and get on to yesterday. She was poisoned. I was pretty sure of that when I found that tablet on the ground, and our fellows confirm it. But I'm here to say, hard as it sounds, that if her murderer had left well enough alone, I believe that Charlie Elliott would have gone to the chair.

"She was feeble. She had this heart trouble. And I doubt if she'd have lived until the trial came up.

"Here the peculiar psychology of any intelligent killer comes to our aid. No killer is content to let well enough alone. That's probably why they return to the scenes of their crimes. And this killer of ours was in a bad way; lying awake at night wondering if he had covered his tracks. Thinking of this, afraid of that. God knows whether there's a hell or not, but the killer doesn't need one. He lives it on earth.

"And remember, Miss Juliet hadn't mentioned that newspaper in her statement.

"Let's go back over that original scheme. I'm inclined to think that Herbert originated the idea. I know this much: he was to get five thousand down, and another five when he had drowned himself, or pretended to.

"The scheme was, of course, to get away from here, and to make a new start. The Lenz girl was to go with him, and as far as I know, it may have been her idea."

"It's the sort of thing she would think of," I agreed.

"Now that's all very pretty. You can see Hugo falling for it. But I have an idea that the original amount was not to be so large; enough to pay

Herbert what he was to get, pay Miss Juliet's debts, and leave enough for the servants' legacies. One of the things which looked odd was Hugo's astonishment when he learned that a hundred thousand dollars was involved. I believe he was frightened, from that time on.

"Much of the insurance plot I knew or suspected; but it was only yesterday that I learned that the Lenz girl had been Herbert's lady love until he met Paula, early last spring. The plot had preceded that. That brought Florence Lenz in in some way, but I couldn't see how. And there were other things to be worked out. I'd been over that upper room, but without conviction, as you know. So there was the explanation of those night invasions of the Mitchell house, and finding Charlie Elliott back there on Thursday.

"Then there was the searching of Herbert's clothes by Mary and Miss Juliet, and I suppose by Hugo before that. I knew it had been done, but why? Hugo I can understand. Paula had said that Herbert had threatened to leave a letter somewhere, so that, if anything happened to him, she could produce it. He was after that letter. But what were Mary and the old lady looking for?

"That's fairly easy. I think Miss Juliet believed that he had killed himself, and there's a convention about such affairs. At least she believed that there was. All suicides left letters, she believed, and where was Herbert's?

"You get that, of course? All right. Now, she has gone as far as she can, and she is miserable. She has saved the Mitchell house and the Mitchell honor; but she is a sinning woman, and she will have to meet her God before long. She can't stand it. She tells Hugo she is going to confess, she tells Arthur Glenn. And then she doesn't confess after all!

"It wouldn't work, so far as I was concerned, and I began to go back over that poisoning. Why did she have to go? She had done her part. And then, sometime between four and five that afternoon, those two boys you'd held on the roof came in to give me something, and I began to see daylight."

He paused, and poured out another cup of coffee; it was cold by that time.

"Now go over the people involved in this case. Hugo didn't smoke at all. Herbert smoked cigarettes incessantly. There were only two men connected with it at all who smoked cigars. And what those boys had found was an almost entire cigar of a good brand. You have to remember that the press has known almost as much of this case as I have. The D. A. has seen to that." He smiled wryly. "Also a good many of the newspapermen, especially the younger ones, never had believed that Charlie Elliott was guilty. And Elliott was a cigarette smoker.

"But I had to be sure. I had to be sure that Evans hadn't smoked a cigar there the night I got him out on the roof. Well, he had, but it was a stogie, and he still had it in his mouth when he got down the ladder.

"This cigar was under some leaves in the gutter, and we'd overlooked it. But one of these reporters, a fellow named Davidson, crawled out there to see what I was doing below when I threw that ladder away, and he uncovered it. I took it to the laboratory, and while a lot of this Sherlock Holmes stuff about tobacco ashes and so on is only good for fiction, they did think it had been out in the weather three or four days. They didn't know when or how I got it. That was the opinion, anyhow.

"That gave me something. I could imagine that a part of the camouflage in that room which fooled Herbert Wynne on Monday night, and maybe let this unknown get hold of that revolver, was the lighting of that cigar. It hadn't been smoked more than a couple of minutes.

"Well, who smoked cigars on this case? Only two men, and you know who they are."

"Mr. Glenn and the doctor!"

"Precisely. And the whole case came down to which of them profited by Miss Juliet's death. By her will, in other words. Remember, the original modest insurance had been increased to a hundred thousand dollars. Even after Herbert had got his ten, and the servants perhaps five thousand apiece, there was still eighty thousand left. In other words, the old lady had probably made that will when she had a little capital, and Herbert would get what remained after the legacies. But she'd have to provide for the possibility that he might die before her. Well, she did just that."

"And that's when you left the message for Mr. Glenn?"

"It is. He said that the will was in the bank, and he'd get it in the morning."

He finished his coffee, and then looked at me.

"Here's where you come in," he said. "You'd said that whoever saw to it that Miss Juliet got those doses of strychnia yesterday had to know that they would be fatal only in her condition. That looked like the doctor, didn't it? But I happened to know that Arthur Glenn had recently defended a case where something similar had happened; not the same thing, but he had had to read up on toxicology.

"When I set that trap last night, I knew that it was for one of those two men. I didn't know which, but I knew that the Lenz girl was mixed up in it somehow. She knew Stewart; she used to keep books for him. And she knew Glenn. And you had revealed something yesterday afternoon, when you were scolding me! You'd told her that Paula had been trying to get upstairs to get a letter. You weren't looking at her then, but I was. She simply blazed.

"You see, everyone in that plot knew that Herbert had left such a letter, or threatened to. Paula and Charlie Elliott weren't the only people who wanted it, and wanted it desperately.

"But something else, too, had happened yesterday afternoon. Paula told Glenn and Stewart that she had married Herbert Wynne. I didn't know that, or I'd have had her watched last night. But whichever one of them was guilty, Paula had to be done away with before she spread that news. Hugo also. When the Lenz girl and Herbert quarreled, it's almost certain that she ceased being the go-between, and Hugo took it over. That is, Hugo gave Herbert the cash for those insurance premiums.

"It's pretty clear that Herbert didn't know who was providing it. He may have suspected, but I doubt if he knew until he had that visitor on Monday night; the man he knew, so that he was not alarmed, the man who smoked the cigar.

"I didn't know myself. I didn't know which of those two men it was until I ran into that third-floor room last night, and found him where you had knocked him senseless with that door."

"And it was . . . ?"

"It was Arthur Glenn," he said soberly. "He'd been in the market, and he was desperate. Desperate all this week, too. Just how desperate you'll know when I tell you that Miss Juliet Mitchell never dictated that statement you signed. The one she dictated never mentioned Charlie Elliott. What she told was that she had known of that newspaper dodge, and had taken the paper and given it to Mary to hide.

"But Glenn had had a warning of what was coming, and so he prepared another statement, one of his own. He shifted them before you went in that day, and she never knew the difference. She had to go, of course, after that. He had taken a tiger by the tail, and he didn't dare to let go. But I don't know yet whether he substituted those tablets himself, or Florence did it."

"She did it," I said with conviction.

He got up and stretched himself.

"Well, I think she did, at that," he said. "One thing's certain: Glenn went to that house late last Monday night to have a showdown with Herbert. More than that, he went there to kill him, if he had to. The chances are that Florence's getting those keys out of Paula's bag was just a bit of luck; but it may have been more. She wasn't in love with Herbert any more, but she might still have been jealous. I haven't a doubt myself that she knew Paula had the keys, and from that to getting them . . .

"Anyhow, Glenn carried a revolver with him that night as well as Paula's keys; and he had that newspaper in his pocket, all ready in case he needed to leave it behind him, bullet hole and all. If there was a verdict of accidental death, he would be sitting pretty. If it was murder, and he was by any chance involved, he could point to that paper and save his life. If it was suicide—well, it was just too bad, and he was out several thousand dollars and the balance when Miss Juliet's angina killed her.

"Well, he left the paper all right. But he didn't need to use his own gun. There was Herbert's, all ready on the bureau. He may still have worn his gloves, or he used a handkerchief. Anyhow, he left no prints on it.

"He had no trouble getting in or getting out. He knew about that sawed-off bolt on the landing door; maybe from Florence. And he moves lightly, for a heavy man.

"But figure up what happened! The old lady gets that alibi of his, and carts it away! And we guess a murder! Moreover, Mary has hidden the paper even from Hugo, and tells him she has burned it! Whatever is coming to him in the next world, Glenn has had his bit of hell already in this. And get this, too! Florence had got Glenn where she wanted him by that time. I doubt if there was anything she didn't either know or guess. She had him chained, and I think he hated her. It's my guess that, if he confesses, he'll involve her, and involve her plenty!"

I suppose I yawned then, for he got up.

"Well, I owe you a lot, Miss Pinkerton. And not the least is a chance to get some sleep."

I yawned again. I could hardly keep my eyes open.

"I want a week of it," I said. "I want a week of sleep, without a break. And I'm ready to start right now."

He smiled at that, and picked up his hat. But he looked at the canary as he moved to the door.

"Dick," he said, "you know your mistress better than I do. But I regard that as a hint. What about you?"

"Don't be foolish," I said sharply. "I meant that I don't want a case for a week."

"I suppose she knows that there is one case she can have for life, Dick," he said. "But she is a hardhearted young woman, and not looking her best just now at that, Dick. Not looking her best."

He turned around and grinned at me.

"Well, I'll run along. Have to see the D. A. and tell him he's been fishing for a minnow and got a whale. And after that I shall buy and *send*—not deliver—a pair of surgical scissors. Well, that's a policeman's life!"

He opened the door, and stopped with his hand on the knob.

"You can let me know when you want to take a case again, little Miss Pinkerton."

"What sort of case?" I asked suspiciously.

"A very long and hard case, involving a life sentence, chains and what have you," he said.

Then he closed the door, and I could hear him whistling softly to himself as he went down the stairs.

# Haunted Lady

HILDA ADAMS was going through her usual routine after coming off a case. She had taken a long bath, using plenty of bath salts, shampooed her short, slightly graying hair, examined her feet and cut her toenails, and was now carefully rubbing hand lotion into her small but capable hands.

Sitting there in her nightgown, she looked rather like a thirty-eight-year-old cherub. Her skin was rosy, her eyes clear, almost childish. That appearance of hers was her stock in trade, as Inspector Patton had said to the new commissioner that same day.

"She looks as though she still thought the stork brought babies," he said. "That's something for a woman who has been a trained nurse for fifteen years. But she can see more with those blue eyes of hers than most of us could with a microscope. What's more, people confide in her. She's not the talking sort, so they think she's safe. She sits and knits and tells them about her canary bird at home, and pretty soon they're pouring out all they know. It's a gift."

"Pretty useful, eh?"

"Useful! I'll say. What's the first thing the first families think of when there's trouble? A trained nurse. Somebody cracks, and there you are. Or there she is."

"I shouldn't think the first families would have that kind of trouble."

The Inspector looked at the new commissioner with a faintly patronizing smile. "You'd be surprised," he said. "They have money, and money breeds trouble. Not only that. Sometimes they have bats."

He grinned. The new commissioner stared at him suspiciously.

"Fact," said the Inspector. "Had an old woman in this afternoon who says she gets bats in her bedroom. Everything closed up, but bats just the same. Also a rat now and then, and a sparrow or two."

The commissioner raised his eyebrows. "No giant panda?" he inquired. "No elephants?"

"Not so far. Hears queer noises, too."

"Sounds haunted," said the commissioner. "Old women get funny sometimes. My wife's mother used to think she saw her dead husband. She'd never liked him. Threw things at him."

The Inspector smiled politely. "Maybe. Maybe not. She had her granddaughter with her. The girl said it was true. I gathered that the grand-daughter had made her come."

"What was the general idea?"

"The girl wanted an officer in the grounds at night. It's the Fairbanks place. Maybe you know it. She seemed to think somebody gets in the house at night and lets in the menagerie. The old lady said that was nonsense; that the trouble was in the house itself."

The commissioner looked astounded. "You're not talking about Eliza Fairbanks?"

"We're not on first-name terms yet. It's Mrs. Fairbanks, relict of one Henry Fairbanks, if that means anything to you."

"Good God," said the commissioner feebly. "What about it? What did you tell her?"

The Inspector got up and shook down the legs of his trousers. "I suggested a good reliable companion; a woman to keep her comfortable as well as safe." He smiled. "Preferably a trained nurse. The old lady said she'd talk to her doctor. I'm waiting to hear from him."

"And you'll send the Adams woman?"

"I'll send Miss Adams, if she's free," said the Inspector, with a slight emphasis on the "Miss." "And if Hilda Adams says the house is haunted, or that the entire city zoo has moved into the Fairbanks place, I'll believe her."

He went out then, grinning, and the commissioner leaned back in the chair behind his big desk and grunted. He had enough to do without worrying about senile old women, even if the woman was Eliza Fairbanks. Or was the word "anile"? He wasn't sure.

The message did not reach the Inspector until eight o'clock that night. Then it was not the doctor who called. It was the granddaughter.

"Is that Inspector Patton?" she said.

"It is."

The girl seemed slightly breathless. "I'm calling for my grandmother. She said to tell you she has caught another bat."

"Has she?"

"Has she what?"

"Caught another bat."

"Yes. She has it in a towel. I slipped out to telephone. She doesn't trust the servants or any of us. She wants you to send somebody. You spoke about a nurse today. I think she should have someone tonight. She's pretty nervous."

The Inspector considered that. "What about the doctor?"

"I've told him. He'll call you soon. Doctor Brooke. Courtney Brooke."

"Fine," said the Inspector, and hung up.

Which was why, as Hilda Adams finished rubbing in the hand lotion that night, covered her canary and was about to crawl into her tidy bed, her telephone rang.

She looked at it with distaste. She liked an interval between her cases, to go over her uniforms and caps, to darn her stockings—although the way stockings went today they were usually beyond darning—and to see a movie or two. For a moment she was tempted to let it ring. Then she lifted the receiver.

"Hello," she said.

"Patton speaking. That Miss Pinkerton?"

"This is Hilda Adams," she said coldly. "I wish you'd stop that nonsense."

"Gone to bed?"

"Yes."

"Well, that's too bad. I've got a case for you."

"Not tonight you haven't," said Hilda flatly.

"This will interest you, Hilda. Old lady has just caught a bat in her room. Has it in a towel."

"Really? Not in her hair? Or a butterfly net?"

"When I say towel I mean towel," said the Inspector firmly. "She seems to have visits from a sort of traveling menagerie: birds, bats and rats."

"I don't take mental cases, and you know it, Inspector. Besides, I've just come off duty."

The Inspector was exasperated. "See here, Hilda," he said. "This may be something or it may be nothing. But it looks damned queer to me. Her granddaughter was with her, and she says it's true. She'll call you pretty soon. I want you to take the case. Be a sport."

Hilda looked desperately about her, at the covered bird cage, at her soft bed, and through the door to her small sitting room with its chintz-covered chairs, its soft blue curtains and its piles of unread magazines. She even felt her hair, which was still slightly damp.

"There are plenty of bats around this time of year," she said. "Why shouldn't she catch one?"

"Because there is no possible way for it to get in," said the Inspector. "Be a good girl, Hilda, and keep those blue eyes of yours open."

She agreed finally, but without enthusiasm, and when a few minutes later a young and troubled voice called her over the telephone, she was already packing her suitcase. The girl was evidently following instructions.

"I'm telephoning for Doctor Brooke," she said. "My grandmother isn't well. I'm terribly sorry to call you so late, but I don't think she ought to be alone tonight. Can you possibly come?"

"Is this the case Inspector Patton telephoned about?"

The girl's voice sounded constrained. "Yes," she said.

"All right. I'll be there in an hour. Maybe less."

Hilda thought she heard a sigh of relief.

"That's splendid. It's Mrs. Henry Fairbanks. The address is Ten Grove Avenue. I'll be waiting for you."

Hilda hung up and sat back on the edge of her bed. The name had startled her. So old Eliza Fairbanks was catching bats in towels, after years of dominating the social life of the city. Lady Fairbanks, they had called her in Hilda's childhood, when the Henry Fairbanks place still had the last iron deer on its front lawn, and an iron fence around it to keep out the *hoi polloi*. The deer was gone now, and so was Henry. Even the neighborhood had changed. It was filled with bleak boardinghouses, and a neighborhood market was on the opposite corner. But the big square house still stood in its own grounds, surrounded by its fence, as though defiant of a changing neighborhood and a changing world.

She got up and began to dress. Perhaps in deference to her memories she put on her best suit and a new hat. Then, canary cage in one hand and suitcase in the other, she went down the stairs. At her landlady's door she uncovered the cage. The bird was excited. He was hopping from perch to perch, but when he saw her, he was quiet, looking at her with sharp, beadlike eyes.

"Be good, Dicky," she said. "And mind you take your bath every day."

The bird chirped and she re-covered him. She thought rather drearily that she lived vicariously a good many lives, but very little of her own, including Dicky's. She left the cage, after her usual custom, with a card saying where she had gone. Then, letting herself quietly out of the house, she walked to the taxi stand at the corner. Jim Smith, who often drove her, touched his cap and took her suitcase.

"Thought you just came in," he said conversationally.

"So I did, Jim. Take me to Ten Grove Avenue, will you?"

He looked at her quickly. "Somebody sick at the Fairbanks house?"

"Old Mrs. Fairbanks isn't well."

Jim laughed. "Been seeing more bats, has she?"

"Bats? Where did you hear that?"

"Things get around," said Jim cheerfully.

Hilda sat forward on the edge of the seat. Without her nightgown and with her short hair covered, she had lost the look of a thirty-eight-year-old cherub and become a calm and efficient spinster, the sort who could knit and talk about her canary at home, while people poured out their secrets to her. She stared at Jim's back.

"What *is* all this talk about Mrs. Fairbanks, Jim?"

"Well, she's had a lot of trouble, the old lady. And she ain't so young nowadays. The talk is that she's got softening of the brain; thinks she's haunted. Sees bats in her room, and all sorts of things. What I say is, if she wants to see bats, let her see them. I've known 'em to see worse."

He turned neatly into the Fairbanks driveway and stopped with a flourish under the porte-cochère at the side of the house. Hilda glanced about her. The building looked quiet and normal: just a big red-brick block with a light in the side hall and one or two scattered above. Jim carried her suitcase up to the door and put it down there.

"Well, good luck to you," he said. "Don't let that talk bother you any. It sounds screwy to me."

"I'm not easy to scare," said Hilda grimly.

She paid him and saw him off before she rang the bell, but she felt rather lonely as the taxi disappeared. There was something wrong if the Inspector wanted her on the case. And he definitely did not believe in ghosts. Standing there in the darkness, she remembered the day Mrs. Fairbank's daughter Marian had been married, almost twenty years ago. Hilda Adams had been a probationer at the hospital then, and she had walked past the place on her off-duty. There had been a red carpet over these steps then, and a crowd, kept outside the iron fence by a policeman, was looking in excitedly. She had stopped and looked, too.

The cars were coming back from the church, and press photographers were waiting. When the bride and groom arrived, they had stopped on the steps, and now, years later, Hilda still remembered that picture: Marian in white satin and veil, with a long train caught up in one hand, while the other held her bouquet of white orchids; and the groom, tall and handsome, a gardenia in the lapel of his morning coat, smiling down at her.

To the little probationer outside on the pavement it had been pure romance: Marian and Frank Garrison, clad in youth and beauty that day. And it had ended in a divorce.

She turned abruptly and rang the doorbell.


## CHAPTER II

SHE WAS SURPRISED when a young girl opened the door. She had expected a butler, or at least a parlormaid. It was the girl who had telephoned her, as she knew when she spoke.

"I suppose you are Miss Adams?"

Hilda was aware that the girl was inspecting her. She smiled reassuringly. "Yes," she said.

"I'm Janice Garrison. I'm so glad you came." She looked around, as if she were afraid of being overheard. "I've been frightfully worried."

She led the way along the side passage to the main hall, and there paused uncertainly. There were low voices from what Hilda later learned was the library, and after a moment's indecision the girl threw open the doors across from it, into what had once been the front and back parlors of the house. Now they were united into one huge drawing room, a Victorian room of yellow brocaded furniture, crystal chandeliers and what looked in the semi-darkness to be extremely bad oil paintings. Only one lamp was lit, but it gave Hilda a chance to see the girl clearly.

She was a lovely creature, Hilda thought. Perhaps eighteen; it was hard to tell these days. But certainly young and certainly troubled. She closed the double doors behind her, after a hurried glance into the hall.

"I had to speak to you alone," she said breathlessly. "It's about my grandmother. Don't—please don't think she is queer, or anything like that. If she acts strangely, it's because she has reason to."

Hilda felt sorry for the girl. She looked on the verge of tears. But her voice was matter of fact.

"I'm accustomed to old ladies who do odd things," she said, smiling. "What do you mean by a reason?"

Janice, however, did not hear her. Across the hall a door had opened, and the girl was listening. She said, "Excuse me for a minute, will you?" and darted out, closing the doors behind her. There followed a low exchange of voices in the hall. Then the doors were opened again, and a man stepped into the room. He was a big man, with a tired face and a mop of heavy dark hair, gray over the ears. Hilda felt a sudden sense of shock. It was Frank Garrison, but he was far removed from the bridegroom of almost twenty years ago. He was still handsome, but he looked his age, and more. Nevertheless, he had an attractive smile as he took her hand.

"I'm glad you're here," he said. "My daughter told me you were coming. My name is Garrison. I hope you'll see that she gets some rest, Miss Adams. She's been carrying a pretty heavy load."

"That's what I'm here for," said Hilda cheerfully.

"Thank you. I've been worried. Jan is far too thin. She doesn't get enough sleep. Her grandmother . . ."

He did not finish. He passed a hand over his hair, and Hilda saw that he had not only aged. He looked worn, and his suit could have stood a pressing. As if she realized this, the girl slid an arm through his and held it tight. She looked up at him with soft brown eyes.

"You're not to worry, Father. I'll be all right."

"I don't like what's going on, Jan darling."

"Would you like to see Granny?"

He looked at his watch and shook his head.

"I'd better get Eileen out of here. She wanted to come, but—— Give Granny my love, Jan, and get some sleep tonight."

As he opened the door, Hilda saw a small blonde woman in the hall. She was drawing on her gloves and gazing at the door with interest. She had a sort of faded prettiness, and a slightly petulant look. Janice seemed embarrassed.

"This is Miss Adams, Eileen," she said. "Granny is nervous, so she's going to look after her."

Eileen acknowledged Hilda with a nod, and turned to the girl. "If you want my opinion, Jan," she said coolly, "Granny ought to be in an institution. All this stuff about bats and so on! It's ridiculous."

Janice flushed but said nothing. Frank Garrison opened the front door, his face set.

"I wish you would keep your ideas to yourself, Eileen," he said. "Let's get out of here. 'Night, Jan."

With the closing of the door, Hilda turned to the girl. To her surprise Jan's eyes were filled with tears.

"I'm sorry," she said, fumbling in her sleeve for a handkerchief. "I never get used to his going away like that. You know they are divorced, my father and mother. Eileen is his second wife." She wiped her eyes and put the handkerchief away. "He can come only when Mother's out. She—they're not very friendly."

"I see," said Hilda cautiously.

"I was devoted to my father, but when the court asked me what I wanted to do, I said I would stay here. My grandmother had taken it very hard. The divorce, I mean. She loved my father. Then, too"—she hesitated—"he married Eileen very soon after, and I—well, it seemed best to stay. I thought I'd better tell you," she added. "Eileen doesn't come often, but since you've seen her——"

She broke off, and Hilda saw that she was trembling.

"See here," she said, "you're tired. Suppose you tell me all this tomorrow? Just now you need your bed and a good sleep. Why not take me up to my patient and forget about it until then?"

Janice shook her head. She was quieter now. Evidently the emotional part of her story was over.

"I'm all right," she said. "You have to know before you see my grandmother. I was telling you why I am here, wasn't I? It wasn't only because of Grandmother. My mother was terribly unhappy, too. She's never been the same since. They both seemed to need me. But of course Granny needed me most."

Hilda said nothing, but her usually bland face was stiff. The complete selfishness of the aged, she thought. This girl, who should have been out in her young world of sport and pleasure, living in this mortuary of a house with two dismal women. For how long? Six or seven years, she thought.

"I see," she said dryly. "They were all right. What about you?"

"I haven't minded it. I drive out with Granny, and read to her at night. It hasn't been bad."

"What about your mother? I suppose she can read."

Janice looked shocked, then embarrassed. "She and my grandmother haven't got along very well since the divorce. My grandmother has never quite forgiven her. I'm afraid I've given you a very bad idea of us," she went on valiantly. "Actually everything was all right until lately. My father comes in every now and then. When Mother's out, of course. And when I can, I go to his house. He married my governess, so of course I knew her."

Hilda sensed a reserve at this point. She did what was an unusual thing for her. She reached over and patted the girl's shoulder.

"Try to forget it," she said. "I'm here, and I can read aloud. I read rather well, as a matter of fact. It's my one vanity. Also I like to drive in the afternoons. I don't get much of it."

She smiled, but the girl did not respond. Her young face was grave and intent. Hilda thought she was listening again. When the house remained quiet, she looked relieved.

"I'm sorry," she said. "I guess I *am* tired. I've been watching my grandmother as best I could for the last month or two. I want to say this again before you see her, Miss Adams. She isn't crazy. She is as sane as I am. If anybody says anything different, don't believe it."

The hall was still empty when they started up the stairs. The girl insisted on carrying the suitcase, and Hilda looked around her curiously. She felt vaguely disappointed. The house had interested her ever since the day of the wedding so long ago. She had visualized it as it must have been then, gay with flowers and music, and filled with people. But if there had ever been any glamour, it was definitely gone.

Not that it was shabby. The long main hall, with doors right and left, was well carpeted, the dark paneling was waxed, the furniture old-fashioned but handsome. Like the big drawing room, however, it was badly lighted, and Hilda, following the young figure ahead of her, wondered if it was always like that; if Janice Garrison lived her young life in that half darkness.

Outside the door of a front room upstairs, the girl paused. She gave a quick look at Hilda before she tapped at the door; a look that was like a warning.

"It's Jan, Granny," she said brightly. "May I come in?"

Somebody stirred in the room. There were footsteps, and then a voice. "Are you alone, Jan?"

"I brought the nurse Doctor Brooke suggested. You'll like her, Grandmother. I do."

Very slowly a key turned in a lock. The door was opened a few inches, and a little old woman looked out. Hilda was startled. She had remembered Mrs. Fairbanks as a dominant woman, handsome in a stately way, whose visits to the hospital as a member of the board had been known to send the nurses into acute attacks of jitters. Now she was incredibly shrunken. Her eyes, however, were still bright. They rested on Hilda shrewdly. Then, as though her inspection had satisfied her, she took off what was evidently a chain and opened the door.

"I've still got it," she said triumphantly.

"That's fine. This is Miss Adams, Granny."

The old lady nodded. She did not shake hands. "I don't want to be nursed," she said, peering up at Hilda. "I want to be watched. I want to know who is trying to scare me, and why. But I don't want anyone hanging over me. I'm not sick."

"That's all right," Hilda said. "I won't bother you."

"It's the nights." The old voice was suddenly pathetic. "I'm all right in the daytime. You can sleep then. Jan has a room for you. I want somebody by me at night. You could sit in the hall, couldn't you? Outside my door, I mean. If there's a draft, Jan can get you a screen. You won't go to sleep, will you? Jan's been doing it, but she dozes. I'm sure she dozes."

Janice looked guilty. She picked up the suitcase. "I'll show you your room," she said to Hilda. "I suppose you'll want to change."

She did not speak again until the old lady's door had been closed and locked behind them. "You see what I mean?" she said as they went down the hall. "She's perfectly sane, and something *is* going on. She'll tell you about it. I don't understand it. I can't. I'm nearly crazy."

"You're nearly dead from loss of sleep," said Hilda grimly. "What is it she says she still has?"

"I'd rather she'd tell you herself, Miss Adams. You don't mind, do you?"

Hilda did not mind. Left alone, she went about her preparations with businesslike movements, unpacked her suitcase, hung up her fresh uniforms, laid out her knitting bag, her flashlight, her hypodermic case, thermometer, and various charts. After that she dressed methodically: white uniform, white rubber-soled shoes, stiff white cap. But she stood for some time, looking down at the .38-caliber automatic which still lay in the bottom of the case. It had been a gift from the Inspector.

"When I send you somewhere, it's because there's trouble," he had said. "Learn to use it, Hilda. You may never need it. Then again you may."

Well, she had learned to use it. She could even take it apart, clean it and put it together again, and once or twice just knowing she had it had been important. But now she left it locked in the suitcase. Whatever this case promised, she thought—and it seemed to promise quite a bit—there was no violence indicated. She was wrong, of course, but she was definitely cheerful when, after surveying her neat reflection in the mirror, she stopped for a moment to survey what lay outside her window.

Her room, like Janice's behind it, faced toward the side street. Some two hundred feet away was the old brick stable with its white-painted cupola where Henry Fairbanks had once kept his horses, and which was now probably used as a garage. And not far behind it was the fence again, and the side street. A stream of light from Joe's Market at the corner helped the street lamps to illuminate the fringes of the property. But the house itself withstood these intrusions. It stood withdrawn and still, as if it resented the bourgeois life about it.

Hilda's cheerfulness suffered a setback. She picked up what she had laid out, tucked under her arm the five-pound *Practice of Nursing*—a book which, on night duty, induced a gentle somnolence which was not sleep—and went back to Janice's door.

The girl was also standing by her window, staring out. So absorbed was she that she did not hear Hilda, who rapped twice on the door frame before Janice heard her and turned, looking startled.

"Oh!" she said, flushing. "I'm sorry. Are you ready?"

Hilda surveyed the room. Janice had evidently attempted to make it cheerful. The old mahogany bed had a bright patchwork quilt on it; there were yellow curtains at the window; and a low chair by the fireplace looked as if she had upholstered it herself in a blue and gray chintz. But there was little sign of Janice's personal life, no photographs, no letters or invitations. The small desk was bare, except for a few books and a package of cigarettes.

"All ready," Hilda said composedly. "Did the doctor leave any orders?"

For some reason Janice flushed. "No. She's not really sick. Just a sedative if she can't sleep. Her heart's weak, of course. That's why it all seems—so fiendish."

She did not explain. She led the way forward, and Hilda took her bearings carefully, as she always did in a strange house. The layout, so far as she could see, was simple. The narrow hall into which her room and Jan's opened also had two rooms on the other side. But in the front of the house the hall widened, at the top of the stairs, into a large square landing, lighted in daytime by a window over the staircase, and furnished as an informal sitting room. Two bedrooms occupied the front corners of the house, with what had once been a third smaller room between them, now apparently converted into bathrooms.

Janice explained as they went forward. "My uncle, Carlton Fairbanks, and his wife, Susie, have these rooms across from yours and mine," she said.

"They're out of town just now. And Mother has the other corner in front, over the library."

Unexpectedly she yawned. Then she smiled. The smile changed her completely. She looked younger, as if she had recaptured her youth.

"You go straight to bed," Hilda said sternly.

"You'll call me if anything goes wrong?"

"Nothing will go wrong."

She watched the girl as she went back along the hall. In her short skirt and green pull-over sweater she looked like a child. Hilda grunted with disapproval, put down her impedimenta—including *Practice of Nursing*—on a marble-topped table, looked around for a comfortable chair in which to spend the night and saw none, and then finally rapped at her patient's door.

CHAPTER III

HER FIRST real view was not prepossessing. Mrs. Fairbanks was dressed in an ancient quilted dressing gown, and she looked less like an alert but uneasy terrier, and more like a frightened and rather dowdy old woman. Nor was her manner reassuring.

"Come in," she said shortly, "and lock the door. I have something to show you. And don't tell me it came down the chimney or through a window. The windows are barred and screened and the chimney flue is closed. Not only that. There is a wad of newspaper above the flue. I put it there myself."

Hilda stepped inside and closed the door behind her. The room was large and square. It had two windows facing the front of the house and two at the side. A large four-poster bed with a tester top occupied the wall opposite the side windows, with a door to a bathroom beside it. The other wall contained a fireplace, flanked, as she discovered later, by two closets.

Save for a radio by the bed, the room was probably as it had been since the old lady had come there as a bride. The heavy walnut bureau, the caneseated rocking chair by the empty fireplace, even the faded photograph of Henry Fairbanks on the mantel, a Henry wearing a high choker collar and a heavy mustache, dated from before the turn of the century.

Mrs. Fairbanks saw her glance at it. "I keep that there to remind myself of an early mistake," she said dryly. "And I don't want my back rubbed, young woman. What I want to know is how this got into my room."

She led the way to the bed, which had been neatly turned down for the night. On the blanket cover lay a bath towel with something undeniably alive in it. Hilda reached over and touched it.

"What is it?" she asked.

Mrs. Fairbanks jerked her hand away. "Don't touch it," she said irritably. "I had a hard enough time catching it. What do you think it is?"

"Perhaps you'd better tell me."

"It's a bat," said the old lady. "They think I'm crazy. My own daughter thinks I'm crazy. I keep on telling them that things get into my room, but nobody believes me. Yes, Miss Adams, it's a bat."

There was hard triumph in her voice. "Three bats, two sparrows, and a rat," she went on. "All in the last month or two. A rat!" she said scornfully. "I've lived in this house fifty years, and there has never been a rat in it."

Hilda felt uncomfortable. She did not like rats. She resisted an impulse to look at the floor. "How do they get in?" she inquired. "After all, there must be some way."

"That's why you're here. You find that out and I'll pay you an extra week's salary. And I want that bat kept. When I saw that police officer today, he said to keep anything I found."

"I don't take extra pay," said Hilda mildly. "What am I to do with the thing?"

"Take it back to the storeroom. The last door on the right. There's a shoe box there. Put it inside and tie it up. And don't let it get away, young woman. I want it."

Hilda picked up the towel gingerly. Under her hands something small and warm squirmed. She felt a horrible distaste for the whole business. But Mrs. Fairbanks's eyes were on her, intelligent and wary and somehow pathetic. She started on her errand, and heard the key turn behind her, and all at once she had the feeling of something sinister about the whole business: the gloomy house, the old woman locked in her room, the wretched little creature in her hands. The Inspector had been right when he said it all looked damned queer to him.

The storeroom was, as Mrs. Fairbanks had said, at the back of the hall. She held her towel carefully in one hand and opened the door with the other. She had stepped inside and was feeling for the light switch when there was a sudden noise overhead. The next moment something soft and furry had landed on her shoulder and dropped with a plop to the floor.

"Oh, my God!" she said feebly.

But the rat—she was sure it was a rat—had disappeared when at last she found the light switch and turned it on. She was still shaken, however. Her hands trembled when she found the shoe box and dumped the bat into it. It lay there, stunned and helpless, and when she carried it to the hall table and put it down, she stopped and cut a small air hole with her surgical scissors. But she was irritable when, after the usual unlocking, she was again admitted to the room.

"How am I to look after you," she inquired, "if you keep me locked out all the time?"

"I haven't asked you to look after me."

"But surely——"

"Listen, young woman. I want you to examine this room. Maybe you can find out how these creatures get in. If you can't, then I'll know that somebody in this house is trying to scare me to death."

"That's dreadful, Mrs. Fairbanks. You can't believe it."

"Of course it's dreadful. But not so dreadful as poison."

"Poison!"

"Poison," repeated Mrs. Fairbanks. "Ask the doctor, if you don't believe me. It was in the sugar on my tray. Arsenic."

She sat in the rocking chair by the fireplace, looking wizened but complacent. As though, having set out to startle the nurse, she had happily succeeded. She had indeed. Hilda was thoroughly startled. She stood looking down, her face set and unsmiling. Quite definitely she did not like this case. But equally definitely the old woman believed what she was saying.

"When was all this?" she asked.

"Three months ago. It was in the sugar on my breakfast tray."

"You are sure you didn't imagine it?"

"I didn't imagine that bat, did I?"

She went on. She had strawberries the morning it happened. She always had her breakfast in her room. The arsenic was in the powdered sugar, and she had almost died.

"But I didn't," she said. "I fooled them all. And I didn't imagine it. The doctor took samples of everything. It was in the sugar. That's the advantage of having a young man," she said. "This boy is smart. He knows all the new things. If I'd had old Smythe, I'd have died. Jan got young Brooke. She'd met him somewhere. And he was close. He lives across from the stable on Huston Street. It was arsenic all right."

Hilda looked—and felt—horrified. "What about the servants?" she said sharply.

"Had them for years. Trust them more than I trust my family."

"Who brought up the tray?"

"Janice."

"But you can't suspect her, Mrs. Fairbanks."

"I suspect everybody," said Mrs. Fairbanks grimly.

Hilda sat down. All at once the whole situation seemed incredible: the deadly quiet of the house, the barred and screened windows, the thick atmosphere of an unaired room, and the old woman in the rocking chair, telling calmly of an attempt to murder her.

"Of course you notified the police," she said.

"Of course I did nothing of the kind."

"But your doctor . . ."

Mrs. Fairbanks smiled, showing a pair of excellent dentures. "I told him I took it myself by mistake," she said. "He didn't believe me, but what could he do? For a good many years I have kept this family out of the newspapers. We have had our troubles, like other people. My daughter's divorce, for one thing." Her face hardened. "A most tragic and unnecessary thing. It lost me Frank Garrison, the one person I trusted. And my son Carlton's unhappy marriage to a girl far beneath him. Could I tell the police that a member of my family was trying to kill me?"

"But you don't know that it is a member of your family, Mrs. Fairbanks."

"Who else? I have had my servants for years. They get a little by my will, but they don't know it. Not enough, anyhow, to justify their trying to kill me. Amos, my old coachman, drives my car when I go out, and I usually take Janice with me. He may not be fond of me. I don't suppose he is, but he won't let anything happen to Jan. He used to drive her around in her pony cart."

Hilda was puzzled. Mrs. Fairbanks's own attitude was bewildering. It was as though she were playing a game with death, and so far had been victorious.

"Have there been any attempts since?" she asked.

"I've seen to that. When I eat downstairs, I see that everybody eats what I do, and before I do. And I get my breakfasts up here. I squeeze my own orange juice, and I make my coffee in a percolator in the bathroom. And I don't take sugar in it! Now you'd better look around. I've told you what you're here for."

Hilda got up, her uniform rustling starchily. She was convinced now that something was wrong, unless Mrs. Fairbanks was not rational, and that she did not believe. There was the hard ring of truth in her voice. Of course she could check the poison story with Doctor Brooke. And there was the bat. Even supposing that the old lady was playing a game of some sort for her own purposes, how, living the life she did, could she have obtained a bat? Hilda had no idea how anyone got possession of such a creature. Now and then one saw them at night in the country. Once in her childhood one had got into the house, and they had all covered their heads for fear it would get in their hair. But here, in the city——

"Was your door open tonight?" she asked.

"My door is never open."

That seemed to be that. Hilda began to search the room; without result, however. The windows, including those in the bathroom, were both barred and screened, as Mrs. Fairbanks had said, and the screens were screwed into place. The closets which flanked the fireplace revealed themselves as un-

broken stretches of painted plaster, and gave forth the musty odor of old
garments long used. Only in one was a break. In the closet nearest the door
was a small safe, built in at one side, and looking modern and substantial.

As she backed out, she found Mrs. Fairbanks watching her.

"What about the safe?" she asked. "Could anything be put in it, so that
when you open it, it could get out?"

"Nobody can open it but myself. And I don't. There is nothing in it."

But once more the crafty look was on her face, and Hilda did not believe
her. When, after crawling under the bed, examining the chimney in a rain
of soot and replacing the paper which closed it, and peering behind the
old-fashioned bathtub, she agreed that the room was as tight as a drum, the
old woman gave her a sardonic grin.

"I told the policeman that," she said. "But he as much as said I was a
liar."

It was after eleven at night when at last Mrs. Fairbanks agreed to go to
bed. She refused the sleeping tablet the doctor had left, and she did not
let Hilda undress her. She sent her away rather promptly, with orders to sit
outside the door and not to shut her eyes for a minute. And Hilda went,
to hear the door being locked behind her, and to find that a metamorphosis
had taken place in the hall outside. A large comfortable chair had been
brought and placed by the table near the old lady's door. There was a reading lamp beside it, and the table itself was piled high with books and
magazines. In addition there was a screen to cut off drafts, and as she
looked, Janice came up the front stairs carrying a heavy tray.

She was slightly breathless. "I hope you don't mind," she said. "There's
coffee in a thermos. I had Maggie make it when I knew you were coming.
Maggie's the cook. You see, Grandmother doesn't want to be left. If you
went downstairs for supper——"

Hilda took the tray from her. "I ought to scold you," she said severely.
"I thought I sent you to bed."

"I know. I'm sorry. I'm going now." She looked at Hilda shyly. "I'm so
glad you're here," she said. "Now nothing can happen, can it?"

Days later Hilda was to remember the girl's face, too thin but now confident and relieved, the sounds of Mrs. Fairbanks moving about in her
locked room, the shoe box with the captive bat on the table and her own
confident voice.

"Of course nothing can happen. Go to bed and forget all about it."

Janice did not go at once, however. She picked up Hilda's textbook and
opened it at random. "I suppose it's pretty hard, studying to be a nurse."

"It's a good bit more than study."

"I would like to go into a hospital. But of course the way things are . . . It must be wonderful to—well, to know what a doctor means when he says things. I feel so ignorant."

Hilda looked at her. Was it a desire to escape from this house? Or was she perhaps interested in young Brooke? She thought back over the long line of internes she had known. She did not like internes. They were too cocky. They grinned at the young nurses and ignored the older ones. Once one of them had grabbed her as she came around a corner, and his face had been funny when he saw who it was. But Brooke must have interned long after she left Mount Hope Hospital.

She changed the subject. "Tell me a little about the household," she suggested. "Your mother, your uncle and aunt live here. What about the servants?"

Jan sat down and lit a cigarette. "There are only three in the house now," she said, "and Amos outside. There used to be more, but lately Granny—well, you know how it is. I think Granny is scared. She's cut down on them. We even save on light. Maybe you've noticed!"

She smiled and curled up in the chair, looking relaxed and comfortable.

"How long have they been here, Miss Garrison?"

"Oh, please call me Jan. Everybody does. Well, William's been here thirty years. Maggie, the cook, has been here for twenty. Ida"—Jan smiled—"Ida's a newcomer. Only ten. And of course Amos. He lives over the stable. The others live upstairs, at the rear."

"I suppose you trust them all?"

"Absolutely."

"Any others? Any regular visitors?"

Janice looked slightly defiant.

"Only my father. Granny doesn't like callers, and Mother—well, she sees her friends outside. At the country club, or at restaurants. Since the—since the trouble Granny hasn't liked her to have them here."

She put out her cigarette and got up. The box containing the bat was on the table. She looked at it.

"I suppose you'll show that to the police?" she asked.

"That seems to be your grandmother's idea."

Janice drew a long breath. "I had to do it," she said. "I was afraid they would say she was crazy. Have her committed. I had to, Miss Adams."

"Who are 'they'?"

But Janice had already gone. She was walking down the hall toward her bedroom, and she was fumbling in her sleeve for her handkerchief.

Hilda was thoughtful after the girl had gone. She got out her knitting, but after a few minutes she put it down and opened her textbook. What she found was far from satisfactory. Arsenic was disposed of in a brief paragraph:

"Many drugs, such as dilute acids, iron, arsenic and so on, are irritating to mucous lining of the stomach and may cause pain, nausea and vomiting." And death, she thought. Death to an old woman who, whatever her peculiarities, was helpless and pathetic.

She put the book away and, picking up the chart, wrote on it in her neat hand: "11:30 P.M. Patient excitable. Pulse small and rapid. Refuses to take sedative."

She was still writing when the radio was turned on in Mrs. Fairbanks's room. It made her jump. It was loud, and it blatted on her eardrums like a thousand shrieking devils. She stood it for ten minutes. Then she banged on the door.

"Are you all right?" she shouted.

To her surprise the old lady answered at once from just inside the door. "Of course I'm all right," she said sharply. "Mind you, stay out there. No running around the house."

Quite definitely, Hilda decided, she did not like the case. She was accustomed to finding herself in unknown houses at night, with no knowledge of what went on within them; to being dumped among strangers, plunged into their lives, and for a time living those lives with them. But quite definitely she did not like this case, or this house.

The house was not ghostly. She did not believe in ghosts. It was merely, as she said to herself with unusual vigor, damned unpleasant; too dark, too queer, too detached. And the old lady didn't need a nurse. What she needed was a keeper, or a policeman.

## CHAPTER IV

THE RADIO went on until after midnight. Then it ceased abruptly, leaving a beating silence behind it, and in that silence Hilda suddenly heard stealthy footsteps on the stairs. She stiffened. But the figure which eventually came into view was tragic rather than alarming.

It was a woman in a black dinner dress, and she seemed shocked to see Hilda. She stood on the landing, staring. "Has anything happened to Mother?" she half whispered.

Hilda knew her then. It was Marian Garrison, Janice's mother, but changed beyond belief. She was painfully thin and her careful make-up only accentuated the haggard lines of her face. But she still had beauty, of a sort. The fine lines of her face, the dark eyes—so like Jan's—had not altered. Given happiness, Hilda thought, she would be lovely.

She stood still, fingering the heavy rope of pearls around her neck, and Hilda saw that she was carrying her slippers in the other hand.

"It isn't—she hasn't had another——"

She seemed unable to go on, and Hilda shook her head. She picked up a pad from the table and wrote on it: "Only nervous. She caught a bat in her room tonight."

Marian read it. Under the rouge her face lost what color it had had. "Then it's true!" she said, still whispering. "I can't believe it."

"It's in that box."

Marian shivered. "I never believed it," she said. "I thought she imagined it. Where on earth do they come from?" Then she apparently recognized the strangeness of Hilda in her uniform, settled outside her mother's door. "I suppose the shock—she's not really sick, is she?"

Hilda smiled. "No. The doctor thought she needed someone for a night or two. Naturally she's nervous."

"I suppose she would be," said Marian vaguely, and after a momentary hesitation she went into her own room and closed the door behind her. Hilda watched her go. She was trusting no one in the house that night, or any night. But she felt uncomfortable. So that was what divorce did to some women! Sent them home to arbitrary old mothers, made them slip in and out of their houses, lost them their looks and their health and their zest for living. She thought of Frank Garrison with his faded little blonde second wife. He had not looked happy, either. And the girl, Janice, torn among them all—the old woman, Marian, and her father.

The bat was moving around in the box, making small scraping noises. She cut another hole for air, and tried to look inside. But all she could see was a black mass, now inert, and she put down the box again.

She had a curious feeling that the old lady was still awake. There was no transom over the door, but she seemed still to be moving around. Once a closet door apparently creaked. Then the radio came on again, and Hilda, who abominated radio in all its forms, wondered if she was to endure it all night. She was still wondering when the door to Marian's room opened, and Marian came into the hall.

"Can't you stop it?" she asked feverishly. "It's driving me crazy."

"The door's locked."

"Well, bang on it. Do something."

"Does she always do it?"

"Not always. For the past month or two. Sometimes she goes to sleep and it goes on all night. It's sickening."

She had not bothered to put on a dressing gown. She stood shivering in the June night, her silk nightgown outlining her thin body, with its small high breasts, and her eyes desperate.

"Sometimes I wonder if she really is——"

What she wondered was lost. From the bedroom came a thin high shriek. It dominated the radio, and was succeeded by another, even louder one. Marian, panic-stricken, flung herself against the door and hammered on it.

"Mother," she called, "let me in. What is it? What's wrong?"

Abruptly the radio ceased, and Mrs. Fairbanks's thin old voice could be heard. "There's a rat in here," she quavered.

Out of sheer relief Marian leaned against the door. "A rat won't hurt you," she said. "Let me in. Unlock the door, Mother."

But Mrs. Fairbanks did not want to unlock the door. She did not want to get out of her bed. After she had finally turned the key, she scurried back to it and, sitting upright, surveyed them both with hard triumphant eyes.

"It's under the bureau," she said. "I saw it. Perhaps now you'll believe me."

"Don't get excited, Mother," Marian said. "It's bad for you. If it's here, we'll get William to kill it."

Mrs. Fairbanks regarded her daughter coldly. "Maybe you know it's here," she said.

"That's idiotic, Mother. I hate the things. How could I know?"

Hilda's bland eyes watched them both, the suspicion in the old lady's face, the hurt astonishment in the daughter's. It was Marian who recovered first. She stood by the bed, looking down at her mother.

"I'll get William to kill it," she said. "Where were you, Mother, when you saw it?"

"I was in bed. Where would I be?"

"With all the lights on?"

There was a quick exchange of looks between the two, both suspicious and wary. Hilda was puzzled.

"Don't stand there like a fool," said Mrs. Fairbanks. "Get William and tell him to bring a poker."

Marian went out, closing the door behind her, and Hilda, getting down on her knees, not too happily, reported that the rat was still under the bureau, and apparently not too happy about it either. She got up and beat a hasty retreat to the door, from which she inspected the room.

It was much as she had left it, except that the old lady's clothes were neatly laid on a chair. The windows were all closed, however, and the bed was hardly disturbed. It looked indeed as though Mrs. Fairbanks had just got into it. There was another difference, too. A card table with a padded cover had been set up in front of the empty fireplace, and on it lay a pack of cards.

The old lady was watching her. "I lied to Marian," she said cheerfully. "I hadn't gone to bed. I was playing solitaire."

"Why shouldn't you play solitaire? Especially if you can't sleep."

"And have the doctor give me stuff to make me sleep? I need my wits, Miss Adams. Nobody is going to dope me in this house, especially at night."

The rest of the night was quiet. William, an elderly man in a worn bathrobe with "old family servant" written all over him, finally cornered the rat, dispatched it and carried it out in a dustpan. Marian went back to her room and closed and locked the door. Janice had slept through it all, and Hilda, after an hour on her knees, discovered no holes in the floor or baseboard and finally gave up, to see Mrs. Fairbanks's eyes on her, filled with suspicion.

"Who sent you here?" she said abruptly. "How do I know you're not in with them?"

Hilda stiffened. "You know exactly why I'm here, Mrs. Fairbanks. Inspector Patton——"

"Does he know you?"

"Very well. I have worked for him before. But I can't help you if you keep me locked out. You will have to trust me better than that."

To her dismay the old lady began to whimper, the tearless crying of age. Her face was twisted, her chin quivered.

"I can't trust anybody," she said brokenly. "Not even my own children. Not even Carlton. My own son. My own boy."

Hilda felt a wave of pity for her. "But he's not here tonight," she said. "He couldn't have done it. Don't you see that?"

The whimpering ceased. Mrs. Fairbanks looked up at her. "Then it was Marian," she said. "She blames me for bringing that woman Frank married into the house. She was crazy about Frank. She still is. When that woman got him, she nearly lost her mind."

"She couldn't possibly have done it," Hilda told her sharply. "Try to be reasonable, Mrs. Fairbanks. Even if she had come into this room, she couldn't have brought it with her. People don't carry rats around in their pockets. Or bats, either."

It was over an hour before she could leave the old lady. She utilized it to make a more careful examination of the room. The bathroom, which was tiled, did not connect with Marian's room, and its screen was, like the others, screwed into place. The closets again revealed nothing except the safe and the rows of clothing old women collect. Hanging on the door of the one where the safe stood was a shoe bag, filled with shoes. She smiled at it, but days later she was to realize the importance of that bag; to see its place in the picture.

One thing was certain. No rat or bat could have entered that room by any normal means. The old-fashioned floor register was closed. Not entirely. There were, she saw with the aid of a match, small spaces where the iron blades beneath did not entirely meet. The grating over them, however, was tightly screwed to the floor and its openings were less than a square inch in size.

Mrs. Fairbanks lay in her bed, watching her every move. She had taken out her teeth, and now she yawned, showing her pale gums.

"Now you know what I'm talking about," she said. "Put out the light, and maybe you'd better leave the door unlocked. But don't you go away. I wake up now and then, and if I find you're not there . . ."

Outside in the hall Hilda's face was no longer bland. Inspector Patton would have called it her fighting face. She waited until she heard her patient snoring. Then she tiptoed back to her own room, and from what she called her emergency case she removed several things: a spool of thread, a pair of rubber gloves and a card of thumb tacks. These she carried forward and, after a look to see that all was quiet, went to work. Near the floor she set two of the tacks, one in the door frame and one in the door itself. She tied a piece of the black thread from one to the other and, cutting off the ends with her surgical scissors, stood up and surveyed her work. Against the dark woodwork it was invisible.

After that she put the screen around her chair so as to shield it, picked up the flashlight, the gloves and a newspaper Janice had left for her, and very deliberately went down the stairs.

The lower floor was dark. She stopped and listened in the hall. Somewhere a clock was ticking loudly. Otherwise everything was quiet, and she made her way back to the kitchen premises without having to use her light. Here, however, she turned it on. She was in a long old-fashioned pantry, the floor covered with worn linoleum, the shelves filled with china and glassware. A glance told her what she was looking for was not there, and she went on to the kitchen.

It was a huge bleak room, long unpainted. On one side was a coal range, long enough to feed a hotel. There was a fire going, but it had been carefully banked. Nevertheless, she took off the lids, one by one. There was nothing there, and she gave a sigh of relief. After that she inspected a small garbage can under the sink, without result.

It was in the yard outside the kitchen porch that she finally found what she was looking for. It lay on top of a barrel of ashes, and she drew on her gloves before she touched it. When she went upstairs again, it was to place and lock in her suitcase the neatly wrapped body of a dead rat.

Then, having found that the door had not been opened, she calmly moved her chair against it, and picking up the *Practice of Nursing,* opened it at random. "The physician, the nurse and others should report what they see, hear, smell or feel, rather than what they deduce." She read on, feeling pleasantly somnolent.

CHAPTER V

THINGS LOOKED better the next morning. The old house looked somber in the June sunlight but not sinister. Mrs. Fairbanks wakened early and allowed Hilda to bring her a breakfast tray. But she took her grapefruit without sugar, and insisted on opening her egg herself.

In the kitchen, waiting for her tray, Hilda inspected the servants: Maggie, stout and middle-aged, over the stove; Amos outside on the porch, smoking a corncob pipe; William, taciturn and elderly; and Ida, a pallid listless creature in her late thirties, drinking a cup of tea at the table. They were watching her, too, although they ignored her. She was familiar with the resentment of house servants toward all trained nurses; resentment and suspicion. But it seemed to her that these four were not only suspicious of her. They were suspicious of each other. They did not talk among themselves. Save for the clattering of Maggie's pans and stove lids, the room was too quiet.

Hilda Adams was in the pantry when she heard William speaking.

"I tell you I put it there," he was saying. "I'm not likely to forget a thing like that."

"You'd forget your head if it wasn't fastened on." This was Maggie.

"Someone's taken it," said William stubbornly. "And don't tell me it wasn't dead. It was."

When Hilda went back to the kitchen, conversation ceased, but on the porch Amos was grinning.

Janice slept late that morning, but Marian was at the table when Hilda went down for her own breakfast. She looked as though she had not slept at all. The green house coat she wore brought out the pallor of her skin and her thinness, and beside her, Hilda looked once more like a fresh, slightly plump cherub. Marian had already eaten, but after William had served the nurse and gone, she stayed on, nervously fingering her coffee cup.

"I suppose," she said, "that Mother has been telling you how we have tried to murder her."

Hilda looked unruffled. "I wouldn't say that, Mrs. Garrison. She did say there was an incident some time ago. Something about arsenic in the sugar."

Marian smiled grimly. She got a cigarette from a side table and lit it before she spoke. "As it happens, that's true," she said. "That was when Doctor Brooke had the contents of her tray analyzed. It was there, all right. Only I ask you"—she smiled again, her tight-lipped smile—"would we have left it there if we had done it? Everybody handled that tray. My daughter Janice had taken it up to her. I took it out of the room. My brother Carlton carried it to the head of the back stairs and later his wife carried it down. If the servants were guilty, they could have got rid of it. But nobody did." She put out her cigarette. "We may be an unpleasant family, but we are not fools, Miss Adams. We wanted to call the police, but Mother refused."

She shrugged her thin shoulders. "What could we do? If she wanted to think we did it, that was all right with us; but life hasn't been very pleasant since."

"Was there arsenic in the house?"

"We never found any. Of course she suspects us all."

"Why should she?"

"She has the money," Marian said dryly. "She has it and she keeps it. I could leave, of course. I have my alimony." She flushed. "And I have a little place in the country. But Mother wants Janice here, and Jan thinks we ought to stay. That rat last night was merely an accident. As for the bats and all the rest of it . . ."

She shrugged again. Hilda's expression did not change.

"Have you thought that she might be doing some of this herself?" Hilda inquired. "Old women do strange things sometimes. They crave attention and don't get it, so they resort to all sorts of devices."

"How could she?"

"Through one of the servants, possibly. Or, she drives out every day or so, doesn't she? She might have an arrangement—somebody handing her a package of some sort."

Marian laughed, without particular mirth. "Such as arsenic, I suppose!"

"I gather that she didn't take enough to kill her," said Hilda dryly. "She may resent some member of the family and want to make trouble."

"She resents us all," said Marian. "All but Jan, and she uses her until I'm frantic. The child has no life of her own at all." She lit another cigarette and Hilda saw her hands were shaking. "Don't judge us too soon," she went on. "I'd get out and take Jan, but she doesn't want to leave her grandmother. And my brother has no place to go. His business is shot to pieces. He was a broker, but that's all over. He doesn't make enough to buy shoes these days. And he has a wife to support."

She got up. "We're not a bad lot," she said. "Even Susie has her points." She smiled thinly. "None of us would try to kill Mother, or even scare her to death. Now I suppose you'll need some sleep. I'll stay within call, if she wants anything."

Hilda, however, did not go to bed that morning. She saw that Mrs. Fairbanks was bathed and partly dressed, and made up her bed with fresh linen. Then, leaving Ida to clean the room and finish, she changed into street clothing and took a bus at the corner for Police Headquarters. The Inspector was alone in his bare little office, and when Hilda walked in, in her neat tailored suit and small hat, he eyed her with appreciation.

"Hello," he said. "How's the haunted lady today?"

She smiled and deposited the box and the parcel on the desk in front of him. He looked faintly alarmed.

"What's this?" he inquired. "Don't tell me you've brought me cigars?"

She sat down and pulled off her gloves. "The box," she said smugly, "contains one bat. It's alive, so don't open it while I'm here. The other is a dead rat. I got it out of a trash can, at three o'clock in the morning—if that interests you."

"Great Scott! The place sounds like Noah's ark. What do you mean, you got the rat out of a trash can?"

She told him then, sitting across the desk, her hands primly folded in her lap. She began with the arsenic in March, and went on to the events of the night before. He looked bewildered. He stared at the body of the rat, neatly wrapped in its newspaper.

"I see. And this thing couldn't get into the room, but it did. That's the idea?"

"It may not be the same one I saw under the bureau."

"But you think it is, eh?"

"I think it is. Yes."

"What am I to do with it?" he inquired rather helplessly. "What about rats, anyhow? Don't the best houses have them?"

"They carry bubonic plague sometimes."

"Good God," said the Inspector. "What did you bring it to me for?"

"I don't suppose it has any fleas on it now. It's the fleas that are dangerous. I just thought it had better be examined. Certainly somebody is trying to kill Mrs. Fairbanks."

"Just like that?"

"Just like that."

He leaned back and lit his pipe. "I suppose you haven't any ideas?"

She smiled faintly. "All of them have motives. I haven't seen Carlton and Susie, the son and his wife. They're out of town. But Mrs. Fairbanks has the money and apparently holds on to it. Her ex-son-in-law, Frank Garrison, sees her now and then, but I doubt if he gains by her death. The doctor might have a reason, but she was poisoned before any of them knew him, except the granddaughter. She'd met him somewhere. He was called because he lives close by. I haven't seen him yet."

"Why the doctor?"

"I think the girl may be in love with him. And I suppose he could carry more than babies in his bag."

The Inspector laughed. He had a considerable affection for her, and an even greater respect. "You're a great girl, Hilda," he said as she got up. "All right. Go back to your menagerie. And for God's sake don't get any fleas."

She took a bus back to her corner, but she did not go directly to the house. Instead she turned at Joe's Market into Huston Street, and, passing a row of once-handsome houses, now largely given over to roomers and showing neglect, found Dr. Brooke's office in one of them. It was almost directly across from the Fairbanks stable, and a small brass plate, marked "C. A. Brooke, M.D." and in need of polishing, told her where she was.

On the steps she turned and surveyed the outlook. The stable and its cupola concealed the service wing of the house, but the rest was in full view. She could see the porte-cochère, and as far back as Jan's room. So that was why Jan had been gazing out her window the night before!

It was some time before an untidy girl answered her ring. Then she jerked the door open and stuck her head out.

"Is the doctor in?" Hilda asked.

The girl surveyed her, looking astonished. "I'll see," she said, and ducked back.

Hilda followed her into the house. To the left was a waiting room. It was sparsely furnished with a center table, a row of chairs around the wall, and a bookcase which had seen better days. Double doors opened into the consulting room behind, where a young man, with his coat off, was sound asleep behind a desk.

The girl made a gesture. "That's him," she said, and disappeared.

The young man opened his eyes, looked bewildered, then jumped to his feet and grabbed his coat. "Terribly sorry," he said. "Up all night. Please come in."

He was not particularly handsome. He had, however, a nice smile and good teeth. Hilda rather hated disappointing him.

"I'm afraid I'm not a patient," she said.

"No? Well, I didn't really expect one. Sit down, anyhow. It's hot, isn't it?"

Hilda was not interested in the weather. She looked at him and said, "I'm the nurse at Mrs. Fairbanks's. I'd like to ask some questions, doctor."

She thought he stiffened. Nevertheless, he smiled. "I can't violate any professional confidences, even to you, you know, Miss——"

"Adams is my name."

"I see. In a way I'm responsible for your being there, Miss Adams. I was worried about Jan. But I didn't expect her to get a police nurse."

"I'm not a police nurse, doctor. When there is trouble, I report to the police. That's all."

"I see," he said again. "Well, Miss Adams, if you want to know whether or not I think Mrs. Fairbanks is haunted, the answer is no. She's an old woman, and she was always eccentric. Lately she has developed some fixed ideas. One is that her family is trying to do away with her. Scare her to death, as she puts it. I don't believe it. When you know them——"

"The arsenic wasn't a fixed idea, doctor."

He looked unhappy and annoyed. "Who told you about that? The family and she herself have insisted on keeping it to themselves. I argued against it, but it was no good."

"It was arsenic, wasn't it?"

"It was. Arsenious acid. She didn't get a lot, but she got it on an empty stomach. Luckily I got there in an hour. Even at that she was in poor shape —cyanosed, pulse feeble and so on. I washed her out, but she was pretty well collapsed."

"There was no doubt what it was?"

"No. I used Reinsch's test. She'd had it, all right."

He went on. He had wanted to call the police, but look at it! Nobody there but the family and servants who had been there a lifetime. Impossible to blame it on any of them. Impossible to have a scandal, too. And there had been no repetition. All that had happened had been a change in the old lady herself. She had been imagining things ever since. This story of things in her room, bats, rats, sparrows or what have you . . .

When he heard about the night before, he got up and took a turn about the room. "Well, I'll be damned," he said. "I'll be eternally, everlastingly damned! Of course," he added, "things like that won't necessarily kill her. It's not murder. The other time——"

"You thought it was an attempt at murder?"

"She didn't take white arsenic for her complexion," he said grimly.

He went to the door with her, a tall lanky young man who towered over her and who, as she started out, put a hand on her shoulder.

"Look here," he said. "Keep an eye on Janice, will you? She's been under a terrific strain. They're a decent lot over there, but there isn't anything to hold them together. They fight like cats and dogs. If anything happens to her . . ."

He did not finish. He stood still, gazing across the street to where, beyond the fence and the brick stable, the dark rectangle of the Fairbanks house stood in all the dignity of past grandeur.

"Funny, isn't it?" he said. "When I was a kid, I used to stand outside that fence to see the old lady drive out in her carriage!"

Except that she was trusting nobody just then, Hilda would have liked him that day. He had a boyish quality which appealed to her. But she hardened herself against him.

"I suppose you know," she said coolly, "that you are on the list of suspects?"

"Suspects! What on earth have I done?"

"You might have carried a few vermin into Mrs. Fairbanks's room in that bag of yours."

He looked astounded. Then he laughed, long and heartily. "And tried to scare my best and almost only patient to death!" he said. "Come and look, Miss Adams. If ever you've seen a bag of pristine purity, you'll see one now."

She did not go back, however. He showed her a break in the fence near the stable and she took that short cut to the house. Amos was washing a muddy car as she passed him, but he did not look up. He was a short, surly-looking man, and she felt that he was staring after her as she went toward the house. She had an unpleasant feeling, too, that he was grinning again, as he had grinned earlier that morning on the kitchen porch.

She did not go to the front door; instead, she walked to the rear of the house. It was twelve o'clock by that time, and the servants—with the exception of Amos—were already eating their midday dinner in a small room off the kitchen. She stopped in the doorway, and William got up.

"I was wondering," she said blandly, "whether you have a rattrap in the house. If there are rats here——"

"There are no rats in this house," said Maggie shortly.

"One was caught last night."

"You ask Amos about that. He's got them in the stable, if you ask me."

But Amos, arriving and overhearing, grouchily affirmed that there were no rats in the stable. Hilda surveyed them. They were the usual lot, she thought; loyal rather than intelligent, and just now definitely uneasy. Ida glared at Amos.

"What about that arsenic? Maybe there's arsenic in the stable."

Her voice was high and shrill. Amos glared back at her.

"You'd better keep your mouth shut if you know what's good for you."

They were all close to hysteria, but it was left to Maggie, matter-of-fact Maggie, to put the keystone on the arch of their terror.

"If you ask me," she said, "the place is haunted. I've sat with the old lady when Ida and Miss Jan were out, and I've heard plenty."

"What have you heard?" Hilda asked.

"Raps all over the room. Queer scraping noises. And once the closet door opened. The one with the safe. I was looking right at it, and only me and Mrs. Fairbanks in the room—and her asleep."

Ida screamed, and William pounded on the table. "Stop that kind of talk," he ordered sharply. "All old houses creak. Do you want to scare the nurse away?"

Maggie subsided, looking flushed. Ida was pale and plainly terrified. Only Amos went on eating. And Hilda, on her way upstairs, was convinced of two things: that they were all badly scared, and that they were all equally innocent.

## CHAPTER VI

THE OLD LADY'S ROOM, when Hilda reached it, bore no resemblance to the eerie chamber of the night before. Someone—Jan, she thought—had been at work in it.

The sun was pouring in, there were lilacs on a table, the bed had a silk cover over it, and a number of small pillows gave it an almost frivolous look. Even Jan looked better, rested and smiling, and Mrs. Fairbanks herself, dressed now in black silk and sitting in her rocker, was a different creature from the untidy old woman of the previous evening.

Not that she was entirely changed. She was still domineering, even suspicious. Her small eyes were fixed on one of the closets, which contained the safe, and she ignored Hilda in the doorway.

"Come out of that closet, Carlton," she said. "I told you there was nothing there."

Carlton Fairbanks emerged reluctantly. He backed out, dusting his knees as he came, a small dapper man in his forties, his thin face ruffled, his expression stubborn.

"They have to get in somehow, Mother. Why don't you let me look?"

"They're brought in," said Mrs. Fairbanks tartly. "I've told you that. Someone in this house brings them in."

Carlton tried to smile. "If you mean that I did it, I was out of town last night. So was Susie. Anyhow, she's afraid of rats."

"I imagine Susie has seen rats before, and plenty of them," said Mrs. Fairbanks coldly.

This, for some reason, caused a blank silence in the room. Carlton's mouth tightened, and Janice looked uneasy. The silence was broken only by the old lady's tardy recognition of Hilda in the doorway. She looked at her with small malicious eyes.

"You see me surrounded by my loving family, Miss Adams," she said.

"This is my son. He was out of town last night when you came. Or so he says."

Carlton stiffened. He nodded at Hilda and then confronted his mother. "Just what do you mean by that?" he demanded. "I'm doing the best I know how. If things go on the way they are, you must make some plans. As to last night——"

"I'm perfectly capable of making my own plans."

"All right. All right," he said irritably. "As to last night, if you think I need an alibi, I have one. So has Susie. But the whole thing's ridiculous. Why in God's name would anybody carry these things into this room?"

"To scare me to death," said the old lady placidly. "Only I'm pretty hard to scare, Carlton. I'm pretty hard to scare."

Later Hilda tried to recall in order the events of the next few days, beginning with the lunch that followed this scene. Marian, she remembered, had been silent. In daylight she looked even more ravaged than the night before. Janice had seemed uneasy and distracted. Carlton was irritated and showed it. And Mrs. Fairbanks, at the head of the table, watched it all, touching no food until the others had taken it, and pointedly refusing the sugar for her strawberries.

Only Carlton's wife, Susie, seemed to be herself. Hilda was to find that Susie was always herself. She was a big blonde girl, and she sauntered into the room as casually as though an aged Nemesis were not fixing her with a most unpleasant eye.

"Put out that cigarette," said Mrs. Fairbanks. "I've told you again and again I won't have smoking at the table."

Susie grinned. She extinguished the cigarette on the edge of her butter dish, a gesture evidently intended to annoy the old lady, and sat down. She was heavily made up, but she was a handsome creature, and she wore a bright purple house gown which revealed a shapely body. Hilda suspected that there was little or nothing beneath it.

"Well, here's the happy family," she said ironically. "Anybody bitten anybody else while we were away?"

Janice spoke up quickly. "Did you have a nice trip?" she asked. "Oh, I forgot. This is Miss Adams, Susie. She's taking care of Granny."

"And about time," said Susie, smiling across the table at the nurse. But Hilda was aware that Susie's sharp blue eyes were taking stock of her, appraising her. "Time you got a rest, kid. You've looked like hell lately."

She spoke as though Mrs. Fairbanks were not there, and soon Hilda was to discover that Susie practically never spoke to her mother-in-law. She spoke at her, the more annoyingly the better. She did that now.

"As to having a nice trip. No. My feet hurt, and I'll yell my head off if I have to inspect another chicken house. I'm practically covered with lice—

if that's what chickens have. Anyhow, Carl can't buy a farm. What's the use?"

"Are you sure you would like a farm?" Janice persisted.

"I'd like it better than starving to death, honey. Or going on living here."

"Susie!" said Carlton. "I wish you'd control your tongue. We ought to be very grateful to be here. I'm sure Mother——"

"I'm sure Mother hates my guts," said Susie smoothly. "All right, Carl. I'll be good. What's all this about last night?"

Hilda studied them: Marian vaguely picking at what was on her plate, Janice looking anxious, Carlton scowling, Susie eating and evidently enjoying both the food and the bickering, and at the head of the table, Mrs. Fairbanks, stiff in her black silk and watching them all.

"I wonder, Carlton," she said coldly, "if your wife has any theories about some of the things which have been happening here?"

Carlton looked indignant. Susie, however, only looked amused. "I might explain that I've spent the last three days alternating between chicken houses and pigpens," she said to her husband. "I rather enjoyed it. At least it was a change. I *like* pigs."

All in all it was an unpleasant meal. Yet, remembering it later, Hilda could not believe that there had been murder in the air. Differences of all sorts, acute dislikes and resentments; even Susie—she could see Susie figuratively thumbing her nose at her mother-in-law. But she could not see her stealthily putting poison in her food. There was apparently nothing stealthy about Susie.

Marian she dismissed. She was too ineffectual, too detached, too absorbed in her own personal unhappiness. She wondered if Mrs. Fairbanks was right and Marian was still in love with Frank Garrison, and what was the story behind the divorce. But over Carlton Fairbanks she hesitated. Men did kill their mothers, she thought. Not often, but now and then. And his position in the house was unhappy enough; dependent on a suspicious old woman who was both jealous and possessive, and who loathed his wife.

He was talking now, his face slightly flushed. "I'm not trying to force your hand, Mother," he said. "It's a good offer. I think you ought to take it. This neighborhood is gone as residential property. A good apartment building here—well, what I say is that, with war and God knows what, a farm somewhere would be an ace in the hole. We could raise enough to live on, at least."

"Don't talk nonsense. What do you know about farming?"

"I could learn. And I like the country."

There was enthusiasm in his voice. He even looked hopeful for a moment. But his mother shook her head. "This place will never be an apartment house," she said, putting down her napkin. "Not so long as I am alive, anyhow," she added, and gave Susie a long hard look.

Hilda watched her as she got up. Old she was, bitter and suspicious she might be, but there was nothing childish about her standing there, with her family about her. Even Susie, who had lit another cigarette and grinned at her mother-in-law's hard stare, rose when the others did.

Hilda slept a few hours that afternoon. The house was quiet. Susie had gone to bed with a novel. Carlton had driven out in the car Amos had washed. Marian had—not too cheerfully—offered to drive with her mother. And Hilda, looking out her window, saw Janice cross the street to the doctor's office and come out with him a few minutes later, to enter a shabby Ford and drive away.

When she had wakened and dressed, she telephoned the Inspector from the empty library.

"Any news?" she asked.

"I've got the report. Nothing doing. Your Noah's ark is as pure as lilies. Anything new there?"

"No. Nothing."

She hung up. There was a telephone extension in the pantry, and she did not want to commit herself. But she was uneasy. She did not think Maggie's story had been pure hysteria. She put on her hat and went across the street to a small electrical shop. There she ordered a bell and batteries, with a long cord attached and a push button. It took some time to put together, and the electrician talked as he worked.

"You come from the Fairbanks place, don't you?" he said. "I saw you coming out the driveway."

"Yes. I'm looking after Mrs. Fairbanks."

He grinned up at her. "Seen the ghost yet?"

"I don't believe in ghosts."

"You're lucky," he said. "The help over there—they're scared to death. Say all sorts of things are going on."

"They would," said Hilda shortly.

She took her package and went back to the house. It was still quiet. The door to Mrs. Fairbanks's room was open, but the closet containing the safe was locked. She shrugged and tried out her experiment. The push button she placed on the old lady's bedside table. Then she carried the battery and bell out into the hall. To her relief the door closed over the cord.

After that she made a more careful inspection of the room than she had been able to make before. She examined the walls behind the pictures, lifted as much of the rug as she could move, tested the screens and bars at the windows again, even examined the tiles in the walls of the bathroom and the baseboards everywhere. In the end she gave up. The room was as impregnable as a fortress.

She was still there when the door opened and Carlton came in. He had a highball in his hand, and his eyes were bloodshot. He seemed startled when he saw her.

"Sorry," he said, backing out. "I didn't know—I thought my mother was here."

He was looking at her suspiciously. Hilda smiled, her small demure smile. "She hasn't come back, Mr. Fairbanks. I was installing a bell for her."

"A bell? What for?"

"So if anything bothers her in the night, she can ring it. I might not hear her call. Or she might not be able to."

He had recovered, however. "All damn nonsense, if you ask me," he said, swaying slightly. "Who would want to bother her?"

"Or want to poison her, Mr. Fairbanks?"

He colored. The veins on his forehead swelled. "We've only got young Brooke's word for that. I don't believe it."

"He seems pretty positive."

"Sure he does," he said violently. "Look what he gets out of it! An important patient, grateful because he saved her life! If I had my way . . ."

He did not finish. He turned and left her, slamming the door behind him.

Hilda went downstairs. Ida was out, and Maggie was alone in the kitchen. She was drinking a cup of tea, and she eyed Hilda without expression.

"I want to try an experiment," Hilda said. "Maybe you'll help me. It's about those raps you heard."

"What about them? I heard them, no matter who says what."

"Exactly. I'm sure you did. Only I think I know how they happened. If you'll go up to Mrs. Fairbanks's room——"

"I'm not going there alone," said Maggie stolidly.

Hilda was exasperated. "Don't be an idiot. It's broad daylight, and anything you hear I'll be doing. All I want to know is if the noise is the same."

In the end an unwilling Maggie was installed in the room, but with the door open, giving every indication of immediate flight. The house was very quiet. Only a faint rumble of the traffic on Grove Avenue penetrated its thick walls, and Hilda, making her way to the basement on rubber-heeled shoes, might have been a small and dauntless ghost herself.

She found the furnace without difficulty. She could hardly have missed it. It stood Medusa-like in the center of a large room, with its huge hot-air pipes extending in every direction. She opened the door and, reaching inside, rapped the iron wall of the firebox, at first softly, then louder. After that she tried the pipes, but, as they were covered with asbestos, with less hope.

There were no sounds from above, however. No Maggie shrieked. The quiet of the house was unbroken. Finally she took the poker and tapped on the furnace itself, with unexpected results. Susie's voice came from the top of the basement stairs.

"For God's sake stop that racket, Amos," she called. "Don't tell me you're building a fire in weather like this."

Hilda stood still, and after a moment Susie banged the door and went away. When at last Hilda went upstairs to Mrs. Fairbanks's room, it was to find Maggie smiling dourly in the hall.

"That hammering on the furnace wouldn't fool anybody," she said. "You take it from me, miss. Those noises were in this room. And there were no bats flying around, either."

## CHAPTER VII

THAT NIGHT, Tuesday, June the tenth, Hilda had a baffling experience of her own.

Rather to her surprise Mrs. Fairbanks had accepted the bell without protest. "Provided you keep out unless I ring it," she said. "I don't want you running in and out. Once I've settled for the night, you stay out. But don't you leave that door. Not for a minute."

She was tired, however, after her drive. Hilda, taking her pulse, was not satisfied with it. She coaxed her to have her dinner in bed, and that evening she called the doctor.

"I think she's overdone, and I know she's frightened," she said. "Can you come?"

"Try to keep me away," he said. "I use the short cut. One minute and thirty seconds!"

He was highly professional, however, when he stood beside Mrs. Fairbanks's bed and smiled down at her. "Just thought I'd look you over tonight," he said. "Can't have a nurse reporting that I neglect a patient. How's everything?"

"She's not a nurse. She's a policewoman," said the old lady surprisingly. "I'm not easy to fool, doctor. That officer I talked to suggested a companion, and *she* comes. Maybe it's just as well. I don't intend to be murdered in my bed."

He pretended immense surprise. "Well, well," he said. "A policewoman!

We'll have to be careful, won't we? And I've had an eye on the spoons for weeks!"

He ordered her some digitalis and sat with her for a while. But some of his boyishness was gone. Hilda followed him out of the room, and after he went down the stairs, she heard him speak to Jan in the hall below. Their voices, though guarded, carried up clearly.

"We're not so smart, are we, darling?" he said. "Miss Gimlet-eyes up there isn't missing a trick."

"I don't want her to miss anything, Court."

"Are you sure of that?"

His tone was quizzical, but there was anxiety in it too.

"Certainly I am." Jan's voice was defiant. "So are you. But if the police——"

"Look, sweet," he said. "If and when your grandmother dies, it will be a natural death. The police won't come into it at all. Only for God's sake don't tell the family that the Adams woman is on the watch. If there's any funny business going on——"

"You can't suspect them, Court."

"Can't I?" he said grimly. "You'd be surprised what I can suspect."

He went out the side door under the porte-cochère, his head down, his face moody and unhappy. Near the stable, however, he roused. A figure had slid stealthily into the door leading up to Amos's room, and he dropped his bag and plunged in after it. To his dismay it was a woman. She was cowering against the wall at the foot of the stairs and softly moaning.

He let go of her and lit a match, to find Ida gazing at him with horrified eyes. She looked ready to faint, and he caught hold of her.

"Here, here," he said, "none of that! I'm damned sorry, Ida. I didn't know it was you."

He eased her down on the steps. Her color came back slowly, although she was still breathless.

"I was scared," she said. "I saw someone coming at me in the dark, and I thought——" She stopped and picked up a parcel she had dropped. "It's my day out, sir. I was just coming home."

"Better use the driveway after this," he told her. "I'll watch you to the house."

She went on slowly, while he retrieved his bag. But his own nerves were badly shaken. He let himself into the house across the street, to find the slatternly girl in his back office avidly studying the plates in one of his medical books. He strode in and jerked the book out of her hands.

"Keep that filthy nose of yours out of my books and out of my office," he snapped. "Not that I think you have anything to learn, at that. Now get out and keep out."

The girl went out sniveling. He felt ashamed of his anger. And he was tired. He yawned. But he did not go to bed. He picked up a cap from the hall and, after a brief survey of the Fairbanks property across the street, went cautiously back there and moved toward the house.

Inside the house the evening was following what Hilda gathered was its usual pattern. In the small morning room behind the library, Susie and Carlton bickered over a game of gin rummy. Jan, after seeing that Hilda was fixed for the night, went to bed. And Marian, having read for an hour or two in the library, came up to bed. Apparently none of them outside of Jan and Mrs. Fairbanks suspected Hilda's dual role. But Marian paused for a time in the upper hall.

"It isn't serious, is it? Mother's heart, I mean."

"No. Her pulse was weak. It's better now."

Marian stood still, looking at her mother's door. She looked better now, dressed and made up for the evening. Jan's resemblance to her was stronger. Apparently on an impulse, she drew up a chair and sat down.

"I suppose she has talked about me? My divorce, I mean."

"She mentioned it. That's all."

Marian's face hardened. "I begged her not to bring that woman here as Jan's governess," she said. "I knew her type. When she had been here a month, I almost went on my knees to Mother to have her sent away. But she wouldn't. She said Jan was fond of her."

Hilda picked up her knitting. She kept her head bent over it, the picture of impersonal interest. "All divorces are sad," she said. "Especially when there are children."

"I stood it for years. I could see her, day after day, undermining me. I wanted to go away and live somewhere else, but my—but my husband didn't want to leave Mother alone. At least that's what he said. I know better now. Carlton had got out, but I had to stay."

If anyone was to be murdered, Hilda considered, it would probably be Eileen, the second Mrs. Garrison. It was obvious that Marian was bitterly jealous of her successor. She changed the subject tactfully.

"Tell me, Mrs. Garrison," she said, "when did all this begin? I mean, the arsenic and the bats and so on."

Marian's flush subsided. She pulled herself together with an effort and lit a cigarette. "I don't know exactly," she said. "Mother wanted a safe in her room, God knows why. It was installed while I took her to Florida in February. We got home on the ninth of March, and a day or two later she got the poison. If it was poison."

"And the bats?"

"I don't know. She didn't tell us about them at first. She said she opened the screens, and let them out. That was before she had her screens fastened.

None of us believed her, I'm afraid. After all, bats and birds and rats do get into houses, don't they?"

She smiled faintly, and Hilda smiled back at her. "I suppose the raps come under the same category," Hilda said mildly.

Marian looked startled. "Raps? What raps?"

"The servants say there are noises at night in your mother's room. I talked to Maggie. She doesn't strike me as a neurotic type."

But Marian only shrugged. "Oh, Maggie!" she said. "She's at a bad time of life. She can imagine anything. And you know servants. They like to raise a fuss. Their lives are pretty drab, I imagine. Anything for excitement."

She got up and put out her cigarette. She was slightly flushed. "We have trouble enough without inviting any, Miss Adams," she said. "I don't give the orders in this house, but I'd be glad if you didn't take the servants into your confidence."

She went on into her room, her head high and the short train of her black dress trailing behind her. Hilda, watching her, felt that something like the furies of hell were bottled up in her thin body: hatred for the woman who had supplanted her, resentment toward her mother, scorn and contempt for Susie, indignation at her brother. She put down her knitting—she loathed having to knit—and considered one by one the occupants of the house: Marian, frustrated and bitterly unhappy; Carlton, timid toward his mother, slightly pompous otherwise, certainly discontented; Susie, shrewd, indifferent and indolent. Jan she left out, but she considered Courtney Brooke for some time.

The girl would probably be an heiress when Mrs. Fairbanks died, and he had known her before the poisoning incident. If he was earning more than his rent, she would be surprised. And he had been very glib about the arsenious acid, very sure of what it was. Perhaps she had not been meant to have it at breakfast? Suppose she had had it at night, with her door locked and unable to call for help? One thing was certain. He was afraid of her, Hilda. That remark about Miss Gimlet-eyes had left her rather annoyed. On the other hand . . .

By midnight the house had settled down. In his room, next to his mother's, Carlton was snoring comfortably. Janice was apparently asleep. From Susie's open door came a light and the odor of a burning cigarette, and Marian had not reappeared. Hilda went cautiously into the old lady's room and stood listening. She was asleep, breathing quietly, but the air in the room was close and hot. Mrs. Fairbanks had refused to have a window open. She stood in the darkness, worrying. There should be air. Heart cases needed oxygen. She tiptoed to a window and suddenly stopped.

There was a sound behind her, a faint scraping sound as though something had been moved. She turned sharply, but the room was as it had been.

The old lady had not stirred. Then she saw it. The door to the closet which held the safe was slowly moving. In the light from the hall it edged out six inches or more, creaking as it came.

She stared at it incredulously. Then she took a quick step forward, and as carefully as it had opened it began to close again. Not entirely. The latch did not click. But close it did, and she found herself staring at it, the very hair in her scalp lifting with horror. She did not dare give herself time to think. She walked over with buckling knees and stood outside of it.

"Come out," she said in a low voice. "Whoever is in there, come out or I'll raise an alarm."

There was no reply, and when she tried the door, it swung open easily in her hand. The closet was empty. The shoe bag hung undisturbed, the safe was closed, the row of dresses harbored no lurking figure. She felt deflated, as though all the breath had gone out of her. It's a trick, she thought furiously. A part of the campaign to terrify the old lady. A trick! A dirty trick! And it's been tried tonight because her heart hasn't been too strong. If she had wakened and seen it . . .

She hurried out into the hall. Nothing there had changed, however. Carlton was still snoring, and when she went back along the hall to Susie's open door, that lady put down a magazine with a lurid cover and stared at her.

"Hello!" she said. "Anything wrong?"

Hilda studied her, the gleam of cold cream on her face, the half-smoked cigarette in her fingers.

"Somebody's playing tricks around this house," she said. "And don't tell me I imagine it, or that it's done with mirrors. It's got to stop. I've got a patient to consider."

Susie sat up in bed. "What sort of tricks?" she inquired, with interest.

"Were you in your husband's room just now, Mrs. Fairbanks?"

Susie raised her eyebrows and grinned. The connecting door into Carlton's room was open, and through it came the unmistakable snoring of a sleeping man, which begins softly and rises gradually to an ear-splitting snort.

"Listen to that," she said. "If you think Carl is in any mood for amorous dalliance . . ."

Hilda left abruptly. The amused smile was still on Susie's face. Jan was in bed, sleeping like a tired child. Marian's door was locked. And there was nobody else. In a cold rage she got her gun from the suitcase and took it forward. In the same rage she folded back the screen, so that it gave her an unimpeded view of the hall. And still in the implacable anger of a woman who has been the victim of a cheap trick she crept into Mrs. Fairbanks's room and examined the closet again, this time with her flashlight.

There was no break in the plaster, no place where anything could have been introduced to open the door and close it again.

She spent the remainder of the night in baffled indignation. Her patient slept. No sounds came from the door. At seven she heard the servants going down the back staircase, and shortly after, Ida brought her a cup of coffee. She asked the girl to take her place for a few minutes.

"I want to go up to the third floor," she said. "I thought I heard somebody up there last night."

Ida looked surprised. "There was nobody up there, miss. Not in the front of the house."

"Well, I'll look at it anyhow," she said, and climbed the stairs.

The upper floor was much like the second. Two large rooms across the front and a smaller one above Carlton's were evidently guest rooms. They were long unused, however. Dustcloths covered the furniture and beds, and a faint film of dust showed that rooms and baths were given only periodical cleanings. Hilda paid particular attention to the one over Mrs. Fairbanks. It had a fireplace, like the room below, but it had evidently been long unused. The dust on the hearth was undisturbed, and the flue in the chimney was closed.

There was a closet there, similar to the one below, and this she examined minutely, going over the sides and floorboards. But she discovered nothing out of the way. She thought dejectedly that she would have to come to the theory of a ghost after all.

## CHAPTER VIII

YOUNG BROOKE looked tired that morning. Jan was sleeping late, and she was still not around when he made his morning call. He stood over the old lady's bed, and protested her intention of getting up.

"You're not as young as you used to be," he said, smiling down at her. "If you won't take care of yourself, we have to do it for you, Mrs. Fairbanks."

"I've got the Adams woman to do that," she retorted dryly. "I don't trust any of the rest of you. And I've noticed that she doesn't bring any bats in with her. I can't say that of anybody else."

Very gravely he offered to let her look into his bag, and the bit of foolery seemed to amuse her.

"Get on with you," she said. "If you'd wanted to kill me, why would you have pumped the poison out of me?"

It was rather grisly, but she seemed to enjoy it. Outside the door, however, young Brooke lost his professional cheerfulness. He glanced about and lowered his voice.

"I wish you'd tell Jan something for me," he said. "Just tell her it's all right. She will understand."

"I'm not so sure it's all right, doctor."

Then and there Hilda reported the incident of the closet door. He was puzzled rather than alarmed.

"Of course, a house as old as this——"

"It had nothing to do with the age of the house," she said tartly. "Something opened it and then closed it. I was there. I saw it."

He did not answer. He picked up his bag and glanced back toward Jan's room.

"Don't forget to tell her," he said. "Nobody was around the place. She's got a fool idea that somebody gets in at night. Well, tell her that nobody did. Or tried to."

"You mean you watched all night?"

"You and me both, Miss Adams," he said, with a return of his old manner. "You and me both."

She had a strong feeling that she should report the door incident to the Inspector. There was some sort of pernicious activity going on. When she went back to Mrs. Fairbanks's room, she took the first opportunity to examine the closet door. It could be opened, she thought; a string tied to the knob and carried out into the hall might do it. But she could see no way by which it could be closed again.

Jan relieved her for sleep, but she did not go to bed. The June day was bright and warm, so she wandered into the grounds. Outside the garage, Amos was tinkering with one of the three cars, and she wandered over in that direction.

"Good morning," she said. "I can remember this place when they kept horses."

"Pity they ever changed," said Amos grumpily.

"Mind if I look around a bit?"

He muttered something, and she went inside.

Behind the former carriage house was the tack room, and then came seven or eight fine old box stalls, now empty save for Amos's gardening implements and two or three long pieces of rubber hose.

Amos had stopped work and was watching her. She was aware of his hard, intent stare. But her eyes were fixed on the hose. A motor going in the garage at night, a long hose leading into the house, perhaps to the furnace, and Mrs. Fairbanks's windows closed. All the other windows open where people slept, but the old lady . . .

Amos was still watching her. She smiled at him blandly. "Mind if I go upstairs?" she said. "I've always longed to see out of that cupola."

"I live up there."

"You don't live in the cupola, do you?"

She had a strong impression that he did not want her to go up. Then he shrugged and gave her a faint grin. "All right," he grunted. "But you won't find anything."

So Amos knew why she was there! She felt uneasy as she started up the stairs, and even more so when she discovered that he was behind her. He did not speak, however. He merely followed her. But at the top he ostentatiously reached for the key of the door leading to his own quarters and locked it. What was left was only the old hayloft, and over it the cupola, dusty and evidently unused for years. There was a ladder lying on the floor, but Amos made no move to lift it.

"What's up there?" she asked.

"Nothing. Used to be pigeons. I've boarded it up. None there now."

She abandoned the idea of the cupola, and took a brief look at the loft itself. It was dark, but she could see that it was filled with castoffs of the house itself. She could make out broken chairs, a pile of dusty books, an ancient butterfly net, a half dozen or so battered trunks, and a table with a leg missing. Days later she was to wish that she had examined the place thoroughly that morning. But Amos was there, surly and watchful. She gave it up, and another event that afternoon drove it entirely from her mind.

Marian, looking bored, had taken her mother for a drive, and Janice, after seeing them off, had slipped out of the house on some mysterious errand of her own. Hilda, undressing for bed, heard her rap at the door.

"I'm going out," she said. "If they get back before I do, please don't say I'm not here. I'll get in somehow."

Hilda watched from the window. The girl did not go to young Brooke's office, however. She took a bus at the corner, and Hilda finally went to bed. She slept until five o'clock. Then, having missed her luncheon, she dressed and went down the back stairs for a cup of tea, to find the kitchen in a state of excitement, Maggie flushed with anger, William on the defensive, and Ida pale but quiet.

"Why did you let her in?" Maggie was demanding.

"What else could I do?" William said. "The child brought her in and asked for her grandmother. When I said she was still out in the car, she took her into the library. She looks sick."

"She has no business in this," Maggie said furiously. "After the trouble she made! She has a nerve, that's all I've got to say."

They saw Hilda then, and the three faces became impassive.

A few minutes later, Hilda carried her cup of tea to the front of the house.

Everything was quiet there, however, and she was puzzled. Then she saw what had happened. A woman was lying on the couch in the library. Her hat was off, lying on the floor, and her eyes were closed. But Hilda knew at once who it was.

She went in, putting down her tea, and picked up a limp hand. "Feeling faint?" she asked.

Eileen opened her eyes and, seeing who it was, jerked her hand away. "You startled me," she said. "I thought you were Jan."

Hilda inspected her. She was pale, and her lips, without lipstick, were colorless. Seen now in the strong daylight, she looked faded and drab. Resentful, too. There was a tight look to her mouth.

"Jan's getting me some brandy," she said in her flat voice. "We were—we were walking near here, and all at once I felt faint. I'll get out as soon as I can. Marian would have a fit if she found me here."

She tried to sit up, but just then Jan came in, carrying a small glass of brandy and some water. She looked worried, but her small head was high and defiant. "You're not getting out until you're able to go," she said. "Here, drink this. It will help."

Eileen drank, taking small ladylike sips, and Jan looked at Hilda. "I'm sorry, but you'd better let me handle this," she said. "I was taking her to see Doctor Brooke, but he was out and she got faint. That's all."

Thus dismissed, Hilda went up the stairs. She prayed devoutly that Eileen would be out of the house before Marian and her mother got back. But the family would have to work out its own problems. She had one of her own. If, as she now fully believed, someone was trying to get rid of Mrs. Fairbanks, either directly or by indirection, it was up to her to shut off every possible method. As she expected, the closet door was locked, and a careful examination of Carlton's behind it revealed nothing but his clothes in orderly rows and his shoes lined neatly on the floor. The register in the floor in Mrs. Fairbanks's room, however, did not close entirely. She found a screwdriver in the storeroom as well as a piece of pasteboard, and was in the act of fitting the latter into place when she heard the car drive in. After that there was a moment or two of quiet below. Then she heard Marian coming up the stairs and a moment later she slammed and locked her door.

Hilda shrugged. It was trouble, but it was not hers. She was screwing down the grille over the register when she heard Jan in the hall outside.

"I must speak to you, Mother. I must."

There was no immediate answer. Then Marian's door flew open, and her voice shook with rage when she spoke.

"How dare you, Jan? How dare you do a thing like this to me?"

"I couldn't help it, Mother. She was sick."

"Sick! I don't believe it."

"She was. Ask Miss Adams. Ask Grandmother."

"She can put anything over on your grandmother. As for you, forever hanging around her——"

"Listen, Mother. She telephoned me. She doesn't want Father to know yet, but—she's going to have a baby."

There was a brief stunned silence. Then Marian began to laugh. It was a terrifying laugh, and Hilda got quickly to her feet. Before she reached the door, however, Marian had vanished into her room, and the laughter, wild and hysterical, was still going on.

Jan was standing in the hall. She was trembling, and Hilda put an arm around her.

"Never mind," she said. "Don't worry, child. She'll get over it."

"I didn't think she'd care," said Jan blankly, and went down the stairs again.

That evening, Wednesday, June the eleventh, Marian left the house, bag and baggage. Nobody saw her go except Ida, who carried down her luggage. She left while the family was at dinner, and she told nobody where she was going.

## CHAPTER IX

JAN TOOK her mother's departure very hard. She found the room empty after dinner and Hilda, seeing her as she came out, realized that she was badly shocked.

"She's gone," she said. "Mother's gone. I don't understand. Why would she do a thing like that?"

"I wouldn't worry. She'll come back."

"You don't know her," said Jan. "She hates Eileen. She's made life pretty hard for her, and for my father too. I'm . . ." She steadied herself by a chair. "I guess I'm frightened, Miss Adams."

Hilda tried to send her to bed. She refused, however. She spent the evening trying to locate Marian at the hotels in town and at the place she owned in the country. But there was no sign of her. She had not registered anywhere, and the caretaker on the small farm had had no word from her. Jan, giving up finally, looked wan and despairing.

"You don't think she would do anything dreadful?" she asked Hilda. "She's been so terribly unhappy."

"I doubt it," said Hilda briskly. "She's had a shock. She'll get over it."

The old lady took Marian's departure rather philosophically. "What did she expect? They're married, aren't they? If they want a child . . ."

On the whole, Hilda thought, the old lady was pleased rather than resentful. As though Marian were getting the punishment she deserved. But she carried through her usual routine that night: an hour or so with her door locked, the radio on, and her game of solitaire.

During that interval Hilda found Carlton in the library and told him about the night before, the noises and the moving closet door.

His reaction rather surprised her. He was alone, the evening paper on his knee but his eyes fixed on the empty fireplace. He stared at her without replying when she had finished. Then he walked to the portable bar and poured himself a drink. When he came back, he looked more normal. "I wouldn't listen to servants' gossip, Miss Adams," he said.

"I heard the sounds myself. And I saw the door move, Mr. Fairbanks."

In the end he went upstairs to his mother's room. It was some time, however, before she admitted him. The room was as usual, the card table set out in front of the hearth and the cards lying on it, but she looked annoyed.

"Really, Carlton, at this time of night."

"It isn't late, Mother."

"It's my time for bed."

"Miss Adams heard something in here last night. I want to find out what it was."

She was quiet after that, although she watched him grimly. Reluctantly she allowed him in the closet with the safe, but he found nothing there. After that he concentrated on the fireplace. At Hilda's suggestion he tore the paper wadding out of the chimney. Nothing resulted but a shower of soot, however. No bricks were loose, and when at last he turned a grimy face to his mother, it was to find her coldly indignant.

"Now that you have ruined my room, perhaps you'll get out."

"If somebody is trying to scare you——"

"Who would be trying to scare me out of this house? Who wants to sell this place? Who wants to live on a farm? Not Marian. Not Janice. Certainly not the servants. Then who?"

He looked at her, soot and all, with a queer sort of dignity. "I'm sorry, Mother," he said. "I'm trying to protect you, that's all. As to the farm, I've given that up. Don't worry about it."

He went out, carrying his coat, and Hilda watched him go. It was impossible to think of him, mild and ineffectual as he was, in connection with poison, or even with a mild form of terrorism. It was indeed impossible to think it of any of them: of Jan, young and evidently in love with Courtney Brooke; of Susie, cheerful and irresponsible; of Marian, involved in her own troubles. Even Frank Garrison and Eileen—what had they to gain by the old lady's death?

As it happened, it was Susie who told Hilda about Frank and Eileen that same Wednesday night. Told it with considerable gusto, too, while smoking an endless chain of cigarettes. She came wandering along the hall at one in the morning, in a pale blue negligee over a chiffon nightdress, and wearing an outrageous pair of old knitted bedroom slippers.

She pulled up a chair and took a chicken sandwich from the supper tray. "God, how my feet hurt!" she said. "Try walking over farm fields in spike heels and see how you like it."

"I don't think I would try," said Hilda, picking up her knitting. "I have to take care of my feet."

Susie looked at Marian's door. "Funny about her running off," she said. "Look here, you look like a regular person. What do you make of Eileen Garrison coming here today? Why did the old"—here Susie caught herself, and grinned—"witch see her, anyhow?"

"I don't know the circumstances, Mrs. Fairbanks. Of course she was feeling faint."

"Yeah. She's in a chronic state of feeling faint. Can't do any housework. You ought to see the way they live!" She finished the sandwich and lit another cigarette. "Well, if you ask me, it's damned queer. First Mrs. Fairbanks drives her out with curses—same like me, only I don't go. For years she doesn't speak her name or let us speak it. Then Jan brings her here and she talks to her. No wonder Marian screamed. She's still crazy about Frank. I could be myself, without half trying."

Hilda glanced at her. "I thought you knew. Mrs. Garrison is going to have a baby."

"Oh, my God!" said Susie. "That spills it. That certainly spills it—for Marian."

It was some time before Hilda got Susie back to where she had left off. She sat grinning to herself over another sandwich until a question brought her back.

"If she was crazy about Mr. Garrison, why did she divorce him?"

Susie finished her sandwich. "Why? Well, the Fairbanks have got their pride, or haven't you noticed? She'd caught him in Eileen's room, I guess. Maybe nothing to it, but there it was. So she goes off to Reno, and Frank, the poor sap, thinks he's got to marry the girl."

There was much more, of course. Susie, according to herself, might be from the wrong side of the tracks. She was, she said. Her father was a contractor in a small way, who liked to eat in his shirt sleeves. But Eileen was worse.

"Not her family," she said. "They're all right, I suppose. They live in the country. But they managed to get Eileen an education. However, she couldn't get a job, so she went back to the farm. And believe you me," Susie added, "there's nothing like a country girl who once gets to town.

The one thing she won't do is go back to the farm. She'll grab a man of her own if she can, and if she can't, she will grab some other woman's. She tried for Carl, but I slapped her face for her. After that she let him alone. But Frank, the big softie . . ."

She put out her cigarette. "I don't know just how Eileen came in the first place. The old lady wanted a nice country girl, I guess. Anyhow, Marian was jealous of her from the start. She soft-soaped everybody. The servants liked her, and she was the nearest to a mother Jan ever had. Marian was pretty much the society girl in those days. But Eileen was on the make all the time. . . . Well, I'd better go bye-bye."

She rose and stretched. "Good heavens," she said. "I've eaten all your supper! I'll go down and get some more."

Hilda protested, but she went down, padding up the stairs a few minutes later with a laden tray. She looked indignant.

"That William ought to be fired," she said. "He left the kitchen door unlocked. I'll tell him plenty in the morning."

Hilda ate her supper, but she was uneasy. She got up and went to the window which lighted the stairs. Outside, a faint illumination from the street lamps showed the trees which bordered the place, and the garage. Joe's Market on its corner was closed and dark, but there was a small light in the house where young Brooke had his office. Below her was the roof of the porte-cochère, and beyond it the vague outline of the stable.

Then she stiffened. A figure was moving stealthily from the stable toward the house. It seemed to be carrying something bulky, and whoever it was knew its way about. It kept off the driveway and on the grass, and as she watched, it ducked around the rear of the building toward the service wing.

She hesitated. The thought of the huge dark rooms below was almost too much for her. But this was why she was here and, after locking Mrs. Fairbanks's door and taking the key with her, she picked up her flashlight and went swiftly back to her room. There she got the automatic and, as quietly as she could, made her way down the back stairs.

There was no question about it. Someone was trying the kitchen door. She did not turn on her light. She listened, and the footsteps moved on to the pantry. Here whoever it was was trying to pry up a window and—with her gun ready—she threw the light of her flashlight full in his face.

It was Carlton Fairbanks, and at first he seemed too startled for speech. Then he recovered somewhat. "Get that damned light out of my face," he shouted furiously. "And who locked the kitchen door?"

Hilda, too, had recovered. "Your wife found it open. If you'll go around, I'll let you in. I thought you were a burglar."

She turned on the kitchen lights and admitted him. He was in a dressing gown and slippers, and whatever he had been carrying was not in sight.

His anger was gone. He looked embarrassed and uneasy, especially when he saw the automatic in her hand.

"Always carry a thing like that?"

"I got it out of my suitcase when I saw you coming from the garage."

He relaxed somewhat. "Sorry if I scared you," he said. "I ran out of cigarettes, and I'd left some in the car. What on earth," he added suspiciously, "was my wife doing down here?"

Hilda explained. He seemed satisfied, but he did not leave her there. He watched her up the stairs and then went back, ostensibly to get some matches. Wherever they were, he was a long time finding them. When he came up, he said a curt good night. But he did not close his door entirely, and she sat in the hall through the rest of the night, convinced that he was still awake, listening and watching her.

She reported to Inspector Patton the next morning. He looked relieved when she laid no parcel on his desk.

"What? No livestock?"

She shook her head. She looked very pretty, he thought, but also she looked devilishly tired. "No. No livestock. But I'm worried."

"You look it. What's going on there?"

"Everything, from a ghost that opens and closes doors to a family row. Also breaking and entering. And of course a love affair." She smiled faintly. "That makes it perfect, I suppose."

"Just so long as it isn't yours. I—we can't afford to lose you, you know."

He was grave enough, however, when she told her story. "Any idea what Carlton was carrying last night?"

"No. I looked around this morning. I couldn't find anything. Whatever it was, he hid it before he came upstairs."

"Bulky, eh?"

"Maybe two feet high and a foot or so across. That's merely a guess."

"Seem heavy?"

"I don't think so, no. He's a small man. If it had been——"

"Do you think everything centers about the safe? Is that it?"

"She has something in it," Hilda said stubbornly. "She gets me out of the room, sets up a card table and pretends to play solitaire. I don't believe she does."

"What does she do?"

"She gets something out of the safe and looks at it. She locks me out of the room and turns on the radio. But I have pretty good ears. She goes to the closet and opens it. I can hear it creak. Then she moves back and forward, to the card table, I think. It takes about an hour."

The Inspector whistled. "Hoarded money!" he said. "That's the first time anything has made any sense. And it's the money you're to guard, not the old lady."

"It might be both," said Hilda, and got up.

He did not let her go at once, however. "You talk about family rows, and so on. Why? I mean—why did Marian Garrison stay there? She could live on her alimony, couldn't she? She gets ten thousand a year, tax free. I've been in touch with Garrison's lawyer. Says the poor devil's business is gone—he's an architect—and it's about all he has."

"Ten thousand a year!" Hilda looked shocked.

"That's right. She takes her pound of flesh every month, and these are hard times on the alimony boys. The damned fool could probably get it reduced by court order. It seems he refuses. But if you want a motive for a murder, there it is, Miss Pinkerton. Maybe that arsenic was meant for Marian, after all."

"And the bats?"

"Oh, come, come, Hilda," he said impatiently. "Carlton wants to sell the place for an apartment building. He wants to live on a farm. If he tries to scare his mother into moving, what has that to do with murder?"

"I'd like to know," said Hilda quietly, and went home.

It was that night that Susie fainted.

The day had gone much as usual. No word had come from Marian, and Jan, looking pale and tired, went with her grandmother for her drive that afternoon. On her return she came back to Hilda's room as she was getting into her uniform, but at first she had little to say. She stood gazing out the window, to where, across Huston Street, young Brooke had his shabby offices. When she turned, her young face looked determined.

"We must seem a queer lot to you, Miss Adams," she said. "Maybe we are. Everyone pulling in a different direction. But we're fond of one another, and we're all fond of Granny. That is, none of us would hurt her. You must believe that."

Hilda was pinning on her cap. She took a moment before she replied. "I would certainly hope so."

"My father is devoted to her. He always was."

"So I understand," said Hilda quietly.

Jan lit a cigarette, and Hilda saw her hands were trembling. She took a puff or two before she went on.

"Then what was he doing outside our fence last night? On Huston Street? He was there. Courtney Brooke saw him."

She went on feverishly. Brooke had had a late call. When he came back, he had seen a figure lurking across the way. He had gone inside and, without turning on the light, had watched from his window. It was Frank Garrison. His big body was unmistakable. Now and then a car had lighted it, and he had moved a bit. But he had stayed there from midnight until two o'clock in the morning. Then at last he had gone.

Hilda thought quickly. That was when Carlton had come from the stable. Had he been watching Carlton? Or had he some other reason? What on earth could take a man out of bed and put him outside the Fairbanks fence for two hours? But Jan had not finished.

"There is something else, too," she said. "Court says someone with a flashlight was in the stable loft at that same time. It might have been Amos, of course. He's a bad sleeper."

"Did you ask Amos?"

"Yes. He says nobody was there. He'd have heard whoever it was. And I've been to the loft. It's just the same as usual."

"There's probably some perfectly simple explanation for it all," Hilda said, with her mental fingers crossed. "Ask your father when you see him."

Jan looked at her wistfully. "You don't think he wanted to see Mother? He might have thought she was out, and waited for her to come in. If Eileen told him she had been here . . ."

"That's something I wouldn't know about," said Hilda firmly, and went forward to her patient.

These people, she thought resentfully, with their interlocking relationships, their loves and hates—what had they to do with the safety of a little old woman, domineering but at least providing a home for them? They only cluttered up the situation. There was Carlton, annoyed with Susie about something and hardly speaking to her all day. And Marian, alone somewhere with her furious jealousy and resentment. And now Frank Garrison, probably hearing of Eileen's visit and trying to make his peace in the small hours of the night.

It was eleven o'clock that night when Susie fainted.

There had been no gin rummy. Carlton had come up early and gone to bed. Jan had gone out with young Brooke. Even Mrs. Fairbanks had settled down early, and the quiet was broken only by Carlton's regular snoring. Hilda had picked up the *Practice of Nursing* and opened it at random.

"When an emergency arises," she read, "a nurse must be able to recognize what has happened, think clearly, act promptly, know what to do and how to do it."

That was when Susie screamed and fell. Hilda, running back, found her lying on the floor, in the doorway between her room and that of her husband. She was totally unconscious. As Hilda bent over her, she heard Carlton getting out of bed.

"What is it?" he said thickly. "Who yelled?" Then he saw his wife and stared at her incredulously. "Susie!" he said. "Good God, what's happened to her?"

"She's only fainted."

"Get some water," he yelped distractedly. "Get a pillow. Get the doctor. Do something."

"Oh, for heaven's sake keep quiet." Hilda's voice was taut. "She's all right. Keep her flat and let her alone. She's all right."

He got down on his knees, however, and tried to gather her big body to him. "I'm sorry, old girl," he said hoarsely. "It's all right, isn't it? You know I love you. I'm crazy about you. It's all right, darling."

Susie opened her eyes. She seemed puzzled. "What's happened to me?"

"You fainted," said Hilda practically. "You screamed and then you fainted. What scared you?"

Susie, however, had closed her eyes. "I don't remember," she said, and shivered.

## CHAPTER X

MRS. FAIRBANKS was murdered on Saturday night, the fourteenth of June; or rather early on Sunday morning. Marian had been gone since Wednesday evening, and no word whatever had come from her. The intervening period had been fairly quiet. There were no alarms in the house. On Friday, Hilda caught up with her sleep, and Carlton was once more the loving husband, spending long hours beside Susie's bed. He had insisted that she stay in bed.

But Susie was not talking, at least not to Hilda. She eyed her dinner tray sulkily on Friday evening. "Take that pap away and get me an honest-to-God meal," she said. "I'm not sick. Just because I banged my head——"

"What made you do it, Mrs. Fairbanks? Why did you faint?"

"Why does anybody faint?"

"I thought possibly something had frightened you. You shrieked like a fire engine."

"Did I?" said Susie. "You ought to hear me when I really let go."

But her eyes were wary, and Hilda, bringing back the piece of roast beef and so on that she had demanded, was to discover Carlton on his hands and knees, poking a golf club under her bed. He got up, looking sheepish, when Hilda came in.

"My wife thinks there is a rat in the room," he explained carefully.

"A rat!" said Susie. "I've told you over and over . . ."

She did not finish, and Hilda was left with the baffled feeling that the entire household had entered into a conspiracy of silence.

By Saturday, save for Marian's absence, the house had settled down to normal again. Susie was up and about. At dinner that night she persuaded Carlton to take her to the movies, and they left at eight o'clock. At eight thirty Courtney Brooke came in, announcing that he had made three dollars in the office and was good for anything from a Coca-Cola to a ham on rye and a glass of beer.

Mrs. Fairbanks chuckled. "If that's the way you intend to nourish my granddaughter——" she began.

"I?" he said. "I am to nourish your granddaughter? What will *you* be doing while she starves to death?"

She was more cheerful than Hilda had ever seen her when at last he left her and went downstairs to where Jan waited for him in the library.

Looking back over the evening later, Hilda could find nothing significant in it. Mrs. Fairbanks had locked her door at ten o'clock and pursued her usual mysterious activities until eleven. Hilda took advantage of part of that hour of leisure and of Carlton's absence to examine both his and Susie's rooms carefully. She found nothing suspicious, however, and save for Jan's and young Brooke's voices coming faintly from below, and the distant rumble of thunder, the house was quiet. It was appallingly hot, and when she was at last allowed to put Mrs. Fairbanks to bed, she opened a window.

"You need the air," she said, "and I'll be just outside."

She drew a sheet over the thin old body, feeling a sense of pity for it, that age had brought it neither serenity nor beauty, nor even love.

"Sleep well," she said gently, and went out, closing the door behind her.

It was a quarter after eleven when the doorbell rang, and Jan answered it. Immediately there were voices below, Jan's and another, high-pitched and hysterical. It was a moment before Hilda realized that it was Eileen's.

"So I came here, Jan. I didn't know where else to go. I can leave to-morrow," she added feverishly. "I can go back home. But tonight . . ."

Hilda started down the stairs. Eileen, white-faced and trembling, was in the front hall, a suitcase beside her on the floor. Jan was staring at her.

"I can't believe it," she said slowly. "Why would he leave you, Eileen?"

"He was furious because I came here the other day. He's hardly spoken to me since."

"But even then——"

"He's gone, I tell you. He packed a bag and left. He didn't even say good-bye."

Jan looked bewildered. Eileen sat down on a hall chair and took off her gloves. Her hysteria was gone now. She looked stubbornly determined.

"I can't go to a hotel," she said. "I have no money. Anyhow, your grandmother told me to let her know if I was in trouble. She said that the other day. You heard her, Jan."

Hilda inspected her. She looked sick. Her color was high, and she was breathing fast. And that was the moment when Carlton and Susie arrived. They stopped and stared at the scene before them.

Susie spoke first. "What's wrong, Eileen? Frank left you for another woman?"

And then Eileen threw her bombshell. "If you care to know," she said, "I think he's somewhere with Marian."

Jan suddenly looked young and rather sick. "You know that's a lie, Eileen," she said and, turning, went stiffly up the stairs.

After that, what? Hilda tried to sort it out in her mind. Carlton went up to consult his mother, and there were loud voices from the old lady's room. Eileen leaned back in her chair, her eyes closed. Susie smoked, casually dropping her ashes into a vase on the hall table, and young Brooke came out of the library, felt Eileen's pulse, and suggested that she be put to bed as soon as possible.

"You can make other plans tomorrow, but what you need now is rest."

Her eyes opened. "That's kind of you, whoever you are," she said faintly. "If I could have my old room for tonight——"

Unexpectedly Susie laughed. "Not tonight, darling," she said. "Carlton sleeps there now, and Carlton sleeps alone."

After that Carlton came down the stairs. He looked irritated, but he was civil enough. "Mother thinks you'd better stay here tonight," he said. "She suggests that you take Marian's room. It's ready. She doesn't want the servants disturbed at this hour."

Susie had giggled, but no one else smiled.

Then what? There had been the procession up the stairs, the doctor supporting Eileen, Carlton carrying her suitcase, Susie following with an amused smile on her face. Nothing unusual had happened then, certainly, unless one remembered Jan. She was waiting outside her mother's room, silent but resentful. She had switched on the lights, but that was all. The bed was not turned down.

Eileen stopped and looked at her. "I'm sorry, Jan," she said. "I shouldn't have said what I did. I was excited."

"That's all right," Jan said awkwardly. She turned abruptly, went back along the hall to her room and closed the door.

What else happened? Hilda tried to remember. Eileen unlocked her suitcase and got out a nightgown, but when Hilda offered to unpack for her, she refused curtly.

"I'm leaving in the morning," she said. "Anyhow I hate anyone pawing over my things."

It was all over pretty quickly. Eileen settled, the doctor went back to speak to Jan. Susie went to bed, still smiling her cool smile. And Hilda, going into Mrs. Fairbanks's room, found her sitting up in bed, her eyes bright with excitement.

"So he's left her at last!"

"So she says."

"I hope it's true. But it wouldn't be like Frank to leave her. Now especially. Tell her I want to talk to her. I've got to get to the bottom of this."

Eileen did come, although not with any great rapidity. She sat on the side of her bed and thrust her feet into slippers, yawning widely. Then she put on a dressing gown of Marian's from the closet and surveyed herself in the mirror.

"You needn't tell her I wore this," she said. "She'd burn it if she knew."

The idea seemed to amuse her. She tucked the gown around her—it was too long for her—and went into Mrs. Fairbanks's room. The old lady's voice was shrill.

"Come in and shut the door," she said. "Now what's all this nonsense?"

Eileen stayed for half an hour. Hilda could hear their voices, Eileen's soft, Mrs. Fairbanks's high and annoyed. And there was a brief silence, during which she heard the closet door creak. When Eileen came out, she looked indignant. She closed the door and leaned against it.

"The old devil," she said, in a low voice. "She tried to buy me off! Look, may I have a little of that coffee? I need it."

"It will keep you awake."

"I don't expect to sleep anyhow. Not in that room."

Mrs. Fairbanks was excited when Hilda went in again, but she was certainly alive. She demanded to know why Eileen had told that cock-and-bull story about Frank being with Marian, and she said that she had told Eileen she must leave in the morning. Hilda got her settled with difficulty. She was not sleepy, and she turned on the radio as the light was switched off.

"Get that woman out of the house in the morning," she said. "Get her out, or somebody will murder her."

That was at midnight. Eileen was quiet, the light out in her room. Courtney Brooke was still with Jan. Susie was reading in bed, her door open, and Carlton had gone back to the library, where he was presumably settling his nerves with the usual highballs.

At a quarter after twelve Mrs. Fairbanks turned off the radio, and soon after, young Brooke, looking concerned, left Jan's room and came cautiously forward along the hall.

"She's taking this very hard," he said. "She says her father would never have left his wife, especially since she's going to have a child. She's afraid something has happened to him. I think I'll stay awhile. Where is Mr. Fairbanks?"

"He hasn't come up yet. In the library probably."

He looked about him, at Hilda's tray, at the screen which shielded her from the draft, her easy chair. He thrust his hands into his pockets and took a turn or two across the hall and back.

"What about Jan's father?" he said abruptly. "Of course I know who he is. Who doesn't? Designed the Courthouse, didn't he? But what sort is he? Jan's so damned loyal——"

"I've only seen him for a minute or two."

"Still in love with his first wife?"

"I wouldn't know about that," Hilda said primly.

"Sort of fellow who'd get in a jam and jump out of a window? Or put a bullet through his head?"

She considered that carefully.

"I don't think so. He had a good war record, I believe. I wouldn't think he lacked courage."

"Oh, rats!" he said roughly. "It takes the hell of a nerve to kill yourself."

He went downstairs after that, his hands still in his pockets, his head bent in thought; a tall, lanky, worried young man, his hair on end as though he had been pushing his fingers through it. The picture, Hilda thought, of every interne she had ever known, but somehow likable. He reminded her of one in the hospital where she had been a probationer. He had found her once in a linen closet and kissed her. It hadn't meant anything, of course. It had been spring, and the windows had been open. She had slapped him.

She drew a long breath and began to fill in her records.

The house was quiet after that. Below she could hear the two men's voices, faint and far away. The radio was still. She looked at her watch. It was well after midnight. And then something happened which surprised and startled her.

The hall had a chandelier which was seldom used. It was an old-fashioned affair of brass and glass pendants, and now the pendants were tinkling. She looked up at them. They were moving, striking together like small bells, and she got cautiously to her feet. Someone was up there on the third floor, moving stealthily about, and a moment later she had a considerable shock.

From the foot of the stairs she saw a vague figure. It disappeared almost instantly and without a sound, and when she reached the upper hall, it was empty. She fumbled for a light, but she could not find one. The doors into the guest rooms were closed as usual. The long hall to the servants' quarters was a black tunnel, and at last she went down again, to find everything as she had left it. To her surprise she found that her knees were shaking. She sat down and poured herself a cup of coffee from the tray. One of the servants, she thought, curious about what was going on. Or maybe the house was haunted, after all. She remembered the opening and closing of the closet door, and found herself shaking again. Of all the absurd things! Maybe she needed glasses. But what about the chandelier?

Afterward she was to time that absence of hers; to do it with the police holding a stop watch on her. Three minutes, almost to the dot. Time to drive a knife into an old woman's thin chest, but hardly time to reach the room, commit the crime and escape. And who could know that she would go upstairs at all? Eileen drowsy or asleep, her door closed and her light out. Susie and Jan far back along the hall, and the two men in the library below.

Yet then or later . . .

It was half past twelve when Eileen opened her door. She looked panicky. "I've got a pain," she said. "Do you think anything's wrong?"

"What sort of pain?"

Eileen described it, and Hilda got up. "The doctor's still here," she said. "I'll get him."

Eileen, however, was not listening. She was doubled over, holding herself, and Hilda put her back to bed. She lay there, softly moaning, while Hilda went downstairs. The two men were still in the library. Carlton, a highball in his hand, was looking strained; Courtney Brooke was at the telephone. He put it down when she told him about Eileen, and got briskly to his feet.

"I'd better look at her," he said. "We don't want her to abort. Not here, anyhow."

"No. For God's sake get her out of the house before that happens. Or before Marian comes back." Carlton looked alarmed.

Eileen was watching the door as they came in. She was a pathetic figure as she lay there in her worn nightgown, her face contorted with pain.

"I'm sorry to be such a bother," she said. "I suppose it's the excitement. And my suitcase is heavy. I carried it to the bus."

The doctor examined her briefly and straightened. "You'll be all right. I'll give you a hypo," he said. "Do you mind boiling some water, Miss Adams?"

He followed her out into the hall. Carlton had come up the stairs. He asked briefly about Eileen and then went into his room. Hilda hesitated.

"I don't usually leave Mrs. Fairbanks alone," she said. "If I do, I lock the door. But if you'll watch her——"

He grinned at her. "Old Cerberus will have nothing on me," he said. "Do you think I want anything to happen to my best patient?"

"Something did happen. Once."

She left him with that, his bag open on the table, his hands fumbling in it for his hypodermic case and the tube of morphia sulphate. But his light-ness had gone. He looked thoughtful, even grave.

Downstairs the house was dark, and the huge dingy kitchen was eerie even when she had turned on the lights. It was a quarter to one, she saw by the kitchen clock. She was there for some time. The fire in the range was low, and it was perhaps fifteen minutes before she succeeded in boil-ing the water in a small aluminum pot and carried it up the stairs.

Courtney Brooke was where she had left him. He had poured himself a cup of coffee from her thermos jug, and was holding it. But he was not drinking it. Some of the coffee had spilled into the saucer, and he was staring up at the landing on the third floor. He said nothing, however. He fixed the hypodermic and gave it to Eileen, still moaning in her bed.

"I don't think you'll lose your baby," he told her. "After all, it's only a few months, isn't it? You're pretty safe. Just get some sleep. You'll be all right in a day or two."

"I can't stay here, doctor."

"You'll stay until you're able to leave."

He did not leave at once. He stood in the hall, looking uncertain and uneasy, but he merely finished his coffee. He was putting down the cup when, without warning, Mrs. Fairbanks's radio began to play. He started and almost dropped the cup.

"Does she do that often, at this hour?"

"She turns it on when she can't sleep. I suppose she's excited tonight."

"No good suggesting that it bothers the rest of the household, I suppose?"

"None whatever," Hilda told him wryly.

He went back into Eileen's room before he left. She was still awake, but she said the pain was better. She thought she could sleep now. Hilda opened a window for her, the one over the porte-cochère, and tucked the bedclothes around her: Marian's monogrammed sheets, Marian's soft luxurious blankets. Eileen's hand was icy cold when she touched it.

"I'll leave tomorrow," she said. "Tell them not to worry. I'll not bother them long."

Outside in the hall the radio could still be heard. Courtney Brooke picked up his bag and prepared to go. He looked young and tired.

"Tell Jan not to worry," he said. "I'll be on the job. But I'd give my neck to get her out of this madhouse."

HILDA WAS quite clear as to what followed. The doctor had hardly let himself out of the house when Carlton's door banged open. He came into the hall, tying his dressing gown around him, his hair rumpled and his face scowling. "Good God!" he said. "Why don't you turn that thing off?"

"Your mother likes it when she can't sleep."

"Well, she might let the rest of us have a chance," he said, and pushed savagely past her.

With the door open the noise in the hall was appalling, and he closed it all but an inch or so. He said "Mother," but Hilda heard no reply. The radio ceased abruptly, so that the silence was almost startling. But Carlton did not come out immediately. Later she was to be queried about that.

"How long did he stay? A minute? Two minutes?"

"Not more than two, at the most."

"But more than long enough to go around the bed and shut off the radio?"

She was miserably uncomfortable. "I don't know. I heard something creak, and I thought he had opened the door to one of the closets. His mother's safe was in it. The door always creaked."

They timed her on that, too. One of the men walked into the room, turned the radio switch and came back.

"Longer than that?"

"Yes. I'm afraid—I think it was. I know I had time to uncork the thermos jug and pour some coffee, and I had taken a sip or two before he came out."

"How did he look?"

"I didn't really look at him. He closed the door and said his mother was asleep. He must have gone to sleep himself soon after. I could hear him snoring."

It had commenced to rain after Carlton went back to his room, a summer storm, with rolling thunder and sharp lightning. The rain was heavy. It poured down in solid sheets, and with it came gusts of wind which set the trees outside into violent motion. Somewhere, too, something was banging. Not a door. The sound was too light for that. Hilda decided to look for it and then abandoned the idea.

She ate her supper mechanically. The radio was still silent, and her watch said two o'clock when, having finished, she carried her tray to the back-stairs landing to be picked up in the morning.

The sound was still going on when she went back to her post. It would stop just long enough for her to hope that it was over. Then, with a fresh gust of wind, it would start again.

She was listening for it when there was a crash from the back stairs, followed by a startled "damnation" in what was unmistakably a feminine voice. When she reached the landing, she opened the door to find Susie standing there, a Susie with soaking hair, wearing a wet raincoat over a bedraggled nightdress. She was standing on one foot and anxiously examining the other.

"Why the hell did you leave that thing there?" she demanded furiously. "I've damned near cut a toe off."

In the light from the front hall Hilda grimly surveyed her, from her sodden blonde hair to her slippers, one of which she held in her hands. One of her toes was bleeding, and a cup lay shattered on the tray.

"Better let me put some iodine on that," Hilda said. "Where on earth have you been?"

"I went out to the garage. I'd left my cigarettes in the car."

"It seems to be a family habit," Hilda observed dryly. "Mr. Fairbanks did that a night or two ago. When you locked him out."

Susie fixed a pair of sharp blue eyes on her. "Oh," she said. "So Carl said that, did he?" Suddenly she giggled. "Not very original, are we?"

She limped forward, and Hilda put her in a chair and dressed her foot, with its pink-painted toenails. But she did not go to bed at once. Nor did she produce any cigarettes. Later Hilda was to know that Susie had done a superb piece of acting that night; that she had been frightened almost out of her senses when she came racing up the stairs. Now, however, she was herself again.

She glanced at Eileen's door and laughed. "Good heavens," she said, "when I think what would happen if Marian found her there, in her bed!"

Hilda deliberately picked up her knitting. She had an idea that camouflage was not necessary with Susie, but it did no harm to try. "I don't suppose she would like it," she said absently, counting stitches.

"Like it! Don't underestimate our Marian, Miss Adams. She's a tigress when she's roused. She'd do anything. What on earth is that noise?"

The slapping had started again. It seemed now to come from Eileen's room, and while Susie watched her, Hilda opened the door cautiously. Eileen was asleep, her face relaxed and quiet, but one of the screens, the one of the window Hilda had opened over the roof of the porte-cochère, was unhooked. It swung out, hesitated, and then came back with a small sharp bang. The rain was coming in, wetting the curtains, and Hilda, having hooked the screen, closed the window carefully.

Susie had not moved. She was examining her foot. "What was it?" she inquired.

"A window screen."

"That's funny. Marian always keeps them hooked. She's afraid of burglars. That roof outside——"

She stopped suddenly, as if she had just thought of something. "What about Eileen? Is she asleep?"

"She's had a hypodermic. She's dead to the world."

"She couldn't have opened it herself?"

"Not for the last hour or so. Anyhow, why would she?"

But the open screen worried Hilda. She took her flashlight and went back into Eileen's room. It was as she had left it, Eileen's suitcase on the floor, the window closed, and Eileen still sleeping. She went to the window and examined the screen. It could have been unhooked from the outside. A knife blade could have done it. But if there had been any marks on the roof beneath, the rain had washed them away. One thing struck her as curious, however. A thin light piece of rope was hanging down from one of the old-fashioned outside shutters. It swayed in the wind and now and then one end of it slapped against the window itself. The other end was out of sight. But although it seemed to serve no useful purpose, it might have been there for years.

She left the window and opened the bathroom door. The bathroom was empty, and so, too, was Marian's closet, save for the row of garments hanging there. When she went back into the hall, Susie was still there.

"Find anything?"

"No. How long has that rope been fastened to the shutter over the porte-cochère?"

"Rope?" said Susie blankly. "What rope?"

Hilda was worried. Useless to tell herself that nobody could have entered Mrs. Fairbanks's room that night. Useless to recall all the precautions she had taken. Her bland cherubic expression was gone now. Instead she looked like an uneasy terrier.

"I'm going in to see Mrs. Fairbanks," she said. "She can't do any more than take my head off."

She opened the door and went in. The room was cool and dark, but outside the wind had veered and the curtains were blowing out into the room. She put down the window and then turned and looked at the bed. Afterward she only remembered dimly that Susie was standing in the doorway; that there was a brilliant flash of lightning, and that all at once Susie was pointing at the bed and screaming. Loud piercing shrieks that could be heard all over the house.

She herself was only conscious of the small old figure on the bed, with the handle of a common kitchen knife sticking up from the thin chest.

Carlton was the first to arrive. He bolted out of his room in pajamas, and stopped Susie by the simple expedient of holding his hand over her mouth.

"Shut up," he said roughly. "Have you gone crazy? What's the matter?"

Susie stopped yelling. She began to cry instead, and he looked helplessly at Hilda, standing rigid at the foot of the bed.

"I'm sorry, Mr. Fairbanks," she said. "Your mother——"

"What's happened to her?"

"I'm afraid," she said, her voice sounding far away in her own ears, "I'm afraid she's been killed."

He shoved Susie aside, switched on the lights and went into the room. He did not say anything. He stood looking down at the bed, like a man paralyzed with horror. Not until he heard Jan's voice outside did he move.

"Don't let her in," he said thickly. "Keep everybody out. Get the police." And then suddenly, "Mother, *Mother!*"

He went down on his knees beside her bed and buried his face in the covers.

When he got up, he was quieter. He looked what he was, an insignificant little man, small and shrunken in his pajamas, but capable, too, of dignity.

"I'd better look after my wife," he said. "She has had a shock. Will you—do you mind calling the police? And the doctor? Although I suppose——"

He did not finish. He went out into the hall, leaving Hilda in the room alone.

She did not go downstairs at once. She went to the bed and touched the thin old arm and hand. They were already cool. An hour, she thought. Maybe more. She had sat outside and eaten her supper, and already death had been in this room, in this body.

Automatically she looked at her wrist watch. It showed a quarter after two. Then her eyes, still dazed, surveyed the room. Nothing was changed. The card table and rocking chair were by the empty hearth. The door to the closet with the safe was open only an inch or two, and when she went to it, being careful not to touch the knob, the safe itself was closed. Nothing had disturbed the window screens. They were fastened tight. And yet, into this closed and guarded room, someone had entered that night and murdered an old woman.

She was very pale when she went out into the hall. The household was still gathering. William and Maggie, in hastily donned clothing, were coming along the back hall. Ida was halfway down the stairs from the third floor, clutching the banisters and staring, her mouth open. Jan was standing, wearing a dressing gown over her nightdress, her eyes wide and horrified, and Susie was in a chair, with Carlton beside her, tears rolling down her cheeks.

Hilda surveyed them. Then she closed the door behind her, turned the key in the lock and took it out.

"I'm sorry," she said. "Nobody is to go in until the police get here. I'll call them now."

But she did not call them at once. Eileen, roused from her drugged sleep, had opened her door. She stood there swaying, one hand against the frame.

"What is it?" she said dazedly. "Has something happened?"

It was Carlton who answered, looking at her without feeling, as if he could no longer feel anything, pity or love or even anger. "Mother is dead," he said. "She has been murdered."

Eileen stood very still, as if her reactions were dulled by the drug she had had. She did not look at Carlton. It was as though she saw none of them. Then her hold on the door relaxed and she slid in a dead faint to the floor.

## CHAPTER XII

HILDA LEFT her there with Jan and Ida bending over her. She felt very tired. For the first time in her sturdy self-reliant life she felt inadequate and useless. She had failed. They had trusted her and she had failed. Jan's shocked face, Carlton's dazed one, Susie's tears, even Eileen's fainting showed how terribly she had failed.

And it was too late to do anything. What use to call the doctor—any doctor—or even the police? The best they could do would be to exact justice. They could not bring back to life a little old lady who, whatever her faults, should not be lying upstairs with a kitchen knife in her heart.

She sat down wearily at the library desk and picked up the telephone. Even here things were wrong. It was some time before she got young Brooke's office. Then the girl she had seen there answered the phone indignantly.

"Give a person time to get some clothes on," she snapped. "What is it?"

"I want the doctor."

"You can't have him. He's out."

Eventually she learned that a woman had been knocked down at the corner by a bus, and Doctor Brooke had gone with her to a hospital. The girl did not know what hospital.

"Tell him when he comes back," Hilda said sharply, "that old Mrs. Fairbanks has been killed, and to come over at once."

"Jesus," said the girl. "There goes the rent."

Hilda hung up, feeling sick.

After that she called Inspector Patton at his house. Her hands had stopped shaking by that time, but there was still a quaver in her voice. To her relief he answered at once.

"Yes?"

"This is Hilda Adams, Inspector."

"Hello, Pink. What's wrong? Don't tell me you've found some goldfish!"

Hilda swallowed. "Mrs. Fairbanks is dead," she said. "She's been stabbed with a knife. It couldn't have happened, but it did."

His voice changed. There was no reproach in it, but it was cold and businesslike. "Pull yourself together, Hilda. Lock the room, and hold everything until I get there. Keep the family out."

"I've done that. I——"

But he had already hung up.

She went slowly up the stairs. Ida and Maggie had got Eileen into bed and were standing over her, the door to the room open. In the hall the group remained unchanged, save that Carlton was sitting down, his head in his hands.

"I've got the police," Hilda said. "The doctor's out. If you'd like me to call another one——"

Carlton looked up. "What's the good of a doctor?" he said. "She's gone, isn't she? And I want that key, Miss Adams. You're not on this case any more. She's my mother, and she's alone. I'm going in to stay with her."

He got up, looking determined, and held out his hand.

"No one is to go in there," Hilda said. "Inspector Patton said——"

"To hell with Inspector Patton."

It might have been ugly. He was advancing on her when a siren wailed as a radio car turned into the driveway. Susie spoke then.

"Don't make a fool of yourself, Carl. That's the police."

William went down the stairs. He looked old and stooped, and his shabby bathrobe dragged about his bare ankles. When he came back, two young officers in uniform were at his heels. They looked around, saw Eileen in her bed and started for the room. Hilda stopped them.

"Not there," she said. "In here. The door's locked."

She gave them the key, and they unlocked it and went in, to come out almost immediately. One of them stayed outside the door, surveying the group in the hall with an impassive face. The other went down to the telephone. With his departure everything became static, frozen into immobility. Then Jan moved.

"I can't bear it," she said brokenly. "Why would anybody do that to her? She was old. She never hurt anyone. She . . ."

She began to cry, leaning against the screen and sobbing brokenheartedly, and with the sound the frozen silence ended. There was small but definite movement. Carlton lifted his head, showing a white face and blank eyes. Susie felt in her draggled raincoat for a cigarette and then thought better of it. And Hilda pulled herself together and went in to look at Eileen. She was conscious, but her pulse was thin and irregular, and Hilda mixed some aromatic ammonia with water and gave it to her.

Eileen looked up at her. "Let me out of here," she gasped. "I'm all right. I want to go home."

"Better wait until morning, Mrs. Garrison. You've had a shock. And anyhow you oughtn't to move about. You know that."

Eileen's eyes were wild. They moved from Maggie and Ida back to Hilda. "I'm frightened," she gasped. "You can slip me out somehow." She tried to sit up in the bed, but Hilda held her down.

"I'm afraid that's impossible," she told her. "The police are here. They may want to talk to you."

"But I don't know anything about it," Eileen gasped. "I've been dead to the world. You know that."

"Of course I know it," Hilda said gently. "They'll not bother you much. I'll tell them."

Eileen relaxed. She lay back against her pillows, her eyes open but the pupils sharply contracted from the morphia. "How was she killed?" she asked.

"Never mind about that. Try to be quiet."

The second policeman had come up the stairs, and from far away came the sound of another siren. Hilda walked to the window over the porte-cochère and looked out. The rain had almost ceased. It was dripping from the roof overhead, but the wind had dropped. The room was hot and moist. She raised the window and stood staring outside.

The screen she had fastened was open again. It hung loosely on its hinges, moving a little in the light breeze, but no longer banging.

She did not fasten it. She went back to the bed, where Eileen lay with her eyes closed, relaxed and half asleep. "I'm sorry to bother you, Mrs. Garrison," she said. "Did you open a window tonight? Or a screen?"

"What screen?" said Eileen drowsily. "I didn't open anything."

Ida got up. She had been sitting by the bed. "Better let her sleep if she can, miss," she said. "Why would she open a screen?"

All at once the hall outside was filled with men, some of them in uniform. They came up the stairs quietly but inevitably, carrying the implements of their grisly trade: the cameramen, the fingerprint detail, the detectives in soft hats and with hard, shrewd eyes. A brisk young lieutenant was apparently in charge.

He nodded to Carlton. "Bad business, sir," he said. "Sorry. Can you get these people downstairs? In one room, if that's convenient."

Carlton looked overwhelmed at the crowd. "We'd like to get some clothes on," he said.

"Not yet, if you don't mind. The Inspector will be here any time now. He'll want to see you all."

They shuffled down, accompanied by an officer: the three servants, Susie, Jan and Carlton. Only Eileen remained, and Hilda, standing in her doorway. The lieutenant looked at her, at her uniform and at the room beyond her.

"Who is in there?"

"Mrs. Garrison. She can't be moved. I'm looking after her."

He nodded, and with a gesture to two of the detectives, went into the dead woman's room and closed the door. The others stood around, waiting. A cameraman lit a cigarette and put it out. One or two yawned. Hilda closed the door into Eileen's room and stood against it, but they showed no interest in her. Not, at least, until the Inspector came up the stairs.

He took one look at her and turned to the uniformed man who had come with him. "See if there's any brandy in the house," he said. "Sit down, Hilda. Bring a chair, somebody."

They looked at her then. The hall was filled with men staring at her. Their faces were blurred. She had felt this way her first day in the operating room. White masks staring at her, and someone saying, "Catch that probationer. She's going to faint." She roused herself with an effort, forcing her eyes to focus.

"I'm not going to faint," she said stubbornly.

"You're giving a darned good imitation, then," he said. "Sit down. Don't be a little fool. I need you."

The brandy helped her. When she could focus her eyes, she found the Inspector gone. But the phalanx of men was still in the hall, watching her with interest. She got up unsteadily and went into Eileen's room. To her surprise Eileen was up. She was trying to get into her clothes, and the face she turned on Hilda was colorless and desperate.

"I've got to go," she said. "If Frank goes home and finds I'm gone—I must have been out of my mind to come here."

"I can telephone, if you like. You can't leave, of course. They won't allow anyone to leave the house."

"You mean—we're prisoners?"

Hilda's nerves suddenly snapped. "Listen," she said. "There's been a murder in this house. Of course you're not a prisoner. But you're getting back into that bed and staying there if I have to put a policeman on your chest."

That was the situation when there was a rap at the door. The Inspector wanted her, and Hilda went out.

In the old lady's room nothing had yet been disturbed. Only the detectives were standing there, touching nothing. The Inspector nodded at her.

"All right," he said. "Now look at this room. You know how you left it when Mrs. Fairbanks went to bed. Is anything changed? Has anything been moved? Take your time. There's no hurry."

She gazed around her. Everything was different, yet everything was the same. She shook her head.

"Try again," he insisted. "Anything moved on the table? Anything different about the curtains?"

She looked again, keeping her eyes from the quiet figure on the bed. "I think Mrs. Fairbanks left that closet door closed," she said finally.

"You're not sure?"

"I'm sure she closed it. She always did. It's the one with the safe in it. But I think Mrs. Fairbanks opened it at night. I don't know why."

He took out a handkerchief and pulled the door open. He examined the safe, but it was closed and locked. "Anyone else in the house have access to it?"

"I don't think so. She was rather queer about it. She didn't really like anybody to go into the closet, and she locked it when she went out."

"I suppose this is the closet where——"

"Yes."

He showed her the knife, still in the dead woman's chest. She forced herself to look at it, but she was trembling.

"Ever seen it before?"

"I may. I wouldn't know. It looks like a common kitchen knife."

"There wasn't such a knife upstairs, for instance? Lying about?"

She shook her head, and he let her go, saying he would talk to her later. As she went out, the men in the hall crowded in, to take their pictures, to dust the furniture and the knife for prints, to violate—she thought miserably—the privacy of fifty years of living. And why? Who in this house would have killed an old woman? No one seeing the household that night could doubt that they were shocked, if not grieved. And who else could have done it?

Her mind was clearer now. The radio had been turned on before young Brooke left, so she was alive then. Who else? Carlton? He had gone in and shut off the machine. He could have carried the knife in his dressing-gown pocket. But—unless he was a great actor—he was almost broken by his mother's death. He had gone down on his knees by the bed. He . . .

Who else? Marian was away. Jan was out of the question. Eileen was sick and under the influence of the hypodermic. Susie? But how could Susie get into the room? How could anyone get into the room?

She went back carefully over the night. Eileen had left Mrs. Fairbanks at midnight and Hilda had put her to bed. At a quarter after twelve she had shut off her radio and apparently gone to sleep. It was almost half past twelve when Courtney Brooke had gone down to have a drink with Carlton in the library, and soon after that Eileen had complained of pain.

During all that time she, Hilda, had left the door unguarded only for the brief excursion to the head of the stairs to the third floor, along the back hall to carry her tray back, and later when Susie crashed into it. True, she had been in the kitchen for some time, but Mrs. Fairbanks had been alive after that. Witness the radio.

Her mind was whirling. She had been in Eileen's room once or twice, but only for a matter of seconds. In any case she could have seen Mrs. Fairbanks's door, and any movement outside. Susie? But the old lady had been dead for some time before Hilda left Susie in the hall to close Eileen's screen. An hour at least; maybe more.

She leaned her head back in her chair. On the table still lay her equipment for the night, the heavy textbook, her knitting bag, the thermometer in its case, the flashlight, her charts and records. She could see the last thing she had written, after Eileen's visit. "Patient nervous. Not sleepy. Refuses sedative." She felt sick again.

From beyond the closed door came the muffled sounds of men moving about, and the soft plop of the cameramen's flash bulbs. A car drove in below, a bell rang, and a man with a bag came up the stairs. The Medical Examiner, she knew. But what could he find? A little old lady on her back, with her arms outstretched and a knife in her heart.

He was a brisk youngish man with a mustache, and he was in a bad humor when the Inspector came out to meet him. "Pity you fellows can't move without a Panzer division," he said. "I had the devil of a time getting my car in."

"Well, we won't keep you long," said the Inspector. "Stab wound in the chest. That's all."

"How do you know that's all?"

"It seems to have been enough."

The Medical Examiner ignored Hilda. He went inside the room, followed by the Inspector, and was there five minutes. He was still brisk when he came out, but his irritation was gone. He seemed depressed.

"So that's the end of old Eliza Fairbanks," he said, tugging at his mustache. "Who did it? You can bet your bottom dollar she didn't do it herself."

"No," said the Inspector. "No, I don't think so. How long ago, do you think?"

The Medical Examiner looked at his watch. "It's half past three now," he said. "I'd say two hours ago. Maybe more. Say between one and two o'clock, at a guess. Nearer one, perhaps, from the body temperature. Hard to tell, of course. Rigor sets in earlier in warm weather. I'll know better after the autopsy. What time did she eat last?" He looked at Hilda.

"She had a tray at seven thirty," she said. "She didn't go down to dinner. Poached eggs, a green salad, and some fruit. She was alive a little after one o'clock."

"How do you know that?" he asked sharply. "See her?"

"No. She turned on her radio."

He was still brisk as he went down the stairs. This was his job. Always, when he went to bed, he left his clothing ready to put on, the cuff links in his shirt, his shoes and socks beside the bed, his tie on the dresser. Even his car had a permit to stand out on the street all night. He lived like a fireman, he would say. But now he was slightly shocked. Mostly his work took him to the slums. Now there was a murder in the Fairbanks house. Somebody had jabbed a knife into old Eliza. Well, he'd be damned. He'd be doubly damned.

The Inspector watched him down the stairs. Then he got a straight chair and sat down, confronting Hilda. There was no softness in his face. He looked angry and hard. Hard as nails.

"All right," he said. "Now let's have it. And it had better be good. No use saying it couldn't happen. It has."

She braced herself. She had failed, and he knew it. He wanted no excuses. He wanted the story, and she gave it as coherently as her tired mind would allow: Eileen's arrival, her story and subsequent collapse; Mrs. Fairbanks's demand to see her, and after that the usual settling of the old lady for the night. Then came Eileen's pain, the two trips downstairs—one to speak to the doctor, the other to boil some water, leaving the doctor on guard—and the later discovery of Eileen's open screen slapping in the wind. But it was over Susie's appearance, wet and bedraggled, that he spent the most time.

"What about this Susie?" he asked. "Devoted to the old lady and all that?"

In spite of herself Hilda smiled. "Not very. Mrs. Fairbanks disliked her, and Susie—well, I thought she tried to annoy her mother-in-law. But that's as far as it went."

"What about this excursion of hers? For cigarettes in the rain? Do you believe it?"

"It might have been true. She smokes a good bit."

"But you don't think so?"

"I don't know. I don't think she's particularly scrupulous. But I doubt if she would kill anybody. She and her husband wanted to leave here and buy a farm. Mrs. Fairbanks objected. Still that's hardly a reason——"

"Any chance she could have unhooked this screen over the porte-cochère? Earlier in the night?"

"She didn't come upstairs after dinner. She and Mr. Fairbanks went to the movies."

"What about later? After the Garrison woman came?"

"She wasn't in the room at all. She hates Eileen Garrison like poison."

"What's she like? Strong? Muscular?"

"She looks pretty strong. She's a big woman."

He looked back along the hall. The screen which usually protected Hilda's chair had been folded against the wall, and he had an uninterrupted view. "Where is her room?"

Hilda told him, and he went back and inspected it, including the door to the service staircase.

"You didn't see her leave?"

"No. The screen was in the way."

"So," he said thoughtfully, "she was outside for nobody knows how long. She's big enough to handle a ladder, and she had no reason for loving her mother-in-law. People have gone to the chair for less!"

All at once Hilda found herself defending Susie. She was too direct, too open. She was—well, she was simply Susie.

"Suppose she did get into Eileen's room? Eileen Garrison was there. She was awake until she had the hypodermic. And after that, how could she get into Mrs. Fairbanks's room? I was here, in this chair. When we found the body at half past two, it was already—cool."

Nevertheless, he sent an officer to locate a ladder, in the house or on the grounds, preferably wet. He did not sit down again after that. He stood still, frowning thoughtfully.

"What about this radio?" he asked abruptly. "Sure the old lady turned it on herself? Somebody might have used one of these remote-control affairs. They operate as far as sixty feet."

"Don't they have cables, or something of the sort?"

"Not the new ones."

The men were coming out now. Inspector Patton let some of them go and detained two of the detectives.

"I want every room in the house searched," he told them. "Look for one of those remote radio controls. Look for a phonograph, too. And for anything suspicious, of course. Miss Adams will have to go into the room here in front. There's a sick woman there."

They moved off, quiet and businesslike. From the driveway below came the sounds of cars starting as the fingerprint men and cameramen departed.

No voices came from the library, and Hilda could imagine the group hud-dled there, stricken and dazed. She got up.

"Now?"

"If you please."

She went into Eileen's room. Eileen was asleep, but she roused at Hilda's entrance.

"What is it?" she said peevishly.

"I'm sorry. I'll have to search the room. All the house is being searched. I won't bother you."

"Go ahead. What are they looking for?"

But the net result was nothing. The suitcase revealed a dress or two and some undergarments, most of them showing considerable wear. The closet, hung with Marian's luxurious wardrobe, provided a bitter contrast, but that was all. And Eileen, yawning, looked bored and indifferent.

"I wish you'd get out and let me sleep."

"How do you feel?"

"How do you expect me to feel?"

She was half asleep when Hilda left the room.

The search was still going on when she closed the door behind her. One of the detectives was on his way to the third floor, and she gathered nothing had been found. There was a uniformed guard outside Mrs. Fairbanks's door, and two men in white were inside by the bed with a long wicker basket.

So Eliza Fairbanks was leaving the home to which she had come as a bride, going in a basket, without the panoply of flowers and soft music, without even dignity or any overwhelming grief.

Standing in the hall, Hilda swore a small and very private oath: to help the police to avenge this murder, and to send whoever had done it to death. "So help me God."

CHAPTER XIII

THE FAMILY and servants were still in the library when she went down-stairs. They paid no attention to her. It was as though the knife, now wrapped in cellophane and in the Inspector's pocket, had cut them all away from their normal roots, their decent habits of living. When Hilda entered, only Jan looked up, her eyes swollen, clutching a moist handkerchief in her hand.

"Are they through?"

"Not quite."

"But this is dreadful. We're not prisoners. None of us would have hurt Granny."

"I don't see how it's possible for anyone to have done it."

Carlton turned his head and looked at her with bloodshot eyes. He was holding a highball, and it was evidently not his first.

"Where were you?" he demanded. "I thought your job was to protect her. What do we know about you? How do we know you didn't do it yourself?"

"Oh, shut up, Carl," Susie said wearily. "Why would she?"

Watch them all, the Inspector had said. They'll have the gloves off now. Watch Carlton. Watch his wife. Watch the servants, too. They may know something. Tell them about the ladder and the screen. That may make them sit up.

She sat down. The servants were huddled in a corner: Maggie stiff and resentful, Ida staring at nothing, her hands folded in her lap, and William on the edge of a chair, his head shaking with an old man's palsy.

"Someone may have got in from outside," she said. "Mrs. Garrison's screen was open. They're looking now for a ladder."

She thought Carlton relaxed at that. He even took a sip of his drink. "Plenty of ladders about," he said. "Police have some sense, after all."

Only Jan showed a sharp reaction. She sat up and stared at Hilda wildly. "That's absurd," she said. "Who would want to do such a thing? And even if they did, they couldn't get into Granny's room. Miss Adams was always in the hall."

Hilda watched her. She was not only terrified. She knew something. And Susie was watching her, too.

"Don't take it too hard, Jan," she drawled. "They've got to try everything. No use getting hysterical. That won't help."

It sounded like a warning. Again Hilda wondered if there was a conspiracy among them, a conspiracy of silence. As if, whatever had once divided them, they were now united. She got no further, however. Outside an ambulance drove away, and immediately after, the Inspector appeared at the door.

"I'd like to talk to you," he said to the room in general. "There are some things to be cleared up. If there's a place where I can see everybody, one at a time . . ."

Carlton got up. His truculence had returned, and he was feeling the whisky.

"I'd better tell you," he said thickly. "I suppose this Adams woman has already done it. I was in my mother's room tonight. I went in to turn off the radio. But I didn't touch her. I thought she was asleep. I——"

"We'll talk about that later. You're Mr. Fairbanks, I suppose?"

"Yes."

"And don't be a fool," said Susie unexpectedly. "He didn't kill her. He was fond of her, God knows why. Anyhow he hasn't got the guts for murder. Look at him!"

Her tone was half contemptuous, half fiercely protective. The Inspector ignored her.

"If there is a room, I'll talk to you there, Mr. Fairbanks. And I'll ask you to come along, Miss Adams, to check certain facts."

"I'm not talking before her," Carlton snapped.

"Miss Adams is one of my most able assistants, Mr. Fairbanks. If you prefer to go to my office . . ."

But the fight was out of Carlton. He looked at Hilda and shrugged. "All right. God knows I have no secrets. Come in here."

He led the way to the small morning room behind the library, and the Inspector closed the door.

Carlton's story, as it was dug out of him, offered little or nothing new. He had been in bed when his mother's radio went on. It was very loud. It wakened him. He had gone in and shut it off. The room was dark. He had seen only her outline, but she had not moved.

"You came out immediately?"

"I did."

"Are you sure of that? Didn't you open a closet door while you were in the room?"

The question took him by surprise. He looked uncomfortable. "I closed it," he said. "It was standing open."

"Wasn't that rather curious? I mean, why do a thing like that?"

"My mother liked it closed. Her safe was there."

"Did you stop to examine the safe?"

He hesitated. "Well, I took a look." He glanced at Hilda. "I didn't know anything about Miss Adams. I just wondered . . ." He tried to smile and failed. "My mother was rather peculiar in some ways," he said. "I've never seen inside the safe. But if she had money there . . ." His voice trailed off again.

"I thought she was crazy," he said heavily. "All this talk about bats and things. But I might have known better. Somebody tried to poison her this spring. I suppose you know about that?"

"Yes. And she told me about the bats herself."

Carlton looked stunned. "Are you telling me she went to the police?"

"I am. I saw her last Monday, and I sent Miss Adams at her request. She believed that someone in this house was trying to scare her into a heart attack—and death."

"That's absurd." He lit a cigarette with unsteady fingers. "Who would try a thing like that? It's silly on the face of it."

He looked profoundly shocked, however. Hilda, watching him, thought that for the first time he was really apprehensive. But the Inspector shifted his questions.

"Do you know the combination of the safe?"

"No."

"Who benefits by her death?"

"That's the hell of it. We all do."

"Even the servants?"

"I'm not certain. I haven't seen her will. Her lawyer, Charles Willis, has it. They may get a little. Not enough to matter."

"Have you any idea of the size of the estate?"

The shift had brought some color back to Carlton's face. He put out his cigarette and straightened. "I don't know, and that's a fact," he said bitterly. "My father left about three million dollars. She must have quite a lot left. I wasn't in her confidence. I tried to talk to her, about her taxes and so on, but she wouldn't listen. She always thought I was a fool about money. But lately she's been cutting down expenses. I don't know why. She should have had a fair income."

"What do you mean by fair?"

"Oh, forty or fifty thousand a year."

The Inspector smiled faintly. To him that amount represented capital, not income. There was a brief silence. Hilda looked at her wrist watch. It was half past four, and the early June dawn was already outlining the trees outside the windows. When the Inspector spoke again, his face was grave.

"The Medical Examiner sets the time of death as sometime between one and two o'clock. Nearer one, he thinks. He may be able to tell us more accurately after the autopsy. The only person known to have entered your mother's room during that time was yourself, Mr. Fairbanks."

Carlton leaped to his feet. "I never touched her," he said shrilly. "I thought she was asleep. Ask Miss Adams. I wasn't in the room more than a minute or two."

He was in deadly earnest now, and cold sober. Hilda felt sorry for him. Of all the family, she thought, he was the only one outside of Jan who had had any affection for the old lady. Marian had resented her, had blamed her for the failure of her marriage. Susie had frankly flouted her. Even Eileen had called her an old devil.

"You went into the room, walked around the foot of the bed, turned off the radio, came back and closed the closet door. That right?"

"That's right."

He would not change his story, and at last he was allowed to go. The Inspector looked at Hilda. "True or false?" he said.

"Partly true, anyhow. If he closed the closet door, who opened it? He's keeping something back. Something he's not going to tell."

"Any idea what it is?"

"Not the slightest. Unless he knows his wife was outside in the rain. He's very much in love with her."

He got out the knife and laid it, still in its cellophane envelope, on the table beside him. "Let's show this to Maggie," he said.

But Maggie, having worked herself into a fine state of indignation, repudiated it at once. "It's none of mine," she said. "And I'd like to say that I've been in this house for twenty years and never before——"

"All right," said the Inspector. "Get out and send in the butler and the other woman, Ida. And make some coffee. I've got some men who need it, too."

Maggie, considerably deflated, went out, and William and Ida came in. Neither of them recognized the knife; both had been in bed when Susie's shrieks wakened them; both were—according to the Inspector's comment after they left—pure as the driven snow and innocent as unborn babes.

"But behaving according to rule," he said dryly. "Always more emotional than the family in a crisis. Watch it sometime."

Susie bore this out when she was sent for. She looked faintly amused as she wandered in, a cigarette in her fingers and her raincoat still covering her draggled nightgown.

"I suppose the dirty work begins now," she said, sitting on the edge of the table and ignoring the knife. "I didn't like her. I've had to take her charity and her insults ever since Carl's business failed. I thought she was an old bitch and I've said it. So I suppose I'm the leading suspect."

The Inspector eyed her, the nightgown, the stained bedroom slippers, her hair still damp and straight. "Not necessarily," he said dryly. "I'd like to know why you were out in the rain tonight."

"Your lady friend has told you, hasn't she? I went out to get some cigarettes from the car, and that damned storm caught me."

"There were cigarettes all over your room, Mrs. Fairbanks. I saw them there. I don't believe that was the reason you were outside."

Susie stared at him. "So what?" she said defiantly. "I didn't kill her, if that's what you want to know."

"But you admit you didn't like her."

"Good God! I don't like you, but I don't intend to cut your throat."

"That's very reassuring," he told her gravely. "And I haven't accused you of killing your mother-in-law. I want to know if you were in Mrs. Garrison's room tonight."

Susie's surprise was apparently genuine. "Eileen's? I should say not. I sat in the hall while Miss Adams fastened her screen. She was asleep, thank God. That's as near as I came to her, and nearer than I wanted to be."

"You don't like her, either?"

"She's another bitch," said Susie with feeling.

But she was evasive after that. Hilda, watching her, was certain she was frightened, that her assurance covered something close to panic. She stuck to her story, however. She had gone out for cigarettes and the storm had caught her. The garage was locked, as was the door to the stairs leading to Amos's quarters. She had stood under the eaves of the stable for a while. Then she had made a dash for the house.

"That's all?"

"That's all," she said defiantly.

The Inspector took a piece of paper from his pocket and unfolded it. "'At five minutes before two,'" he read, "'a woman yelped under my window. I raised it and looked out. She was standing still, but someone else was going out through the break in the fence. I think it was a man. The woman was Mrs. Carlton Fairbanks. She was rubbing her arm. I watched her until she went back to the house.'"

Susie's bravado was gone. She pushed back her heavy hair. "Amos, the dirty skunk!" she said. "All right, I wasn't going to say anything, but I can't help you at that. There was a man there. I was trying the door to the stairs when he grabbed me by the arm. I yelled and he beat it. But I don't know who it was."

She stuck to that. He had been behind her when he caught her. He hadn't spoken, and the rain was like a cloudburst. All she knew was that he let go of her when she screamed, and disappeared. She hadn't said anything to Miss Adams. No use scaring a woman who had to be up all night. But she had had a shock. She hadn't felt like going to bed. She had sat in the hall, and then Mrs. Fairbanks had been killed.

She pulled back the sleeve of her raincoat and showed her forearm. "Take a look at that if you don't believe me," she said.

There were two or three small bruises on her arm, as if made by fingers, and they were already turning purple. "I bruise pretty easy," she said.

Nothing shook her story. The sun had risen and birds were chirping outside when at last she was dismissed. With a warning, however.

"I think you know who the man was, Mrs. Fairbanks," the Inspector said soberly. "I want you to think it over. It is bad business to keep anything back in a case of this sort."

She went out, and he looked at Hilda.

"All right, Miss Pinkerton," he said. "What about it?"

"She's a fine actress and a pretty fair liar," Hilda said. "She's protecting somebody." She hesitated. "It may be the doctor. He lives across Huston Street, and he uses that break in the fence. But it might have been innocent enough. He's in love with Jan Garrison. He may have meant to meet her. Or even"—she smiled faintly—"to look up at her window. I believe people in love do things like that."

The Inspector, however, had jumped to his feet. "The doctor!" he said. "He's in love with the girl, she inherits under the will, and he was alone outside Mrs. Fairbanks's door for fifteen or twenty minutes. Where the hell is he?"

"He took an injured woman to the hospital. He may be home now. But he couldn't have done it. The radio——"

"Oh, blast the radio," he said.

He went out into the hall and sent an officer to Courtney Brooke's house. After that he sent for Janice. She came in slowly, her eyes still red, and Hilda felt a wave of pity for her. Before going to bed she had wrapped the long ends of her hair in curlers, and they made her look childish and naïve. Even the Inspector spoke gently.

"Sit down, Miss Garrison," he said. "You know we have to ask all sorts of questions in a case like this. You needn't be afraid. All we want is the truth."

"I don't know anything."

"I don't suppose you do. You were asleep when it happened, weren't you?"

"I don't know when it happened, but I wasn't asleep when Susie yelled. I wasn't sleepy, and Granny's radio had been turned on full."

"You hadn't expected to go out? Into the grounds, I mean?"

Jan looked puzzled. "Out? No. Why should I?"

"Let's say, to meet someone?"

It took her by surprise. She stared at him. Then a look of horror spread over her face. She looked wildly about the room, at Hilda, at the door. She even half rose from her chair.

"I don't know what you mean," she managed to gasp.

The Inspector's voice was still quiet.

"Suppose you meant to meet someone by the garage. Then it rained, and you didn't go. That would be understandable, wouldn't it? He came, but you didn't."

"Nobody came. I don't know what you're talking about."

"Would you swear on oath that you had no appointment to meet Doctor Brooke by the garage tonight?"

She only looked bewildered. "Doctor Brooke!" she said. "Certainly not. He can see me whenever he wants to, here in the house."

He let her go, watching her out with a puzzled look on his face. "Well, what scared *her?*" he demanded. "Do I look as formidable as all that, or—— What about this Amos, anyhow? Think he's reliable?"

"He's a mischief-maker. Stubborn and sly. He's probably honest enough."

"What is 'honest enough'?" he inquired quizzically.

But Hilda was thinking. She was remembering Jan's story that Courtney Brooke had seen her father outside the fence a night or two before. That, she was convinced, had been behind Jan's terror just now. Yet there were so many other things that she felt dizzy. The coldness for a day or so between Carlton and Susie, and Susie's fainting. Her idiotic story about going to the garage for cigarettes. Carlton, earlier in the week, carrying something from the stable and being locked out. The bats and so on in Mrs. Fairbanks's room, and the closet door which opened and closed itself.

They must make a pattern of some sort. Only what had they to do with an old woman dead of a knife thrust in a closed and guarded room?

It was just before young Brooke's arrival that one of the detectives from upstairs came down and stood in the doorway. He looked rather sheepish.

"There's a bat in that room where the old lady was," he said. "It was hanging to a curtain, and it acts like it's going crazy."

"It hasn't a thing on me," said the Inspector, and sighed.

It was bright daylight when Courtney Brooke arrived. He looked tired and puzzled, and like Susie he showed evidence of having been caught in the storm. His collar was crumpled and his necktie a limp string.

"What's wrong?" he said. "I've just come back from the hospital. Is Mrs. Fairbanks——"

"Mrs. Fairbanks is dead," said the Inspector dryly. "She was murdered last night."

The doctor stiffened and looked wildly at Hilda. "Murdered! All I ordered for her was a sleeping tablet if she couldn't sleep. If she got anything else——"

"She was stabbed. Not poisoned."

The full impact seemed to strike him with that. He sat down, as though his legs would not hold him.

"I'd like an account of what you were doing last night, doctor," said the Inspector smoothly. "Begin, if you please, with Mrs. Garrison's trouble, when you were sent for. You decided to give her a hypodermic. Then what?"

He made an effort to collect himself. "I didn't notice the time. She was having pain. She was afraid of a miscarriage. I asked the nurse here to get me some sterile water. She went downstairs. It took some time, and I——"

"You remained outside Mrs. Fairbanks's door during all that time?"

He looked unhappy. "Well, yes and no," he said. "I went back and spoke to Janice Garrison. She had been uneasy about her father. Her stepmother said he had left her, but Jan didn't believe it. She thought something had happened to him."

"Did you stay in the hall? Or did you go into Miss Garrison's room?"

"I went in. I was there only a minute or two. Long enough to reassure her."

"You agreed to guard the door," Hilda said. "Like Cerberus. You remember?"

"Well, look," he said reasonably. "Only the family was in the house. Nobody would have had time to get in from the outside. And it was poison she was afraid of. Not—being stabbed." He became suddenly conscious of his appearance. He put a hand to his collar. "Sorry I look like this," he said.

The Inspector eyed him. "Never mind how you look. This isn't a party. It's a murder investigation." He cleared his throat. "That's all, is it? You stepped into Miss Garrison's room and out again. Right?"

"I might have been there five minutes," he admitted. "I'd been telephoning around for her, and——"

"You saw nothing whatever that might be useful? Nobody moving about?"

For an instant he seemed to hesitate, and Hilda remembered the coffee spilled in the saucer and his strange expression as she came up the stairs. But he shook his head.

"Nothing," he said.

He had gone home after giving Eileen the hypodermic, he said. It was raining a little, and he had taken the short cut by the stable and the break in the fence. He saw no one lurking there. And he was in bed asleep when a man from Joe's Market rang the bell and said a woman had had an accident at the corner.

"What time was that?"

About two, he thought. It was storming hard by that time. He had telephoned for an ambulance, taken his bag and gone to the corner. The woman was lying on the pavement, with one or two people around her. She was pretty badly hurt. He had done what he could, and then gone with the ambulance to the hospital.

"I stayed while they operated," he said. "It's my old hospital, Mount Hope. They all know me."

"At ten minutes of two you were in bed?"

"I was in bed when this fellow rang the bell. I opened a window and he called up to me."

"You were undressed?"

Brooke grinned. "I'll say I was. I haven't got much on now, under this suit."

"You didn't run into Mrs. Susie Fairbanks at the garage, at five minutes of two, and catch hold of her?"

He looked astounded. "Good God, no! Why should I?"

But he lost some of his spontaneity after that. He was wary. He answered the routine questions more carefully, and at last the Inspector shrugged and let him go. He was irritable, however.

"What's the idea?" he said to Hilda grumpily. "That fellow knows something. Everybody around here knows something—except me. Even you, probably." He looked at her keenly. "I wouldn't put it past you, you know. You've held out on me before."

"Only when I thought it was necessary," she said, smiling up at him delicately.

But he had had enough. He had had too much. He got up and banged the table. "God damn it, Hilda," he roared, "if I thought you had any pets around here and were protecting them, I'd—I'd turn you over my knee."

## CHAPTER XIV

IT WAS eight o'clock in the morning before they could rouse Eileen enough to interview her. Carlton, unshaven and still only partially dressed, was at the telephone trying to locate his sister. Susie had brought him a cup of coffee, but it sat untouched beside him.

"Hello. That you, Blanche? Sorry to bother you. Did Marian happen to tell you where she was going to stop while she's away? It's rather urgent."

He would hang up after a minute or two, feverishly thumb the telephone book and commence all over again.

In the morning room, Courtney Brooke was trying to comfort Jan, a Jan who lay face down on a long davenport and refused to be comforted. One of the curlers on the end of her long bob had come loose, and he sat turning the soft curl over a finger.

"Believe me, darling, it's all right. You mustn't go on like this. You break my heart, sweet."

"Granny's dead." Her voice was smothered. "Nothing can change that."

"It's a bad business, Jan. I know that. Only try to face it as it is, not as you're afraid it is. You're not being fair. Even the police don't condemn people until they have the facts."

"I saw him. I spoke to him." She turned over and sat up, her eyes wide with fear. "Now it will all come out, Court. She had it in the safe. She told me so. They'll open it, and—then they'll know."

"Whoever did it, didn't open the safe. It's still there, sweet."

She got up, and as he steadied her, he thought how thin she was, how badly life had treated her. His arm tightened around her.

"If it's still there," she said excitedly, "do you think we could get it? Oh, Court, can't we get it? She must have had the combination somewhere. She never trusted her memory."

"We can make a try anyhow. Able to get upstairs?"

"I could fly, if I thought it would help."

They were a sorry-looking pair as they went up the long staircase, Jan's eyes still swollen, her rumpled nightgown hanging below her bath-robe, her feet still bare. Young Brooke was not much better, a disreputa-ble figure in a suit which had been soaked with rain, his hair standing wildly in all directions, and his collar melted around his neck. They did not notice the uniformed man in the lower hall, standing stolidly on guard, and there was hope in both of them until they reached the upper hall, to confront a policeman parked outside Mrs. Fairbanks's door, smoking a surreptitious cigarette.

He put it out quickly, and he did not see the dismay in their faces.

Brooke left soon after that. Eileen was still sleeping. The house was quiet. But outside in the grounds, one or two men were quietly exam-ining the pillars and roof of the porte-cochère, and a detective in plain clothes, bent double, was going carefully over the ground around the stable and near the fence.

He looked up as the doctor neared him. "Got permission to leave the place?"

"I'm the doctor," Brooke said stiffly. "My office is across the street. Anything to say about that?"

He was in a fighting mood, but the detective only grinned. "Not a word, brother. Not a word. Might like a look at your feet. That's all."

"What the hell are my feet to you?"

"Not a thing. You could lose 'em both and I wouldn't shed a tear. Lemme look at those shoes, doc."

Brooke was seething, but after a glance at the shoes, especially the soles, the detective only shrugged.

"Went out of here after the rain started, didn't you?" he said. "All right. That checks. I'll see you later. Those shoes could stand some work on them."

Brooke was still furious as he started across the street. For the first time he realized the excitement in the neighborhood. There was a large crowd around the entrance to the driveway on Grove Avenue, and the windows on both streets were filled with men in their shirt sleeves, and women hastily or only partially dressed. To add to his rage, the slovenly girl from the house where he had his offices was on the steps, surrounded by a group of laughing boys.

He caught one of them and shook him. "Get out of here," he said. "Get out and stay out, all of you." He jerked the girl to her feet. "Go inside and do some work, for once," he ordered. "If I catch you out here again . . ."

He knew it was useless. It was the ugly side of all tragedy, this morbid curiosity and avid interest which deprived even grief of privacy. But he could not fight it. He went upstairs and took a bath, as though to wash it away.

In the dining room at the Fairbanks house the Inspector was eating a substantial Sunday-morning breakfast of sausages and pancakes, and a long rangy captain of the homicide squad was trying to keep up with him. Hilda, unable to eat, eyed them resentfully. Men were like that, she thought. They did not project themselves into other people's troubles as women did. All this was just a case, a case and a job. It did not matter that a family was being torn apart, or that some one member of it was probably headed for the chair.

William had just brought in a fresh supply of pancakes when Amos came in. His small sly eyes were gleaming.

"Fellow out in the yard says to tell you he's got a footprint," he said. "It's under the big oak, and he's got a soap box over it."

The captain got up, eying his last pancake ruefully. "I guess you win, Inspector," he said. "Thirteen to my eleven. I suppose you'll want a cast."

He went out, and the Inspector took a final sip of coffee and put down his napkin. "I'm feeling stronger," he announced. "Nothing like food to take the place of sleep."

"I should think you could stay awake for the next month," said Hilda tartly.

He got up and lit a cigarette. "Don't be crabbed," he said. "It doesn't suit you. You are the ministering angel, the lady who knits while people pour out their troubles to her. Which reminds me, how about the Garrison woman? I'll have to see her. What do you think of her?"

"As a suspect? All I can say is that women don't usually murder when they're threatened with a miscarriage and under the influence of morphia."

"Don't they?" He eyed her with interest. "How much you know! But you'd be surprised, my Hilda. You'd be surprised at what some women can do."

Eileen was still in her drugged sleep when Hilda, leaving the Inspector outside, went into her room. It was not easy to rouse her, and when she did waken, she seemed not to know where she was. She sat up in bed, looking dazedly around her.

"How on earth did I get here?" she demanded, blinking in the light.

"You came last night. Don't you remember?"

She stretched and yawned. Then she smiled maliciously. "My God, do I remember!" she said. "Did you see their faces?"

But she was not smiling when the Inspector came in. She sat up, drew the bedclothing around her and stared at him suspiciously. "Who are you?" she said. "I don't know you, do I?"

He looked down at her. A neurotic, he thought, and scared to death. Heaven keep him from neurotic women.

"I'm sorry, Mrs. Garrison. I am a police officer. I want to ask you a few questions."

But he did not ask her any questions just then. She seemed profoundly shocked as full recollection came back to her. She looked, indeed, as though she might faint again, and when at last she lay back, shivering under the bedclothes, she could tell him nothing at all.

"I remember Susie screaming. I got up and went to the door. Somebody said Mrs. Fairbanks was dead—murdered. I guess I fainted after that."

"Did you hear anyone in this room last night? Before it happened."

"I don't know when it happened," she said petulantly. "Ida was here, and the doctor. And the nurse, of course."

"Did you unhook the window screen over there, for any purpose?"

She went pale. "My screen?" she said. "Do you mean——?"

"It was open. Miss Adams heard it banging. She came in and closed it."

Suddenly she sat up in bed, wide-eyed and terrified. "I want to get out of here," she said. "I'm sick, and I don't know anything about it. I wouldn't have come if I'd had any other place to go. They'd pin this murder on me if they could. They all hate me."

"Who hates you?"

"All of them," she said wildly, and burst into loud hysterical crying.

It was some time before he could question her further. But she protested that she had not even heard the radio, and that Mrs. Fairbanks had been as usual when she talked to her.

"She didn't seem nervous, or apprehensive?"

"She seemed unpleasant. She never liked me. But she did promise to look after me when my—when my baby came."

She made no objection when he asked to take her fingerprints. "Part of the routine," he told her. She lay passive on her pillows while he rolled one finger after another on the card. But she did object when he asked her to stay in the house for a day or two longer.

"I'm better," she said. "I'm all right. The doctor said——"

"I'll let you go as soon as possible," he told her, and went out.

It was in the hall outside her door that Hilda remembered about the figure at the top of the third-floor stairs.

The Inspector was about to light his pipe. He blew out the match and stared at her. "Why in God's name didn't you tell me that before?" he demanded furiously.

She flushed. "You might remember that I've had a murder on my hands, and a lot of hysterical people. I just forgot it."

He was still indignant, however. He went up the stairs, with Hilda following. But nothing was changed. The guest rooms with their drawn shades were as she had last seen them; the hall stretched back to the servants' quarters, empty and undisturbed. A brief examination showed all the windows closed and locked, and the Inspector, wiping his dusty hands, looked skeptical.

"Sure you didn't dream it?"

"I came up and looked around. There wasn't time for anyone to have gone back to the servants' rooms. I thought it was Maggie or Ida, curious about Mrs. Garrison."

"When was all this?"

"Before I went down to boil the water for the hypodermic. I was gone only a minute or two. I hardly left the top of the stairs."

He was still ruffled as he went back along the hall. There were closets there, a cedar room and a trunk room. All of them were neat but dusty, and none showed any signs of recent use as a hiding place. He lit matches, examined floors, and, still ignoring Hilda, went on back to the servants' quarters. Compared with the rest of the house they were musty, with the closeness of such places even in June, the closed windows, the faint odor of cooking from below, of long-worn clothing, and unmade beds.

Two of the rooms were empty, but Ida was in hers. She was sitting by a window, her hands folded in her lap and a queer look on her long thin face as Hilda went in. "I was nervous and Maggie sent me up," she said. "But there's no use of my going to bed. I couldn't sleep."

It was the appearance of the Inspector which definitely terrified her, however. She went white to the lips. She tried to get up and then sank back in her chair.

"What is it?" she asked. "I don't know anything. What do you want with me? Can't I get a little rest?"

Hilda tried to quiet her. "It hasn't anything to do with Mrs. Fairbanks's death, Ida," she said. "I thought I saw someone in the upper hall last night, before—before it happened. If it was you, it's all right. We're only checking up."

Ida shook her head. "It wasn't me, miss."

"Would it have been William? Or Maggie?"

She was quieter now. "I wouldn't know about that. They usually sleep like the dead."

But Hilda was remembering something. She was seeing the household gather after Susie screamed, and seeing Maggie and William come along the back hall on the second floor, while Ida was standing still, looking down from the front stairs to the third floor. She did not mention it. Quite possibly Ida as the housemaid used those stairs habitually. She tucked it away in her memory, however, to wonder later if she should have told it. If it would have altered the inevitable course of events.

Neither of them could change Ida's story. She sat there, twisting her work-worn hands in her lap. She had been in bed. She had seen nobody, and she had liked the old lady. She had looked after her as well as she could. Tears welled in her eyes, and the Inspector left her there and went out, muttering to himself.

"Damn all crying women," he said. "I'm fed up with them."

That was when he timed Hilda, making her leave her chair in the hall, go up, look around for a light switch and come down again. He put his watch back in his pocket and looked at her grimly. "Three minutes," he said. "A lot can happen in three minutes, my girl."

He left at nine o'clock, driving away with his uniformed chauffeur. The men who had been scattered over the grounds had disappeared, but one officer was on duty on Huston Street beside the break in the fence. Another was holding back the crowd at the gate, and two still remained in the house. Hilda watched the car make its difficult way through the crowd.

"It's disgusting," she said to the tall young policeman on duty in the lower hall. "They ought to be ashamed."

He smiled indulgently. "They like a bit of excitement, miss," he said. "There's a lot of reporters out there, too. I caught one carrying in the milk bottles early this morning."

As she went up the stairs, she could still hear Carlton at the library phone.

"Hello, George. I'm trying to locate Marian. She's out of town somewhere. I suppose you and Nell haven't heard from her?"

She was very tired. When she looked into Eileen's room, Ida was running a carpet sweeper over the floor. Eileen's hair had been combed and fresh linen put on her bed. She looked better, although she was still pale.

"If you're all right, I'll go to bed for an hour or two, Mrs. Garrison," Hilda said. "I haven't had much sleep lately."

"I'm perfectly all right. I told that fool of a policeman, but he wouldn't listen."

Hilda went back toward her room. But she did not go to bed. Maggie was carrying a tray into Jan's room, and she followed her. Jan was standing by a window, fully dressed. She looked at the tray and shook her head.

"I'm afraid I can't eat," she said. "Thanks anyhow. I'll have the coffee."

Maggie put down the tray firmly. "You'll eat," she said. "Somebody's got to keep going around here." Her voice softened. "Try it anyhow, dearie," she said. "Just remember she was old. She hadn't long anyhow."

Jan's chin quivered. "She liked living."

"Well, so do we all," said Maggie philosophically. "That don't mean we can go on forever." She went out.

Jan looked at Hilda. "I've been trying to think. How are we to get word to Mother? I don't suppose it is in the papers, is it?"

"I hardly think so. There wasn't time."

"And there are no evening papers today," Jan said desperately. "She may not hear it until tomorrow. And she ought to be here. Uncle Carl's no good at that sort of thing, and Susie's asleep. I went in and she was dead to the world. I wanted to talk to her. I . . ."

Her voice trailed off. Her hands shook as she tried to pour the coffee. Hilda took the miniature pot from her and poured it for her.

"Why not waken her?" she said quietly. "After all, if it's important——"

"Important!" Jan's voice was bitter. "You've seen her. You've heard her. You know she hated Granny. She hated living in the house with her. Uncle Carl wanted a farm, and she adores him. They can have it now," she added hopelessly. "They'll have my grandmother's money. First Susie tried to scare Granny to death, and when that wasn't any good——"

"What do you mean by that?" Hilda demanded sharply. "Scaring her to death."

"Those bats and things. You don't think they got in by themselves!" Jan was scornful. "It was just the sort of thing she would think of. Scare Granny out of the house, or into a heart attack. What did she care?"

Hilda was thoughtful. In a way Jan was right. Susie was quite capable of it. It might even appeal to her macabre sense of humor. The murder, however, was different. She could not see Susie putting arsenic in the old lady's sugar or driving a knife into her heart.

"She had the chance last night, too," Jan went on. "She could have heard Courtney come back to talk to me while you were downstairs. She could have slipped through Uncle Carl's room and around the screen. Nobody would have seen her."

She stopped, looking startled. Susie was in the doorway, cigarette in hand and her sharp blue eyes blazing.

"So I did it!" she said. "You little idiot, didn't I lie my head off last night for you?" She threw back the sleeve of her dressing gown and showed her arm. "You know who did that, don't you? Suppose I'd told the police your precious father was here in the grounds last night? And his wife inside the house with the screen over the porte-cochère open? Suppose I'd said that the whole thing was a plant to get Eileen into this house, so Frank Garrison could get in, too?"

Hilda watched them, her blue eyes shrewd. Neither of them seemed aware of her presence. She saw that Jan was on the verge of collapse.

"He wouldn't kill Granny. Never. You know it. Deep down in your heart you know it."

Susie eyed her. Then she shrugged. "All right, kid," she said. "I didn't tell the police. I won't either, unless you go around yelling that I did it. Or Carlton." Suddenly she sent a shocked look at Hilda. "Good God, I forgot. You're police yourself, aren't you?"

"Not all the time. I'm a human being, too." Hilda smiled faintly.

"Well, forget it," said Susie. "I was just talking. The kid here made me mad. Maybe he thought Eileen was here. He might have come to find out."

She went back to her room, and Jan caught Hilda by the arm. "That's why he came," she said desperately. "I swear it is. I'll swear it by anything holy. My window was up, and he called to me. He said, 'Jan, do you know where Eileen has gone? She's not in the apartment.' When I told him she was here and—and sick, he seemed worried. But he wouldn't come in. He went away again, in the rain. In the rain," she repeated, as though the fact hurt her. "I can't even telephone him," she went on. "Uncle Carl's still using the phone. And if the police find it out——"

"Why worry about that? He had no reason for wishing your grandmother—out of the way, had he?"

"Of course not." She lit a cigarette and smoked it feverishly. "He was devoted to her. But he doesn't know what's happened. He ought to know. He ought to be able to protect himself. Look," she said, putting down the cigarette, "would you be willing to tell him? To go to his apartment and tell him? It wouldn't do any harm. He can't run away. That's all I want—for him to know."

It was a long time before Hilda agreed, but the girl's sick face and passionate anxiety finally decided her. Also she was curious. There was something behind all this, something more than a distracted husband trying to locate a missing wife in the middle of the night. Why had he not come in when he learned that Eileen was sick? Surely that would have been the normal thing to do.

She knew she had very little time. The police had the cast of the footprint under the oak. They would be working on it now. They would have examined the shoes of the men in the house, measured them, perhaps photographed them. And if Amos knew more than he had told . . .

She hurried to her room to dress. As she opened the door, she had the feeling that something had moved rapidly across the floor. Whatever it was, she could not find it, and she dressed rapidly and went down the stairs. Evidently the officer there had no orders to hold her, for he smiled and opened the door.

"Out for a walk?"

"I need some air," she said blandly.

Under the porte-cochère, however, she stopped. The crowd was still on the pavement, held back by the guard, and a photographer was holding up his camera. She turned quickly toward the stable and the broken fence. Amos was not in sight, but the soap box lay on its side under the oak tree, some fifty feet away. She hurried to the break in the fence, and straightened, to look into the lens of a camera. A grinning young man thanked her. She made a wild snatch at the camera, but he evaded it.

"Naughty, naughty," he said. "Papa slap. Now, what's your name, please?"

"I have no name," she told him furiously.

"Must be a disadvantage at times. How do they get you? Say, 'Here, you'?"

He took another flash of her indignant face before she could stop him, and she was moving rapidly toward the corner when she became aware that the crowd was coming toward her. It moved slowly but irresistibly, as though propelled by some unseen power from behind. A half-dozen small boys ran ahead of it.

"That's the nurse!" one of them yelled. "She's got her cap off, but I know her."

"Hey, nurse! What's happened in there?"

The reporters were in the lead now. In an instant she was surrounded by eager young faces. She could see her bus a block away, and she stood haughtily silent, like a small neat Pekingese among a throng of disorderly street dogs. "Have a heart, sister." "Come on, how was the old lady killed?" "Has anyone been arrested?"

She was driven to speech, in sheer desperation. "I have nothing to say," she told them. "If you care to follow me while I get some fresh uniforms and look after my canary, that's all the good it will do you."

They laughed but persisted until the bus came and she got on. Looking back, she could see them, returning discouraged to take up their stations again, to wait and hope for a break, to be able perhaps to get a new angle on the story and maybe a raise in salary. She felt unhappy and guilty, as though she had failed them. As, of course, she had.

She reached the Garrison apartment at ten o'clock. No one answered the bell, and at last she tried the door. It was unlocked, and she stepped inside, to find herself in a long gallery, paved with black and white marble. A fine old tapestry hung at the end. It surprised her, as did the drawing room when she saw it; a handsome room carefully furnished, but with every sign of extreme neglect. The grand piano showed dust in the morning sun, the brocaded curtains were awry, the windows filthy, the rugs askew on the floor. Old magazines and papers lay about, and a vase of flowers on a table had been dead and dried for days.

Her tidy soul revolted. No wonder men left women who surrounded themselves with dirt and disorder. But there was no sign of Frank Garrison. The place was quiet and apparently empty. Not until she had investigated most of the apartment did she locate him, in a small room at the far end of the gallery. He was in a deep chair, and he was sound asleep.

Whatever she had expected, it was not this. She inspected him carefully. He was in pajamas and bathrobe, and the Sunday papers were scattered around him. A cluttered ash tray and an empty coffee cup were beside him, and he had the exhausted unshaven look of a man who had slept little or not at all the night before.

When she touched him on the shoulder, he jerked awake. Not fully, however. "Sorry," he mumbled. "Guess I dozed off." He looked up at her and blinked.

"Thought you were my wife," he said. "My apologies." He got up slowly, his big body still clumsy with sleep. Then he recognized her. He looked alarmed.

"Miss Adams! Has anything happened? Is Jan——"

"Jan's all right." She sat down. "I have other news for you, Mr. Garrison, unless you already know it. Jan wanted me to tell you. Mrs. Fairbanks is dead."

He looked surprised. "Dead!" he said. "Just like that! Jan will take it hard. Still, I suppose it was to be expected." He looked down at his pajamas. "I'd better dress and go over. I didn't expect a visitor. What was it? Heart, I suppose?"

"No," said Hilda.

"No? Then what——"

"She was murdered, Mr. Garrison."

He stared at her. He had been in the act of picking up a cigarette. Now his hand hung frozen over the box. The incredulity in his face gave way to sick horror. "Murdered!" he said hoarsely. "I don't understand. Not poison again?"

"She was stabbed. With a knife."

He still seemed unable to take it in. "I don't understand," he repeated. "Who would kill her? She hadn't very long to live. And nobody hated her. Even the servants . . ."

He did not finish. He got up and went to the window. "Is Jan all right?" he asked without turning.

"She's worried, Mr. Garrison."

He swung around. "Worried! What do you mean, worried?"

"You were outside the house last night, and Mrs. Carlton Fairbanks knows it."

"Susie! So it was Susie!" he said, and gave a short laugh. "She scared the insides out of me."

"Jan thought you ought to know," Hilda said patiently. "There may be trouble. The police have found a footprint. I imagine it's yours. I promised to tell you before they got here—if they come at all. Susie won't talk, but Amos might. He looked out the window. He may have recognized you."

He began to see the seriousness of his situation. Yet his story was coherent and straightforward. He had had what he called a difference with Eileen, on Wednesday night. He had packed a bag and gone to his club, and on Saturday morning he had taken a plane to Washington.

"Things haven't been very good," he said. "I needed a job, and I thought with all this government housing I might get something. I happen to be an architect. But it was a Saturday, and summer"—he smiled—"and the government doesn't work on June weekends."

He had got back to the apartment at midnight the night before, to find Eileen gone and her suitcase missing. They had had to let the maid go, and he didn't know what had happened to Eileen.

"I thought Jan might know," he said. "But I didn't want to telephone her and rouse the house. So I went over. It was about one o'clock when I left here. I've done that before—talked to Jan at night, I mean. Her window was up, although it was raining cats and dogs, and I called to her. She said my wife was there, so I came back here."

"Meeting Susie on the way?"

"Meeting Susie on the way," he said, and smiled again. "She yelled like an Indian."

She considered that. It might be true. She had an idea, however, that it was not all the truth.

"You didn't go back again? To the house?"

He looked at her oddly. "See here," he said. "What's all this about? They don't think *I* killed the old lady, do they?"

"Somebody killed her," Hilda said dryly, and got up.

He saw her out, apologizing for the dust, the evident disorder. He owned the apartment. He couldn't sell it, worse luck. Nobody could sell anything nowadays, even a tapestry. But she felt that behind all this, his confident manner, the composure on his good-looking face, his mind was far away, working hard and fast.

She was on a corner waiting for a bus when she saw the Inspector's car drive up to the door of the apartment building and two or three men get out. So Amos had talked, after all.

She was not surprised, on her return to the Fairbanks house, to learn from William that the police had taken away the window screen from Eileen's room. But she was rather astonished to find Carlton, in a morning coat, striped trousers and a black tie, wandering around upstairs and carrying a hammer and an old cigar box filled with nails.

"Thought I'd nail up the other screens," he said vaguely. "Can't have people getting in and out of the house. Not safe."

He went into Eileen's room, a dapper incongruous figure, and Hilda followed him. Eileen was sitting up in bed. She looked better, although she was still pale; and she managed an ironical smile when Carlton told her what he was doing.

"You're a little late with that, aren't you?" she said.

"Some of us still want to live, Eileen."

"You can do that now, can't you?" she said maliciously. "Live the way you like, get your Susie safe on a farm away from other men, raise pigs, do anything you damn well please."

He stiffened. "That was entirely uncalled for. If you were not a sick woman——"

"If I were not a sick woman, I wouldn't be here."

He finished his hammering and later Hilda, remembering that day, was to hear the noise as he moved from room to room, and even to smell the putty and white paint with which he neatly covered the signs of his labors.

He finished at eleven thirty, which was almost exactly the time Patton and his henchmen were leaving Frank Garrison. He had told a straight story, but the Inspector was not satisfied. He stood in the long marble-floored gallery and put his hat on with a jerk.

"I'll ask you not to leave town," he said. "Outside of that, of course, you're free. I suppose you have no idea where your first wife is? We'd like to locate her."

"I am not in her confidence," he said stiffly. "I would be the last person to know."

## CHAPTER XVI

### POLICE DEPARTMENT

From: Commanding Officer, 17th Precinct
To: Medical Examiner
Subject: Death of Eliza Douglas Fairbanks, of Ten Grove Avenue.

1. On June 15, ——, at 2:20 A.M., a report was received from Inspector Patton that a Mrs. Eliza Douglas Fairbanks, aged 72 years, had been found dead in her bed as a result of a stab wound in the chest.

2. Case was reported at once by Inspector Patton and usual steps taken. Inspector Patton and Captain Henderson of Homicide Squad were assigned to case.

The Inspector had this document in front of him that noon. In such brief fashion, he thought, were the tragedies of life reported. Men and women died of violence. Tragedy wrecked homes. Hatred and greed and revenge took their toll. And each of them could be officially recorded in less than a hundred words.

Nor was the report of the autopsy more human. An old woman had died, cruelly and unnecessarily. Died in a closed room, with access to it almost impossible. And the autopsy, after recording her pathetic age, her shrunken weight, and the entirely useless examination of her head, abdomen and thorax, merely reported the cause of death as an incised wound with a tract of two and one-half inches, which, on being carefully dissected, was shown to have reached the heart. And that the approximate time of death had been between twelve thirty and one thirty in the morning.

He put it down. After all, murder was an inhuman business, he thought, and began again to look over the reports and his own memoranda, which had accumulated on the desk. Considering that the day was Sunday they covered considerable ground.

The house: No sign of entrance by roof of porte-cochère. Blurred prints on window screen, one identified as belonging to Miss Adams, nurse. Three ladders on property, none showing signs of having been out in the rain. No indication pillars had been climbed. All doors and windows on lower floor closed and locked. No phonograph or remote control for radio found. Knife not belonging to kitchen. (Evidence of one Margaret O'Neil, cook.) At seat of crime, fingerprints only of dead woman, servants and family, including those of Mrs. Eileen Garrison on back of chair. None of Mrs. Carlton Fairbanks. Prints of Carlton Fairbanks on foot of bed and closet door. Prints of dead woman on safe. No others.

On the people in the house at the time of the crime his notes were brief, mostly written in his own hand.

Carlton Fairbanks: Son of deceased. Member of prosperous brokerage house until 1930. Business gradually declined until 1938, when it was liquidated. Married in 1930 to Susan Mary Kelly. Came to live with mother in 1938. Wife disliked by Mrs. Fairbanks and daughter Marian. Both Carlton Fairbanks and wife anxious to leave and buy farm. Is supposed to inherit, along with sister and niece, Janice Garrison, under will. Admits entering room at or about 1:15 to turn off radio.

Susan Mary Fairbanks: See above. Reason for visit to stable-garage that night not known. Did not enter, as encountered Garrison and was scared away. No cigarettes in her car, although given as reason for night excursion. Does not conceal dislike of mother-in-law. Father contractor in small way. Family lives at 140 South Street in plain but respectable neighborhood. On good terms with them. Probably does not inherit under will but would share husband's portion.

Marian Garrison: Quarreled with mother and left home last Wednesday evening, June eleventh. Present address unknown. Thirty-eight years of age, thin, dark, usually dressed in black. Taxicab which called for her took her to Pennsylvania Station. No further information. According to servants, bitterly resentful over husband's second marriage. Has lived at Grove Avenue house since marriage in 1921, as mother refused to be left alone. Divorced in 1934 at Reno, Nevada.

Janice Garrison: Age 19. Probably inherits under will. Friendly with father and second wife. Apparently devoted to grandmother. No motive, unless money. Is supposed to be interested in Doctor Courtney Brooke.

Courtney Allen Brooke, M.D.: Age 28. Office and house at 13 Huston Street. Graduate Harvard Medical School. Interned two years Mount Hope Hospital. In private work one year. Small practice, barely earning expenses. First called to attend deceased March tenth, when treatment was given for arsenic poisoning. Has attended deceased at intervals since. Apparently in house during time of crime, in attendance on Mrs. Eileen Garrison, who was threatened with abortion. Alibi given by nurse Hilda Adams: the dead woman turned on her radio before his departure.

Eileen Garrison: Age 35. Married in 1934 to Francis J. Garrison, following divorce. Formerly governess to Janice Garrison. Small, blonde, nervous temperament. Born on farm near Templeton, thirty miles from city, where parents still live. Not liked by Fairbanks family, although Janice Garrison remained friendly. Could expect nothing under will. In house at time of crime, but sick and under influence of morphine administered at or about one o'clock.

Francis Jarvis Garrison: Well-known architect. Age 42. Inherited money. Supposed to be wealthy until 1929. Since then heavy losses. Pays ex-wife ten thousand a year alimony, tax free. Owns large apartment, but behind on maintenance charges. Divorced in 1934. Married daughter's governess soon after. Produces ticket stub to prove plane trip to Washington Saturday. Admits being in grounds night of crime and says he talked to daughter, to learn his wife's whereabouts. Uncertain of time. Thinks between 1:30 and 2:00 A.M. Encounter with Mrs. Fairbanks Jr. purely accidental. Admits footprint his. Expects nothing under will.

There were brief reports on the servants, but he glanced at them casually. Only Ida's he picked up and examined.

Ida Miller: Country girl born in Lafayette County. Age 40. Ten years in Fairbanks house. Hysterical since murder. Possibly not telling all she knows.

He was still looking at it when the commissioner came in. The commissioner had expected to play golf, and he was in a bad humor. The Inspector offered him a chair, which he took, and a cigar, which he refused.

"Never smoke them," he said. "What's all this, anyhow? I thought you'd put that woman of yours to watch the Fairbanks house."

"Not the house," said the Inspector politely. "Mrs. Fairbanks herself."

"So she lets her be killed! It's the hell of a note, Patton. I may be new to this job, but when you guarantee to protect a woman—and a prominent woman at that—I want to know why the devil she wasn't protected."

"She was, as a matter of fact. It couldn't have happened. Only it did."

"Don't give me double talk," said the commissioner, the veins in his forehead swelling. "She's dead, isn't she?"

It was some time before the Inspector could tell the story. He went back to the attempt to poison Mrs. Fairbanks, and to the mystery of the bats and so on in the room.

"They got in somehow," he said. "I've been over the place. I don't see how it was done. But it was."

"Carried in," said the commissioner. "That's easy. Carried in while she was out and left there. Room wasn't locked, was it?"

"Not during the day."

"All right. Get on with it."

He sat with his eyes closed while the Inspector got on with it, reading now and then from his notes. At the end he sat up, eying the Inspector with unexpected shrewdness.

"You've got only two suspects, Patton. Frank Garrison's out. Why would he kill the old woman? He had nothing to gain. Anyhow, I know him. He's a damned decent fellow."

"I've known——"

"All right. Who have you got? This young doc and Carlton Fairbanks. The doctor's out. So Carlton's left. Know him, too. Always thought he was a stuffed shirt."

"That wouldn't go far with a jury." Patton smiled unhappily. "Anyhow, he doesn't seem to me the type. Of course——"

"Type? Type! Any type will kill for a half of three million dollars. That's what old Henry Fairbanks left his widow when he died. In bonds, Patton! No hanky-panky, no cats and dogs, no common stocks. Bonds!"

"It sounds like a lot of money," said the Inspector. "Maybe you'd like to talk to Fairbanks yourself."

The commissioner got up hastily. "Not at all," he said. "I've got an engagement. And I guess you have your own methods. Better than mine, probably!"

With that he departed, and the Inspector felt that he was left virtually with a rubber hose in his hand.

Back at the Fairbanks house, Hilda had not gone to bed. She took off her shoes and rubbed her tired feet, but she was not sleepy. The sense of failure was bitter in her. Yet what had she done? She had left the door to go up to the third floor, a matter of three minutes or so. She had been fifteen minutes, maybe twenty, in the kitchen, but the doctor had agreed to stand guard. And Mrs. Fairbanks had been alive then. She had turned on the radio after that, turned it on loudly, as if the movements in the hall outside the door had exasperated her.

What else? Hilda had taken her tray to the back staircase, and later on Susie had stepped in it. She had gone back and found her there. How long had that taken?

She got up, and to the astonishment of the officer in the hall, paced it off in her stocking feet, carrying her watch in her hand. She could hardly believe it when the second hand showed only a minute and a half. Then what? She and Susie had sat in the hall, until the slamming screen had taken her into Eileen's room. Eileen had been asleep, and she had closed and hooked the screen. And after that she had found Mrs. Fairbanks dead, and her hands were already cool.

It was Carlton, then, after all. It had to be Carlton.

She went back to her room and stood looking out the window. Amos, in his best clothes and with a smug look on his face, was coming toward his Sunday dinner. Birds were busy on the grass after the rain the night before. The crowd outside had diminished somewhat as the meal hour arrived, but it was still there.

Carlton, she thought wretchedly. She could see him now, dressed in his striped trousers and black coat and wearing a mourning tie, trying to fill in the time with a hammer and an old cigar box filled with nails. Did men kill their mothers and then go puttering around fastening screens? Decent quiet little men who liked the country and growing things?

The unreality grew when she sat at the midday dinner table, watching him carve a roast of beef into delicate slices.

"Well done or rare, Miss Adams?"

"Medium, please."

Not Carlton, she thought, looking around the table. Not any of them. Not Susie, in a black dress, with little or no make-up, and for once not smoking. Not Jan. Oh, certainly not Jan, looking young and tragic and not eating. Not even young Brooke, watching Jan and making such talk as there was. Certainly not Eileen, sick and hysterical in her room upstairs. Not William, his head still shaking as he passed the food. Not Ida, pale but efficient. Not any of them, she thought drearily. Then who?

The guards were taken out of the house that afternoon, but Mrs. Fairbanks's room was left locked and sealed. There was still no news of Marian, and Jan, after a talk with her father on the telephone, had at last gone to bed and to sleep.

It was three o'clock in the afternoon when Carlton was taken to police headquarters for questioning.

Hilda was in the lower hall when it happened. He said nothing to anybody. When she saw him, he was carefully selecting a stick from a stand, and he spoke to her quietly.

"If my wife asks for me," he said, "tell her I have some things to do downtown. I may be late, so ask her not to wait up for me."

She saw the car outside, with Captain Henderson and a detective waiting, and felt sorry for him, adjusting his hat in front of the mirror. When he turned, she saw he was pale.

"I was fond of my mother, Miss Adams," he said strangely, and without looking back, went out to the officers and the waiting car.

At four o'clock that same afternoon, Marian Garrison came home.

## CHAPTER XVII

SHE ARRIVED apparently unwarned. Her first shock came when the taxi, violently honking its horn, tried to make its way through the crowd. The police officer drove the crowd back, but when the driver stopped under the porte-cochère, he found her collapsed in the seat and rang the doorbell.

"Lady here's in poor shape," he told William. "Want me to bring her in?"

William ran down the steps, to find her with her eyes shut and her face colorless.

"What is it? What's wrong, William?"

"I'm sorry, madam. Mrs. Fairbanks is dead."

"Dead? But the crowds! What's wrong? What happened to her?"

"It was quite painless. Or so they say. She was asleep when it took place. If——"

She reached out and caught him by the arm.

"Not poison, William? Not poison!"

He hesitated, his old head shaking violently.

"No, madam. I'm afraid—it was a knife."

She did not faint. She drew a long breath and got out of the car. The driver and William helped her into the house. But she could not walk far. She sat down on a chair inside the door, snapping and unsnapping the fastening of her bag, her eyes on William.

"Who did it?" she asked, in a half whisper.

"Nobody knows. Not yet. The police——"

She got up. "I want to see Jan," she said wildly. "I must talk to her. I'd better try to go up to my room."

William caught her by the arm. "Not right away, Miss Marian," he said in his quavering voice. "You see——"

She shook him off. "What's the matter with you?" she demanded. "I'm going up to my room. Get Jan and tell her I'm here, and don't act the fool."

That was the situation when Jan ran down the stairs: Marian standing angry and bewildered, and William evidently at a loss to know what to do.

She gave them one look and kissed her mother's cold face. But Marian did not return the caress.

"Why can't I go upstairs in my own home, Jan? What is all this?"

It was on this tableau that Hilda appeared: Marian's face flushed, Jan's pale and her young body stiff.

"I'm sorry, Mother. We'll get her out as soon as we can. You see——"

"Get whom out?"

"Eileen. She's sick. She is in your room, Mother."

Marian's frail body stiffened. "So that's it," she said. "You've brought her here and put her in my room. The woman who ruined my life, and you couldn't wait until I was gone to get her here!"

She would have gone on, but Hilda interfered. She took her into the library and gave her a stiff drink of Scotch. All the fire had gone out of her by that time. She seemed stunned. The liquor braced her, however, although she listened to Jan's story with closed eyes. But her first words when Jan finished her brief outline were addressed to Hilda.

"So you let it happen after all!" she said. "I left her in your care, and she was killed."

She was badly shaken, but she was frightened, too. Hilda was puzzled. She caught Marian watching Jan, as if the girl might know something she was not telling. Marian was more frightened than grieved, she thought. But she was coldly determined, too.

"Get that woman out of here," she said. "At once, Jan. Do you hear? If she can't walk, carry her. If she won't be carried, throw her out. And if none of you can do it, I'll do it myself. Or strangle her," she added.

That was the situation when Hilda got the Inspector on the telephone. He seemed annoyed, as though he resented the interruption, but he agreed to let Eileen go.

"She's hardly a suspect," he said. "Sure. Better get young Brooke's okay on it first."

She called the doctor, who agreed unwillingly, and went to Eileen's room. To her surprise Eileen was already out of bed and partly dressed. She was sitting in a chair while Ida drew on her stockings, and she was smiling coldly.

"I heard the fuss and rang," she said. "Tell them not to worry. I'm leaving. She can have her room. She can have the whole damned house, so far as I am concerned." She slid her feet into her pumps and stood up. "I suppose," she said, "my loving husband has come back, too."

"He came back last night. From Washington."

Eileen looked at her sharply. "From Washington? How do you know?"

"I saw him this morning."

"Where? Here?"

"I went to the apartment. Jan asked me to. He had been here last night and she was worried."

A flicker of alarm showed in Eileen's face. "What do you mean, he was here? In the house?"

"In the grounds. He says he didn't know where you were, so he came and called up to Jan's window to find out."

Eileen sat down on the bed, as though her knees would not hold her. "When—when was that?"

"Between one thirty and two, I think," Hilda said. "His plane got in at midnight, but he went home first. Then he walked here. It's quite a distance."

Eileen's face had turned a grayish color. She seemed to have difficulty in breathing. "Do the police know that?" she asked, her lips stiff.

"They know he was in the grounds. He admits it himself." And then, because Hilda was sorry for her, she added, "I wouldn't worry too much about it, Mrs. Garrison. Of course, they're suspecting everybody just now. I'd better order a taxi. I can go with you if you like."

Eileen, however, wished for no company. When Hilda came back from the telephone, she was looking better, or at least she was under control. She was in front of Marian's table, eying herself in the mirror. Almost defiantly she put on some rouge and lipstick, and finished her dressing. Ida had carried down her suitcase, and at the door she turned and surveyed the room.

"Did you ever know what it is to pray for somebody to die?" she said bitterly. "Did you ever see someone riding around in a car in the rain while you walked, and wish there would be an accident? Did you ever lie awake at night hating somebody so hard that you hit the pillow? Well, that's what Marian Garrison has done to me. And he still cares for her. After seven years he's still in love with her. He'd even go to the chair for her! The fool. The blind stupid fool."

Carlton had not come home when Eileen left the house. He was still in the Inspector's office, his dapper look gone, but his head still high.

"Just go over that again, Mr. Fairbanks. You went into the room, went around the foot of the bed, turned off the radio and came directly out again. How could you see to turn off the radio? Did you light a match?"

"I didn't need to. It's an old one. We've had it for a long time. I knew where the switch was. And of course there was some light from the door into the hall."

"You still claim that you didn't speak to your mother?"

"I did not. She had a habit of going to sleep with the radio on. I've gone in and shut it off many times."

"You came out at once?"

"I did. Immediately. Ask the nurse. She was there."

But he was tired. He had eaten almost nothing that day, and although they gave him water when he asked for it and he was well supplied with cigarettes, he needed a drink badly. There was a cold sweat all over him and his mouth was dry. He moistened his lips.

"You had no reason, for instance, to investigate the closet where the safe is?"

"Why should I? It's been there for months."

"And the closet door?"

"Oh, for God's sake! How can I remember? What does it matter? Suppose it was open and I shoved it out of my way? What has that got to do with my mother's death?"

"Do you think anyone could have been hidden in the closet?"

"Who? My niece? My wife?"

"I'm asking the questions, Mr. Fairbanks," said the Inspector. "You are the only person known to have entered your mother's room at or about the time she was—the time she died. I know this is painful, but we have to get on with it. If you had nothing to do with it, you will want to be helpful. Nobody is trying to railroad you into"—he coughed—"jail. Now. You have said that you are one of the heirs to the estate."

A little of Carlton's dignity had returned. He was even slightly pompous. "I presume so. My sister and myself. Probably there is something for my niece, Janice Garrison. I don't know, of course. My—my mother managed her own affairs."

"You must have some idea of the value of the estate."

But here he was on surer ground. "It was a very large one at one time. Some values have shrunk, but it was carefully invested. Mostly in bonds."

"Did she keep those securities in the safe?"

"I don't know. I hope she didn't. She used to have several safe-deposit boxes at her bank. I suppose she still has them."

But always they went back to the night before. The knife. Had he seen it before? Had he bought it anywhere? Of course knives and sales could be traced. He would understand that. And he didn't like the city, did he? He and his wife wanted a farm. Well, plenty of people wanted farms nowadays. He brightened over that.

"Certainly I wanted a farm," he said. "There's a living in it, if you work yourself. A man can keep his self-respect. I've studied it a good bit. These fellows who go out of town and play at it—they'll only lose their investments. They'll fix up the houses and build fancy chicken houses and pigpens, and in three or four years they'll be back in town again."

"The idea was to be independent of your mother, wasn't it?"

"Not entirely. But what if it was? There's nothing wrong about that."

They took him back to the attempt to poison Mrs. Fairbanks on her return from Florida. He was indignant.

"I never believed she was poisoned. Not deliberately. Some kinds of food poisoning act the same way. I looked it up. She'd come back from Florida the day before. She might have eaten something on the train."

"The doctor doesn't think so."

"That young whippersnapper! What does he know?"

The Inspector picked up a paper from his desk. "This is Doctor Brooke's statement," he said. He read: " 'Showed usual symptoms arsenical poisoning, heat and burning pain; was vomiting and very thirsty. When I saw her, her pulse was feeble and she showed signs of collapse. Had severe cramps in legs. I gave her an emetic and washed out her stomach. Reinsch's test later showed arsenious acid, commonly known as white arsenic. I also found it in the sugar bowl on her tray. At request of family made no report to the police.' "

"Oh, my God!" said Carlton feebly.

He sat clutching the arms of his chair, hardly hearing what they asked him. He looked smaller than ever, as though he had been deflated, and his replies were almost monosyllabic.

"Do you know anything about this campaign to terrify your mother? The bats, I mean."

"No. Nothing."

"Nor how they were introduced into the room?"

"No."

"I'll ask that another way. Have you any suspicions as to how or why they were being used?"

And at that he blew up. "No. No!" he shouted. "What are you trying to do to me? Make me confess to something I never did? I didn't poison my mother. I didn't kill her with a knife. I don't know anything about your damned animals. I don't know anybody cruel enough to——"

His voice broke. Tears rolled down his cheeks. He mopped at them helplessly with his handkerchief. "I'm sorry, gentlemen," he said. "I didn't mean to make a fool of myself. I was up all night, and I haven't eaten anything today."

They gave him a little time. He lit a cigarette and tried to smile. "All right," he said. "I guess I can take it now."

But they got nothing of importance from him, except a pretty thorough idea that he was keeping something back. They did not hold him, however. At eight o'clock that night the Inspector drove him home. They stopped and had something to eat on the way, and Carlton drank two neat whiskies. He looked better when they reached the house.

There was no one in sight. Marian, after having her room cleaned and aired, had retired to it and locked her door. Jan had gone with Courtney Brooke to see Eileen, and Hilda was packing her suitcase, preparatory to leaving, when she got the word. But Susie was waiting in the library. When she heard the car, she flew out at the Inspector like a wild creature.

"So *you've* had him!" she said. "The only one in this house who loved his mother, and you pick on him! If you've done anything to him, you'll be sorry. Good and sorry."

"I'm all right, Susie," Carlton said mildly. But she was not to be placated. "Why didn't you take that nurse of yours? Or Frank Garrison? Or me? I could have told you some of the things that have been going on."

"Oh, shut up, Susie," Carlton said wearily. "There's been too much talking as it is."

They were in the house by that time. He gave her a warning look, and she subsided quickly.

"What's been going on?" the Inspector inquired.

"Marian's back, if that interests you. She raised hell until Eileen got out." She lit a cigarette and grinned at him. "Nice place we've got here," she said airily. "Come and stay sometime, if you ever get bored."

He left them downstairs, Susie mixing a highball and Carlton lighting a pipe. It would have been quite a nice domestic picture, he thought, if he had not known the circumstances.

Hilda was in her room when he went up the stairs. She was standing by her window, looking out, and her suitcase was packed and closed on a chair. He scowled at it.

"You're not leaving," he said. "I need you here."

"I have no patient."

"You'll stay if I have to break a leg. Get young Brooke to put the girl to bed. Nervous exhaustion. Anything, but you're staying." He looked at her. "Anything attractive outside that window?"

"No. I was just thinking."

"About what?"

She had again assumed her cherubic look, and he eyed her with suspicion. "Not much. Just a can of white paint."

"What?"

"A can of paint. Of course people do queer things when they're worried. They play solitaire, or bite their fingernails, or kick the dog. I knew one man who cut down a perfectly good tree while his wife was having a baby. But paint is different. It covers a lot of things."

"I see. Who's been painting around here?"

"Carlton Fairbanks. This morning. He nailed the screens shut and then painted over the marks he made."

"Very tidy," said the Inspector.

"But he fastened his mother's screens weeks ago. I would like to know whether he painted them, too."

He laughed down at her indulgently. "What you need is a night's sleep," he told her. "Go to bed and forget it. And remember, you're not leaving."

But she was stubborn. She wanted to see Mrs. Fairbanks's screens, and at last he unsealed and unlocked the door, and gave her the key. The room was as it had been left, the bedding thrown back, print powder showing here and there on the furniture. She went straight to a window.

"You see, he didn't."

"I'm damned if I know why that's important."

"I don't know myself. Not yet."

"All right. Go to it," he told her, still indulgent, and left her there, a small intent figure in that ghostly room, still gazing at the screens.

He yawned as he got into his car. The crowd outside the fence had practically disappeared. Only a scant half dozen men still stood there, the diehards who would not give up until all hope of further excitement was over. He did not notice them. What on earth had Hilda meant about white paint? What had white paint to do with murder? The thing nagged him all the way back to his office and, later on, even to his bed.

Back in Mrs. Fairbanks's room, Hilda switched off the lights and prepared to leave. She knew death too well to be afraid, but the impress of Mrs. Fairbanks's small old body on the bed had revived her sense of failure. She stood still. What could she have done? What had she failed to do?

And then she heard it again, a faint scuffling noise from the closet.

## CHAPTER XVIII

SHE JERKED the door open, but the closet was empty. The shoe bag still hung on the door, the safe was closed, and the sounds had ceased. Save for the low remote voices of Carlton and Susie from the library below, the house was silent.

Out in the hall she felt better. This noise, whatever it was, had not been what she had heard before, and turning briskly, she opened the door of Carlton's room and went in. She stopped abruptly.

There was a man in the closet. He was standing with his back to her, and fumbling among the clothes hanging there. She felt for the light switch and turned it on, to see William emerging, blinking.

"Is anything wrong, miss?" he asked.

She was surprised to discover that she was trembling.

"No. I was in Mrs. Fairbanks's room and I heard a noise. I thought——"

He smiled, showing his excellent set of false teeth.

"It was me in the closet," he explained. "I look after Mr. Carl's clothes. He wants a suit pressed, and he got paint on the toes of these shoes this morning. I'm sorry if I scared you. I am afraid we are all in a bad state of nerves. If you'll excuse me . . ."

She felt exceedingly foolish as he passed her with his usual impeccable dignity, but in doing so he dropped one of the shoes. She picked it up and looked at it. It was an old tan one, with a smear of white paint across the toe, and the ones Carlton had worn that morning had been black. There could be no doubt of it. She could see him now: his black shoes, his morning coat and striped trousers, as he moved from room to room, carrying his cigar box and hammer, and later the small can of white paint.

William had not noticed. He thanked her and went out, and she turned off the light behind him. She did not go out, however. She stood still until she heard him going down the back stairs. Then she closed the door, fumbled for a box of matches and, getting down on her knees, began systematically to examine the row of neatly treed shoes on the closet floor.

She did not hear the door opening behind her. Only when the light went on did she realize that Carlton had come into the room. She turned, still on her knees, the smoldering match in her hand, to see him coming at her, his face contorted, the veins on his forehead swollen with fury. For a moment she thought he was going to attack her. She got up quickly.

"I'm sorry," she said. "I was in your mother's room, and I heard a noise in here. I thought it might be another rat."

He did not believe her. She saw that. He took a step or two toward her and stopped.

"Aren't you through here? In this house?" he said, his voice thick with anger. "My mother doesn't need you any more. Eileen Garrison has gone. Are you supposed to stay indefinitely, snooping around about what doesn't concern you?"

"Are you so sure it doesn't concern me?" she inquired. "The police sent me here, at your mother's request. And they haven't released me yet. I assure you I am more than willing to go."

He got himself under control with difficulty. He walked past her and closed the closet door. When he faced her again, his voice was more normal. "At least I can ask you to keep out of the family rooms," he said. "There are no rats in the house, and if anything of this sort happens again, I advise you to notify the servants."

She left with such dignity as she could muster. As she opened the door of her room, she heard again the soft slithering sound she had heard before, but she was too shaken to investigate it. She stood at her window for some time, trying to think. It was very black outside. With the disappearance of the crowd, the guards had evidently been removed, for by the light of the lamp on Huston Street she could see no one there. The stable was dark, as though Amos was either out or asleep.

She was astonished when the luminous dial of her watch showed only ten o'clock.

She was still there a few minutes later when Marian rapped at her door and slipped inside. "Don't turn on the light," she said. "It's too hot. Miss Adams, you were here. You saw it all. Who did it? Who killed my mother?"

Hilda could not see her. She was only a vague figure in the room, but her voice was hard and strained.

"I wish I knew, Mrs. Garrison."

"That woman—why did she come here?"

"I think Mrs. Fairbanks had told her——"

"Nonsense," Marian said sharply. "She had some purpose of her own. That statement that Frank was with me!—I suppose she was after money. Did Mother give her any?"

"I wasn't in the room. She may have."

Marian took a case from the pocket of her housecoat and lit a cigarette. In the light from the match she looked more haggard than ever, but it was Jan's eyes, dark and tragic, that looked out from her raddled face.

"I don't understand anything," she said. "Why did they put her in my room? The whole third floor was empty. And why have the police taken the screen from one of my windows? They have it, haven't they?"

"There is a chance somebody got into the house last night through that window," Hilda said guardedly. "I found it open. It could have been done from the roof of the porte-cochère. It was only a hook, and the blade of a knife—or of course it might have been opened from within, by someone in the room."

Marian dropped her cigarette. "Oh, God!" she said. "Frank, of course. They think it was Frank, and she let him in! Have they arrested him yet?"

"No. They've talked to him. That's all."

"They will arrest him," she said in a flat voice. "Jan says he was outside. They will arrest him, and what defense has he? He could have climbed to the roof. He's very strong. I've seen him do it, on a bet. They'll say she let him into her room and hid him there. But he didn't do it, Miss Adams. He cared for my mother. He's the kindest man on earth. He's had the patience of God himself, and I ruined his life. I was a jealous fool. I let him go. I made him go. So now . . ."

Hilda let her talk. Mentally she was back at the window of Marian's room the night before, and something was whipping about in the wind outside. She looked at Marian. "When I closed the screen in your room last night, before I found your mother, there was a light rope fastened to one of the outside shutters. Do you know anything about it?"

"A rope? Something that could be climbed? Good heavens, are you trying to say that Frank——"

"It wasn't strong enough for that. Or long enough. I just wondered about it."

But Marian was vague. "I wouldn't know," she said. "It might have been there for years. I don't remember it."

Hilda went back with her to her room. It had changed, she thought, since Eileen was in it. The bed had a silk cover and small bright-colored pillows. The dressing table where Eileen had so defiantly made up her face only a few hours ago still had the gold toilet set, but it was crowded now with creams and perfumes. A silver fox scarf had been tossed on a chair, and sheer undergarments, unpacked but not put away, lay on the chaise longue.

"Ida wasn't well," Marian said indifferently. "I sent her to bed."

She had apparently forgotten the rope. But Hilda looked for it, raising the window to do so. It was gone.

Marian shrugged when she told her. "Maybe you only imagined it."

"I didn't imagine it," said Hilda dryly.

Back in her room she tried to fit the pieces of the puzzle together, but she got nowhere. The rope had been there. Now it was gone. It must be important, must mean something. Had Eileen taken it away, and if so, why? Or had someone in the family removed it? Not Carlton. He had been away after Eileen left and Marian arrived. Not Jan. She had gone to see Eileen and had not come back. Susie? She was quite capable of it, if it was important. She would have no scruples, Susie. But why would it be important? A rope and a bit of white paint on a tan shoe. They must fit somehow. Or did they?

She felt the need of action. For days, she thought, things had been going on around her. Not only the murder; small stealthy movements, doors opening and closing, people talking and saying nothing, going out and coming in, and always she had been merely the watcher, seeing but not comprehending. The night Carlton had carried the bundle from the stable, the figure at the top of the stairs, the open screen in Eileen's room, and now—of all silly things—a missing rope.

She looked across the hall. Susie's light was on. It showed over the transom, and she went over and knocked lightly at the door. But she did not go into the room. Standing there she could hear Susie crying, childish sobs that were as unrestrained as everything else about her.

She got her flashlight from her suitcase and went down the stairs. The doctor's car had just driven in. There was no mistaking its rattle, or the cough of its ancient engine. Young Brooke did not come into the house, however. Jan opened the door and stood there, her voice cool.

"I don't understand you, that's all," she said.

"I've told you. I'm not living off any woman. You're going to have money now, and I'm peculiar about money." His voice was stubborn. "I'll support my own wife, or I won't have one."

"I wouldn't use the money, Court."

"There's where you're wrong, my darling. You think you wouldn't. You think you'd go hungry and without shoes. You wouldn't. I watched you this afternoon and tonight, cleaning up the mess at your stepmother's. You didn't like it, did you? And that's luxury, my child. One week of boiled beef and cabbage——"

"You can't see anything but your perfectly sickening pride, can you?" said Jan, and closed the door on him.

Hilda went back to the kitchen. Unless the police had taken the rope, it should be somewhere in the house, or the yard. She tried the trash cans and the garbage pails outside without result. Then, rather reluctantly, she went down to the basement. She did not like to turn on the lights, and her flash made only a small pool of illumination in the darkness. There was rope there, a large coil of it in a preserve closet for some reason, but it was thick and heavy.

When she did find it, it was in the furnace. A small fire had been built around it at some time, but it was only charred, not consumed. She pulled it out and turned the light on it, some eight feet of thin blackened rope, which must be important since someone had attempted to destroy it. She went back over the night before, when she had seen it: Eileen asleep in her bed, the pouring rain, the slapping screen. And Susie in the hall, drenched to the skin.

She felt the ashes in the furnace. They were still faintly warm. Quite recently then—within two or three hours—someone had tried to destroy it. She tried to think what it meant, but she was tired. She had slept little that afternoon and since then she had been going around in circles.

Nobody saw her as she carried it upstairs. She wrapped it in a piece of newspaper and laid it in the top of her suitcase. Maybe tomorrow her mind would be clearer, or the Inspector would fit it into his puzzle. All she wanted now was to go to bed.

She undressed by the open window, for the sake of the breeze. That was how she happened to see Jan when she left the house. Even in the darkness there was no mistaking her slim figure, the easy grace with which she moved. On her way to Courtney Brooke, she thought comfortably. To make it up, to say she was sorry, to effect a compromise between his pride and her own. Then she stared. Jan was not crossing Huston Street. There was no sign of her under the street light. She had gone into the stable.

Hilda never quite understood the fear which made her snatch up a dressing gown and her flashlight and follow her. The lights were out in the lower hall, but the door to the porte-cochère was open. She was in her bare feet as she ran across the grass. Once at the stable, however, she began to feel foolish. The doors to the garage were closed and Amos's windows overhead were dark. There was no sound to be heard, and it was not until she turned on her light that she saw the door to the staircase standing open. She stepped inside and looked up. It seemed to her that there was a small flickering light above in the loft.

Then it came, a crash from overhead that sounded as though the roof had fallen in. She was too shocked to move at first. She stood still, staring up. Her voice sounded thin and cracked when it came.

"Jan!" she called. "Jan! Are you there?"

There was no answer, and she ran up the stairs. At the top she turned the flashlight into the loft.

Jan was lying without moving on the floor, blood streaming from a cut on her forehead, and the heavy ladder was lying beside her.

## CHAPTER XIX

SHE WAS not dead. That was the first thing Hilda ascertained. Her pulse was rapid but strong, and she was breathing regularly; and Hilda's heart, which had been trying to choke her, settled back into its proper place. The cause of the accident seemed obvious. For some reason Jan had used the ladder to reach the cupola, and it had slipped. The cut was from an old bird cage on the floor beside her.

Hilda's first impulse was to go to the house for help. Amos was evidently out. His door was standing open and his rooms dark. But she felt an odd reluctance to leave the girl there alone. She made her way across the small landing into Amos's rooms, turned on the lights and found the bathroom. There she got a clean towel and a basin of water, and was turning back when she heard the far door quietly closing.

At first she thought it had closed itself. She put down the basin and towel and pulled at it. It did not yield, however, and at last she realized that it was locked. Someone had reached in while the water was running, taken out the key and locked it from the outside.

Hilda was frantic. She beat on the door, but there was only silence beyond. Then her practical, rational mind began to assert itself. She opened a window and looked out. There was no one in sight save a woman whistling for a dog across Huston Street, and the distance was too great for her to drop. But there must be some method of communication with the house. She looked about, and found a house telephone beside Amos's bed. Even then she was not too hopeful. It probably rang in the kitchen or back hall, and the household was upstairs. To her relief, however, it was answered almost at once.

Carlton's voice, sounding resentful, came over the wire. "What the hell's the matter, Amos?" he said. "Place on fire?"

"It's Hilda Adams, Mr. Fairbanks," she told him. "Jan's had an accident in the stable loft, and I'm locked in."

His reaction was slow. "What do you mean, you're locked in?"

"Someone has locked me in Amos's rooms. And Jan's hurt. She's in the loft. I don't know what's happening, but hurry. I——"

He did not wait for her to finish. From the window she saw him emerge from the house and come running across the lawn, his dressing gown flapping around his legs. She stood inside the door as he climbed the stairs, but he went on to the loft. There was a brief silence, while he scratched a match or two. Then his voice, outside the door.

"She must have fallen," he said. "I'll get Brooke."

"Don't leave her there," she said. "Not alone. I don't think she fell. There's someone around, Mr. Fairbanks. She's not badly hurt. Not yet anyhow. But don't leave her."

"What on earth am I to do?"

"Look around for the key. It may be out there, or on the stairs."

He found it finally. It had been dropped just outside the door. But he had used his last match. When Hilda emerged, it was into darkness, and the loft also was dark.

"My flashlight," she said. "I left it here."

"No light when I got here. See if Amos has a candle, or matches. I'll get the doctor."

She felt her way to Jan. She was still unconscious, but when Hilda touched her, she moved slightly. She sat down on the floor beside her in the dark, and she was still there when Carlton came back, bringing Courtney Brooke with him.

After that there was a good bit of confusion. The two men carried Jan to the house, the family was roused, and Susie, to everybody's discomfiture, went into violent hysterics. Hilda gave her a good whiff of household ammonia and Susie, choking for breath, came out of it. She looked up, tears streaming from her eyes.

"It's my fault," she said. "I knew I ought to tell. But Carl——"

"What should you have told?"

Susie did not say. She closed her eyes and went into a stubborn silence. Across the hall Courtney was sitting beside Jan's bed, holding an ice pack to her head. Instead of a shirt he wore the coat of his pajamas, and his face was grim.

"Someone tried to kill her," he said. "She fell first. Then she was struck, evidently with the flashlight. There was blood on it when we found it."

Marian stared at him from across the bed, her face filled with horror. "But who would do that to her?" she demanded. "Who would want to kill her?" She leaned over the bed. "Jan. Jan! Who hurt you? What happened to you?"

"I'd let her alone," he said. "She is coming out of it. The quieter she is, the better. She'll be all right, Mrs. Garrison."

At midnight Frank Garrison arrived. Carlton, telephoning wildly, had finally located him at his club. He came into the room, his tall figure seeming to fill it, and Marian went pale when she saw him.

"What are you doing here?"

"She is my child, Marian," he said politely.

"You deserted her. You deserted us both."

He ignored that. He asked about Jan, and Courtney gave him his place beside the bed. Marian got up, her face a tortured mask.

"You are driving me out of this room. You know that, don't you? Why don't you go back to your woman? Jan is nothing to you. Less than nothing."

"Sit down, Marian," he said gravely. "This is our girl. We have at least that in common. And be quiet. I think she is coming out of it."

But Jan, coming out of it, was not much help. After her first wondering gaze around the room, she simply said that her head ached, and after that she went to sleep. She was still sleeping when, at three in the morning, her father left the house, and the doctor sent Hilda to bed.

"She's all right," he said. "She'll have a day or two in bed, but that's all. You'd better get some sleep. You look as though you need it. I'm staying anyhow."

She slept for three hours. Then she got up and put on her uniform. In Jan's room Courtney Brooke was asleep, as was Jan herself, and she went downstairs and let herself out without disturbing anyone.

Amos had returned to the stable. Even before she climbed the stairs, she heard him snoring. A dim light from the cupola showed her the loft as they had left it: the ladder lying across the floor, the trunks, the broken furniture. But lying where Jan's body had fallen was something she had not noticed the night before: a large piece of unbleached muslin some four feet square. She picked it up and examined it. It looked fairly new, and it had certainly not been there when Amos showed her the loft some days before.

She put it down and was stooping over the ladder when Amos appeared. He had pulled a pair of trousers over his nightshirt, and he was in a bad humor.

"What are you doing here?" he asked suspiciously. "If a man works all day and can't get his proper sleep——"

She cut him short. "Lift this ladder, Amos. I want to look at the cupola."

"What for?"

"That's my business. Miss Jan was hurt here last night. I want to know why."

"Hurt? Not bad, is it?"

"Bad enough. She'll get over it."

The cupola, however, revealed nothing at first. It was floored, save for the square opening for the ladder. Such light as there was, was admitted by slotted openings on the four sides. Except that in one place the dust of ages seemed to have been disturbed, it appeared empty. Then she saw something: an old pair of chauffeur's gloves. They had been shoved back into a corner, but she managed to reach them. She showed them to Amos when she climbed down again.

"Are these yours?"

He stared at them. Then he grinned. "So that's where they went!" he said.

"You didn't put them up there?"

"Why would I put them up there?" he demanded truculently. "I lost them two or three months ago. I thought somebody stole them."

He wanted them back, but Hilda, to his fury, took them back to the house with her. One part of the mystery, she felt, was solved. But before she left, she turned to him.

"I suppose you can account for your own movements last night?"

He took a step toward her, looking ugly. "So I hurt her, did I?" he said harshly. "Like my own daughter, and I try to kill her! Sure I can account for where I was last night, if that's any of your business. You don't have to come out to the stable to find your murderer, Miss Police Nurse. Look in the house."

Jan was better that morning. Outside of a headache, some bruises and a small cut, she had suffered no ill effects. She even drank a cup of coffee and ate a piece of toast. But she had no idea what had happened to her, except that she thought the ladder had slipped.

She had not gone to bed. She had quarreled with Courtney and she could not sleep. She had decided to go over and see him. She had reached the stable when she heard a sound overhead. She thought it was Amos, and called to tell him that the door to the staircase was open. Amos, however, had not answered, so she had climbed the stairs.

She was not frightened. She had thought for some time that the bats in her grandmother's room might have come from the cupola.

"There were slits in the shutters," she said. "Pigeons couldn't get in, but bats might."

What she thought she heard, she said, might have been bats flying around. No, she couldn't describe it. It was just a sound. Not very loud, either. She knew the loft well. She had played there as a child. She didn't even light a match until she got there.

To her surprise the ladder was in place. She decided to investigate the cupola, and she struck a match and climbed it. She was near the top when it gave way under her.

"I felt it going," she said. "I couldn't catch anything. I—well, I guess I just fell. I don't remember."

They let her think that. She was not told that it had probably been jerked from under her, or of the savage attack on her with the flashlight.

Hilda saw the Inspector later that morning. She sat across from him and placed on the desk between them the piece of muslin, the gloves, a small can of white paint and the piece of charred rope.

Patton eyed them solemnly. "You're slipping," he said. "No snakes? No guinea pigs?"

He looked tired. He had slept badly, and it almost annoyed him to see Hilda, bland and fresh, her hands neatly folded in her lap.

"You're not human," he said. "And what in God's name does all this stuff mean?"

"Somebody tried to kill Janice Garrison last night."

He almost leaped out of his chair. "What?" he yelled. "And you didn't call me? See here. I'll be damned if I'll have you running this case. You've let one murder happen, and now you tell me——"

He choked, and Hilda looked more bland than ever. "I thought you needed your sleep," she said calmly. "And the family didn't want you." She smiled faintly. "They said they had had enough of you to last a long time."

"Who said that?"

"I think it was Carlton."

She told her story after that, the attack on Jan, her own discovery of the girl, being locked in Amos's rooms, and Carlton coming to the rescue.

"So he was downstairs, was he?"

"He was. Probably getting a drink."

Patton leaned back in his chair. "You don't think he is guilty, do you?"

"I think he was fond of his mother."

Their eyes clashed, the Inspector's hard, Hilda's blue and childlike, and stubborn.

"He had the motive and the opportunity."

"You couldn't get an indictment on that, could you? No grand jury——"

"All right," he said resignedly. "Now what's all this stuff?"

Hilda smiled. "I don't know about the rope. Not yet, anyhow. But suppose you wanted to scare an old lady, maybe bring on a heart attack. And suppose she's afraid of bats. Other things, too, like rats. You might get a supply of them, put them in an old bird cage covered with a piece of muslin and hide them where nobody ever went."

"The cupola?"

"The cupola. But bats—and other things—have teeth. So you use a pair of heavy gloves. You might look at those gloves. They have small holes in them."

"Where would you get the bats—and so forth?"

"Out of the cupola itself. I didn't see any. I probably scared them away. But there's a butterfly net in the loft. I suppose it would be possible."

He threw up his hands. "All right. You win," he said. "But how did they get into the room?"

"I imagine that's where the paint comes in," she said tranquilly.

She was there for some time. When she got up, the Inspector went to the door with her. Always she amused him, often she delighted him, but that morning there was a new look of admiration in his eyes.

"You're a highly useful person, Miss Pinkerton," he said, smiling down at her. "If I didn't think you'd slap me, I'd kiss you."

"It wouldn't be the first time."

"Which?" he said quizzically. "Slap or kiss?"

"Both," she said, and went out.

Ida was dusting the lower hall when she got back. She did not look up, and Hilda did not speak to her. She had no idea that it was to be the last time she would see the girl alive.

## CHAPTER XX

THE INQUEST was held at two o'clock that afternoon. It was very brief. Carlton Fairbanks identified his mother's body, and nothing new was developed. Susie came home looking sick and went to bed, but Marian stayed downtown to make arrangements for the funeral and to buy the conventional black.

She was still out when the Inspector arrived at four that afternoon. Jan was better, sitting up in bed, with Courtney Brooke in and out of the room, but mostly in. They did not talk much. It seemed to content them merely to be together. And Carlton was in the library. He had had a drink or two, but he was entirely sober.

He did not seem surprised to see the Inspector. He stood up stiffly. "I rather expected you," he said. "Jan's accident, and all that. But I want to ask you not to judge us on what may seem unusual. If any one of us has been at fault . . ."

Here, however, his voice failed him. It was a moment or so before he pulled himself together. "I know things look bad," he said. "When I saw the paint was gone—— But it has nothing to do with my mother's death. Nothing. I am innocent, and so—God help her—is my wife."

He followed the Inspector up the stairs. Hilda, watching them come, thought Carlton would not make the top. He rallied, however, when she unlocked the door of the death room, although he did not look at the bed.

The Inspector was brisk and businesslike. He went at once to the closet and, ignoring the safe, got down on his knees and examined the baseboard. He used a flashlight, and he rapped on it and listened, his head on one side, while Carlton stood mutely by.

When he got up, his voice was brisk. "All right," he said. "Now I'd like to see your room, please."

This time Carlton led the way. He looked shrunken, incredibly aged. Once inside, he closed the door to Susie's room, but when the Inspector opened his closet door, he spoke for the first time.

"I give you my word of honor," he said bleakly, "that I knew nothing about this until yesterday morning. I would have told you before, but it involved"—he swallowed—"it involved someone very dear to me."

He said nothing more. He stood silent while the Inspector took out the row of neatly treed shoes. Even the tan ones were there, although the paint had been removed. The Inspector picked up his flashlight and turned it on the baseboard.

"How does this open?"

"It slides—toward the fireplace. It's nailed now."

"Since yesterday?"

"Since yesterday. I nailed and painted it yesterday morning."

The white paint was dry. The Inspector produced from his pocket one of those small arrangements in which a number of tools are carried inside the handle. He fitted one and went to work. Carlton said nothing. A breeze from the open windows blew the curtains into the room. Outside, the traffic of a busy Monday moved along the streets, and Joe's Market was filled with women, shopping and gossiping.

"That police car's back. Look, you can see it."

"Much good it will do. They don't arrest people like the Fairbanks for murder."

It took some time to slide the panel. The paint held it. But at last it moved and the Inspector picked up his flashlight. He saw a small empty chamber, the thickness of the wall, and beyond it a flat wooden surface fastened to the floor with hooks and screw-eyes. He opened it, and saw, as he had expected, that it was the baseboard of Mrs. Fairbanks's closet. On his right was the safe. He could touch it, but he could not reach the dial. The whole aperture was only seven inches high.

He got up, dusting his hands. "I suppose that accounts for a number of things," he said. "Not only for the attempts to frighten your mother. It could account for something else, Mr. Fairbanks."

"For what?"

"A cable for a remote control to the radio in your mother's room. I suggest that your mother was killed earlier in the night, that you turned on the radio from here, that you later re-entered the room, ostensibly to shut it off, but actually to disconnect the cable, and that when you went to the closet, it was to place the cable there, so you could withdraw it quietly from this side."

"Before God I never did."

That was when Susie burst into the room. She came like fury, ready to spring at Patton. "You fool!" she said. "You stupid fool! He never knew about it until yesterday."

Carlton roused at that. "Be still," he said. "Don't make things worse. They're bad enough. Go back to your room. I'll——"

She paid no attention to him. She was panting with anger and fear. "Don't listen to him. I did it. I had it done. He'd never have found it if I'd had a chance to close it all the way. But if you think I put those creatures in his mother's room, I didn't." Her voice was shrill. She was trembling. "Someone else in this house did that. Not me. I wouldn't touch them with a ten-foot pole."

She came out with her story. Nothing would have stopped her. Carlton had turned his back and was staring out the window. The Inspector listened. Hilda watched.

It had started late the winter before, she said. She had been in the bank, and she had seen Mrs. Fairbanks receive a large bundle of currency.

"She didn't see me," she said. "I saw her go down to her safe-deposit box, and I knew she was hoarding money. I told Carl, but he didn't believe me. Anyhow, he said it was his mother's business."

Then came the matter of the safe. Why did she want a safe in her room? And she had changed in other ways, too. She became stingy with money. She had sent away the kitchenmaid and the second housemaid.

"I was scared," Susie said. "I knew damned well why she wanted a safe in her room. Maybe I was raised on the wrong side of the tracks, but I had a pretty good idea what she was doing—selling her securities and turning them into cash to save taxes. And now she was going to keep it in the house!

"I got my brother-in-law the job of doing the carpentry work," she said defiantly. "The safe was to be built into the wall, and I told him what I thought. Suppose she had two or three million dollars in cash in this house? A lot of people might know—her banks, her brokers. Things like that leak out. It wasn't safe. *We* weren't safe. Even if there was a fire . . ."

Her brother-in-law had suggested that she could at least keep an eye on things. "You can't change her," he said, "but you can watch her. Then, if she's doing it, you can get that son of hers to work on her. If she's trying to escape her taxes, she ought to go to jail."

Mrs. Fairbanks and Marian were in Florida, Jan was visiting a school friend, and she and Carl were out of town for days at a time looking for a farm. He had no difficulty in doing the work. And when the old lady came back, Susie learned a good bit. Mostly by listening. Mrs. Fairbanks would drive out, come back and put something in the safe. After a time, as the money apparently accumulated, she developed a new habit. She would lock her door at night, set up a card table, and apparently count over her hoard.

"I didn't dare to open the baseboard all the way," Susie said, "but I'd push it out an inch or so. She kept her shoes in a shoe bag on the door, so they didn't bother me. She'd pretend to be playing solitaire, but she didn't fool me! But when I tried to tell Carl, he wouldn't believe it. I didn't dare to tell him how I knew."

As to a possible cable to the radio and a remote control, she dismissed that with a gesture. "That's crazy," she said. "He never knew the thing was there until after his mother was dead and he hunted out some black shoes yesterday morning to wear with his morning coat. Then he gave me hell, and yesterday he nailed it up." She went over and put a hand on Carlton's arm. "The one thing he suspected me of I didn't do," she said softly. "He thought I was keeping the bats in the stable. He found a bird cage up there, wrapped in a cloth, and he was bringing it to me when the nurse saw him. He had to take it back!"

She eyed Hilda without rancor. "You're pretty smart," she said, "but you missed that, didn't you? That's why I went out there in the rain that night. Carl had told me about it, and I wanted to see if it was still there, and what was in it."

"But you never got there?"

"I was scared off," said Susie, suddenly wary. "Somebody grabbed me. . . ."

Down in the kitchen, Maggie was looking at the clock. "I'd like to know what's keeping Ida," she observed. "She said she'd be gone only an hour, and it's five now." She poured William a cup of tea and took one for herself. "She's been queer lately," she said. "Ever since the old lady's death, and before."

"She'll be all right," said William. "Maybe she went to a movie."

But no one upstairs was thinking of Ida. Not then, certainly. Carlton did not know the combination to his mother's safe, and the Inspector was anxious to open it.

"I think she would have written it down," Carlton said worriedly. "Her memory wasn't very good lately. Perhaps you have seen it, Miss Adams."

Hilda, however, had seen nothing of the sort. She had never seen Mrs. Fairbanks open the safe, and in the search of her room which followed, nothing developed. They took the pictures from the walls, raised the rug at its edges, looked through the bed and under the paper lining the drawers of her table and bureau. They even examined the few books lying about, the vases on the mantel, the back of the clock and the radio, as well as the cards with which—according to Susie—she had merely pretended to play solitaire.

They were almost friendly, the four of them, during that interval. At least a common cause united them. When Maggie came to the door at a quarter to six, it was to see Mrs. Fairbanks's room completely dismantled, Susie on a chair examining the top of the draperies at the window, and an inspector of police lying under the bed, with only his legs protruding.

She looked apologetic. "I didn't mean to disturb anybody," she said, highly embarrassed. "It's about Ida. She went out at one o'clock for an hour or so, and she hasn't come back yet."

The Inspector had crawled out. He stood up and dusted his clothes. "Does she often do that?"

"Never before, to my knowledge."

"Did she say where she was going?"

"She said she needed some darning silk. I wanted her to eat her lunch first. She looked sick. But she wouldn't wait."

The Inspector looked at his watch. "It's almost six now. Five hours. I wouldn't worry. She'll probably show up."

Ida did not show up, however. Marian came home from her shopping and her interview with the mortician, looking exhausted. Refusing dinner, she lay on her chaise longue, her eyes closed and her face bitter.

Carlton was closeted with Susie in her room, and Jan and Courtney had a double tray on the side of her bed, achieving the impossible of balancing it, holding hands and still doing away with a considerable amount of food.

When Hilda carried it out, Courtney followed her. "See here," he said. "What's been going on? What's this about Ida being missing?"

"I don't know that she is, doctor."

"Well, what's the row about? Maggie says you've practically torn up the old lady's room."

"We've been trying to locate the combination of her safe."

He whistled and looked back at Jan's door. "I wouldn't tell her that, Miss Adams," he said. "It might upset her."

He declined to elaborate, and Hilda had that to puzzle over during the evening, as well as Ida's continued absence. At eight o'clock William had sent a wire to her people in the country, and he and Maggie were waiting in the kitchen for an answer. Young Brooke, having eaten his dinner, left for his office hours but came back at nine. Marian went to bed, and Carlton and Susie were in the library. Hilda, not needed anywhere, sat in her room and watched the twilight turn into night. She had gathered up a lot of odds and ends, but where did they take her? She was no nearer the solution of the crime than she had been before.

Ida? What about Ida? She could have discovered the opening into Mrs. Fairbanks's room; the panel not entirely closed, and Ida on her knees, washing the floor of the closet. She could even have slipped the bats into the room. She was a country girl. She would not be afraid of such things. But why? What would be her motive?

She went back to the morning after the murder; Ida in her room by the window, her hands folded in her lap and a queer look on her long thin face as Hilda and the Inspector entered. She had been afraid, so afraid that she tried to rise and could not. And now she was missing.

In the next room the young people were talking. Hilda got up and, moving carefully, went to the front hall. Above her the third floor loomed dark and empty, and the long passage to Ida's room was ghostly. As the evening cooled, the old house creaked, and Hilda, remembering the figure she had seen at the top of the stairs, felt small goose pimples on her flesh.

Once back in the girl's room, however, she felt better. She turned on the light and looked about her. There was no indication that Ida had intended to leave. A pair of washed stockings hung over the back of a chair; a discarded blue uniform lay on the bed; and a battered suitcase stood on the closet floor.

The wastebasket was empty, except for a newspaper, but under the pine dresser she found a scrap of paper. It was part of a letter, and it contained only two words. On one line was the word "sorry" and below it "harmless." Nowhere could she find any other bits, and at last she gave it up and put out the light.

She went quietly forward and down to the second floor. To her surprise the door into Mrs. Fairbanks's room was open, and she stepped inside. Young Brooke was there. He had opened the drawer of the table and had taken something out.

He started violently when he saw her. Then he grinned. "Looking for cards," he said. "Jan and I want to play some gin rummy."

He showed her the cards, but Hilda held out her hand for them. "I'll take those," she said. "My orders are that nothing is to leave this room."

"Oh, have a heart. A pack of cards——"

"Give them to me, please. There are cards downstairs."

He gave them up reluctantly. "And what will *you* do with them?" he inquired.

"Put them back where they belong," she said stiffly, "and lock this door." When he had gone out, she locked the door and took the key.

At midnight the telegram came. Ida had not gone home. And Hilda, getting Marian some hot milk to enable her to sleep, found the servants still in the kitchen: Maggie, William and Amos, who was smoking a pipe by the door. They were, she thought, both worried and watchful.

Maggie was convinced that Ida was dead. "She was a good girl," she said tearfully. "A good Christian, too. And she minded her own business."

Amos shook the ashes out of his pipe. "Did she now?" he said. "Sure of that, are you? Then what was she doing in my place yesterday, after the old lady was killed?"

"You're making that up."

"Am I? I found her in my bedroom, looking out of the window. She was a snooper. That's what she was. I never did trust her."

"You never trusted anybody," said Maggie scornfully. "What would she want in your room anyhow?"

"That's what I asked her. She said she had brought me some blankets. I've been here thirty years and she's been here ten. It's the first time she's been interested in my bed."

He seemed to think that was humorous. He grinned, but Maggie eyed him disdainfully.

"You might at least be grateful."

"Grateful? For blankets at the beginning of summer? Them blankets were an excuse to get in my room, and don't tell me different."

That night Hilda discovered why Susie had fainted a few days before.

Jan had sent Hilda to bed, and she went gladly enough. All she wanted, she thought, was a hot bath and sleep, and tomorrow she could go home, to her bird and her sunny sitting room. She had done all she could. She had not solved the murder, but she had solved one mystery. She locked the bit of paper from Ida's room in her suitcase, got out a fresh nightgown, and after some hesitation put the key to Mrs. Fairbanks's room under her pillow.

Then she undressed and reached into the closet for her bedroom slippers. Curled up in one of them was something cold and clammy, and as she touched it, it slithered out across her feet and under the bed.

She was too paralyzed to move for a moment. Then she put on her slippers and, going across the hall, rapped at Susie's door. Susie was in bed, the usual cigarette in one hand, the usual lurid magazine in the other.

"You might tell Mr. Fairbanks," Hilda said coldly, "that the thing that scared you into a faint the other night is under my bed. I believe it's harmless."

"Harmless!" Susie said. "I put my hand on it in that damned peephole, and it nearly scared me to death. It's a——"

"Yes," said Hilda calmly. "It's a snake. It would be nice to know who put it there."

## CHAPTER XXI

### OFFICE OF CHIEF MEDICAL EXAMINER
### REPORT OF DEATH

Name of deceased: Unknown
Last residence: Unknown
Date and time of death: June 17, ———. 1 A.M.
Date and time examiner notified: June 17, ———. 2 A.M.
Body examined: June 17, ———. 8 A.M.
Reported by: City Hospital
Place of death: City Hospital
Body found: At Morgue
Pronounced dead by: Dr. Cassidy
Sex: Female
Age: Approximately 40
Color: White

Notes: Woman reported discovered in great pain in rest room of Stern & Jones department store at 4 P.M. Store physician called and gave treatment for shock. When taken to City Hospital (see police report) was in state of collapse. Reached hospital 5:10 P.M., June 16th.

The body is that of a thin but sufficiently nourished female. From condition of hands believe worked at domestic service, office cleaning or similar occupation. Clothing revealed nothing. There was no sign of violence on body.

There was no suicide note to be found. That the deceased was not anticipating death is possible, as a small paper bag containing darning silk was found in her purse. Also the report of the maid in said rest room, who states that the deceased was conscious when found, and said that she had been poisoned.

In view of the circumstances I am of the opinion that the cause of death was:

Administration of arsenical poison by person or persons unknown: Homicide.

(Signed) S. J. Wardwell
Chief Medical Examiner

### AUTOPSY

Approximate age: 40 years
Approximate weight: 105 lbs.
Height: 5' 3"
Stenographer: John T. Heron

I hereby certify that on the 17th day of June, ———, I, Richard M. Weaver, made an autopsy on this body seven hours after death, and said autopsy revealed:

No injury on body, which is that of a white female, apparently 40 years of age. Examination of viscera revealed characteristic symptoms of arsenical poisoning. Due to use of stomach pump, impossible to tell time of last food taken. Possibly twelve hours before death.

Arsenic present in considerable amount in viscera.

(Signed) Richard M. Weaver
Assistant Medical Examiner

It was noon of the day after Ida disappeared before she was found at the morgue. The autopsy was over by that time, and Ida's tired hands were resting peacefully on a cold slab in the morgue when Carlton was taken there to identify her.

He gave one look and backed away. "It's Ida, all right," he said hoarsely. "For God's sake, Inspector! What's happening to us?"

"I imagine Ida knew too much," said the Inspector, motioning the morgue master to push the body out of sight. "It's a pity. It's a cruel death."

He eyed Carlton thoughtfully. "I've seen the reports," he said. "She went out yesterday without eating her lunch. At three o'clock or somewhat later she bought some darning silk at the notion counter of Stern and Jones. The saleswoman says she looked sick, and complained of cramps. The girl advised her to go to the rest room. She did. She sat in a chair at first. Then the maid got her to a couch, and called the store doctor. He says she didn't give her name or address, and by the time she got to the hospital, she wasn't

able to. It looks as though sometime between the time she left the house
and when she was found in the rest room she got the poison."

With Carlton looking on, he examined the clothing Ida had worn when
taken to the hospital. It revealed nothing. Her bag, however, provided a
shock. It contained no lipstick or powder. The coin purse had only a dollar
or two. But tucked in a pocket behind a mirror were five new one-hundred-
dollar bills.

The two men stared at them incredulously.

"You don't pay her in money like that?"

"Good heavens, no. Where did she get it?"

The notes were in series, and the Inspector made a record of their numbers. Then he sealed them in an envelope and ordered them put in the
safe. Carlton was still unnerved when they reached the street. He lit a cigarette with shaking hands. But he was still fighting. He drew a long breath.

"At least this murder lets us out," he said. "None of us would kill the girl.
And as for that money——"

"I suppose you were all at home yesterday afternoon after the inquest?"

Carlton flushed. "You were there. You saw us. Except my sister. She was
out shopping. But she would have no reason— You can't suspect *her* of
this. She——"

The Inspector cut in on him. "Where does she usually shop?"

"At—I don't know. All over town, I imagine. What difference does it
make? She was in Atlantic City when Mother died. And she was fond of
Ida. You can't go on like this," he said, raising his voice. "You can't suspect
all of us. It's damnable. It's crazy."

"We have had two murders," said the Inspector stolidly. "There's a restaurant in Stern and Jones, isn't there?"

"I don't know. Marian ate her lunch before she left."

They parted there, Carlton stiffly to hail a taxi and go home, the Inspector to go back to his office and call up certain banks. He found the one
Carlton Fairbanks used, and asked them to check his account. After a brief
wait he got the figures.

"Balance is three hundred and forty dollars. He drew out seventy-five in
cash last week. That's all. Not suspecting him, are you, Inspector?"

"No record of a withdrawal of five hundred in one-hundred-dollar bills
in the last month or so?"

"No. He never has much of a balance."

It was one o'clock when the Inspector reached the Fairbanks house again.
He interviewed the servants first. They were subdued and frightened.
Even Amos had lost some of his surliness, and when they learned that Ida
had been poisoned with arsenic, there was a stricken silence. But they had
nothing to tell him. Ida had taken Mrs. Fairbanks's death hard. She had

eaten nothing in the house the day before except her breakfast, "and little enough of that." Asked where she kept her savings, they agreed that she had an account at a downtown bank.

None of them believed for a moment that she had committed suicide. "Why would she?" said Maggie practically. "She had a steady job and good pay. She wasn't the sort anyhow. Every month she sent money to her people in the country. This will just about finish them," she added. "They're old, and farms don't pay any more. I suppose they've been notified?"

"Not yet. I want their address."

He took it down and asked for Hilda. William said she was in her room, and led him upstairs. She was sitting in a chair with her knitting in her lap, and he went in and closed the door behind him.

"I suppose you know?"

"Yes. There's a family conclave going on now in Marian's room."

"Overhear any of it?"

"I didn't try," she told him primly.

They went up the back stairs to Ida's room. Save for the preparations for lunch going on below, the house was quiet, and Ida's room was as Hilda had seen it the day before. He searched it, but he found nothing of any importance. When he had finished, Hilda handed him the piece of paper she had discovered.

" 'Sorry,' " he read, "and 'harmless.' Part of a letter, isn't it? What do you suppose was harmless?"

"I think," said Hilda mildly, "that it was a snake. You see, the bats and the other things hadn't worked, so she tried a snake."

"Who tried a snake?"

"Ida."

"What on earth are you talking about? If you can make a snake out of the word 'harmless'——"

Hilda smiled. "I didn't. I found one in my closet last night."

He was startled. "Good God! How do you know it was harmless?"

"Well, there was that piece of paper, of course. And I saw it myself. Just a small garden snake. I wanted to take it out to the yard, but Carlton Fairbanks killed it. With a golf club," she added.

He inspected her, standing there in her neat white uniform, her face sweet and tranquil, and he felt a terrific desire to shake her.

"So it's as simple as that." he said caustically. "Ida puts it in your closet and Carlton kills it with a golf club." His voice rose. "What the hell has a snake got to do with two murders? And stop grinning at me."

"I'm not grinning," said Hilda with dignity. "I don't think Ida put it in my closet. I think it escaped from that hole in the wall, and it nearly scared

Susie to death. But I do think Ida brought it here; it and the other things."

"Why?"

"Well, she was a country girl. She lived only thirty miles out of town, and she went there once a month or so. I was wondering," she added, "if I could go there this afternoon. They may know of her death, but they are old. It will be hard on them."

He gave her a suspicious look. "That's all, is it? You wouldn't by any chance have something else on your mind?"

"It wouldn't hurt to look about a little," she said cautiously. "I think Doctor Brooke would drive me out."

He went to the window and stood looking out. "Why would she do it?" he asked. "She had little or nothing to gain by the will."

"Oh, I don't think she killed Mrs. Fairbanks," Hilda said quickly. "She hated the house. The work was too heavy, for one thing. She may have wanted to scare her into moving."

"But you don't believe that?"

"No. Nor do I believe she killed herself."

Before the Inspector left, he saw Carlton. "In view of what has happened," he said, "I'd like to keep Miss Adams here for a day or two longer. You need not pay her. I'll attend to that."

"So we're to have a spy in the house," Carlton said bitterly. "What can I do about it? Let her stay, and the hell with it."

## CHAPTER XXII

OLD ELIZA FAIRBANKS was buried that afternoon from St. Luke's, with a cordon of police to hold back the crowd, and photographers, holding cameras high, struggling for pictures of the family. Her small body in its heavy casket was carried into the church, and in due time out again. A long procession of cars drove up, filled and drove away.

"What is it, a wedding?"

"Sh! It's a funeral. You know, the old woman who got stabbed."

Marian came out, her face bleak under her mourning. Carlton and Susie, Susie unashamedly crying. Jan, wan and lovely, but keeping her head high, and Courtney Brooke holding her arm. Nobody noticed Frank Garrison. He sat at the rear of the church, thinking God knows what: of his wedding, perhaps, in this same church, with Marian beside him; of Jan's christening at the font, a small warm body in his arms; of Sunday mornings when he sat in the Fairbanks pew, and a little old lady sat beside him.

He got out quickly when it was over.

It was five o'clock when the family returned from the cemetery, and six before Hilda had got Marian to bed and was free. She went quietly out the side door and past the stable to Huston Street, to find Courtney waiting for her in his car.

"I hope we make it," he said. "The old bus does all right in town. When it stops, I can have somebody fix it. But a trip like this . . ."

Hilda got in and settled herself. "We'll make it," she said comfortably. "We've got to make it."

Yet at first there seemed nothing to discover. Two elderly, grief-stricken people, Ida's parents were only bewildered.

"Who would want to do that to her?" they asked. "She was a good girl. She minded her own business. And she was fond of the family, miss. Especially Mrs. Garrison, Mrs. Marian Garrison. That's her picture there." Hilda looked. On the mantel was a photograph of Marian taken some years ago. "She was pretty then," the mother said. "Ida used to help her dress. She——"

She checked herself abruptly, and Hilda thought the father had made a gesture. She got nothing further from them. They knew nothing of any bats or other creatures, and Hilda, watching their surprise, was sure that it was genuine. They sat in the old-fashioned parlor, with an organ in the corner and a fan of paper in the empty fireplace, and denied that Ida had ever carried anything of the sort into town. "Why would she?"

"Some laboratories buy such things," Hilda said mendaciously, and got up. "Someone had been keeping things in a bird cage in the Fairbanks stable. Never mind. I'm only sorry. If there is anything I can do . . ."

Courtney had not gone into the house. He was standing by the car when she came out.

"Funny thing," he said. "There was a boy over by the barn. I started over to him but he beat it. Well, how did they take it?"

"It's broken them," she said wearily. "I suppose it was the boy who did it."

"Did what?"

"Caught the bats and so on and gave them to Ida."

He almost put the car into a ditch. "So that's it," he said. "It was Ida! But why, and who killed her?"

"Are you sure you don't know, doctor? On the night Mrs. Fairbanks died, you saw someone on the third floor, didn't you? You were holding a cup of coffee. It spilled."

He passed a truck before he replied. "That's as preposterous a deduction as I've ever heard," he said. "If that's the way the police work——"

"I'm not a policewoman," she told him patiently. "You saw someone, didn't you?"

"I've already said no."

He was lying, and he was not a good liar. She did not pursue the subject. She was very quiet the rest of the way back to town. Her face no longer had its bland cherubic expression. She looked dispirited and half sick. When young Brooke politely but coldly offered her dinner at a roadhouse, she refused it.

"I'm not hungry," she said. "Thanks just the same. I want to get back as soon as possible."

Yet for a woman in a hurry she did nothing much when she reached the Fairbanks house again. She did not get into uniform. She merely took off her hat and sat down in her room. When Jan, on her way to bed, rapped at her door, she was still there in the dark.

"Good gracious!" Jan said. "Don't you want a light? And did you have anything to eat?"

"I didn't want anything, Jan."

"Just what were you and Courtney cooking up this evening?" Jan asked curiously. "I saw you, you know. You were gone for hours."

"I was telling Ida's people about her," said Hilda. "It was rather sad. I hate to carry bad news."

She looked at the girl. How would she bear another blow? Suppose she was right, and Ida had been put out of the way because she knew what Hilda thought she knew?

It was midnight before she made any move. The household was asleep. Even Amos's light in the stable was out by that time. But she took the precaution of slipping off her shoes. Then, armed with a flashlight, she went up to the third floor. She did not go back to Ida's room, however. She went into the guest rooms, one after the other, examining the floors and the bathrooms, and removing the dust covers from the beds.

It was in the room over Carlton's that she found what she had been afraid to find.

She went to bed and to sleep after that, but she carried a sort of mental alarm clock in her head, and promptly at six she wakened. Nobody was stirring in the house when she went down to the library and called the Inspector at his bachelor apartment. His voice was heavy with sleep when he answered.

"It's Hilda Adams," she said carefully. "I want you to do something. Now, if you will."

"At this hour? Good heavens, Hilda, don't you ever go to bed?"

"I do, but I get out of it. Will you have someone check the hotels in town for a woman who got there early Sunday morning and left that afternoon?"

"Sunday? Sure. But what's it all about?"

"I'll tell you later. I can't talk here."

She hung up and went upstairs again. She had been stupid, she thought.

She should have known all this before. Yet she also had a sense of horror. It was still written all over her when she sat in the Inspector's office that Wednesday morning.

"How did you guess it?" he said.

"Then it's correct?"

"Correct as hell. She checked in at five Sunday morning and left that afternoon. She left Atlantic City on Saturday."

She drew a long breath. "I should have known it before," she said. "The figure at the top of the stairs and the chandelier shaking. I think young Brooke saw it, too, although he denies it. But the rooms looked the same. Only Ida had cleaned a bathroom, and she couldn't put back the dust. I suppose that cost her her life. If she had only raised a window and let the dirt in——"

In spite of himself Patton smiled. "The world lost a great criminal in you, Hilda," he said admiringly.

He looked over his notes. Marian had registered at one of the big Atlantic City hotels the night she had left home. She had remained most of the time in her room, having her meals served there, and she had left on a late train on Saturday.

"It checks," he said thoughtfully. "She came home late and Ida probably admitted her and told her Eileen was there. She smuggled her up the back stairs to the third floor and settled her there. Then what? Did she come down while young Brooke was with Jan, and stab her mother? It's—well, it's unnatural, to say the least."

Hilda sat very still. "I'm not sure," she said at last. "She was there. I don't know where she hid while the house was searched. Maybe in the stable. Anyhow she got away, and after you let Ida go, I suppose she made up the bed."

"What put you on the track?" he asked curiously.

"I don't know exactly." She got up to go. "Ida's parents said she was devoted to Marian. And then the doctor—I just wondered if Ida had seen Marian at Stern and Jones on Monday."

He looked at her with shocked surprise. "You don't mean that, do you?"

"It could be," she said rather dismally, and went out.

He read over his notes carefully after she had gone. The waitresses in the restaurant at Stern & Jones did not remember Ida. But they did remember Marian, who was well known in the store. She had come in at three o'clock and had a cup of tea. But she had been alone. As to the will, in a long-distance call to Mrs. Fairbanks's lawyer, Charles Willis—who was in Canada fishing for salmon—Willis said that the old lady had kept all three copies, but that Carlton was substantially correct. The estate was divided between Marian and Carlton, with Marian's share in trust for Janice.

"Although there was a hundred thousand dollars for the girl," he said. The will had been made seven years ago. He did not think Mrs. Fairbanks had changed it.

After that the Inspector went to Mrs. Fairbanks's bank, and had some difficulty in getting information. In the end, however, he learned that over the past year or two she had been selling bonds and converting the results into cash. This she apparently deposited in the safe-deposit boxes in the basement, of which she rented several. If she had removed this cash, the bank had no knowledge of it. It was not an unusual procedure, especially when the customer was a woman. Women resented both income and inheritance taxes, always hoping to escape them. And here the bank added a human note. "As do most people," it said.

Back at his office the Inspector made a brief chronological chart:

In January, Susie had seen Mrs. Fairbanks remove cash from the bank and take it to her box.

In February, Mrs. Fairbanks and Marian had gone to Florida, while the safe was installed, and Susie's brother-in-law built the peephole.

On the night of the ninth of March Mrs. Fairbanks came home. The next morning she was poisoned with arsenic. The arsenic was shown to have been in the sugar.

She was suspicious of her household afterward, making her own breakfast and at other meals eating only what they ate. But the attempt had not been repeated. From that day in March until the beginning of May everything had been as usual.

After that the so-called hauntings began. It was the first of May when she found the first bat in her room. Later there were two more bats, two sparrows, and a rat over a period of a month, and when another bat was discovered, she had gone to the police.

"Someone is trying to kill me," she had said, sitting erect in her chair. "I have a bad heart, and they know it. But I'm pretty hard to scare."

He put his notes away and went thoughtfully out to lunch.

He saw Courtney Brooke that afternoon, and he laid all his cards on the table. He liked the boy, but he sensed a change in him when it came to the safe and the money possibly in it. He stiffened slightly.

"I don't care a damn for the money," he said. "As a matter of fact it bothers me. I'd rather marry a poor girl. I suppose you can open the safe, sooner or later?"

"It won't be easy. But the makers will send somebody if we don't find the combination. I'm putting a guard in the grounds tonight. If the money is there, it won't leave the house."

But Brooke still looked uneasy, and Patton changed the subject. He asked about arsenic. It could be obtained without much trouble, the doctor said; from weed killers, of course, but also it could be soaked out of fly-paper, for instance, or even out of old wallpapers and some fabrics. But on the subject of the attack on Jan, he waxed bitter.

"Who would want to kill her? The old lady and Ida—well, the old lady had the money and Ida probably knew something. But to try to kill Jan——"

"I don't think anyone tried to kill her."

Brooke stared.

"Look at it," said the Inspector. "She could have been killed. She was unconscious, and the nurse was locked up in Amos's rooms. But she wasn't killed. She probably began to come to, and she was struck to put her out again. Somebody was there who didn't want to be seen."

Brooke said nothing. He gazed out the window, looking thoughtful, as though he were comparing all this with some private knowledge of his own. When he turned to the Inspector, it was with a faint smile.

"Funny," he said. "I've been scared to hell and gone. You've relieved me a lot. I've been hanging around under her window every night since it happened."

But the smile died when he was asked about the night of Mrs. Fairbanks's death. "I didn't see anybody on the third floor," he said flatly. "That's Miss Adams's idea. Just because I spilled some coffee——"

"I think you did," said the Inspector, his face grave. "I think you saw Marian Fairbanks, and she saw you."

"How could I? She wasn't there."

"Just whom did you see, doctor?"

"Nobody," he asserted stubbornly. "Nobody at all."

## CHAPTER XXIII

IDA HAD been poisoned on Monday, and Mrs. Fairbanks was buried on Tuesday. It was Wednesday morning when Hilda made her report, and it was the same night when Frank Garrison was arrested for murder.

Late on Wednesday afternoon Patton went back to the Fairbanks house. He intended interviewing Marian, and he dreaded doing it. If she had killed her mother and a servant and attacked her own child, she was an inhuman monster. Unhappy and bitter as she was, he did not believe she was guilty. Nor, he thought, did Hilda.

He did not interview her, however. Marian was in bed, under the influence of a sedative, and he found Hilda back in uniform at her old post in the hall. An absorbed Hilda, who was not knitting or reading the *Practice of Nursing,* but instead had set up a card table and was patiently laying out a pack of cards.

"And people pay you money for this!" he said. "I wish my job was as easy."

She nodded absently, and he watched her as she gathered up the cards, closely inspected the edges, and then began to lay them out again. He sat down and watched her.

"What is all this?"

"I'll tell you in a minute." She was intensely serious. "It's the order," she said. "Clubs first don't do. Maybe it's the other way. Spades."

"Nothing has disturbed you, has it? You feel all right? No dizzy spells? Anything like that?"

She did not even hear him. She spread the cards again, gathered them up, looked at the edges, spread them slightly, and then handed him the pack. There was something written on one side, and she looked rather smug.

"I think it's the combination to the safe," she said complacently.

Patton examined the cards. Thus arranged, they showed a series of letters and numbers, plainly written in ink. Shuffled in the ordinary fashion, they were not detectable, but in their present order they were perfectly clear. He gave her an odd look. Then he took out an old envelope and wrote down the letters and numbers.

"So that's the solitaire she played," he said thoughtfully. "Good girl, Hilda. How did you think of it?"

"Courtney Brooke thought of it first," she told him.

He eyed her sharply, but her face told him nothing.

He sent for Carlton before they opened the safe. He had little or nothing to say. He did not even ask how they had found the combination. Hilda unlocked the door, and Carlton followed them in. The room was as it had been left after the search, and he carefully avoided looking at it. There was still daylight, but the closet was dark and Hilda brought a flashlight. Using it, the Inspector turned the dial, but he did not open the door.

"I'd rather you did this, Fairbanks," he said.

He stepped out of the closet and Carlton stepped in. He pulled open the door and looked speechlessly inside. The safe was packed to the top with bundles of currency.

He made a little gesture and backed out of the closet. He looked small and singularly defenseless. "All right. It's there," he said dully. "Do what you like with it. I don't want to look at it. It makes me sick."

It required some urging to send him back again.

"Look for your mother's will," Patton said. "Bring out any papers you find. We may learn something."

The will was there, in a compartment of its own. It was in a brown envelope sealed with red wax, and it was marked "Last Will and Testament" in the old lady's thin hand. Carlton almost broke down when he read it. But there was another paper in the envelope, and he opened and read it, too. He stood, against the absurd background of fusty dresses and shoes in the bag on the door, holding the paper and staring at it. But neither Hilda nor the Inspector was prepared for his reaction to it.

"So that's why she was killed," he said thickly, and collapsed on the floor before they could reach him.

Frank Garrison was arrested late that night at his club. He was evidently living there. His clothes were in the closet, his brushes on the dresser, and he was in pajamas when they found him.

He said little or nothing. The Inspector had sent the detectives out, but remained in the room while Frank dressed. Once he said he had better take his bag "as he might not be coming back soon." And again he spoke of Jan.

"Tell the poor kid to take it easy, will you?" he said. "She's had enough trouble, and she's—fond of me."

He puzzled the Inspector. He offered no explanation of his being at the club. He offered nothing, in fact. He sat in the car, his fine profile etched against the street lights, and except once, when he lit a cigarette, he did not move. He seemed to be thinking profoundly. Nor was he more co-operative when they reached the Inspector's office, with two or three detectives around, and a stenographer taking down questions and answers.

He was perfectly polite. He denied absolutely having been in the Fairbanks house the night Mrs. Fairbanks was killed, although he admitted having been in the grounds.

"I came home late from Washington. The apartment was empty—we had not had a maid for some time—and my wife was not there. I knew Jan was friendly with Eileen, so I went there to ask if she knew what had happened. We had quarreled, and I was afraid she—well, she's been pretty nervous lately. But Jan—my daughter—said she was there. I talked to Jan at her window. I did not enter the house."

"What did you do after that?"

"I walked around for a while. Then I went home."

"What time did you talk to your daughter?"

"After one. Perhaps half past. I didn't get back from Washington until twelve o'clock."

"Did your daughter tell you where your wife was? In what room?"

He colored. "Yes. In my former wife's bedroom. I didn't like it, but what could I do?"

"She told you your wife was sick?"

"Yes."

"You didn't come in, to see how she was?"

"We had quarreled before I left. I didn't think she'd care to see me. Anyhow, her light was out. I thought she was asleep."

"You have since separated?"

"Not exactly. Call it a difference."

"She is going to have a child."

He showed temper for the first time. "What the hell has that got to do with this?"

But although he was guardedly frank about his movements the night of Mrs. Fairbanks's murder, he continued to deny having entered the house, through Eileen's window or in any other way. He had not climbed to the roof of the porte-cochère to reach one of the windows. And when he was shown the knife, he stated flatly that he had never, to his knowledge, seen it before. He admitted, however, knowing that the safe was in Mrs. Fairbanks's room. "Jan told me about it." But he denied any knowledge whatever of its contents.

The mention of the safe, however, obviously disturbed him. He seemed relieved when the subject was changed to the attack on Jan in the loft of the stable; but he was clearly indignant about it, as well as puzzled.

"If I could lay my hands on whoever did it, I—well, I might commit a murder of my own."

"You have no explanation of it?"

They thought he hesitated. "None whatever. Unless she was mistaken for someone else. Or," he added slowly, "unless someone was there who didn't want to be seen."

They shifted to Ida's death. He seemed puzzled.

"You knew her?"

"Of course. She had been in the Fairbanks house for years."

"She was attached to your first wife?"

"I don't know. I don't care to discuss my first wife."

"You are on good terms?"

"Good God, leave her out of this, can't you? I won't have her dragged in. What has she got to do with it, or my—feeling for her?"

He was excited, indignant. The Inspector broke the tension.

"Mr. Garrison, did you at any time in the last few weeks supply this woman, Ida Miller, with certain creatures to introduce into Mrs. Fairbanks's room?" He picked up a memorandum and read from it. " 'Five bats, two sparrows, one or more rats, and a small garden snake.' "

The detectives grinned. The stenographer dropped his pen. And Frank Garrison unexpectedly laughed. Only the Inspector remained sober.

"Is that a serious question?"

"It is."

"The answer is no. I thought the old lady had imagined all that."

"Have you at any time had in your possession a poison called arsenious acid? White arsenic?"

"Never."

"Can you account for your movements Monday afternoon? Say, from one o'clock on."

The quick shifts seemed to bother him, but he managed to make a fair statement. He had lunched at the club. After that he went to see a man who was taking over some housing work in Washington. When he went home, his wife was still in bed. She had been "difficult." He had told her he would send her a maid. After that he had packed a bag and left. They had not been getting on for some time. Perhaps it was his fault. He wasn't accustomed to being idle.

"Did you at any time Monday go to Stern and Jones? The department store?"

"I stopped in and bought a black tie. I was going to Mrs. Fairbanks's funeral the next day."

"At what time?"

"After I saw the man I referred to. Maybe two thirty or three o'clock."

"Did you see the girl, Ida, at that time?"

He looked puzzled. "Where? Where would I see her?"

"In the store."

"No. Certainly not."

"Have you a key to the Fairbanks house?"

"I may have, somewhere. I lived there for a good many years. I don't carry it."

It lasted until half past one. The questions were designed to confuse him, but on the whole he kept his head. It was not until the Inspector lifted a paper from the desk and handed it to him that he apparently gave up the fight. He glanced at it and handed it back, his face set.

"I see," he said quietly. "I was there that night. I could have got into the house, by key or through my wife's window, and I had a motive. I suppose that's enough."

"You knew about this agreement?"

"Mrs. Fairbanks told me about it at the time."

"Who else knew about it?"

"My first wife. She signed it, as you see. Mrs. Fairbanks and myself."

"No one else knew about it?"

"Not unless Mrs. Fairbanks told about it. I don't think she did."

The Inspector got up. He looked tired, and for once uncertain. "I'm sorry about this, Garrison," he said. "We're not through, and I'll have to hold you. We'll see that you're not too uncomfortable."

Garrison forced a smile and stood. "No rubber hose?" he said.

"No rubber hose," said the Inspector.

There was a momentary silence. Garrison glanced around the room. He seemed on the point of saying something; something important. The hush was breathless, as if all the men were waiting and watching. But he decided against it, whatever it was.

"I suppose it's no use saying I didn't do it?"

"No man is guilty until he has been found guilty," said the Inspector sententiously, and watched the prisoner out of the room.

Carlton broke the news to the family the next morning, telling Susie first, staying with Jan until she had stopped crying, and then going to Marian. He was there a long time. Hilda, shut out, could hear his voice and Marian's loud hysterical protests.

"He never did it. Never. Never."

When the Inspector came, she refused at first to see him, and he went in to find her sitting frozen in a chair and gazing ahead of her as though she were seeing something she did not want to face. She turned her head, however, at his crisp greeting.

"Good morning," he said. "Do you mind if we have a little talk?"

"I have no option, have I?"

"I can't force you, you know," he said matter-of-factly. "All I would like is a little co-operation."

"Co-operation!" she said with her face set and cold. "Why should I co-operate? You are holding Frank Garrison, aren't you? Of all the cruel absurd things! A man who loved my mother! The kindest man on earth! What possible reason could he have had to kill my mother?"

"There was a possible reason, and you know it, Mrs. Garrison," he said unsmilingly.

He drew up a chair and sat down, confronting her squarely. "At what time did you reach here, the night your mother was killed?" he asked.

It was apparently the one question she had not expected. She opened her mouth to speak, but she could not. She tried to get out of her chair, and the Inspector put his hand on her knee.

"Better sit still," he said quietly. "You had every right to be here. I am not accusing you of anything. Suppose I help you a little. You came home during or after the time your husband's present wife had arrived. Either you saw her, in the hall downstairs, or one of the servants told you she was here. However that was, you decided to stay. It was your house. Why let her drive you out? Is that right?"

"Yes," she said, with tight lips. "It was Ida. I opened the side door with my latchkey. There was no one around, so I went back to get William to carry up my bags. I met Ida in the back hall. She told me."

She went on. She seemed glad to talk. She had been angry and indignant. She didn't even want to see Jan. It was Jan who had brought it about. Jan had said that Eileen was going to have a baby, and had even brought her to the house. That was why she had gone away. To have her own mother and her own child against her—! And now Eileen had invented some silly story and sought sanctuary here.

"I wasn't going to let her drive me away a second time," she said. "She had ruined my life, and now at my mother's orders they had put her in my room. I couldn't believe it at first, when Ida told me."

Ida, it appeared, had got her to the third floor by the back staircase, and made up the bed. They had to walk carefully, for fear Carlton would hear them in his room below. But she did not go to bed. How could she, with that woman below? She did manage to smoke, sitting by the open window. She was still sitting there when Susie began to scream.

"That was when Ida came to warn you?"

"She knew something was terribly wrong. Neither of us knew what. I thought at first the house was on fire. I sent her down, and listened over the stair rail. That's how I knew what had happened."

She sat back. Her color was better now, and the Inspector, watching her, thought she looked like a woman who had passed a danger point safely.

"No one but Ida knew you were in the house?" he persisted.

"No one. Not even Jan."

"Are you sure of that? Didn't you come down the stairs while Doctor Brooke was in the hall?"

"Never."

But she looked shaken. Her thin hands were trembling.

"I think you did, Mrs. Garrison," he told her. "He was standing outside your mother's door. You spoke to him from the stairs. You told him to get Eileen away, out of the house, in the morning, didn't you?"

"No! I did nothing of the sort," said Marian frantically. There was complete despair in her face. She looked beaten. "I never spoke to him at all," she said in a dead voice. "When I saw him, he was coming out of Mother's room."

The rest of her story was not important. She told it with dead eyes and in a flat hopeless voice. Brooke had not seen her, she thought, and Ida had helped her to get out of the house before the police took charge. She had used the back stairs and had gone out through the break in the fence. She had taken only the one bag which she could carry, Ida hiding the other, and she had spent what was left of the night at a hotel.

"I was afraid to stay," she told them. "After what I'd seen, I didn't want to be questioned. I had Jan to think of. I still have Jan to think of," she added drearily. "Courtney Brooke killed my mother, and I've ruined Jan's life forever and ever."

## CHAPTER XXIV

BROOKE WAS INTERROGATED at Police Headquarters that afternoon. Inspector Patton found him in his back office, dressing a small boy's hand.

"All right, Jimmy," he said. "And don't fool with knives after this."

The boy left, and Patton went in. Young Brooke was putting away his dressings, his face sober.

"What's this about Mr. Garrison being held, Inspector?" he said. "I was just going over to see Jan. I hear she's taking it badly."

The Inspector did not relax. "You've been holding out on us, doctor," he said stiffly. "That's a dangerous thing to do in a murder case."

Brooke flushed. He still held a roll of bandage in his hand. He put it down on the table before he answered. "All right. What's it all about?"

"You were in Mrs. Fairbanks's room at or about the time she was killed."

"Why not?" He looked defiant. "She was my patient. I had a right to look at her. She'd had a good bit of excitement that night, and I didn't go all the way in. I opened the door and listened. She was alive then. I'll swear to that. I could hear her breathing."

"Why didn't you tell about it?" said the Inspector inexorably.

Brooke looked unhappy. "Sheer funk, I suppose. I told Jan, after it all came out, and she didn't want me to. Not that I'm putting the blame on her," he added quickly. "I was in a cold sweat myself. In fact, I still am!"

He grinned and, pulling out a handkerchief, mopped his face. "I thought I had as much guts as the other fellow," he said. "But this thing's got me."

He looked incredulous, however, when the Inspector asked him to go with him to headquarters. "What for? Are you trying to arrest me?" he asked suspiciously.

"Not necessarily. We'll want a statement from you."

"I've told you everything I know."

He went finally, calling to the slovenly girl that he would be back for dinner, and slamming the door furiously behind him as he left the house. He was still indignant when he reached the Inspector's office. A look at the room, however, with the stenographer at his desk and Captain Henderson and the detectives filing in, rather subdued him.

"Third-degree stuff, I suppose," he said, and lit a cigarette. "All right. I'm a fool and a coward, but I'm no killer. You can put that down."

"No third degree, doctor. Just some facts. Sit down, please. We may be some time."

They were some time. Before they were through, he was white and exhausted.

"Did Janice Garrison know of the document in the safe?"

"Yes. Why drag her in? She hasn't done anything."

"She was fond of her father?"

"Crazy about him."

"You knew that she was to inherit a considerable sum of money?"

"I did."

"What were your exact movements, the night Mrs. Fairbanks was killed? While the nurse was downstairs boiling water?"

"I cleaned the hypo with alcohol. After that I looked in at Mrs. Fairbanks. She was breathing all right, so I went back to see Jan. I was there about five minutes. I went back and poured some coffee. I was drinking it when the nurse came up with the water."

"At what time did you see Marian Garrison?"

He was startled.

"Marian Garrison! She wasn't there. She didn't come until the next day. Sunday."

"She was there, doctor. She saw you coming out of her mother's room."

"Oh, God," he said wretchedly. "So she was there, too. Poor Jan!"

But his story was straightforward. He had not seen Marian when he came out of Mrs. Fairbanks's room. Later, however, as he poured the coffee, he had felt that someone was overhead, on the third floor. The glass chandelier was shaking. He had looked up the staircase, but no one was in sight.

They showed him the knife, and he smiled thinly. "Never saw it before," he said. He examined it. "Somebody did a rotten job of sharpening it," he said.

"It seems to have answered," the Inspector observed dryly. "Have you ever done any surgery, doctor?"

"Plenty."

"You could find a heart without trouble? Even in the dark?"

"Anybody can find a heart. It's bigger than most people think. But if you mean did I stab Mrs. Fairbanks, certainly not."

He explained readily enough his search and Jan's for the combination of the safe.

"Jan knew the agreement was there. The old lady had told her. She was afraid it would incriminate her father. When nobody could open the safe, I happened to think of the cards. Mrs. Fairbanks played solitaire at night. But maybe she didn't. Jan believed she locked herself in and then opened the safe, and we thought the cards might have the combination. I'd seen them with pictures painted on the edges. You arranged them a certain way and there was the picture."

"The idea being to get this document?"

"Well, yes. She was worrying herself sick. But the nurse was too smart for us. She took the cards and locked the door."

It was five o'clock before he was released, with a warning not to leave town. He managed to grin at that. He got out his wallet and some silver from his pocket.

"I could travel—let's see—exactly five dollars and eighty cents' worth," he said. "I've just paid the rent."

The Inspector looked at Henderson after he had gone. "Well?" he said.

"Could have," said Henderson. "But my money's on the other fellow. Garrison is broke too, but he wouldn't be without the alimony."

"Why didn't he have it reduced? It would have been easier than murder."

"Still in love with the first wife," said Henderson promptly. "Sticks out all over him."

"Oh," said the Inspector. "So you got that, too!"

Alone in his office he got out the document he had shown to Garrison the night before, and studied it. Briefly it was an agreement written in the old lady's hand, signed by Marian and witnessed by Amos and Ida, by which Marian's alimony from her ex-husband was to cease on her mother's death. "Otherwise, as provided for in my will, she ceases to inherit any portion of my estate save the sum of one dollar, to be paid by my executors."

He had a picture of Mrs. Fairbanks writing that, all the resentment at Marian and the divorce and its terms in her small resolute body and trembling old hand. He put it back in his safe, along with the knife and Hilda's contributions: a can of white paint, a pair of worn chauffeur's driving gloves, a bit of charred rope, a largish square of unbleached muslin, and now a pack of playing cards. To that odd assortment he added the paper on which he had recorded the numbers of the new bills in Ida's purse, and surveyed the lot glumly. "Looks like Bundles for Britain," he grunted.

He saw Eileen late that afternoon. She was in bed, untidy and tearful, and she turned on him like a wildcat.

"I always knew the police were fools," she shrieked. "What have you got on Frank Garrison? Nothing, and you know it. I didn't let him in through my window. I didn't let anybody in. I was sick. Why don't you ask the doctor? He knows."

He could get nothing from her. She turned sulky and then cried hysterically. She didn't know about Mrs. Fairbanks's will. She had never heard of any agreement. What sort of an agreement? And they'd better release Frank if they knew what was good for them. She'd get a lawyer. She'd get a dozen lawyers. She would take it to the President. She would take it to the Supreme Court. She would——

This new conception of the Supreme Court at least got him away. He left her still talking, and when the maid let him out, he suggested a doctor. "She's pretty nervous," he said. Which was by way of being a masterpiece of understatement.

On the way downtown he thought he saw Hilda in one of the shopping streets, but when he stopped his car and looked back, she had disappeared.

He might have been surprised, had he followed her.

## CHAPTER XXV

Hilda was at a loose end that afternoon. Carlton had recovered from his collapse and had gone out, still pale, to drive around in his car and think his own unhappy thoughts. Marian's door had been closed and locked since the Inspector's visit. Jan wandered around the house, worried about her mother and ignorant of what was going on. And Susie, recovered from her fright about her husband, had settled down on her bed with a magazine.

"I'd better loaf while I can," she told Hilda. "It's me for the pigpens from now on. If you think Carl will change his mind now that he gets some money, you can think again."

Hilda was standing in the doorway, her face bland but her eyes alert. "What do you think about the police holding Mr. Garrison?" she asked.

"Me? They're crazy. Carl says that paper they found will convict him, but I don't believe it. If you ask me——" She stopped abruptly.

"If I ask you, what?"

"Nothing," said Susie airily. "If I were you, I'd take a look at the radio by Mrs. Fairbanks's bed. Maybe you can make something out of it. I can't."

"What's wrong with it?"

"I don't know. It's set to a blank spot on the dial. That's all. Carl says he didn't move the needle."

She went back to her magazine, and Hilda went to the old lady's room. She closed the door, went to the radio and switched it on. There was a faint roaring as the tubes warmed up, but nothing else. She was puzzled rather than excited. But she had already decided to go out, and now she had a double errand.

Her first errand was to the ladies' room of Stern & Jones. The attendant was the same woman who had looked after Ida, and she was immediately loquacious.

"A friend of hers, are you?" she said. "Wasn't it dreadful? And nobody knowing who she was all that time!"

"Was she very sick when she got here?"

"She looked terrible. I asked her if she had had anything that disagreed with her, and she said only a cup of tea. I called up the tearoom right away. Some of the girls had gone, but nobody remembered her. Anyhow, our tea is all right. It could not have been that, or a lot of other people would have been sick, too."

"Is that all she said?"

"Well, she tried to tell me where she lived. She wanted to go home. Grove Avenue, I think she said. But after that she got so bad she couldn't talk at all."

Hilda was filled with cold anger when she left the store. The thought of Ida, dying and unable to tell who she was, enraged her. And now the radio assumed a new importance. If it had been turned to a blank spot on the dial and still played, the whole situation changed. Mrs. Fairbanks might already have been dead when it was turned on.

She visited a number of stores where radio sets were sold, including Stern & Jones. Some of them had remote controls. The boxes they showed her were only a foot long and four inches wide, and they operated as far as sixty feet from the instrument.

"You can set it out in the street," said one salesman, "and turn your radio on and off with it. Magic, ain't it?"

Sixty feet! That would include even Marian's room. But when she told the make and age of the machine, the man shook his head.

"Sorry," he said. "It wouldn't work on one of those old ones. Not a chance."

It was the same everywhere. The machine in Mrs. Fairbanks's room was too old. And the remote controls which used cables were not only modern, they required considerable time for adjustment. But in the end she found something.

She was tired and her feet ached when, at six o'clock, she got back to the house, going directly to the kitchen. William was on the back porch, relaxing in the summer sun, and Maggie was baking a cake. She turned a red face from the oven when Hilda drew a chair to the kitchen table and sat down. But some of Maggie's suspicions had died in the last few days. She even offered her a cup of tea.

Hilda, however, was definitely off tea, at least for a time. "I'd like a glass of water," she said. "Then I want to talk about Ida."

"I'm not talking about Ida," Maggie said stiffly. "If anyone thinks she got that stuff here in this house——"

"I'm not asking about her death. That's for the police. It's just this. Have you any idea why she carried those blankets out to Amos?"

"No. He didn't need them."

"Can you remember what happened that day? It was the day after Mrs. Fairbanks was killed, wasn't it?"

Maggie considered this. "You know how she was that morning. She was so bad I sent her up to rest. She came down later, and that was when Amos says she carried out the blankets. I didn't see her myself. All I know is, she didn't eat any lunch. She left when we were sitting down."

Hilda drank her water and went out to the stable. To her annoyance Amos, in his shirt sleeves, was smoking a pipe inside the garage. He was reading the paper, his chair tilted back. He looked up when he saw her.

"Anything I can do for you, miss?"

He grinned with his usual slyness, and Hilda regarded him with disfavor.

"You can come up to the loft with me," she said coldly. "And don't smirk at me. I don't like it."

Thus reduced, Amos followed her up the stairs. There was still light enough to see around, and to her shocked surprise she found the entire place had been swept and put in order.

"Who did this?" she said sharply.

He grinned. "I did," he said. "Anything to say about it, Miss Policewoman? Any reason why I can't clean the place I live in?"

She ignored that, looking around her carefully. She had had very little hope at any time, but she disliked giving up. Amos was grinning again, pleased at her discomfiture.

"This isn't funny," she said. "I want some answers, and if I don't get them, the police will. When you cleaned this place, did you find anything that didn't belong? That you hadn't seen here before?"

The mention of the police sobered him. "Nothing new. Only the bird cage was on the floor. It used to be in the cupola, when Ida kept her bats and things in it. Wrapped it in a cloth, she did. I threw it out."

"Oh!" she said blankly. "You knew it was Ida, did you?"

"Well, when a woman gets an old bird cage and a net and keeps climbing at night into that tower up there, I didn't think she was after butterflies, and that's a fact."

"Did you tell anybody, Amos?"

"Not me," he said negligently. "Bats don't hurt anybody. Let her have her fun, said I. She didn't have much."

She looked at him. He was incredible, this stocky individualist who had believed in letting Ida have what he called her fun, and who apparently knew far more than he had even indicated. It amused him to tell her so, leaning against one of the trunks and now and then sucking at his dead pipe. Indeed, once started it was hard to stop him. He said that one night Carlton came and, getting the cage, carried it to the house. It was empty, as he—Amos—happened to know. But he had brought it back before morning. He said it was Frank Garrison who had caught Susie by the garage the night Mrs. Fairbanks was murdered. He'd seen him. And he observed cheerfully that he knew Marian had been in the house that same night.

"Funniest sight I most ever saw," he said, his shrewd eyes on hers. "Her streaking across the grass in her nightgown when the police cars were coming in. I slid down and unlocked the door, but she never saw me. She hid in the loft until Ida brought her clothes and bags. Toward morning, it was."

"Why didn't you tell it at the time, Amos?"

"Nobody asked me."

She felt helpless before the vast indifference, the monumental ego of the man. But she had not finished with him. "Why did Ida have those creatures, Amos? Was it to scare Mrs. Fairbanks away? After all, she had worked here for years."

He grinned at her slyly. "Maybe she didn't like her," he said. "Or maybe she didn't like the stairs. Lots of climbing in the house. May have wanted her to move to an apartment. I've heard her say as much."

"I suppose you know how she got them into the room, too?"

"Sure," he said, and grinned again. "Through Mrs. Carlton Fairbanks's peephole in the closet."

She left him then. She felt that even now he might have certain reserves, certain suspicions. But he did not intend to tell them. She could see that in his face.

"So they've arrested Mr. Garrison," he said as she went down the stairs. "Mr. Garrison and the doc across the street. Don't let them fool you, Miss Policewoman. They'll have to eat crow before they're through." He seemed to think this was humorous. He laughed. "But I'd like to know how Ida felt when she got that snake," he said. "I'll bet she didn't like it."

"So there *is* something you don't know!" said Hilda coldly, and went back to the house.

Nevertheless, she had a curious feeling about Amos as she left him. As though he had been trying to tell her something. As though he hoped that she would see what he could not tell her. And there had been something in his small sly eyes which looked like grief; a deep and tragic grief.

When she went upstairs, she found Jan in the upper hall. "She's still sleeping," she said. "I suppose she needs it, Miss Adams. They won't hold Father long, will they? They must know he didn't do it."

Evidently she did not know about Courtney, and Hilda said nothing. She tried the door to Marian's room and found it locked.

"How long has she been asleep, Jan?" she asked.

"I don't know. She's been in there since the Inspector left. It's seven now."

Hilda rapped on the door. Then she pounded hard and called. There was no response, however. Jan was standing by, looking terrified.

"You don't think she's . . . ?"

"She's probably taken an overdose of sleeping medicine," Hilda said briskly. "Get a doctor. If you can't get Courtney Brooke, get someone else. And hurry."

It was Brooke who came, running across the yard and reaching the house as Amos and William were lifting a ladder to the porte-cochère. He shoved them aside and climbed up. A moment later the screen gave way and he unlocked and opened the door into the hall.

"She's still breathing," he said. "Go away, Jan. I don't want you here. She'll be all right."

Hilda went in, and he closed the door behind her. Marian was lying on the bed, not moving. She looked peaceful and lovely, almost beautiful, as though that deep sleep of hers had erased the lines from her face and brought back some of her youth. But she was very far gone.

Brooke examined her and threw off his coat. "Come on, Miss Adams," he said. "We've got to get busy if we're going to save her."


CHAPTER XXVI

AT NINE O'CLOCK that same night a young man carrying a parcel arrived at the house and asked for Hilda. William brought the message to Marian's door.

"Tell him to wait," she said briefly. "Put him in the morning room and close the door. Tell him he's to stay if it takes all night."

William hesitated, his old head shaking. "How is she, miss?"

"A little better."

"Thank God for that," he said and tottered down the stairs.

It was ten o'clock when Courtney Brooke went out into the hall and, bending over, kissed Jan gently. "It's all right, darling. You can see her for a minute. Don't talk to her."

When Jan came out, he was waiting. He took her back to her room and put his arms around her. "My girl," he said. "Always and ever my girl, sweet. Hold on to me, darling. You need somebody to hold on to, don't you? And I'm strong. I'll never let you down."

"I've had so much, Court!"

"You've had too much, sweet. But it's all over. There won't be any more."

She looked up into his eyes, steady and honest, and drew a long breath. "Why did she do it, Court? Was it because Father . . . ?"

"Your father's all right. Take my word for it, darling."

"Then who——"

"Hush," he said, cradling her in his arms. "Hush, my sweet. Don't think. Don't worry. It's all over. You're to rest now. Just rest." He picked her up and laid her gently on the bed. "Sleep if you can. Think of me if you can't! Look out, darling. There's a moon. I ordered it for tonight, for you."

She lay still, after he had gone, looking at the moon. She felt very tired, but she was peaceful, too. It was over. Court had said so. She wrapped herself in his promise like a blanket, and fell asleep. She was still asleep when, at eleven, the Inspector drove in under the porte-cochère.

Susie and Carlton were in the library. Carlton's face was haggard, and even Susie looked stricken. She could accept murder, but she could not face suicide, or the attempt at it. Life was too important to her, the love of it too strong. She sat beside Carl, his head drawn down on her shoulder, her eyes soft.

"Don't be a jackass," she said. "Of course she didn't do it."

"Then why would she try to kill herself?"

"Because she's the same kind of fool I am. Because she's a one-man woman." She sat up and lit a cigarette. "Let's forget it," she said. "Let's think about a farm. You can raise what you want, and I'll raise pigs. I rather like pigs," she said. "At least they're natural. They don't pretend to be anything but pigs."

"So long as you're around, old girl," he said huskily. "So long as you're around."

They did not hear the Inspector as he went up the stairs and tiptoed into Mrs. Fairbanks's room, closing the door behind him. He did not turn on a light, or sit down. Instead, he went to a window and stood looking out. The whole thing was not to his taste. He had come at Hilda's request, and it was not like her to be dramatic. So Marian Garrison had tried to kill herself! It might be a confession, or the equivalent of one. And where the hell was Hilda, anyhow?

He was rapidly becoming indignant when suddenly, without warning, the radio behind him roared into action. He almost leaped into the air with the shock. It was playing the "Habañera" from *Carmen,* and the din was terrific. He was turning on the lights when Hilda came in.

For the first time in his experience she looked frightened. She shut off the machine and confronted him.

"That's how it was done," she said, and sat down weakly in a chair.

"What do you mean, that's how?"

She did not answer directly. She looked tired and unhappy. "It's a phonograph. You set the radio dial on a certain place and turn it on. It's a blank spot, where there's no station. Nothing happens, of course. But if you've got this machine plugged in on the same circuit, even in another room, it plays through the radio. As it did here."

"There was no phonograph in the house that night," he said stubbornly.

"I think there was."

"Where was it? We searched this house for one. We didn't find it."

When she did not answer, he looked at her. She was sitting still, her tired hands folded in her lap, her blue eyes sunken, the life gone out of her.

"I hate this job," she said. "I hate prying and spying. I'm through. I can't go on. I can't send a woman to the chair."

He knew her through long association. He realized that in her present mood he could not push her. "It was a woman?" he said quietly.

She nodded.

"How was it done, Hilda?"

"It had to be done by someone who knew the house," she said slowly. "Someone who knew the light circuits. Someone who knew this radio and had a chance sometime to discover how to adjust the remote-control phonograph. It didn't need much. It could be done in a few minutes. After you find the blank spot on the radio, all you have to do is to turn the dial to that spot. Then you can start the record, and it will play here."

"Where was it played from just now?"

"There's a young man in Carlton's room," she said dully. "I promised him ten dollars to come tonight. I'd better pay him and let him go."

He gave her the ten dollars, and she went out. She was gone a considerable time. When she returned, she looked so pale that the Inspector thought she was going to faint.

"He left the machine," she said. "He'll get it in the morning. If you want to see it . . ."

"See here, I think you need some whisky."

"No. I'm all right. If you'll come along, I'll show you."

She got up heavily and led the way. Carlton was still downstairs with

Susie, but his room was lighted. Sitting on the floor by a base outlet was what looked like a small phonograph, about a foot in diameter, with a record on it. It was plugged into the wall, and the Inspector, picking up the record, saw that it was the "Habañera" from *Carmen*. He started it and, going to Mrs. Fairbanks's room, switched on the radio. Almost immediately the "Habañera" started. He switched it off, and went back to Hilda. She was still there, standing by a window.

"How long have you known about this?" he demanded.

"Only today. Something Susie said. I saw the radio set where it is, and—I wondered about it. You see, there are almost no stations on the air at one or later in the morning, and when they are, it's dance music. I had just remembered it was something from *Carmen* that night. I should have thought about that sooner," she added, and tried to smile.

He had an idea that she was playing for time. He was wildly impatient, but he did not dare to hurry her.

"You see, it didn't take long," she went on. "I've timed it. Two minutes was enough to use the knife and turn the radio dial to the blank spot. And the doctor was in Jan's room for five minutes, maybe more. Even at that she took a chance. A dreadful chance," she said, and shivered. "She wasn't quite normal, of course. Those bats and things——"

"Listen," he said roughly. "Are you trying to tell me that Ida did all this?"

"Ida? No. She used them, of course. Amos saw her in the cupola. I suppose she was given a reason. Maybe to get Mrs. Fairbanks to leave the house. Maybe something worse, to scare her to death. And she hid the machine in the loft of the stable the next day. She carried it out in some blankets. That was why Jan was hurt, and I was locked in. The machine was hidden there, behind some trunks, or in one, I don't know. It had to be taken away, of course. She was in the loft when Jan got there. She had to get out."

She looked at her watch, and Patton at last lost patience.

"Haven't we played around enough?" he said. "What is all this? Are you giving someone a chance to get away?"

She shook her head. "I don't think so. No. I . . ." She closed her eyes. "Ida had to die, you see. She knew too much, so she got arsenic in a cup of tea. In the sugar, I suppose. The way Mrs. Fairbanks got it. If it hadn't been for Ida——"

Downstairs the telephone was ringing. Hilda got up and opened the door. Carlton was talking over it in the library. He sounded excited, and a moment later he slammed out the side door. Hilda was standing very still, listening while the Inspector watched her. Her eyes were on the stairs when Susie came running up. She was gasping for breath, and her eyes were wide with shock.

"It's Eileen," she gasped. "She's killed herself with Frank's service re-volver."

Then Hilda fainted. The Inspector caught her as she fell.

## CHAPTER XXVII

Two NIGHTS LATER Inspector Patton was sitting in Hilda's small neat living room. The canary was covered in his cage, and the lamplight was warm on the blue curtains at the windows and on the gay chintz-covered chairs. Hilda was knitting, looking, he thought, as she always did, blandly inno-cent. Only her eyes showed the strain of the past two weeks.

"Why did you do it, Hilda?" he said. "Why did you telephone her that night?"

"I was sorry for her," said Hilda. "I didn't want her to go to the chair."

"She wouldn't have done that. After all, a prospective mother——"

"But, you see, she wasn't," said Hilda. "That was her excuse to get into the house."

He stared at her. "How on earth did you know?"

Hilda looked down at her knitting. "There are signs," she said evasively. "And it's easy to say you have a pain. Nobody can say you haven't."

"But Garrison didn't deny it."

"What could he do? She was his wife, even if he hadn't lived with her for some time. I suppose he'd suspected her all along, after the arsenic. I knew he was watching her. He'd followed her there at night, maybe when she went to see Ida. In the grounds, perhaps."

"Then she knew about the agreement? That if Mrs. Fairbanks died, the alimony ceased?"

She nodded. "He must have told her. If they quarreled and she taunted him because he was hard up, he might, you know."

"How did she get the arsenic into the sugar?"

"Maggie says she came to the house the day before Marian and her mother returned from Florida. Jan was home by that time. She came to see her. But Mrs. Fairbanks's tray was in the pantry, and she went there for a glass of water. She could have done it then."

"But the poison didn't kill Mrs. Fairbanks. So then it was the terror. That's it, of course."

"The terror. Yes. Ida had told her about the hole in the wall, and—I think she had something on Ida. Maybe an illegitimate child. There was a boy at the farm, and Eileen's people lived nearby. She'd have known."

"It was the boy who brought in the bats and the rest of the zoo, including the snake?"

"Well, I can't think of any other way," Hilda said meekly. "She may have told him she sold them, or something. Of course it was Ida who got Eileen the position as Jan's governess."

"And got a cup of poisoned tea as a reward!"

"She got the five hundred dollars, too. Don't forget that. In new bills that Mrs. Fairbanks gave Eileen the night she was murdered. Maybe Eileen thought she could buy Ida's silence with them. I don't know. But she couldn't stand for the stabbing anyhow, poor thing. Remember how she looked the next morning? And she must have had the phonograph in her room while we were there. She must have been scared out of her wits. It wasn't until later that she took it to the loft, under the blankets, and hid it there."

"Where Eileen retrieved it the next night. And nearly killed Jan. That's right, isn't it?"

"Yes." Hilda looked thoughtful. "It's odd, but I saw her. I didn't know who it was, of course. I raised the window and she was across Huston Street. She pretended to be calling a dog."

Patton got up, lifted a corner of the cover and looked at the bird. It gazed back at him with small bright eyes, and he dropped the cover again.

"You're a funny woman, Hilda," he said. "In your heart you're a purely domestic creature. And yet—well, let's get back to Eileen. How and when did she use this radio-phonograph? Have you any idea?"

"I knew she had it," she said modestly. "I found the man who sold it to her. She said it was to go to the country, so he showed her how to use it. As for the rest, I think she killed Mrs. Fairbanks and set the dial by her bed while the doctor was with Jan. Then he gave her the hypodermic and left her. That's when the music started. He was in the hall."

"Where did she have the thing?"

"Anywhere. Under the bed, probably. There's a baseboard outlet there. She let it play until Carlton went in and turned off his mother's radio. If he hadn't, she would have stopped it herself. She didn't even have to get out of bed to do it. But of course things went wrong. I was there, in the hall. She hadn't counted on my staying there every minute. And Ida was busy with Marian. I suppose that's why she fainted when she did. She hadn't got rid of the machine, and I'd found the body. She had thought she had until morning."

"So it was there under the bed when you searched her room!"

"It was nothing of the sort," Hilda said indignantly.

"All right, I'll bite. Where was it?"

"Hanging outside her window on a rope."

He looked at her with admiration, not unmixed with something else. "As I may have said before, Hilda, you're a smart woman," he said, smiling. "My safe looks like a rummage sale. I'll present you with some of the stuff if you like. But I'd give a good bit to know why you interfered with the law and telephoned her."

"Because she hadn't killed Jan," Hilda said. "She could have, but she didn't."

"What did you say over the phone? That all was discovered?"

She went a little pale, but her voice was steady. "I really didn't tell her anything," she said. "I merely asked her if she still had her remote-control radio-phonograph. She didn't say anything for a minute. Then she said no, she'd given it away."

There were tears in her eyes. He got up, walked over to her and put his hand on her shoulder. "Oh, subtle little Miss Pinkerton," he said. "Lovable and clever and entirely terrible Miss Pinkerton! What am I to do about you? I'm afraid to take you, and I can't even leave you alone."

He looked down at her, her soft skin, her graying hair, her steady blue eyes.

"See here," he said awkwardly, "Jan and young Brooke are going to be married. Susie and Carlton Fairbanks are going on a second honeymoon, looking for a farm. And unless I miss my guess, Frank Garrison and Marian will remarry eventually. I'd hate like hell to join that crew of love-birds, but—you won't object if I come around now and then? Unprofessionally, of course, little Miss Pinkerton."

She smiled up at him. "I'd prefer even that to being left alone," she said.

After he had gone, she sat still for a long time. Then she determinedly took a long hot bath, using plenty of bath salts, and shampooed her short, slightly graying hair. Once more she looked rather a rosy thirty-eight-year-old cherub, and she was carefully rubbing lotion into her small but capable hands when the telephone rang. She looked desperately about her, at the books she wanted to read, at her soft bed, and through the door to her small cheerful sitting room with the bird sleeping in its cage. Then she picked up the receiver.

"Miss Pinkerton speaking," she said, and on hearing the Inspector's voice was instantly covered with confusion.